PRAISE FOR THE
Blade Runner ™
NOVELS OF K. W. JETER

"Jeter's Blade Runner books combine the spirit of Dick's original with the often brilliant touches found in Jeter's own writing."
—*The Washington Post*

"A serious novel, well written and imaginative . . . it remains faithful to its roots and becomes a story Jeter can call his own."
—*The Magazine of Fantasy & Science Fiction*

"Jeter fully exploits the Dickian paradoxes of illusion vs. reality, man vs. machine, that the film only hinted at."
—*San Francisco Chronicle*

"A really rare animal . . . highly recommended for anyone looking for a good read."
—*The Commercial Appeal,* Memphis

"A good, fast-moving story . . . Jeter also plays with readers' heads the way that [Philip K.] Dick loved to."
—*The Orlando Sentinel*

ALSO BY K. W. JETER

NOIR

K.W. JETER

BANTAM BOOKS

NEW YORK TORONTO LONDON SYDNEY AUCKLAND

NOIR
A Bantam Spectra Book

PUBLISHING HISTORY
Bantam Spectra hardcover edition published November 1998
Bantam Spectra paperback edition / September 1999

SPECTRA and the portrayal of a boxed "s" are trademarks of Bantam
Books, a division of Random House, Inc.

Grateful acknowledgment is made for permission to reprint from the following:

Selection on page 1 used as epigraph from *The Birth of the Modern* by Paul
Johnson. Copyright © 1991 by Paul Johnson. Reprinted by permission of
HarperCollins Publishers, Inc.

Selection on page 161 used as epigraph from *God Bless You, Mr. Rosewater* by
Kurt Vonnegut, Jr. Copyright © 1965 by Kurt Vonnegut, Jr. Used by
permission of Delacorte Press/Seymour Lawrence, a division of Random
House, Inc.

Bantam Books are published by Bantam Books, a division of Random
House, Inc. Its trademark, consisting of the words "Bantam Books" and the
portrayal of a rooster, is Registered in U.S. Patent and Trademark Office and
in other countries. Marca Registrada. Bantam Books, 1540 Broadway, New
York, New York 10036.

PRINTED IN THE UNITED STATES OF AMERICA
OPM   10   9   8   7   6   5   4   3   2   1

TO

MARSHA MANNING AND PETER ALLER,

WHO HEARD IT FIRST

You take my life
When you do take the means
whereby I live.

—WILLIAM SHAKESPEARE
The Merchant of Venice (1597),
Act IV, Scene I

. . . there's nothing like a kiss long
and hot down to your soul
almost paralyses you . . .

—JAMES JOYCE
Molly Bloom's soliloquy
from *Ulysses* (1922)

PART ONE

But, at this birth of the modern world, roamed by predatory men armed with increasingly effective means of killing and traveling at speeds which accelerated each year, most assaults on nature went unheeded, and crimes against humanity remained unpunished. The world was becoming one, the wilderness was being drawn into a single world commercial system, but there was as yet no acknowledged law. Who was to play the world policeman?

—PAUL JOHNSON

The Birth of the Modern:
World Society 1815–1830
(HarperCollins Publishers,
New York, 1991)

ONE

SEX BURNED A WIRE

At that moment, as the blue spark of sex burned a wire through his tongue, the heavens rained fire. At that moment, all the other moments rushed inside his head. He turned from the kiss that filled his mouth, the hot copper taste of coded flesh, and fell against the glass; the window shivered with fear and mirrored his own ghost face back at him.

He knew what was happening outside the window. That the fear was his alone, as much as the ghost and the kiss were; that the transit authorities had sent another drone aloft, over whatever city lapped around this building like a hectic gray ocean; that the *Noh*-flies had found the idiot projectile in their airspace—all air was theirs—and were busily devouring it, SCARF'd shards falling on the streets below and the face of anyone stupid enough to look up. Mere coincidence, apocalyptic phenomena synch'd-up with the battery salt leaking through his teeth.

This must be how women feel, thought Travelt.

Not real women, but the women of ideal and dream. Men's dreams, their dream of women's dreams. He had felt himself go all weak at the knees, a kinesthetic cliché as much as the racing heart under his breastbone, when the soul kiss had started to eat him up. He'd put his tongue in the other's mouth, as though his lips were the aggressor's, the conqueror's; he'd made the connection inside another's flesh, that point where electrode and neuron were one fated synapse—

And had been conquered in turn. Battered and ravaged. That dream of rape, in which the raped are dreaming still, in which the dreaming turn their faces upward and see their own faces above them, spread out on a luminous sky like the disintegrating airplanes above the ring of cities and the uncaring, dreaming ocean. Where every hot bit of metal struck and hissed into steam, sharp as his own intake of breath, drifting into unlit depths and turning into adornment for dolphins' skeletons.

Calm down, Travelt told himself. *You're burning up.* The window sweated against his cheek.

Did the other sweat as well? His vision had blurred, everything that close out of focus, and he couldn't tell if the other's face was as wet and shining as his own felt. The kiss hadn't ended, his tongue was still there, locked in bandwidth rapture; the room around him had defocused, the city beyond the window threatened to go any second. Not that it mattered, not now.

No now; all *then.* Memory and spasm; what had happened, what had been brought back to him. What he tasted in the mercury pool of the other's tongue. His own tongue lodged in the hinge of the other's throat, diving toward the other's heart, as though the secret that drove the sweat through his pores could be read there among the obscure saline atoms.

His legs had turned to gelatin, trembling with desires satiated and yet-hungry. The other had to hold him up, its hands locked in his armpits, pinning him against the glass, the crumbs of the eaten drone sizzling transmuted gold on the other side, an inch from his liquefying spine. His tongue in its mouth, their kiss, his senses and being penetrated by the inrush that left him limp and sweetly crucified. Invisible stigmata blossomed in his palms and groin, the feedback of flesh distant in time and space. The flesh that the other had touched, grasped and squeezed blood and lubricating mucus from, like overripe fruit trickling to the points of his elbows. He felt that now, the other's gift to him, rape of him.

Slow down—Travelt murmured the subvocal command and plea. Locked so tight in the other's embrace, its reflected image in the glass next to his, that he could feel the sympathetic flutter of its larynx. As though his words had strummed the other's vocal cords like taut guitar strings, a chord of surrender and supplication.

It obeyed him, or seemed to; he knew the other's response was as synchronous and acausal as the heated shrapnel falling outside. But the inrush slowed, torrent to stream, and separated into layers of incident and event, became an inventory of all that the other had gone out to seek and had brought back to him. He had smelled it on the other's skin-like skin, that muscled substance that passed for its flesh. When it had returned and let itself in to his cubapt, its key imbedded in its stained fingertips—he had smelled it then, as it had walked through one room after another and into this one with the high-luxury window overlooking the anonymous city below. The mingled overlays of sweat and semen, stale cigarette smoke and endorphins breaking down to burning, dysfunctional molecules, the shards of the other's flight through a sunless sky. Collagen derivatives, pharmaceuticals that tasted like metal and the perspiring of schizophrenics, virginal lipstick and Chernobyl mothers' milk, original sin and its photocopies—a wind from that other atmosphere, ten degrees lower than his own body temperature, had swept ahead of the other as it had strode toward him.

He had turned from the window where he had stood waiting, turned upon the sense and smell of its arrival—no sound, it walked so softly, silent as that other world—and had seen the smear of blood on its brow, Cain-marked and Lilith-born, the great wisdom of indulgence in its idiot eyes. Which had scanned and judged him, like the lenses of the watching security cameras at every corner of every building. First from across the room, as he had felt the first tremors of fear move out from his gut, then inches away, then less than that as it had stood right in front of him. The other's eyes had been round dark mirrors in which he had seen himself, perhaps more clearly than ever before.

That was then, just a few minutes ago—or perhaps only seconds. In any death, even the smallest, there was no east or west or other measurement of time, no gauge of stars or the earth's rotation. In this now, the inrush had slowed and become subject to inventory; he could sort one thing out from the next. What the other had brought back to him. The Christmas morning of the genitals, each bright ribbon-bow coming loose inside his head.

This is what he received from the other's kiss. What he saw, felt, inhaled in acidic, mingled pheromones:

- A vision of black-ink tattoos that slowly woke and shifted beneath a woman's skin, pale as unsunned

cave fish, white as Bible pages, dimly phosphores-
cent;

- The swarming of those tattoos, like decorative koi
  or human-eyed piranha, attracted by the shadow of
  a man's hand over the world in which they swam;

- Their nuzzling beneath the palm laid on the
  woman's skin, their kisses' delineated teeth, the
  tingle of each electric micro-surge, the release of
  musky encapsuled opiates, the blood warmth of a
  close-enough approximation of real human flesh;

- All of these and more. The pumped-up techly stuff
  and the straight old-fashioned, the redheaded idiot
  in the cave of wonders, the soft wet hand of normal coitus. Normal as it gets.

Thought Travelt: *I'll have to work on this*. Now he knew
why people started doing this sort of thing. What the attraction was.

Metal fingertips, disconnected from anything but rising
tendrils of SCARF smoke, clicked against the window. And
fell, pieces of the *Noh*-eaten drone. The larger pieces, of
engine manifold and wing panels, would plummet next,
fiery meteors sweeping the streets clean of any watchers.

He was falling as well, the connection between his
tongue and the other's mouth broken, that blue spark snuffed
by his pink-tinged saliva. His jaws felt hot and vacant as the
other, working off some consumer-protection coding, lowered him gently to the fleece carpet.

Shame, or something like it, turned his face away from
the other's gaze above. He couldn't bear to be seen, even by
something empty and soulless as the autonomic truck that

came every morning to change the building's air hoses. Especially by something as empty as that, as empty as the other standing over him. Judged by machines, by their hard flat scrutiny, the iris of an onrushing train. *Iris* and *inrush;* the two words remained inside his head, like prophylactic debris washed up, pearlescent and luminous, on a moonlit beach. Maybe that was how women felt as well; he didn't know. No way he would. He put his arm up across his face, as though shielding himself from the sun.

The name of the flower had left its image, an intricately petaled construction, in his memory. Maybe one of the tattoos that the other had brought back to show him; he could almost see it opening in the white field of the woman's skin. Opening the way flesh opened, the dew at the petal's edge a perfect magnifying lens.

I'm making that part up. That part didn't happen, thought Travelt. Or maybe it had; he didn't know.

The other watched him, waited for him, for whatever he might choose to do next. The other was in that part of its operative cycle; it had gone and fetched, it had brought back, and now it waited. With the flat empty gaze of coins, of metal that had been on fire and then extinguished, smoldering to cold lead. He might stand back up on his trembling, bone-loosened legs, stand up and kiss the other again, insert part of himself into the other again, let the blue spark snap and sing piercingly high, into his throat and down along his spine, penetrated by the other and what it had brought him. The iris, the eye and the flower, each opening, flesh opening, the mouths of the tattooed koi nibbling at the other's palm, the warmth of the dead-white flesh and skin, the ocean in which they swam . . .

It was all there. Waiting for him. Watching him.

I'll get better at this. The first time, for anything, was the hardest. He turned on his side, drawing his knees up against his chest. Closing his eyes, so he wouldn't have to see. Anything but what the other had brought home and bestowed upon him.

On his tear-wet cheek, he felt fire, heat through the window's glass. The last of the drone plane fell from the sky and rolled its black smoke and insect swarm of sparks along the building's flank.

TWO

BITS OF DEAD AIRPLANES

You people shouldn't have called me." McNihil stepped over pieces of blackened metal. The shapes littering the sidewalk were the size of dental fillings, with the same odd combinations of rounded curves and ridges. They might have fallen from junkies' rotting teeth, but he knew they hadn't. "I don't do this kind of work anymore."

The DZ flunky trotted alongside him. The man took the exact same steps as McNihil, at the exact same speed, but looked as if he were running to keep up. If he'd had the end of his own leash clamped in his jaws, it would've been perfect. "What kind of work do you do?"

McNihil was aware the question came from no need, no

desire other than to make talk, to fulfill the rep's junior-exec
schmooze training. He'd run into the type before.

"I don't," he said, "clean up other people's messes."

The metal bits of dead airplanes crunched under the soles
of his shoes. Mess was, categorically, one of the basic components of this universe he lived in, like hydrogen atoms.
Gray newspapers with significant headlines—*Dewey Defeats
Truman; Pearl Harbor Bombed*—moldered in the gutters, or
were nudged along the broken sidewalks by the same night
wind that cut through McNihil's jacket.

"Careful," warned the flunky, but it was already too late.
A piece of hard reality poked through the merely optical;
McNihil hit his knee on some larger contortion of metal,
which hadn't yet been filtered into his black-and-white vision.

"Thanks." McNihil gritted his teeth, as the pain ebbed
and condensed into a drop of blood trickling down his shin.
Now he could see what had done it, a sharp-edged fragment
of a wing panel, its glistening alloy crumpled like a soft mirror. It stuck out into his path all the way from where the
downed jet had dug a trench through the strata of trash,
plowing back the asphalt and concrete below. The singed
metal carcass, the biggest piece at least, lay in the street like a
barbecued whale. The engine, some fairly recent Boeing-
CATIC thrust device, showed the circled fins of its air-intake
snout, the merge of Chinese design and American tech resulting in something delicate as that whale's sifting baleen.

In less than a second, McNihil's vision rolled an overlay
across the broken aircraft, transforming it from the hard
world into what he usually saw. A flash of color had reflected
off the shiny metal; now that had drained away, down to
monochrome. Not even a jet anymore, but a Curtiss P-40,
camo-mottled in dark green and desert sand. The propeller
blades had snapped where they'd scythed into the street's
asphalt. His eyes worked up the most appropriate images they

could; the China suggestion must've evoked this Flying Tigers historical.

As McNihil continued walking, limping a bit, long-fin-
gered dwarves, swaddled up in their homemade *chernober-*
alls—lead-lined against the residual radiation—and their eyes
goggled with aplanatic/achromatic darkfield jeweler's loupes,
crawled out of the littered wreckage's tight spaces and skittered off to some nearby recycling souk. Leaving the jet's
bones behind for the janitors to sweep up, the janitors that
never came. The squat-limbed figures were gone around the
corner before McNihil's eyes could assimilate them into pe-
riod-detail Hell's Kitchen ragamuffins.

"Here we are," announced the DZ flunky. "This is the
place."

"No shit."

Some things just slid right in, from one world to any
other, without any alteration necessary. Even in a moonless
night, a building like this one cast a shadow, a black negative
ooze across the sidewalk. But not enough to hide the ragged
strips of human skin fluttering maypolelike from the exterior
walls, stitched into long banners. The office tower looked
like a vertical snake, shedding its extorted skin.

At one time—McNihil had seen it—the skin segments,
mandatory employee donations, had fit tight on the building.
That sort of thing was the apotheosis of the Denkmann
book's management style, which corporate execs were always so keen on. But bad weather and poor taxidermy had
taken their toll.

One gossamer pennant draped itself across McNihil's
sleeve. Between the curling edges, he saw a faded tattoo, an
initialed heart entwined with a scroll-like banner. Which
had, just as he expected, some trite company slogan: *Enthusi-*
asm is job component number . . .

He didn't catch the rest, as the wind fluttered the dangling scrap away from him.

McNihil didn't look up to see where the building's needle peak scratched at the stars. "Come on," he said, pushing open the door into the lobby. Sinister buildings were regular items in the world he saw. "Let's get this over with."

Going up in the elevator, McNihil continued brooding about the junk in the street. It helped him give off his own lethal gamma rays, a black aura that curdled the marrow of sensitive little corporate types and further convinced them that he wasn't happy about being here at all. That it'd been a mistake dragooning him in on this.

"It's not really a mess." Fidgeting, all nerves and wetly blinking eyes, the flunky thumbed one of the numbered buttons. "I mean, there's not like blood and stuff." The elevator's machinery, transformed to antiquity in McNihil's perceptions, clanked and groaned. "And we wouldn't have called you if it wasn't important."

That was the wrong tack to take with him. "If it's important," said McNihil, "then it's a mess." He knew how these things worked.

A solid minute passed before the elevator doors opened. Which meant nothing, he also knew; they could still be on the ground floor. They could be in the basement, with high-up views of the city dicked onto the windows, with fine-enough resolution almost to be convincing. He loathed that aspect of the building as well.

The elevator had opened onto a standard corridor. "This way," said the flunky. Like an idiot, as if there were any other way to go. The corridor was lined with doors, to all the cubapts on this level. As McNihil's eyes moved over them, they turned into the kind with worn brass doorknobs and pebbly windows bearing the names of insurance agencies and dentists in chipped gold leaf. The optical trigger hooked in a keyed olfactum; he caught the evocative perfume of dust-fuzzed ceiling light fixtures, unswept and threadbare hallway carpets, stoic despair, and file-cabinet scotch.

"Here we go." The flunky pushed at one of the doors.

Which opened onto a room full of people. Or enough of them to make a crowd in the small space. What had looked like some kind of office on the outside—the flaking gold on the glass had read Derrida & Foucault, Certified Public Accountants—was on the inside a luxury cubicle-apartment, nicely enough appointed in the usual corporate style. McNihil loathed spaces like this; these company-supplied cubapts, more artifacts out of the Denkmann book, were one of the things that had always kept him freelancing.

The DZ flunky stood back, letting McNihil walk in ahead. Nobody said anything, though some of the business suits recognized him, knew him. The business suits in the room would've expected that his lip would curl as soon as he walked in. *But they wanted me to see it,* thought McNihil. *Where all the bad stuff came down.* Whatever it was.

Their cold eyes watched as McNihil strode through the room, head down into his shoulders and face set in its bad-mood angles. One of them stuck a hand out, but McNihil avoided it. All these executive types, especially at this level, would have those annoying expanded handshake transmitters wired into their palms. Worse, he had a receptor in his own hand, a souvenir from his old job. Coming in on his skin's nerve endings, it slid past the optical override—the flunky, when he'd come around to McNihil's place, had caught him off-guard and had downed on him before McNihil had been able to pull his arm back. For the next five minutes, the tactile printout had itched away at McNihil's left thigh, the nerve endings tingling with a dot-matrix scan of the flunky's business card. McNihil had let it flash up inside his eye, but the only thing he'd read from it was the stylized DynaZauber logo and the company motto, something about all men being customers. What did he care what the flunky's name and real job title were?

With the execs' collective gaze on his back, McNihil

walked over to the tall view window at the opposite side of the cubapt's living area.

He stood with his nose almost touching the window, looked out and saw the Gloss stretched out far below. He licked the tip of his index finger with his tongue, then rubbed wet a spot of the glass. There was no pixel blur; the space was as high up as it appeared to be.

"You got spit on the window." Harrisch, a silver-haired senior exec that McNihil had encountered before, stood behind him now. "That's DynaZauber property. Not even leased; we own this puppy."

McNihil glanced over his shoulder. "I like to know where I am. Altitude-wise."

"What does it matter?"

"In case I fall." He shrugged. "I want to know how long until I hit."

"You might find out." Harrisch matched him in grumpy radiation, even though a smile like an open wound surfaced across his even teeth. "You're a bad guest. You know that, don't you?"

"I try to be. It saves time."

He'd actually hoped that things would get this ugly, this fast. If nothing else, it meant that none of the other execs would try to introduce themselves. Which meant he wouldn't have to fend off any more of those hearty 'spandshakes. The verified rumor was that execs like these had the data circuits wired over to their genitalia, where the nerves were clustered thick enough for almost instantaneous readout. Stuff like that gave a whole new meaning and impetus to the old yuppie concept of networking; less reliable rumors talked about social events jammed tight with suits, all of them shaking hands and exchanging business-card data with each other until their faces shone like rain-wet stoplights and the smell of semen hung in the heavy-breathing

air. McNihil didn't care to give any of the people in the
room even part of that kind of thrill.

"I knew it." Harrisch looked disgusted, as though the
spit on the window were some personal graffitied message
about the nature of the universe. "We shouldn't have asked
you to come here."

"See? I told you." McNihil turned all the way around, so
he could speak right into the face of the DZ flunky, who'd
materialized at his elbow. "Fine by me. I'm gone." He
pushed past both men and headed for the cubapt's door.

"But as long as you're here." Harrisch snagged him by
the arm and deflected him toward the group of other men at
the center of the living space. They were all standing around
something that looked like a bundle of rags at their feet.
"You might as well let us know what you think."

Not rags; it never was. Not when the bundle was lying in
the middle of a medium-to-expensive gray carpet with taste-
ful black flecks woven in. Laundry, dirty or not, always migrated to the corners of rooms. Nobody ever stood around
laundry or rags, watching with carefully blank-to-hostile ex-
pressions as some intruder was steered their way. Two of the
suited execs stepped back, partly in deference to their boss's
approach, mainly to let McNihil see what was lying there.

Which was what he'd expected to see. At least the gaze
in the filmed-over eyes didn't broadcast contempt for everything that still had breath in its lungs, that managed to live
without benefit of stock options. The corpse stared up at the
ceiling with the patient manner of the truly dead, the ones
who weren't going to return on some battery-driven install-
ment plan. An adult male, younger than anybody else in the
room, including McNihil, excluding the overeager corporate
rep. Christ would've been younger than the creaking execs
who watched from the corners of their eyes as McNihil bent
over the one who now wasn't going to get any older.

"What's all this shit?" He pointed to the corpse's open

shirt. It'd been unbuttoned and folded back, to show the
corpse's chest equally and neatly opened. An incision ran
from under its throat to past its navel, terminated somewhere
below the elastic waistband of the plain-white, non-designer
underpants. The surgical cut might as well have had buttons
and holes along its edges; they had been turned almost
bloodlessly away from the bones and connective tissues of the
corpse's sternum. Gurgling pipes and tubes, small machinery
like burrowing chrome rats, had snuggled in and nested
among the various organs. Selectively permeable gas mem-
branes around the exposed heart and lungs; the human bits
glistened and shone like the contents of the plastic trays at an
upscale butcher's counter. The resemblance was extended by
the drop in temperature—McNihil could feel it just by holding his palm an inch above the corpse's chest—carefully regulated by the devices' programming.

Stuff like that couldn't be overlaid; no analogues existed
in McNihil's monochrome world. The little machines continued their work, visibly, like some nightmare of a future
that had already arrived.

McNihil pointed to the busy wound. "Why's he all
prepped for transplant harvesting?"

"That's just standard procedure." The flunky had hesitated a moment before speaking up, in case Harrisch or any
of the other brass had felt like explaining. "Procedural standards, for the company."

"That's what we do," said one of the other execs. His
voice was a dog's growl in a man's nasopharynx. "That's the
kind of organization we are."

"Condition of employment." Whenever any of the brass
spoke, the flunky bounced on the balls of his feet for a
moment, as though the invisible leash had been yanked.
"Public service sort of thing. Your organs are company property. All the suites and cubes and efficiencies have in-built
Detect-&-Dissect™ kits keyed to the employees' vital signs;

they drop, you're popped." The flunky had settled down, but his quick laugh jerked him up again, marionettelike. "Usable pieces get stitched into deserving orphans."

"Why waste 'em?" The one brass rumbled again.

"True." McNihil looked the man in the red-rimmed eye. "If nothing else, you could serve them over rice in the executive lunchroom."

No laugh or smile. "If we wanted to," the brass agreed quietly.

Harrisch, the senior exec, had hung back, letting the lower rankings have a go at the asp-head they'd invited here. Their relative positions on the DZ corporate ladder were obvious to McNihil, just from the density of the swarms of E-mail buzzing around their heads. Some of the execs had only two or three of the tiny holo'd images yattering around them for attention; the bottom rungs had enough that their faces could barely be seen past them. Swatting did no good; every once in a while, one of the junior execs would have to turn away, crouching over in a corner and downing enough of them, muttering quick responses into his Whisper-Throat™ mike, to get a few seconds of relief. Harrisch had none; either the corporation was paying for max'd-out filtration or he was high up enough to have gone on an elite paper-only status. He at least was at no risk of being overloaded, prostrate on the floor and buried under a thickening flock of messages, like a dead cowboy beneath vultures in a Western landscape à la John Ford.

McNihil looked back down at the corpse and poked it with the toe of his shoe. "What was this poor bastard's name?"

"Travelt." The flunky bobbed helpfully at his side. "His name was Travelt."

"First name?"

Silent and unrepeated, the question went around the cubapt's living space. The execs looked vaguely embarrassed, either from not knowing or knowing and not wanting to admit it.

A wallet was in the corpse's jacket pocket; McNihil had spotted the flat rectangular shape. He stood back up, flipping the soft leather open. "William," he announced, reading it off a company ID card. "In case you were wondering." The driver's license was—in McNihil's vision—a nice overlaid replica of what somebody would've been carrying around circa the Eisenhower administration. The tiny photo showed the corpse's face above an early IBM-white dress shirt and blue-striped tie. In life, the late Travelt had looked like a version-in-training of the older and harder ones standing around watching. At that stage, he'd still looked more human than not.

McNihil tapped the image with his forefinger. He knew that would trigger the ID codes embedded in the card, over in the hard world beneath the one he saw.

"Assembling tomorrow today," spoke a bass-enhanced voice. The words sounded as confident as they would have if the speaker had still been alive. "Add value and evolve—"

"Whatever." He flipped the wallet closed. The ID card/driver's license mumbled for a second longer, then was quiet. He handed the wallet to the flunky, who looked at it as if it were the chilled spleen from the corpse's viscera. "Obviously not a close friend of yours."

"That's not important," said Harrisch.

He made no reply. For a moment, McNihil felt as if the temperature level of the refrigerant devices had seeped out and clamped around his own guts. And from there, across the re-created cubapt's manicured spaces, through the tall windows and out over the world at large. Though he supposed it had less to do with the dead thing at his feet than with the other ones standing around him, who were still capable of motion and speech, however limited. If his blood had dropped a few degrees, it was their proximity effect that had caused it.

The corpse's eyes were shiny enough to make little curved, silvery mirrors. McNihil saw now, as he looked down, that the eyes weren't just filmed over by death; another film had been laid over them, a chilling membrane like the ones wrapped around the corpse's heart and kidneys. Preserving the corneas for those lucky orphans. But which now made the dead eyes into even better mirrors, as though polished by silversmiths; he could see his face in them, doubled. The two miniature faces gazing back up at him looked old and tired, the fatigue producing the age rather than the other way around. He wished even more that he hadn't come here, hadn't let himself be bullied into coming.

"So what do you think?" Harrisch loomed up beside him. "Think you can help us on this one?"

He saw that an edge of the corpse's opened shirt, only lightly stippled with blood and other fluids, lay across the tip of the exec's glossy handmade shoes. McNihil looked up and shook his head. "Like I was trying to tell the boy you sent to get me. I don't do this kind of work."

"But you could if you wanted to. If we made it the kind of job you'd want to take on. You're still on the agency's list, as a licensed operative."

Another shake of the head. "Wake up and smell the burning corpses of your dreams, pal. I don't know what the connect you're thinking of. This is way off-zone for me. I don't take care of this kind of shit; I've never taken care of this kind of shit. Even when I was working for the Collection Agency—and I'm not now—" As if they didn't know that. "But when I was, I never showed up when people were already dead and sorted out their problems. That's not what asp-heads do. Even if I were one anymore. And I'm not." McNihil widened his eyes, to ensure that the message went as straight as possible into the other man's. *"Natterkopf bin ich nicht.* Got it?"

Harrisch didn't give up. "You have special qualifications. You have to admit that—"

"I don't have to admit anything. Except I'm ready to say good-bye now."

"Oh, please." Harrisch widened his smile. Now it looked like the result of trying to carve a Hallowe'en pumpkin with a single stroke of a machete. "We're just starting to enjoy your company. I take back what I said about you before."

Harrisch's eyes, the center of them, were black mirrors instead of silvered, but they showed the same thing as the corpse's blank gaze. In the two dark curves, McNihil saw his tiny reflections again. If that face looked tired and disgusted, and not easily talked into taking this kind of a job, McNihil figured it had a right to. He'd already been connected over enough in this lifetime, in the world he'd started out in and the one he saw in his taken-apart-and-stitched-together eyes. Maybe the guy on the floor, or what was left of him, had had the same kind of luck. Maybe the guy had connected up. One way or another. It didn't really matter.

"Special qualifications," repeated Harrisch. "That's why we asked you to come here."

Little black mirrors. Like looking straight into the exec's skull and seeing nothing, or worse than that, the big Nothing with the capital *N*. The swallower, the negative soul, the extinguishing substance of which was in all the other execs' eyes. That walked amongst them in the cubapt, slipping between their bodies like laughing smoke, that strode through the corridors of all the other ghost buildings in the chain of cities, that hauled the steel cables of the unnumbered elevators like ringing an empty cathedral's bells.

"We asked you to come here because we figured you could help us. We know you can."

McNihil pulled himself back from his own bleak musing, focusing his gaze and attention on the senior exec standing in front of him. The centers of Harrisch's eyes still looked like black holes.

"I don't know what kind of 'special qualifications' you're talking about." He wasn't having any problem resisting the imploded gravitational pull that the exec was radiating in his direction. "You got one of your lower ranks zipped, that's not the kind of thing I was ever concerned with. Are you tracking on this?" McNihil tilted his head and peered at the exec from the corner of one eye. Just for sarcastic effect. "Sometimes people get all confused about other people, about what it is they exactly do. I wouldn't have thought somebody in your exalted position would have that kind of problem, but still. If you think that just because there were dead bodies, or parts of them, left over after I got done with any particular job, that just because of that I must have some kind of general connection to stiff meat . . . then you've really gotten your wires crossed. It doesn't work that way. Even with asp-heads who are still in the business." Another tilt of the head, angled down toward the corpse between them. "Why don't you just get the police to take care of this? They're cheap enough."

"Police don't have the . . ." The ugly executive non-smile appeared again. "The qualifications that you do."

"Again with the qualifications." McNihil shook his head. He glanced toward the cubapt's tall view window and the gray sky on the other side of the glass. *Let the fire fall,* he told himself. He'd be willing to let it rain on his own head, if that would've meant being able to get out of this sucked-airless space. "If sheer connecting nausea were a qualifica-tion"—he let his voice shift into a dull-toothed rasp—"then I'd be your man."

"Oh, you're our man, all right." Harrisch's thing-like-a-smile tugged into a snarl at one corner. "You just don't know it yet."

"You will, though." The little flunky piped up. "Just wait."

"If you don't mind," said McNihil, "I'll wait at home." He turned and headed toward the door.

Not fast enough. Harrisch caught him again by the arm. "I think," said the exec, "that if you just took the time to exercise some of those special qualifications—special even for asp-heads—then you'd have a better idea. About why we wanted you to come here."

A microsuspicion tickled at the back of McNihil's skull. The other man had carefully pitched his voice, its faint hinting undertones, not so that it was rich with implications, but just enough to be an appetizer, the bait on the hook. He peeled the other's hand from him. "What do you mean?"

"Come on." Harrisch stepped back and gestured toward the corpse. "You haven't even really checked it out. Simple dead means nothing. You might as well take a good look. Before we do let the police come and take it away."

He knew he should just turn and start walking again, and make it all the way to the door this time. There would be no stopping him; none of the execs would say anything more to him. Harrisch and the rest would scratch him off their list and move on to Plan B, whoever else they figured they could rope in on their problems. Whatever they were.

McNihil knew that was what he should go ahead and do. But he didn't.

"All right." He was already regretting the impulse, the momentary weakening of resolve. "You win. This much: I'll check this poor bastard out."

He didn't care if a little triumphant smile got passed around the room, from one smug company exec to another. If it did, he didn't see it; that was all that mattered. McNihil had already got down on one knee, that much closer to the corpse. And to its face, the empty, gray-silvery gaze focused on nothing. *As I am,* said the corpse inside McNihil's thoughts. *So will you be.* To which McNihil answered, *Not me, pal. I'll kill myself first.* Some way that left nothing but ashes.

Almost a kiss; he had brought his face that near to the corpse's. McNihil had known what he would find, that there wouldn't be any surprises. There never were. That was why he'd wanted to leave, to have no part of this. No matter how much the company might have been willing to pay.

He smelled it. Not how the man had died. McNihil didn't care about that. But what this Travelt person had been doing when he was alive. That mattered.

A slow exhalation, the way the dead breathed; so slow, the air didn't stir, but hung suspended in their mouths. The corpse's bluish lips were slightly parted, as though it wanted to whisper something more to the face above its own.

It didn't need to speak. McNihil had already caught the trace, the sparse molecules inhaled down his throat, past the receptors of taste and scent and into his memory. He'd smelled it before. Something like wet metal, sulphuric corrosion on battery terminals, the ion discharge of aroused and insatiable desire. He could taste the metal on his tongue, as though he could spit out a bright rolling bead of mercury.

He hooked a thumb behind the corpse's teeth and pried its stiff jaw open. Wide enough that McNihil could run the tips of two fingers across its tongue. Through the film of congealed saliva, he felt the tiny scars, as though the wet flesh had been nicked again and again with the corner of a razor blade. They weren't scars; he knew what they were. The living Travelt's habits had evoked new sensory channels from his own flesh, at the center of his head, close as possible to the red jelly of his brain. It wasn't the worst case McNihil had ever encountered; he'd come across other corpses where the tongues had felt like some kind of stitched and restitched corduroy, the channel tracks wide as the tip of his little finger. Those were the ones who'd indulged themselves for so long that they might just as well have rewired their entire nervous systems, like ancient embroideries from which the word *human* had been picked out and some new, unreadable word needlepointed in.

The space around him had subtly diminished; McNihil looked up and saw Harrisch and the other company execs, even the little corporate rep, standing closer to him. Their faces formed a circle, the base of an inverted cone, with its point set right between his own eyes.

"So?" Harrisch smiled as unpleasantly as before. "What did you find out?"

A bit of metal glittered at the corpse's throat. Four-armed and golden, bilaterally symmetrical, strung on a thin chain. McNihil passed his hand across the cold skin, shielding his movements with his own back. When he took his hand away, the bit was gone, the broken chain slithered out from the white shirt collar.

McNihil stood up; the cone collapsed into a circle, his head at the center, the watching execs all around the circumference. Every one of them had the same hungry dark inside his eyes. The little black mirrors: McNihil could have turned slowly around and seen the tiny reflection of his face, over and over . . .

If only, he thought. If his own face were all that he saw. It was their faces that bothered him. And what he saw there.

He saw the same thing, of which he'd caught the scent on the corpse's non-breath. Tasted on the back of his tongue when he'd inhaled. Metal and spit, mercury and a blue dancing spark. It was in the glistening of their lips, the knowing half-smiles, the smug certainty that badged a brotherhood of the senses.

They're all in on it, thought McNihil. It hadn't been just the late Travelt, the corpse at the bottom of the well their

expensive suits and corporate white shirts formed. That was
why Harrisch and the other execs had wanted him to check
it out, to kneel down and bring his special qualifications to
bear on the dead thing in their midst. So he'd have that scent
in his nostrils, that inhaled taste at the back of his mouth,
when he'd stood back up and looked at them.

"You see?" Harrisch's voice poked at him again. "It
really is the kind of job for which you have a special knack. It
fits into your realm of experience. If not professionally, then
personally. Or perhaps at that point where professional and
personal meet."

Hated the guy before, hated him even more now;
McNihil weighed the consequences of just leaning back and
cocking his fist, unloading it in the exec's face. Satisfaction
would be high, the grief afterward higher, the payment at the
end close to total. People like Harrisch walked around invio-
lable, secure in their perch on the ladder. They invited fists,
they hung their faces out like smiling targets, asking for it.
Knowing that if you fired one off, the blow your arm ached
to deliver, they had ways of paying you back a thousandfold.
And if you didn't, if you just let your white-knuckled fist
hang at your side like a rock extracted from the sweating core
of the earth, the knot in your gut was their reward. They got
you either way.

That was how they worked it. McNihil knew that. He'd
worked for Harrisch, and for people just like him. The only
thing to do was to turn and walk away, to push past the
encircling wall of suits and carry your fist, heavy as lead, out
the door and down the unnumbered elevator, all the way to
the little space called home. Where you could soak your fist
in alcohol and morphine, applied from the inside out,
through gut and vein. Until you forgot, or forgot enough.

They wanted me to know, thought McNihil. *What they do
for fun.* They weren't ashamed; on the contrary. Harrisch and
the other company execs had wanted him to know, had

wanted McNihil to catch the same scent from them as he had from the corpse's mouth. Spit and mercury and blood. All of that and more, and none of it. The only marks on their bodies would be the scars on their tongues, the channel tracks, the contact points, the rain-wet battery terminals of their pleasures. The place where the blue spark leapt from emissary to recipient. *The kiss,* he thought, *that passeth understanding.* From one to the other, from the other to the one.

He let his fist unclench itself. These things didn't bother him so much anymore; they just made him feel older and more tired and disgusted. McNihil scanned across the faces of the execs waiting for his answer.

"Well?" Harrisch smiled at him. And didn't smile.

"Connect you, mother-connector." McNihil felt even more disgusted than before. "I'm outta here." He turned and walked. The circle broke, the nearest execs stepping back out of his way, before he could even shove them aside. Depriving him of that justifiable pleasure.

Harrisch called after him. "There's some details you should know about. Before you make your final decision."

Fingers touching the door's brass knob, McNihil stopped and glanced over his shoulder. "I already have."

"Perhaps." The smile didn't waver. "Though there's one more thing you should see. One more detail." He stepped back and reached down to the corpse, his hand drawing away the tousled shirt from one side, where the skin was still intact above the curve of ribs. "Our late friend seems to have gotten around." Harrisch watched for McNihil's reaction. "Quite a lot, wouldn't you say?"

He could see what the exec was showing him, from all the way across the room. A tattoo, the old-fashioned kind that didn't move around. Big and dark enough that McNihil, standing by the door, could easily make out what it was.

A classic banner scroll, curling around at each end, with some name or word that McNihil couldn't make out inscribed inside. That wasn't the important part; what mattered was the emblem above the banner. An ornate capital V, its point at the corpse's bottom rib, the serifed arms reaching to either side of his armpit. Exact and intricately detailed, as though the artist had completed half of a slanting cross, redeemer to be added later . . .

All of McNihil's restraining wisdom evaporated. When the red haze had flared, then faded behind his eyes, he saw Harrisch sprawled awkwardly across the corpse. The exec pushed himself up on one arm and rubbed his jaw, smearing the blood leaking out of the corner of his mouth.

That was what they really wanted me to see. McNihil wiped his torn knuckles against his shirt. Nobody in the room had taken a step closer, laid a hand on him. They had gotten what they wanted.

"You're the one, all right." Harrisch sat up, balancing himself with one hand on the corpse's chest. His smile showed red around the edges. "You're the one we want."

McNihil pulled open the door.

"Don't call me," said McNihil. "And I won't call you."

In the corridor outside the cubapt, he sensed someone else watching him, as he turned and headed toward the elevator. A glance over his shoulder and he saw her, down at the end of the hallway's flickering yellow pools of light. McNihil wasn't surprised; there was always one, sometimes several in these buildings. A cube bunny, this one prettier than most, and with large, sad eyes reddened with weeping. For Travelt, he figured; she must know that the object of her mercantile affections was dead.

McNihil could also tell that the cube bunny wanted to talk to him, that she'd been waiting there in the building's hallway to do just that. The girl looked up at him and started to say something; but he didn't feel like talking. Not just now. McNihil kept walking toward the elevator at the opposite end of the hallway, and thumbed the down button soon as he reached it.

The machinery groaned, rising toward him. He pulled the rattling cage open and stepped inside. Falling slowly and out of sight, McNihil dug into his pocket and took out the little golden pendant he'd palmed off the corpse.

A bit of metal like this might have its uses. The kind of thing that would tell him what Harrisch might not want him to know.

McNihil turned the cross-shaped crucifax over at the tips of his fingers and rubbed his thumb along the tiny bar code incised into the metal. In the row of lines, more delicate than his own thumbprint, he could almost read the dead man's profession of faith.

He wondered if—at the end, when the poor bastard's mouth had filled with ashes—it'd done any good at all.

Maybe, thought McNihil. He closed his eyes and let the grinding chain continue lowering him to the earth.

THREE

LOVELY THE WAY THE DEAD ARE

He doesn't have a prayer." The living woman spoke to the dead woman. "They'll get him. And then he'll have to do what they want."

The other woman was only somewhat dead. Technically so. At the center of her eyes, where other people, the living ones, had darkness, she had white and two little black ✖'s. The corneas the woman had when she'd been alive, officially so, had been sliced out and sold when there'd been an upward tick in that segment of the organ market. Now she looked out at the world through crosses tilted on their sides, cheap Taiwanese knockoffs, low-resolution scanning lenses.

"I don't know." The dead woman shrugged. Her hollowed cheekbones had edges sharp as dull knives. "I know

him better than you. I was married to him for years and
years. He's pretty clever. In his way. He could always find
another option."

"Like what?"

The dead woman turned her lovely face—lovely the way
the dead are—toward the living one. "He could always kill
himself."

"Ah."

The dead woman laid a cold hand on the living one's
cheek. "What's your name, child?"

She knows that. The living woman's name was November. Not the name her mother had given her, but the one
she'd given herself and that her friends, when she'd still had a
pack to run with, had endorsed as fitting. Snow touched her
brow, whiter than the yellow-tinged bone beneath the dead
woman's parchment skin. Ice walked through the ventricles
of her heart and down her pale arms, not as an indication of
cruelty—for she wasn't cruel, even when her living came at
the price of others' breath—but as the metaphor of sadness.
When she had nothing better to do—when she was far
enough ahead in her accounts that she didn't have to worry
about her own death, at least for a little while—she could
ride down to the bottom of the Gloss, to the Pacific Rim's
southern crossing, where the trains worked their way across
ice floes and polar fields, past the great sliding glaciers and
over the storm-lashed seas. She could lean her forehead
against one of the luxury cars' triple-sealed windows, feeling
through the layers of glass and vacuum the cold of that world
outside, seeping through her skin and into her flesh, meeting
blood that seemed almost the same temperature. Across the
tiny unfolded table in front of her seat would be twists of
paper and scraps of metal foil, the snowy contents unwrapped and ingested in any appropriate way, molecules un-
locking under a Velcro'd patch of skin, or gums and mucosa
stinging under the attack of microscopic drill-bits tugging

bad-attitude atoms behind them. Getting to her feet as the
first shivering rush hit her, eons of glacial motion compressed into seconds as her spine was measured by endorphins and rage; knocking over the champagne flute of the
man sitting next to her, spilling wet prickling stars into his
lap; stumbling out blind into the swaying center aisle, the
magnified thunder of her pulse knocking her off-balance
more than the train's motion as it tilted through the banked
maglev tracks, under cliffs of ice, her heart seizing as though
its hinges had snagged on hard crystals, lurching into the next
beat by some lower brain-stem force of will—

He could always kill himself.

The dead woman's words echoed inside November's
skull; she could close her eyes and still hear them, rolling like
thunder in the air and the iron wheels of the oldest trains that
ran the circle. She supposed the dead woman was right.
Though there were different ways of killing yourself, ways
that efficiently and tidily left you still alive afterward.

Ways like those in the memory flash that had blossomed
inside her head, thinking about her own name. What came
after the stumbling out into the train's aisle: pushing her way
past the backs of the plush seats, her vision opened into a
blur-rimmed tunnel, tight enough that she didn't have to see
the faces turning up toward her, didn't have to see anything
except the auto-sliding door that led between cars and the
door that didn't open by itself, a smaller one, some kind of
maintenance access, which opened into one of those spaces
that people with a desperate need for privacy and little need
for comfort could always find. The cross-treaded metal was
always littered with orange plastic hypodermic caps, like
thimbles for depraved faery folk, the needles themselves
crackling underfoot like the blood-specked ground of a steel
forest. The Antarctic cold crawled in sharper here, her exhaled breath nebulous in front of her face, inhaled ice burning down into her trachea. Pinpoint metal scratched her

knees when some *teneviki* arbitrageur from the Gloss's Vladivostok zone followed her into the narrow space, put his
capitalist hands on her shoulders, and pushed her down. The
one whose champagne she'd spilled; his crotch still darkly
stained and smelling of wine, the teeth of the zipper and his
polished fingernails glistening wet, his other hand already
tangled in her hair and drawing her closer, his back against
the hidden door, the world tight as a refrigerated coffin.

He doesn't have a prayer . . .

None of them ever did. She knew that was why she was
named November. Even when she was alone again, kneeling
in that little space, the side of her head against the metal
separating her from the snow and ice sailing by outside, with
the taste of salt and chlorine at the back of her throat. In the
world outside, the great big empty one, the ice beheaded the
gray waves, the ground split open in white fissures, the bones
of ancient wooden ships were picked over by the wind. The
train rolled on, or flew a millimeter above the charged tracks,
and through some window that opened inside her skull, she
could see the empty snowscapes, the oceans that chilled
drowning men's hearts to a standstill within thirty seconds;
she could see all that without looking outside, she could see
it without opening her eyes. She could spit out the taste of
the *tenevik,* a clouded wet thing glistening on the needles
around her; she could stand up, a little steadier on her legs as
her muscles recongealed into usability, stand and straighten
out her clothes that the hard, manicured hands had dislodged
through the neckline of her blouse, a simple white button
snapped free and rolling through the hypodermic parapher-
nalia on the metal floor. Stand and push open the hidden
door that led back into the train's heated spaces, where her
breath would no longer be a visible and fading thing, and
walk back to her seat in the luxury car, slide past the elegant
chalk-stripe knees of the man's trousers, the spilled champagne already evaporated from his lap. He wouldn't even

look up from the rows of numbers in the folded-open Bang-
kok edition of *The Wall Street Journal*. Which was as she
preferred it as she sat back in the plush seat and watched
Antarctica unfold outside the insulated windows. It wasn't
the chemicals slowly evaporating from her bloodstream that
had kept her from feeling anything.

"You know my name," she said aloud.

The dead woman made no reply. The white-centered
eyes with the little crosses in them gazed on some interior
landscape, some territory where the man she'd been married
to, and who was still alive, was all unknowingly getting into
deeper shit.

The poor bastard, thought November. She felt sorry for
the man—his name was McNihil—in her usual, nonem-
pathic way. An intellectual process, like watching one ice
floe grind implacably against another, the white fields cracking and splintering as though alive but not sentient. It didn't
make her feel sad—nothing did, or at least not any sadder—but it was still something that had to be figured into her
own calculations. He might get in her way, impede the run
of her business activities. That was what she felt sorry about.
She otherwise felt no hostility toward him. To be fatal and
noncaring at the same time; it just worked that way. The ice
surged and hammered against itself.

November zipped up her jacket, sealing a chrome-dotted
leather skin around herself. Not to keep out the cold—this
wasn't the Antarctic; here, in the territory of the dead, the
sun beat down like sulphurous cake frosting—but to keep her
own coldness bottled around her heart.

Even her being here, the fact of her coming to the dead
land and talking to the dead woman—that was part of the
troubles circling and closing around McNihil. He didn't
know yet, but he would.

"I'm leaving now." She bent down, bringing her face
close to the dead woman's, looking right into the black-and-

white eyes. The room, a tiny space filled with untidily stacked, yellowing papers, windows filmed with dust, ate up her words without echoes. Exactly the sort of room the dead would be expected to live in, or at least exist. She had been in ones just like it, before this; the dead were always a good source of information. It was their business. November straightened up; she could still feel the dead woman's hand where the pale fingers had touched her cheek. "Thanks for everything."

The dead woman looked up at her. "When it happens," she said, "when it all comes down . . . don't be too hard on him."

November laid her own hand against the thin, cheap door behind herself. "Why?" She was only mildly curious. "Do you still love him?"

"Of course not." The dead woman managed a smile. "I never did. But he has his virtues. In his way."

For a long time after that, after she had left the little room and the place where the dead lived, she wondered what the dead woman had meant by that. Then she decided it wasn't important.

When she was on one of the trains again, heading north, back to where living people lived, or at least approximately so—she let a little more memory flash unwind inside her head. To the end of the story, or one of the stories, part of the whole that made up the lapidary, carefully assembled history of her name. She couldn't even remember which one it was, whether it'd been that anonymous *tenevik,* some currency cowboy out of the Nakhodka FEZ, who'd shown up in the first reel of the flash, that one or some other member of the shadow people working the Dow Jones/*nomenklatura* overlap in Vladivostok and points west, or a little-dragons personnel enforcer shuttling antique punched-hole loom cards from Djakarta to the Lima child-labor free-enterprise zones . . . or another one entirely. It didn't matter which

one; they never had faces for her but just cruel, hard, pleasur-
ing hands . . . which was enough for her purposes.

They only had faces if they made the mistake of following her off the train, in whatever city on the circle she'd
decided to make her destination. As if they hadn't gotten
enough of her in that little cramped space rolling across the
ocean and the ice floes; as if there were anything more that
she was willing to give them. *Dream on, loser*—she would
silently transmit the warning behind herself as she pushed
through the crowds in the station, aware of the figure tailing
after, erectile tissue transformed into slow heat-seeking mis-
sile. She'd been in every station along the Gloss's edge—the
Gloss being the shorthand for Glossolalia, which was either
the Greater Los Angeles Inter-Alia or the babel of languages
that faded into one another in the almost-complete urban
circle around the Pacific, which was to say the world. And
every station had its tight private spaces as well, maintenance
closets and walk-in fuse boxes and the women's rest rooms so
far off the main drag that they had been annexed into I.V.-
hype and subcute territory, the needle discards and depleted
osmotic skin-pouches all over the floor, the festooned toilet
paper freckled with blood specks. She made it easy, or at least
faster, on her would-be predators by sliding into one of those
obscured nooks, without even a glance over her shoulder,
then waiting. It only took a few seconds, the number of steps
he'd let stretch out between himself and his prey, the prey
that he'd already caught and savored once. That was the brief
moment in which she might see one of their faces, if there
was light enough.

It didn't matter whether she did, though. Because she
would already be standing with her back against the wall or
the divider panel or the tangled ranks of fuses and wiring, she
would already be reaching up with one hand as the man
pushed the door of the closet or the rest room stall shut
behind himself. He would already be smiling, his eyes nar-

rowed to little hungry slits as her hand touched the side of his
head, her fingertips sliding through his hair and onto the
back of his skull, as though she were going to draw him
toward her for a kiss. But the smile would freeze on his face,
it would still be there but it would mean something else, it
would mean both pleasure and terror at the center of his
eyes, one and the same thing, as she and the mark got into
serious transcranial magnetic stimulation time. The fields
pulsed from the rare-earth devices imbedded in her fingertips, at an exact ten-thousandth-of-a-second cycle, ramping
up to 3+ tesla, more than enough to penetrate human scalp
and skull, and into the top cortical layers. Tight magnet currents sparked and modulated and found their way to the exact cerebral tissue necessary to produce lock-loop orgasm
and a general paralysis, his muscles locking hard onto each
other, his body its own ejaculating prison. She had only
enough battery power in the system to freeze the poor horny
bastard for ten to fifteen seconds. But that was more than
enough; she worked fast. And all she really had to do was
reach into his jacket and pull out the weight of metal she
knew he'd be carrying there, a hammer with fire inside.
They all carried heat when they traveled. She'd put it against
the mark's head where her hands had been, his eyes the only
part that could still move, flicking to watch her, to bring the
big black piece she held into focus. Then she merely had to
pull the trigger, the weight cold inside her fist; the implosion
muzzle formed a perfect repulsion-edged vacuum in the little
zone beyond her wrist, just big enough for the bullet to rush
into soundlessly, the anti-acoustic effect lasting just long
enough to soak up the telltale bang. The only sound that
escaped, that might have been heard outside the maintenance
closet or rest room stall, was the crumpling impact of bullet
through rounded bone of skull, gentle as an egg being
crushed with the poke of a finger. That was how the better
grade of silencers worked on guns: you didn't get absolute

silence, the absence of all sound. Instead, you got the revelation of other sounds, the ones beneath the gun's otherwise masking roar. You got—she got—the crack of skull and the wet swallow of the imploding cerebral tissue beneath, the man's gasp at this new, virginal penetration. He might've been paralyzed but he could still feel. At least for a little while. Until the blood rushed to fill the hole and wash what was left of him out the exit wound on the other side of his head, where the bone splinters, hinged by torn flesh, fanned out like a surgical peony. Resulting in a death bigger than the little one he'd enjoyed before, a death big enough to be the last one needed. She'd let this one, whatever his face had been, fall away from her; the same as the others had fallen, so that she had to step over him to push open the door of the tiny space and stride quickly away. November always left the guns behind; who needed them? The spattered muzzle of the gun would already be soaking a wet spot into the wadded toilet paper on the rest room's floor as she'd insert herself anonymously into the crowd, the station, and then whatever part of the Gloss lay beyond.

The memory ran out, reached its terminus inside November's head. She could call it up anytime she wanted, which wasn't often, and with any face attached, any blurred focus tag as to which particular man it might have been, on which train and in which small space littered with the remnants of other passions. She rarely let it get that specific, though; better to keep that section of her brain's contents vague and generic, sharp only on those moments when she had pulled the trigger and read the bright tea-leaf pattern on each space's low ceiling. If the spots of blood and brain tissue spelled out her name, in some red wet braille . . . she wouldn't have been surprised. Only mildly annoyed, at having to reach up on tiptoe with a scrap of tissue, to wipe away the betraying signature.

November gazed out the train window. Not at the

Antarctic; she was too far north on the circle for that. The
train moved slowly through the city's jumbled outskirts.
Strictly a local, for the short ride down to where the dead
lived—sort of—and then back up to the True Los Angeles
sector of the Gloss. Even now, she wasn't quite sure why
she'd gone down there. To talk to the dead woman, the one
who'd been married once upon a time, when she'd been
alive, to the poor bastard named McNihil. She hadn't found
out anything; she supposed now that that hadn't been the
point of the journey.

He doesn't have a prayer . . .

That was probably true. November looked out at the city
and figured she'd find out soon enough.

FOUR

LIKE A YOUNG IDA LUPINO

The girl was waiting for him inside his apartment. The cube bunny that he'd spotted lurking around in the corpse's hallway.

"How'd you get in here?" McNihil would have felt no particular surprise or anger, even if there hadn't been a slowly dissipating haze of alcohol over his brain. He closed the door, which she'd bypassed somehow, with all its locks and dead bolts in place.

"Oh . . . you know." She gave him a shrug and a timid smile, from where she sat over on the crookbacked, threadbare couch. "There's always ways."

"I suppose so." McNihil slipped his rattling keyring into his pocket, his fingertips brushing against an even smaller piece of metal, which hadn't been there when he'd left this morning. "You want some coffee or something?" With the jacket unbuttoned, hanging shroud-loose from his shoulders, he threaded his way through the apartment's cramped spaces. "Frankly, I need some."

"Sure." The cube bunny sat leaning forward, hands clasped at the corner that her knees made in her worn woolen skirt. The fabric had probably been midnight-blue at one time, but had faded to somewhere closer to nine P.M.; that was the tone of gray it looked like in McNihil's eyes. "That'd be great." The girl didn't draw back as McNihil passed by her, close enough that her skirt was brushed by his trousers leg. She glanced up hopefully. "Would it be real coffee?"

"You're kidding." With his forearm, McNihil pushed aside the stacks of dishes and Chinese-restaurant take-out cartons by the sink, giving himself enough room to assemble the battered chrome sections of the percolator. On the kitchen wall, by the oven's flue outlet, a calendar with days but no year hung, its unlikely mountain scene faded to a curling-edged transparency.

"Mr. Travelt always had real coffee." A slight tone of resentment sounded in the girl's voice.

"Yeah, well, there isn't enough caffeine in the world to get a rise out of him now." McNihil threaded the plug past the unwashed glasses and into the socket in the linoleum behind them.

"No," the cube bunny said mournfully. "No, there isn't."

He figured he knew what came next. That she would start crying, not in a big emotional show, but just a few effective tears, half from real grief over somebody who'd been nice to her—or as nice as could be expected—and half for the effect it should have on her audience. And would have; he didn't see things the way he did, this sad and

mournfully beautiful world instead of the other one with all
the colors, if he weren't also inclined toward its emotional
weather.

McNihil turned his gaze from the doorway and back
toward the things on the kitchen counter, as the girl rooted
through the little black handbag she'd tucked beside her on
the couch. He knew that if he'd gone on watching, he
would've seen her come up with some little cotton handker-
chief with the initials in the corner, which the nonexistent
nuns back in the convent school had taught her to hand-
embroider. Instead of the plastic-wrapped pack of disposables
soaked in heat-activated antivirals that she'd really have on
the other side of the reality line.

He dipped his hand in the water in the sink, then ran his
fingertips across the surface of the just-warming coffeepot.
The wetness made a slightly shinier mirror out of the curved
metal. Shiny things worked better for this than real mirrors;
anything big and intentionally reflective got absorbed too
quickly into this world's firmness. But in little bits of chrome
and silver, sometimes the back of a spoon or a polished door-
knob, he saw a scrap from the other side, a bit of optical leak-
through, colors bleeding into the monochrome.

This time, he saw the girl sitting on the couch. McNihil
turned the metal pot slightly, angling the wet reflective
patch's shot through the kitchen doorway and toward the
apartment's living room. Seeing her this way, the girl didn't
look like a young Ida Lupino anymore. The curls against her
pale cheeks had vanished, along with the general air of brave
vulnerability and period early-forties outfit from Raoul
Walsh's *High Sierra* that'd been laid over her in McNihil's
world. The worn-and-mended woolen skirt, the thin unbuttoned sweater with a zigzag decorative pattern around the
bottom and at the cuffs showing her tiny wrists, the plain
high-collared blouse . . . all that McNihil had already seen

her in had been replaced, at least in the percolator's distorted mirror. Replaced by what was sadly real.

More skin; that was what was mainly noticeable. Still in a skirt, of some kind of black plasticky stuff with the slick sheen of fetish enthusiasms. But hiked nearly pudenda-high, with correspondingly bare arms and cleavage. The neoprene highlights shimmered with the slow fever gleam of neon on a rain-wet nocturnal street. Over on the other side, where the colors were, a girl could freeze to death in an outfit like that, not so much from air temperature as the coldly assessing gazes of men.

Just like a cube bunny, thought McNihil. He hadn't expected anything else. It was no wonder she'd been able to get into his apartment. That was about the only kind of survival skill her species possessed. Beyond, at least, the value of skin and flesh and face.

The little vision, the peek into the girl's hard-side existence, faded as the coffeepot heated up, evaporating the wetness on its curved chrome flank. Which was all right by McNihil. He preferred things—especially human things—in black and white. Hands against the edge of the counter, he closed his eyes and leaned his weight forward, easing out the kinks in his stiff spine as he waited for the pot to sigh in steam.

Overhead, bare lightbulbs dimmed for a second as the coffeepot gurgled wetly. A cranking mechanical noise came from the rear of the apartment, where all the black cables ran. McNihil's generator was the envy of the surrounding apartments. A sleek, grease-fed hummer that he kept swaddled in rags to cut down the residual noise, its intestinelike exhaust sphincter duct-taped to a hole he'd punched in the building's exterior. There were other people in the building who weren't so fortunate; they got by on batteries or candles, or gave up the desire, the need, for light entirely. *Like connecting cave fish,* brooded McNihil; it sometimes gave him the creeps to even think about it. *Creep* being the operative word—he could see them in his brain's interior optic, moving around in the pitch-black with their big lemur eyes or the holes where their vestigial eyes had been, their fingers radiating out in front of them like cockroach antennae. Like roaches in more ways than that: whenever he came back to the building, if he pushed the ground-level door open fast enough, he could hear them fleeing back into the even-darker recesses where they were blindly comfortable. Some of those people—if that word still applied—were so devolved, the charity agencies didn't even make personal deliveries anymore, but just sort of pushed food packets at the end of a long stick into the gloom, and let whatever was in there grab them and be gone.

Waiting for the coffee, McNihil reached down and massaged his aching leg. Climbing five flights to get here, through stairwells and landings palely lit by sputtering fluorescent halos, or with nothing but shadows and ammoniacal piss odors seeping into the ankle-deep fast-food trash and discarded subcutaneous-membrane packs—he'd gotten used to it. If he held himself very still, breath stopped and heartbeat slowed, he could hear inside the thin layers of walls and through the buckling floors. Little creatures and the slightly bigger ones that fed on them were scurrying about on their own errands, guided in darkness by the ripe smells of rain-saturated decay. The human inhabitants of the building, and all the similar buildings clustered around it, scuttled through their various agendas the same way, either in the dark or a wavering, battery-fed glow, flashlights duct-taped to the water-stained ceilings.

"Here you go." McNihil handed a cup, no saucer, to the cube bunny. It was the only cup in the place without a cracked rim.

"Thanks." She held it cradled in both hands. She managed to conceal her distaste for the ersatz as she took a sip.

And even lifted a slightly apologetic smile toward him. "That's not too bad."

"Nothing ever is." McNihil lowered himself into the frayed upholstery of the chair across from her. "Too bad, I mean." He could see himself in the black mirror of his own heavy restaurant-china cup. "It's amazing what people can get used to." He looked the same, he supposed, in this world and the other one. "Take me, for instance. Little while ago, I was inhaling a dead man's breath. As if the poor bastard could breathe at all. And you know what?" McNihil leaned back, watching for her reaction. "It didn't bother me at all."

What he'd said didn't faze her. The cube bunny's eyes were tearless, the lashes' cheap drugstore mascara unsmudged, as she regarded McNihil over the rim of the cup. Which meant, he supposed, that the late Travelt had been more than a meal ticket for her. She'd done her crying in some private place, out on the street. *Private* meaning that out there, no one would take any notice. Tears now would've meant self-pity and the play for her one-on-one audience's sympathy.

She lowered the cup, setting it down on the low table between them. Leaning forward, she peered into the centers of McNihil's eyes, as if her lost tears could be found there. "You don't see me," she said finally. "I mean . . . you don't see *me*."

Not stupid, McNihil grudgingly admitted to himself. That was a mistake people made, to think that someone who lived the way she did would be an idiot. A surface phenomenon: a cube bunny's looks, the way this one looked under the firm overlay he saw, was strictly a survival adaptation. They could be as smart as anyone else. Though that wouldn't save them, either.

"I see you fine," said McNihil. His voice sounded stiff and uncomfortable, even to himself. That was his way of handling personal things. "I see you the way I want to. Or at least the way I'm used to."

"How's that?" She had leaned so close to him, over the table, that she could've kissed him. Inside her eyes, McNihil could see himself, small and duplicated. "I don't understand."

She couldn't tell by looking at him; no one could. Some things were truly invisible. The micron-film inlays inside his eyes—inside the eyes of anyone who'd had the same kind of work done on them—had a refractive index clearer than any air that could be breathed in the Gloss. A scalpel and a set of dentist's picks would've been necessary to dig out the interpreter relays running parallel to his optic nerves. And the stuff farther back, past the optic chiasma and into the soft processors of the occipital gyri and sulci . . . those dark little rooms were a mystery even before any of the other work had been done.

"But I *know*," the cube bunny said softly. "That you don't. See right. I can tell."

McNihil wasn't surprised by that, either. That was what cube bunnies were good at. It wasn't their major job skill—their skin and flesh was that—but it was a major adjunct, anyway. The ability to tell things about people, to figure out in some deep nonverbal way what the score was. And how to profit thereby.

Girls like her confounded the corporations. That's what they'd evolved to do. The whole point of cube life, the logical extension of the system of shuffling employees in and out of workplace cubicles at random, had been revealed back at the millennium turn to be psychological warfare on the corporations' own. What the human-resource managers and company psychs called *optimized transience disorientation*. It was all straight out of Henry Denkmann's magnum opus, *Connect 'Em Till They Bleed: Pimp-Style Management™ for a New Century,* which hadn't so much revolutionized corpo-

rate life as confirmed and blessed what had already been
going on. This particular theory being an extension of the
old New Orleans whore-hustling motto, that they weren't
completely under your control if they still thought they
had names of their own: if employees didn't have a place to
call their own all during the day—if they didn't scent-
mark familiar walls and desks with their family photos and
funny plastic figures stuck on top of their computer
monitors—then it was that much easier to ream out their
heads and stick in whatever behavior patterns the human-
resource departments wanted. The only problem being that
the employees still went home, to the same home over and
over, defeating all the psychs' good work, keeping bad atti-
tudes high, as indicated in the standard measurements of
workplace sabotage, absenteeism and pay agitation, and theft
of office supplies. The cubapts solved all that, or at least most
of it.

Better a freelancer, McNihil had decided a long time ago.
The Collection Agency might've wound up connecting him
over as well, but it'd at least left most of the contents of his
head intact. Shabby as this place was—and he'd had better,
back when the agency gigs had been lining his pockets—at
least he'd never had to shuffle every evening from one com-
pany-assigned anonymous living-space to another, with his
clothes and a little box of irreducible personal belongings
packed and waiting for him when he got home to the next
one. That'd be a stone drag, even at the relatively luxurious
levels that an up-and-coming junior exec got shuffled in and
out of. The corpse, which McNihil had looked at a little
while ago, had been like that. The poor bastard had died on
the company farm.

"You're thinking about him, aren't you?" The cube
bunny was still looking intently into McNihil's eyes. "I can
tell that, too."

"Yeah, I suppose you can." The little ways that cube

bunnies and others in their low-rent quadrant of the sexual-
services industry had. Which drove the corporations' psychs
up the wall. How could you reduce your company's employees to perfect productive zeroes, with no hindering attach-
ments to things or places, if cube bunnies and the like kept
showing up at their doors, or even worse, inside their
cubapts, sailing right past all the locks and security devices?
And the same cube bunny, or the gender-preferenced equivalent, for each employee. When that goes on, the erosion of
nonproductive personality structures—the human-resources
goal that management had taken over from the previous century's old-line drug-rehab programs—and all the other good
things that come from a randomized living environment, all
that gets kicked out on the street. Or some of it, at least.

The cube bunny smiled at him. "I'm good at what I do."

"You must be." There had been a hint in the girl's voice,
about her other job skills. He decided to let that pass for the
time being. "You know," said McNihil, "I see you just fine.
I see you the way I'd rather."

She tilted her head to one side, studying him. "You had
that operation, didn't you?"

"I've had several." McNihil shrugged. "I've led a rough
life. Or maybe just an unlucky one."

"No, silly; you know what I mean. *That* operation. That
thing . . ." The cube bunny hesitated, then pointed to her
own face. "With the eyes and stuff. Where they cut 'em
open and . . . put things in 'em."

" 'Things?' "

"Things you see."

"Well, sweetheart . . ." McNihil took another draw on
the brackish liquid in the cup. "That's what they do, all
right. They stuff whole worlds in there." He returned a
fragment of the smile she'd given him. "They even put *you*
in there."

The rest of the smile had faded away. "I don't understand." She drew back apprehensively. "I don't know what you're talking about. Mr. Travelt didn't have anything like that."

"That's because . . ." McNihil set his cup down on the table. "He was a smarter man than I am. Though it doesn't seem to have done him much good."

She didn't seem to hear the last comment. "Why would you do something like that?" An appalled fascination narrowed her gaze. "Let them do that to you?"

" 'Let them'?" McNihil laughed. "Shit, I *paid* for it. Didn't come cheap, either. It was a while back, when I was doing rather better than I am now." He gestured toward the shabby apartment encasing them. "I could afford to be in at the beginning of a product-introduction cycle."

"What happened?"

"I came down in the world." *In this one and the other,* he thought but didn't say aloud.

"No," said the cube bunny, "I mean with the operation. And your eyes. It must've gone wrong, huh? I heard they do that. And then you're . . . you know . . . not right."

"If I am—" One finger tapped the side of the cup in front of McNihil. "It's not because of my eyes." He picked the ersatz coffee up and drank. "Besides," he said, leaning back, "what do you know about it? I wouldn't have thought there were things like that back in Kansas."

"There ain't shit in Kansas." A little cloud of unsunned memory passed across the cube bunny's face.

"That's where you're from? I was just guessing." McNihil felt sorry for her. On the other side of the reality line, in that world he'd glimpsed in the wet reflection of the chrome percolator, she had all that other world's pretty genetics, a child's face grafted by survival-oriented evolution onto an adult's body, one that hadn't needed to be surgically pumped up to achieve its Blakean lineaments of desire. *Born that way,* thought McNihil. They came out of the rusting

wastelands at the center of the continent, boys and girls together, walking the dead roads of Kansas and Ohio all the
way to the Pacific Rim cities, True Los Angeles and all
around the Gloss to Vladivostok and the Chinese and Southeast Asian zones. Where they had something to sell: themselves and their sheer prettiness, the exact combinations of
size of eye, distance between, angle of nose and space to the
perfect upper lip. The infantile kink, the baby-sex lure, was
seemingly programmed right into the human nervous system. It lodged right down at the base of the spine, where
some kundalinic serpent with icy pederast gaze uncoiled and
went either wet or stiff at the sight of its prey. Even in his
own, he had to admit. Before the vision had faded on the
side of the coffeepot, a needle-eyed weasel had smiled at the
center of his brain.

Maybe that's why, thought McNihil. *I'd rather see her this
way.* Safer emotionally, no matter whatever else might happen. He was still a married man, even though his wife was
technically dead.

"Mr. Travelt told me about them." The cube bunny slid
past the question about where she'd come from, the dry zone
before she'd hit the Gloss. "He knew all about them. In the
company he worked for . . . Dyna-something . . ."

"Zauber," said McNihil. "DynaZauber. Like the song."

That produced a frown. "What song?"

"You know. Beethoven. The Ninth. About how it's all
going to *bind uns wieder.*"

The cube bunny shook her head. "I wouldn't know
about that."

"Just as well. The only reason those people want to do
any *bind*-ing is so they can get into our pockets easier. Just
another word for connecting."

A little flinch; the girl he saw in his eyes was probably
more sensitive to dirty words than the cube bunny underneath. After a moment, she nodded. "Anyway, he used to

work in the division that made that stuff. That's in your eyes. But that was before he got promoted.''

"Too bad he's dead, then. Maybe he could've told me why my debits keep coming back." Every month, he wrote out an actual hard-copy paper check, payment for the firmness-overlay maintenance, and every month it came bouncing back with a form letter about the service having been discontinued, thanks for your patronage, be sure and try our other fine enhanced experiential products, blah and more blah.

"Oh?" Mentioning something about money had perked up the cube bunny's interest.

"This late in the game," groused McNihil, "you'd think companies could get their billing straight." He shook his head. "For a while there, I was putting the money away in another account, until I finally figured, screw it, might as well spend it." That'd been right after he'd gotten bounced off the Collection Agency's operatives list, and things had gotten tight as an anaconda's rectum before he'd lined up another paying gig. "They sort it out and want their money, they can come and get it. Fat chance, though."

The girl didn't know what he was talking about. She was still fascinated, childlike, by his eyes, peering into them and trying to see what she couldn't.

"When you look at me," said the cube bunny after a moment. "What do you see?"

"Another world."

If not a better one, then at least more to his liking. *I've gotten used to it,* McNihil told himself. Like a dream that you know you're dreaming, but don't want to wake up from.

For a few seconds, he let the limits of his vision expand beyond the girl sitting in front of him—the tough little, soft little Lupino clone, one of the compensating gifts that his eyes bestowed on him—and out past the gray walls of the shabby apartment. Past the unlit hallways and the faint smells

of dog-bottle alcohol and sweating bedsheets that seeped out
from under the doors, and out into the night's alleys and
cracked sidewalks, with their pools of streetlamp glow that
didn't reach from one to the other, that left patches of darkness stitched with buzzing neon above the steps of basement
gin mills that you descended like marching into one's grave.

The world in the shabby apartment, that smelled like
burnt coffee and suspicion, and the one outside that McNihil
saw—it was real enough for him. That the cube bunny, and
everyone else, didn't see it made no difference.

"You kinda see me, though," decided the cube bunny.
"I mean, I'm real—I'm really here—and you can see that. So
that's a help."

"Sure is." That was the difference between what he'd
had done and all those old-fashioned total-environment sim-
ulations, that unsubtle virtual bunk that simply substituted
one gross set of cooked-up sensory feed for what came in
unassisted from the real world. The problem with those sim
arrangements, and the reason they'd died a quick, merciful
death on the consumer market even before the bandwidth
and nerve-receptor bugs could be worked out, was that nobody could get any work done with them. Not in the real
world, at least.

Whereas the thin-film insertion surgery that he'd paid
for—and gotten; McNihil still didn't regret it—was basically
a businessman's product. He supposed that some of the exces
that had been standing around the corpse probably had accessible over-layers inside their own eyes. Controlled by the
muscles of the eye socket, the interplay of the rectus lateralis
and the superior and inferior oblique muscles, pulling and
distorting the spheres of aqueous humor—not to focusing on
nearer or farther objects, but activating one inserted layer or
another, switching the perceived world into translucent
spreadsheets or databases floating above the hard objects of
people and other real things.

"That's how it works for them," said McNihil. He'd told
the cube bunny all about it, as he'd gotten up and poured
himself the remainder of the coffee in the pot. He stood
leaning against the side of the kitchen doorway, sipping the
lukewarm, kerosenelike fluid. "Strictly business." It was a big
reason why he had such an aversion to executive types, like
that DZ bunch with Harrisch at their head. "You can be
talking to them," he mused aloud, "and you'll be looking at
them, right in the face, and they're looking back at you. And
then you see the eyes shifting, like they're looking past you
into the distance, or at some place just past their noses. And
you know they're not really looking at you, they're reading
some market-update numbers that'd just crawled in over the
wire." McNihil shrugged. "I've always just found that kind
of offensive."

"But that's not what you see." The cube bunny held her
own empty cup enfolded in her hands. "I mean . . . it's
not some kind of business thing with you."

"Well . . . maybe." McNihil shook his head. "I don't
really know, anymore. I've been seeing things this way for a
long time now. I don't make any distinctions between what
it was I wanted to see and . . ." It was hard to say. "And
what it's useful for me to see. I don't know if those are two
different things."

The cube bunny had another question, very serious and
important, the way children's questions are. "Am I . . .
pretty? The way you see me?"

The way he saw her . . . the way he saw everything.
He supposed there was no way of really telling her. Just what
it was that he saw. There wouldn't be any shared points of
reference between himself and a creature of survival-oriented
sexuality such as the one sitting in front of him, like some
kind of grayed-out butterfly caught in a dingy cardboard box
with his name on it. The whole perceptual system of *hard*
and *firm* and *soft* reality—he might've been able to explain

that, with some effort on both their parts. It was really just
the difference between the hard components of the world,
the things that really existed, that didn't go away even if
you'd wanted them to; and the firm overlay that was programmed in over the hard stuff, that transformed the other
world into the one he felt and saw and smelled and tasted;
and the soft, which was all that he could pick up and move
around, change and destroy. Just as in that world, the unaltered one, on the other side of the reality line: there were
some things you could do something about, and other things
you couldn't.

"You look fine," said McNihil truthfully. "You're absolutely lovely."

"Really?"

"Why should I lie to you?" She did look lovely to him;
better than in the smeared, wavering reflection on the side of
the coffeepot. He'd paid to see a world that was to his liking.
Not beautiful—it was based, after all, on cultural artifacts of
more than a century ago, the bleak and brooding crime and
thriller movies of the 1930s and forties—but with beautiful
things in it. More beautiful, actually, for being surrounded by
constant threat and darkness. So that if he could sit in a
shabby, too-small room that smelled like dust settling on
bare, flickering lightbulbs, if he could sit across from a girl
who looked—at least to him—like an actress from those ancient films that nobody watched anymore, a woman with
heartbreaking eyes . . . that was all right by him. And if she
looked both sad and desperate, fragile and eternal, a mouth
that was softly red even when seen in black and white . . .

Then the money he'd paid to the surgeons had been well
spent.

The cube bunny hadn't said anything, but had smiled at
him. McNihil supposed he'd said the right thing. Even if it
was the truth. Sometimes it worked out that way.

He supposed her smile meant something else as well. *You*

shouldn't think so much, McNihil told himself. *About the things you see. The way you see them.*

"But . . . you don't really know." The cube bunny's smile faded. "If I'm pretty or not. 'Cause you don't really see me." A tear trembled against her lashes. "You just see that stuff that's in there, inside your eyes."

"That's not how it works." McNihil set his empty cup down on the counter and walked back out of the kitchen. "It's a little more subtle than that. It has to be." He didn't imagine he had any way of explaining these things to someone like her. The world she'd come out of was too far different from any he lived in, on either side of the firm line. "Only idiots want to inhabit a world separate from anyone else. I mean literally idiots, would-be idiots; you know, from that *idios kosmos* notion of a private universe." He could see that he'd lost her on that one. "There's just no point in thinking that you're picking up things that don't exist, or talking to people that are just part of some dummied-up sensory load. That kind of stuff died out back in the mini-theme-park days. Kids standing around with big ugly goggles on, swatting away at nothing. That kind of stuff's crap. But seeing the same things that everybody else does, but just seeing them differently . . . hey, that's the way it is for *everyone.*"

"It is?"

"Sure," said McNihil. He was on a roll now. He'd walked over behind the couch, standing just in back of where the cube bunny sat. "There might even be some people who're so connected up . . . that they wouldn't even be able to see how beautiful you are." *Like that other poor bastard,* thought McNihil. *The dead one.* What'd the late Travelt's problem been, that he'd gotten into that prowler shit? When he had someone like this available and willing. Just went to prove something that McNihil had believed for a long time.

That people engineered, with all the craft and will they could summon, their own annihilations.

The cube bunny said nothing. McNihil wondered if she had a name. He supposed he could give her one, something cute and temporary; it only had to last as long as whatever connection existed between them. Which was probably measurable in hours. *If that,* he thought glumly. She was the loveliest thing that had ever been inside the dark, cramped space of his working and living accommodation. Like some self-destructive flower that had bloomed here, begging to be crushed inside anyone's fist.

He wondered how much the late Travelt had ever given in to those provoked desires. A little bruise, partly healed and fading, could be seen at the hinge of her jaw, just below her delicate ear. Given the stupid shit that the dead man had gotten into, it was entirely possible that the mark came from him, that the corpse's thumb and fingers would match up, like an ID handprint to buzz him through the door and into that private space where desires were satisfied.

"Why did you come here?"

She twisted about on the couch and looked back up at him. She shook her head. "I don't have a reason."

"People always have a reason," said McNihil. "At least in the world I live in. The one I see."

"I . . . I don't know." The cube bunny's open gaze locked on to his narrower one. "Maybe . . . I was lonely."

"You came to the wrong place, then. We've already got plenty of that here." McNihil laid his hands on her shoulders. The warmth of her skin rose through the layers of thin cotton and wool and into his palms. "But Mr. Travelt is dead, isn't he?"

She nodded. "Yes . . ."

"Well, I can't replace him for you." He let one hand, with its own will, brush softly against the side of her neck. "I don't have that kind of cash."

"That's all right." The cube bunny gave him an under-standing, forgiving smile. "It'd still be okay."

"Just as long," said McNihil, "as you understand that."

The cube bunny nodded again, without speaking.

He came around to the front of the couch and took her hand, pulling her up toward him. When he'd led her down the apartment's dimly lit hallway, he stopped suddenly at the door of the bedroom. "Wait a second."

Back in the kitchen, McNihil pulled the plug of the coffeepot. The burnt smell of the residue inside had already tinged the air; it could be tasted at the back of the throat, like the awareness of sin. He reached over and pulled the thin chain dangling in the middle of the kitchen, switching off the light.

"You said you were lonely." In the bedroom's darkness, the cube bunny's softness was still wrapped in the firmed Lupino-like illusion. Close to him, she laid her hand against his chest, as though reading his heartbeat. "Who are you lonely for?"

McNihil knew why she asked. So she could try to be that other person, another layer of illusion, for him. It came with the territory: that was part of her job and survival skills as well.

"Don't worry about it," he said. Sitting at the edge of a concave mattress, he brought his face close to the hand he'd combed into her dark hair. His lips grazed the skin of her cheekbone. "Probably just my wife."

The cube bunny drew away from him. "Are you sure you want to do this?"

"Like I said. Don't worry about it." McNihil drew the girl down to the field of the thin blanket. "She's dead." The same hand stroked the girl's brow. "When I tell her about things like this . . . she doesn't mind at all."

The girl said nothing, but reached up for him with her bare arms.

———

Later, when the only illumination in the bedroom was the glow from the cube bunny's skin—McNihil's eyes had adjusted to the darkness, so that a naked woman burned like a faint, ghostly lantern—he sat on the edge of the mattress, watching her sleep. She didn't wake as he drew the thin blanket back from her. Confirming what he'd seen while she'd been in his arms: there was no mark on her body, other than the random bruise.

No tattoos, either moving about or still. The blue-black capital *V,* with its knife-pointed serifs, that he'd seen embossed over the corpse's rib cage . . . if he saw it now, it was only in his memory. The image of the corpse . . . and ones farther back. He closed his eyes, not to see them better, but so they wouldn't be superimposed, branded, on the sleeping girl.

In the bathroom at the end of the apartment's hallway, McNihil heard her gathering up her clothes. He splashed cold water in his face, letting it run down his neck as he raised his head to look at himself in the mirror. Taking his time, giving her time.

She was already gone when McNihil walked out to the kitchen. He pulled the chain dangling from the center of the ceiling, flooding the space with an eye-stinging brilliance. The whole apartment seemed as bare and empty as the specimen freezer in an abandoned morgue.

McNihil leaned back against the sink, arms folded across his chest, the edge of the counter's cracked tile pressing against the skin just above the waistline of the trousers he'd picked up from the bedroom floor and pulled on. The cold from the linoleum, with its worn-through patches like black islands on an unlabeled map, seeped into his bare feet. From here, he could see out the kitchen's tiny window with its tattered roller blind, down to the street in front of the building. The homeless were parading by, in strict formation, just

as they were supposed to do. In that other world, the one he
didn't see anymore, he knew they were all shellbacks, hump-
ing along the personal-sized portable refuges into which they
retreated when off-duty. He'd always hated the sequential
billboards mounted on the shells' hardened exterior casings,
the lights usually spelling out an ad slogan about some sleazy
low-budget operation, like whatever Snake Medicine™
clinic was nearby, with its resident Adder clome offering
everything from minor decorative tattoos to Full Prince
Charles jobs. McNihil was glad he didn't see things like that
anymore; now the homeless parade looked like a long line of
sandwich-board men, trudging down the sidewalk one right
after another, like some Depression-era film that had slipped
loose in the universe's projector, stuttering the same frames
over and over again.

This time, the sandwich boards hanging in front and
back of the shuffling homeless men were advertising something McNihil didn't recognize. There was just one big al-
phabet letter on each board; they spelled out, in sequence,
the word *TLAZOLTÉOTL*.

McNihil wondered what the connect that meant. Maybe
a new Central American restaurant opening up somewhere
in the Gloss. Or maybe nothing at all; maybe the sandwich-
board men had gotten mixed up and out of order, creating
some random anagram out of the actual word. A back part of
McNihil's brain idly worked on it. After a few seconds, a
memory scrap floated to the top of his thoughts. *Tlazoltéotl*
had been the indecipherable word in the banner scroll tattooed on the corpse's abdomen, right beneath the big initial
V.

Probably not a good thing, decided McNihil. He also decided not to think about it anymore.

He didn't bother drawing down the blind, to shut out
the image of the homeless parade going down the street
below. Instead, McNihil closed his eyes and thought about

the things he'd told the cube bunny. Which were all true, as far as they went.

I'm used to it, McNihil thought. The world he saw . . . he wouldn't have wanted it any other way.

There was only one thing he missed.

Just once in a while, he would've liked to have seen daylight again. Instead of this world's eternal, clockless night.

FIVE

RENAISSANCE ANGELS TURNED
TO BURROWING MOLES

Some kind of church service was going on underneath the grates. Underground from economic necessity, not from any actual persecution; big spaces, cathedrals vaulted with sewage pipes and bundles of ancient copper wiring, black-sheathed fiber-optic snakes, suitable for large congregations of the faithful. Of whatever denomination:

- subterranean mosques, like minarets laid on their sides, the cries of the muezzin echoing beneath cracked and patched asphalt;

- Holy Rollers, interbred clans, toothless and fervid, calling on Zion and awash in the blood of a

pompadoured, lazy-eyed lamb of Memphis grace,
wrestling high-voltage cables like Teflon-insulated
serpents;

- supply-side Republicans, cutting each other with
little razor knives and lapping up red puddles
among the discarded condoms;

- post-Reformation Lubavitchers awaiting a messiah
with hands of fire.

The man loitering in the alley felt a shiver of disgust roll
up his arms, mutating into a sour ball of spit at the back of his
tongue. He'd just as soon not have been there at all, listening
to multipartite hymnody—was it Latin? Old Tridentine rit-
ual?—wafting up from below his feet, as though Renaissance
angels had turned to burrowing moles. Flickering candlelight, from staggered ranks of small yellow flames, streamed
up past his legs and across his chest, working his face into a
network of spook-pocked shadows. He'd caught a glimpse of
himself in a black puddle at the alley's edge, the thin water
shimmering with solvent rainbows; his face looked like a
campfire parody, a ghost story with a flashlight under the
chin. The anachronism bothered him more than the actual
visual effect.

Come on, he called out inside his head. *Come on, hurry up.*
An Asian storm-front, edge leakage from monsoons on the
other side of the circle, drizzled under his jacket collar. He
thrust his gloved hands deeper into his pockets as a show of
irritated impatience. He'd left a black Daimler do Brasil repro of a 1936 Mercedes-Benz 540K Special Cabriolet C, a
one-off historic Sindelfingen design, hunkered down at the
mouth of the alley, the machine a top-of-the-line product of
the *maquiladores* on the other side of what had once been the
Mexican border. They did good work in that arc of the

Gloss; the vehicle's finish, rubbed to a deep brilliance by the nimble hands of ten-year-olds, glistened as though it contained infinite space, as though a piece of the night sky complete with stars had fallen there.

Other black shapes, smaller but with the same basic curvature, had started to gather near the Daimler. They were attracted by the residual engine heat seeping out to the damp air. *Connectin' freeloaders*—the appearance of the beetle-armored homeless bugged him even more. The man glowered balefully at the dull black carapaces, made shiny only by the rain, that had been grafted onto the limbs and torsos of the recipients of the do-gooder shelter agencies' charity. The cracks between segments of the shells opened and closed tight again as the vaguely human figures inside jostled for position against each other, getting nearer to the car's attractive force with each squatting step.

The loitering man had turned off the car's various alarms, not so much because there was no point to them—the turtlelike homeless were technically within their rights, moving up on anything left out on the streets—but because he knew that most of them had sonic-energy converters inside their shells. They could suck a few microvolts out of the wailing siren noises that would have otherwise split the air, convert those wisps of energy either into heat for their shoulder-wide homes or battery storage for the Crawlman™ music systems that stoppered their ears.

It's a welfare scam, he brooded as more of the black domes crept along the oil-spattered sidewalks. One of the hard-shell bastards had come across the cigar stub that the loiterer had discarded when he'd started his wait in the alley. A random find; the rain had snuffed out the last orange spark in the saliva'd tobacco, so there hadn't been any thermal trail for the crawler to zero in on. As the man watched, the black dome sealed itself down onto the wet asphalt and cement; a moment later, a puff of blue-gray smoke pulsed out of a tiny

ventilation hatch. The ripe smell of the Cohiba Eisner y
Katzenberg stung the man's nose; he had to resist the impulse
to stride up to the dome, pry it loose and roll it over on its
back, and snatch the cigar butt from the scrounging sonuvabitch. An unpleasant vision came to him, that he'd had before, any time he'd been on a nonprivate street; of the black
beetle shapes swarming up around him, the way they were
doing now with his car, and likewise sucking the heat from
him, the way his old granny had told him that cats did with
the breath of newborn infants in their cradles. He shuddered
from both nausea and moral revulsion.

Luckily, the person for whom he was waiting showed up
then, sliding out of a service doorway beside the deactivated
dumpskers lining the far pocket of the alley. The big cubist
elephant shapes, their dead proboscises rooted in the multi-
stratified trash and garbage they were no longer capable of
snuffling up, towered above the girl's fragile image as she
carefully eased the door back into place. The teeth of the
vertical row of locks snagged back together, as though nothing more than a shadow had passed through them. That was
all part of her talents, the loitering man knew; to go in and
out of places she wasn't supposed to. And to know which
places.

"About time." He let his voice rattle gravel in his throat.
"I was just about to leave. I don't have time to hang around
waiting for people like you."

"Oh, no—" Genuine dismay showed in the cube
bunny's widening eyes. She stepped up close to him and
touched his arm with a child's delicate fingers. "I'm sorry,
Mr. Harris—"

"Harrisch," he corrected. For the hundredth time.
"There's a difference. Try to get it right."

"Gosh, I really *am* sorry. I'm so stupid." The touch
turned into something more, her fingers gripping his forearm just tight enough to transfer heat from her skin into his

flesh. A tiny electrical charge connected with a spot between
his shoulder blades and rolled down his spine. "But he was
talking. You know? He wanted to talk to me—"

"Sure." Harrisch nodded. "Of course he did." The poor
bastard up in one of the building's filthy live/work
spaces—*Christ,* he thought with a shudder, *probably not any
better than out here in the street*—would naturally have wanted
to talk to something like her. A scrabbling down-on-his-luck
asp-head didn't get many chances along those lines. "So you
talked."

Her turn to nod. "Some of the *craziest* stuff, too." She
had a child's squeaky little voice as well, all innocence and
fun. The sound of it made men's teeth grow longer in their
sockets. "Like you never heard."

"Really?" Harrisch supposed it was a good idea to know
what was going on inside McNihil's head. That was the
problem with using these freelancers; you couldn't just ring
up the human-resources department and get a readout on
them. "Such as?"

"Oh . . . all kinds of things." The cube bunny
shrugged her bare, pretty shoulders. Raindrops made soft
jewels on her artfully exposed skin. "Like the way he sees
things. He's got these funny eyes, you know? And the way he
saw me. Stuff like that."

It was pretty much what he expected to hear from her.
Sadly so; in this life, there were no surprises. "And you did
everything else? That you were supposed to?"

The cube bunny nodded happily, perfect white face and
cherry-red lips. "Then I fell asleep—kinda—and he got up
and went to the bathroom. That's what I was waiting for. So
I could get away, without him noticing." An impish glint
appeared in her eyes. "Or at least not right away."

Harrisch smiled back at her. *You little conniver,* he thought
approvingly. He supposed her cute mind was part of her
pretty genetics, her way of getting through this world of

thorns and lust. Who could stay mad at someone like that? It would be like rage directed at the berry you were about to crush between your teeth.

"That's fine," said Harrisch. "It doesn't really matter, anyway. I'm sure you did a good job."

The glint in the cube bunny's eye hardened to steel, or an even hungrier metal. "Does that mean I get paid now?"

"Sure." He reached into his jacket pocket.

From below them, from the grating beneath his and the cube bunny's feet, the wavering candlelight poured upward, as though a new sun had been discovered at the center of the earth. *How good they sound,* thought Harrisch, listening to the hidden chorus. They had shifted keys, to a bright C major, the notes of simple and universal triumph. The basses and tenors had dropped out; the female voices were slowly rising, not toward resurrection but to some even brighter apotheosis. Harrisch felt a little door open inside his heart as he lifted a weight of black metal from his pocket.

"Maybe I could do something like this for you again some time." The cube bunny didn't see what he had in his hand. Her childish and seductive gaze was locked on Harrisch's eyes, looking for some other door to open up inside him. " 'Cause it was easy. All I had to do was tell him the truth. About what happened to poor Mr. Travelt. It wasn't like I had to lie or anything. So it really was easy."

"Great," said Harrisch. "Speaking from the viewpoint of upper management, I think it's good that people get some sense of satisfaction from what they do. Every once in a while, at least." Actually, he didn't care. He raised and aimed the gun at a point equidistant between the cube bunny's small breasts and slightly higher, just below the hollow in her white throat. "But I don't really think you'll be working for us again."

Genuine tears welled at the bottoms of her eyes; the trembling lashes darkened. "That's not fair," she said in a small voice, a whisper almost lost against the choir's gentle murmur.

"No, it's not." He had to agree. He could almost regret the tightening of his finger on the gun's trigger.

"But I did what you asked me to—"

He watched her fly, propelled by the bullet's imparted grace. The unmuffled shot echoed along the alley's walls, shivering dust and bird droppings from the ancient bricks. At times like these—Harrisch had done this before; he never left jobs like this to underlings—time smoothly ratchetted down to slow motion. An occasional pleasure in his stressful executive life; *I deserve this,* he thought. That part at least was fair. For him. The Denkmann book agreed, which was one of the reasons it was popular with high-level execs.

The impact of the bullet had lifted the cube bunny from her feet, tilting her onto her back as though on a feather bed of empty night air, her blond hair coming loose to form a radiant haloed pillow. Her bare arms flung back, as though wings. The petals of an intricate rose spattered against her chin. Then she fell, yards farther from where she had stood in front of Harrisch. She changed from angel to human, a wordless question in her clear eyes, and then to something that had the same shape and thermal signature of human, but wasn't anymore. The pretty thing sprawled in the alley's decaying litter, the side of her face turned against the base of the wall.

Harrisch had preregistered the killing, so he didn't have to wait around if he didn't want to. But he did; he let the weight of the gun dangle in his hand, its fading warmth traveling up the muscles of his arm and into his shoulder. He walked a few steps, working a crick out of his neck and gazing up at the stars. *I should get out more,* he thought vaguely. The choir of whatever church was hidden beneath the grating had piled on fortissimo with the gunshot, as though the noise had been the announcement of their re-

deemer's return. A little of their holiness, however shabby
and subterranean it might have been, resonated inside Harrisch; he felt at peace as the excess adrenaline metabolized
out of his system. *Get more exercise,* he vowed.

Back at DynaZauber headquarters, he knew, some computer in the accounting department was humming almost
silently to itself, deducting the minor cost of the girl's death
from the corporation's stock of pollution credits, specifically
on the urban misery index. Every year, DZ's PR division
planted along the roads enough seedlings—most of which
died or grew into no more than toxin-stunted weeds—to
more than counterbalance necessary operating deaths.
Which proved that the system worked, if you let it.

A franchised black-and-white cruised up alongside the
Daimler repro at the alley's mouth. Harrisch scratched his ear
with the muzzle of the gun as he watched the cop—only one
had shown up on the nonpriority scene—examine the dead
cube bunny. The cop left a tripoded coroner's camera, a
variable-focus lens and digital frame-storage device, spider-
legging around the corpse and clicking away, and strolled
over to talk.

"That's what you used?" The cop nodded toward the
weapon in Harrisch's hand. The cop's voice was affable and
unexcited. "Mind if I take a look at it?"

Harrisch knew he didn't have to do that, either; the cop
had already read off the gun's bar-code ID with a remote
scanner and matched it up with the hit registration on file.
But he didn't mind; he handed the piece over.

"Not bad." The cop nodded in approval. "These three-
fifty-seven parsifals do good work. Neat, as these things go;
you don't have to stand there, pumping away and knocking
little bits off your target." He held the gun back out to
Harrisch. "Ever think of using something not quite so can-
nonlike? Something like that can really climb up in your
hand, if you lose control of it."

"But I don't," said Harrisch. "I've got a pretty firm grip."

"I'm sure you do. Hey, no question about that, pal. But why take the chance? The wear and tear on yourself?" The dead cube bunny was forgotten as the cop warmed to his topic. "Personally, I think you could haul something a little more stylish, something a little more in keeping with your, um, position in life. Now, something like a tosca or a light-weight nine-millimeter, a traviata maybe—"

Harrisch felt his face harden into a sneer. "Those Italian pieces are all pussy guns. Those are for girls."

"Hey . . . hey, I understand." The cop backed off, holding up a mollifying hand, palm outward. "You want to carry major weight, that's cool. I can go with that. It's noth-ing Freudian, you know, it's just an image thing, really. But remember, those aren't your only choices. You want to stick with the Teutonics, hey, I agree." The cop gave an admiring shake of the head. "Nothing fills your hand like those babies. But maybe for a change of pace, you'd like to go with a tristan; that's a sharp piece. Or hey, go bigger; go up to a four-eighty siegfried. Or shit, go all the way to a connectin' götterdämmerung; you just about need a crane to lift it, but I guarantee you, if you'd popped one of those off here, we'd be picking up the evidence with a push broom and a vacuum cleaner. I tell you—"

"Are we about done?" Harrisch interrupted the cop's spiel. "Is there anything more we need to take care of?"

"No. I guess not." The cop looked sullen. He glanced over his shoulder toward the camera at the other end of the alley. "You got what you need?"

"Sure do! Right on!" The camera had a minimal person-ality interface and the voice of an animated cartoon charac-ter. The round blank face of the lens swiveled toward Harrisch and the cop. "We be cookin'!" With fussy arachnoid movements, the tripod picked its way through the low, black dunes of trash.

"Just trying to do a little public service . . ." Under his breath, the cop muttered just loud enough for Harrisch to hear. "And what do you get for it? Connect . . ."

The coroner's office was a low-budget item in the PD's budget; Harrisch wasn't surprised to see an antiquated low-rez LCD screen unfold from the camera's dented and patched thorax. The display blurred through a reconstructive autopsy, extrapolating back from the gridded shots that had just been taken of the dead cube bunny. Her smiling face, near to lifelike, appeared on one side of the screen; the photo that Harrisch had registered before flashed on the other side.

"Pretty good!" pronounced the camera. "Close enough for police work! Everything looks copacetic, folks!"

"I think I'll be on my way, then." Harrisch felt tired and regretful. Not over the cube bunny, but on having let himself linger out here, where he could get latched on to by hustlers like this cop. *Should've just gone straight back to the office,* he brooded. Scenes such as this one were the consequence of mixing business with pleasure, even such innocuous ones as listening to the invisible choir's music with heated metal in his fist. "Call me if there's any other forms I need to fill out."

"There won't be." The cop visibly shifted his glum mood. "Tell you what, though; why don't you take my card?" From one of the dark blue uniform's pockets, he extracted a thin white rectangle. "This is my private sideline business. I've got a little dealership thing going—"

"No shit." Harrisch looked at the card; a 3-D image of a dancing gun winked and pointed to a phone number. He stuck the card inside his jacket, knowing he wouldn't be able to get rid of the cop, otherwise. "I'll keep it in mind."

"Hey, wait a minute." Another voice, ragged and with slurred consonants, broke into the discussion. "This sucks."

Both Harrisch and the cop glanced over at the figure that

had appeared next to them. One of the shellbacked homeless clustering near the Daimler had gotten to his feet and approached them. The segments of the black carapace soft-welded to his skin—the charity agencies did that, to make sure their clients didn't lose any of the pieces of their minimal shelters—glistened in the first of a drizzling rain.

"What's your problem, buddy?" The cop narrowed his gaze to slits. "Why don't you just take it back out to the street? This doesn't concern you."

"The connect it doesn't." The man's face was all bone angles edged with scabs and crusted dirt. His breath was ripe with alcohol and the cheaper grades of paint thinner. "This really sucks." One plated arm gestured floppily toward the alley's depths. "Sonuvabitch here just blew away that poor girl."

As though on a common gear, Harrisch and the cop looked toward the yellow-haired corpse, then back to the homeless figure in his dissembled shell. The cop shrugged. "So?" He looked genuinely puzzled. "What's your point?"

"Connect, man . . ." The red-rimmed eyes were filled with the fury of Old Testament saints. "You're not gonna do anything about it?"

"Of course not," said the cop, deeply offended.

Harrisch tilted his head back and looked up at the night sky. The patchy clouds, tinged with the city's luminescence, still let a few long segments of clear stars through. *This is what I get.* When one's tenderer sentiments were indulged, payment was exacted. The singing from the choir below had stopped, letting silence fill the alley's narrow space again. For all he knew, they had given up their church service for the time being and were listening in on his problems.

"The connect you aren't." Noisily, segments of the interlocking shell clattering against each other, the turtlelike figure rooted through the various grimy pouches and rope-slung sacks on his torso and around his waist. He came up

with a miniature video camera, its silvery plastic smeared
with his black fingerprints. "I got it all down. I'll go witness
status. Then you're in deep doo-doo."

"Bullshit." The cop sneered again. "You're not licensed
for that."

"Yeah?" A gap-toothed smile showed on the gaunt face.
"Check it out." One gnarled hand extended a plastic-lami-
nated card. "You and your little businessman pal here have
got the wrong story going."

"Ah, damn." The cop examined the card, then handed it
back. A sigh born of deep frustration lifted and dropped his
shoulders.

"What's the problem?" Harrisch took one of the cop's
arms and pulled him away from the smirking homeless.
"There's a problem, right?"

The cop tilted his head toward the watching and waiting
figure. Beyond, at the mouth of the alley, a few more of the
homeless had tilted their shells back, the attraction of the
voices' buzz greater than the car's dying heat. "There was
that traffic-monitoring program about six months ago.
Buncha crap, if you ask me. But the transport authorities
issued videocams, little cheap throwaway numbers, to a lot of
these guys; figured they were already on the street, might as
well let them do the counts. The only thing, they had to be
granted temporary citizenry levels as well, something high
enough that the data they collected could go into the public
records. The funding debates on some of these issues are
pretty hot right now. But that's where our problem comes
from." The cop pointed a thumb toward the shellback.
"This guy's temp level hasn't expired yet; it's still got three
days to run. So technically, at this point in time—but not
next week—he *could* enter testimony against you."

"On what?" Harrisch's anger rose. "What charge? I
don't see what his level's got to do with it." This was the
kind of thing that always pissed him off, little unexpected

traps laid in the path of an honest man. "It's her level; that's
what's important." He pointed toward the corpse, gazing up
at the clouded sky, flecks of rain tearlike on her soft cheekbones. "She didn't have any; you know that. I thought that
was the whole reason I was able to preregister this hit."

"You're right. You're absolutely right." The cop tried to
calm him down. "So it's not like you'd get charged with
anything major; it's not a murder or an aggravated-assault
rap. You don't have to worry about *that*."

"Damn straight." Harrisch's temper had come down a
few notches, to a grouchy irritation. "The way I see it, I was
doing my civic duty here. She didn't have any entry permit.
You know she didn't." Which brought it, he knew but
didn't need to bother explaining to the cop, under the "Invisible Wall" sections of the immigration code. The cube
bunny's looks and charm had been her only passport, her
only badge of citizenship—and that had been revocable at a
moment's notice. The parsifal, cold now but still dangling in
Harrisch's fist, had accomplished that much. "So who cares
if this dildo saw what happened?"

"Well . . . it's a technicality." The cop looked uncomfortable. "Even with a preregistration like yours . . . the
actual code is that it has to be done in front of a law-enforce-
ment official. Like me. You call up the dispatcher, I come
out, you do whatever you're going to and I check it off; then
it's all kosher. Now, in practice, it's me and the coroner's
equipment showing up after the fact—that's usually how it's
done. We can always fudge the time stamp on the hit." He
gave a big sigh and a shake of the head. "But with a certified
witness on the scene . . . that makes it a little harder."

"Dig it, jerk-off." With a mottled grin of satisfaction,
the homeless figure folded his plated arms across his chest.
"I'm the crap sandwich on your menu."

"All right." Harrisch's turn to sigh. He turned away
from the cop and toward the other man. He pocketed the

parsifal, then took his wallet from inside his jacket. "What's this going to cost me?"

"Hey . . ." The cop's whisper emerged from between clenched teeth. "Don't let this schmuck hustle you."

"Right. Like you've been so much help."

"Well, at least get a good price from him." The cop retreated next to the camera on its tripod.

The corners of the homeless man's mouth were bright with saliva as he regarded Harrisch's wallet. Harrisch took out a diamond Amex, his own, not the company's. "As I said—how much?"

"Depends." The interlocking plates clacked against each other. "You want to go for straight bribery—you know, buy me off—I could go for a thousand."

"I don't bribe. I buy."

A puzzled look appeared in the other's eyes.

"Come on." Harrisch gestured impatiently. "The tape, the disk, whatever you've got it on."

"Oh. Well, that's gonna run a bit more—"

"Plus your citizenship status."

"Huh?" The largest armor plate, the one over the surgically curved spine, shifted as the figure hunched forward. "What're you talking about?"

"Figure it out," said Harrisch. "You want to be an idiot, fine, but I don't have to. There's no way of proving to me that you haven't already loaded the footage off to some datastore." He used the corner of his wallet to point to the Mini-Cel™ linkem tucked in with the rest of the welfare agencies' tracking devices. "Or some tipscanner down at the networks could be going over it right now. But if you don't have current witness certification, it doesn't mean jack. And that's the way I want it."

"I got ya." The shellback nodded in understanding. "No wonder you're some big exec type. You got brains. Okay, but it'll cost you."

Harrisch let the other man hit him for a mid-five-figure amount. The shellback returned the card after running it through his handheld scanner. He'd already decided to wait until the homeless figure showed some sign of realization; he knew it wouldn't take long.

"Cool." The gaunt-faced man radiated an appreciation of his good fortune. The other black domes, their residents' eager faces peeping out from beneath their edges, crept closer, anticipating some distribution of the largesse. "Nice doing business with you." The gap-toothed mouth barked out a laugh. "Only problem is, now I gotta go down to the charity offices in the morning and reregister. You just bought my whole ID, buddy. I can't even collect my ration tags until I officially exist again . . ." His voice faded out; in his eyes, a new light faded in. Those eyes widened, staring at Harrisch. "Wait a minute . . ."

Harrisch said nothing; he didn't feel like rubbing it in. He saw the shellback's gaze shift to the gun that he'd brought back out of his jacket. The homeless figure's pupils looked almost the same size as the black hole at the front of the parsifal's muzzle. Reflected fire shone bright for the millisecond following Harrisch's squeeze of the trigger, then was gone as the other arced backward and away.

The black shell cracked and splintered against the pavement, a few feet from the Daimler repro. Denuded of the portable shelter, the homeless figure's corpse lay on the wet concrete and asphalt like something extracted from an unhatched egg, the artificial curvature of his spine drawing his limbs cocked above his shattered chest. A red puddle, blackened by the night's limited spectrum and shimmered with the light rain falling, began to spread around what was left of him. The other homeless scurried away, toward darker and safer holes. Most of them speedcrept with their shell's rims lifted only a fraction of an inch above the ground; a few, the more frightened ones, actually got as upright as they could and ran into the city's shadows.

"Jeez," said the cop, shaking his head. "Even I could see that coming. What a dolt."

Harrisch glanced over his shoulder. "Any problem with this one?" He pointed with the gun toward the dead shell-back.

"Nope." The cop gave a shrug. "The guy's off the books. There's nothing to even register."

With the gun put away, Harrisch took the Amex from his wallet and checked the account readout on the back. The charge to the homeless figure had bounced back, marked *Account Canceled*. The whole incident had been a freebie.

Which, as far as he was concerned, was as it should be. A signifier of God's love toward the elect; it was times like this that made the strict interpretations of the Protestant work ethic seem so sensible. If only the choir beneath his feet had started singing again, voices raised in four-part SATB hallelujahs, then the moment would have seemed complete.

The cop took off, leaving the cleanup to the city's sanitation department. Harrisch was left alone in the alley, in silence.

I want something to remember this by, he thought. He supposed he was getting sentimental in his old age. No need for a scrapbook; just some small item that he could keep for a little while, until its evocative power faded, then throw away.

Harrisch walked over to the dead cube bunny. She was as pretty now as before; he knew that some of his colleagues in the company would have thought her more so. Where there had been a red flower between her small breasts, that the gun had blossomed forth, there was now only a fist-sized hole and a congealing wetness around.

He took a little pasteboard rectangle from his pocket—the cop's business card—and leaned down closer to the pretty corpse. He pressed his thumb against a bit of exposed, chilling flesh, then against the back of the card. When Harrisch straightened back up, there was an oval red signature, intricate lines and whorls, on the back of the card. He slipped it into his wallet—there were others like it in there, a little collection, one of them fairly recent—and then walked slowly, meditatively, toward the mouth of the alley and the waiting Daimler. The blank eyes of his witness gazed up at him as he stepped over the bits and pieces littering the ground.

SIX

DOWNLOADING THE ACTUAL BODY
AND BLOOD OF CHRIST

The Bishop of North America lived in a hole nearly as bad as, or worse than, McNihil's apartment.

"Not just North America," said the bishop, hunched over his computer terminal. "The Holy See just added Central America by Proxy to my job description. The appointment—well, elevation's the right word technically, I think, but that doesn't really *seem* right anymore—it fluttered in by E-mail just yesterday morning."

If that wasn't the right word, then *hole* seemed to fit the other well enough. The moldy ceiling of the windowless space came within a half-inch of the top of McNihil's head. If he'd risen on his toes, he could've scraped gray, wet plaster

flakes onto his scalp, like some kind of sebaceous organ donation.

"Forgive the mess," the bishop had said as he'd held
open the warped fiberboard door. "I've been rather busy of
late." He'd gone right back to the terminal and the ministra-
tions to his flock.

"Me too," McNihil had answered. Standing in the center of the dingy room, he tried to keep his shoulders away
from the damp-rot patches that blossomed on the book
spines and disordered stacks of paper lining the swaybacked
shelves. With each breath, fungus spores collected in his nostrils like the silt of an invisible, stagnating river. "That's life
these days."

"It's so much work," moaned the bishop. His forehead,
with its strands of sweat-pasted black hair, nearly touched the
terminal's screen. "I should never have answered the ad on
that matchbook."

McNihil wondered if he'd really heard that last bit, or if
it'd been some overlaid auditory fragment, a piece of his
world that he somehow heard rather than saw. He glanced
around while the bishop went on tapping and clicking, the
little sounds forming a monotonous repeated pattern. He'd
been down here a long time ago, with the same bishop or a
different one—it didn't matter. But it'd been before he had
the surgery done on his eyes, had this perceived black-and-
white world layered in. And the place—he supposed that it
was technically a cathedral, no matter how small, since it was
the official seat of the bishop—had looked exactly the same.
Which meant that it came across the reality line unaltered.
Nothing had to be done to it, no visual alterations, to make
it fit into the world he saw. The hole and its contents were
already dark enough, with all the shabby accoutrements that
made it look like one of the ancient German Expressionist
film sets that'd preceded the old Warner Bros. B-movie
thrillers.

"Think of all the spiritual merit you're accumulating." McNihil didn't care to listen to the bishop's eternal complaints. There was supposedly another world, brighter than this one or the hard reality that everyone else saw, that the bishop's carefully tended faith was supposed to evoke. "You'll get your reward in heaven."

The bishop sighed, hunched shoulders lifting and then collapsing like a deflated black balloon over his shoulder blades. "Sometimes . . ." He shook his head. "I don't think I'm going to make it."

McNihil wasn't surprised by the existence of doubting bishops. He would've been more surprised by any sign of faith at all.

He turned away from the moldering stacks of papers, and looked over the bishop's shoulder. On the terminal screen appeared a low-rez image of a stylized human face, without identity or gender. Then a dialogue balloon with tail, straight out of the ancient comic strips, and the words *Bless me, Father, for I have sinned.*

Mechanically, the bishop went about his pastoral duties, hand shifting back and forth across an old-fashioned clickpad, hitting the *download-confession* button on the screen and waiting as the communicant's compressed file zipped over the wire. McNihil wondered where it went from there; maybe to the bishop's storage unit, or passed along some fiber-optic trunk line to the Vatican bunkers. Surely nobody actually read or listened to these monotonous litanies of transgressions. Maybe the anonymity of the confessional booth was maintained by the wire terminating nowhere, the PVC sheath exposing bare metal at the end, connected to nothing, coiled or slackly dangling in the waste-flow conduits below the Gloss. *Maybe,* thought McNihil, *that's okay, too.* A ubiquitous deity would be able to listen in the sewer as well as anywhere else.

The rest of the communion clicked by. On the terminal

screen, the bishop moved the chalice icon over to the cartoon face's open mouth, then the consecrated-host icon. A
final tap on the blessing button—*log off in peace*—and the
communicant's face disappeared, replaced a split second later
by the next one in the queue.

"Did you come here to ask me something?" The bishop
didn't glance around from the terminal. "It's all right—we
can talk while I'm doing this."

"Yeah," said McNihil. "I need some information. Something I need you to take a look at." He held out the little
metal cross, the one he'd palmed off the corpse, dangling
from his hand. "This one of yours?"

The bishop turned his head just enough to see the cross.
"Probably." He tapped the clickpad again, and another of
the faithful was made one with his or her God. At least for
the time being. "I don't know of any other franchises that've
been allowed to open up in this area. I wish there were—I
could use a smaller congregation."

"Could you check it out?"

Host halfway to communicant, the bishop paused. He
raised one gray-specked frowsy eyebrow as he glanced back
at McNihil. "You know," said the bishop, "that's not strictly
. . . umm . . . kosher. The faithful are enjoined to keep
their devotions private."

McNihil shook his head. "This guy isn't private anymore. He's dead. And I already know his name. I just want
to know a little more."

"In that case, then, it's just expensive." The computer
terminal beeped impatiently; barely glancing at the screen,
the bishop maneuvered the chalice image to the waiting
mouth. "I imagine you expected that, though."

With the cross's chain wrapped around his hand,
McNihil extracted several hard-currency bills from his wallet.
"This'll have to do," he said. "I'm on a budget."

The bishop looked both hungry and disappointed. "Your

employers?" His voice arched hopefully. "Maybe they can be approached regarding unforeseen expenses?"

"There are no employers," said McNihil. "I'm acting on my own, this time."

"How unusual." The bishop regarded him thoughtfully. "I didn't think that was something your kind did. You're an asp-head, aren't you?"

"I used to be." He still was, technically, but it tended to stop questions cold if he said he wasn't.

The bishop's face grew heavy with his deliberations, as if his thoughts were some grainy sedimentary substance collecting in the bags under his eyes and in the folds of his throat. "I wonder about that . . ." He rubbed the bristles of white hairs on his chin. "About that 'used to be.' I wonder if it's as easy as that." One hand gestured toward the terminal. "You see, I deal a lot with the sinful and the guilty." The screen crawled with flashing lights, the line into the confessional stacking up. "I've gotten so I can smell it on people." One black-nailed hand patted the top of the monitor. "Even through something like this."

"Then you should blow your nose," said McNihil. "People who don't care for the Collection Agency . . . they might enjoy imagining people like me suffering all sorts of mental racks. But we don't. So sniff for what you want somewhere else."

"Well . . . it was worth a try." The bishop brought his gaze back around to the terminal and clicked through a couple more on-line communicants. He held out an open palm for the cross. "Lemme see what you got."

McNihil dropped the tiny bit of metal into the other's hand, the fine chain-links piling into a little glistening hill between the ragged life and fate lines.

The bishop swiveled his chair around, holding the crucifax beneath a goose-necked worklamp. "Oh, yes . . ." He nodded. "Definitely one of mine."

"How can you tell?"

"It's a discontinued model—see the little beveling on the ends of the arms?" The bishop dangled the cross from his thumb and forefinger, as though letting McNihil admire it. "Nice touch, but the manufacturer figured the tooling was too expensive for his profit margin. I got a good deal on 'em, down at one of the big trinket liquidators over on La Cienega. I bought all they had; it was a couple gross, complete with mailing envelopes and these little holy cards of Saint Sebastian with the arrows poking out of him. The scriptures on the flip side of the cards were all in some kind of mid-West cracker pidgin—Nebraskonics, I believe—but I didn't think anybody would mind."

With one fingernail, McNihil tapped the cross so it swung back and forth on the chain the bishop held. "What's it say on it?"

"Iesus Nazarenus Rex Iudaeorum . . ."

"Not that. The other bit, on the back. The personal code."

The bishop laid the crucifax in his cupped palm, running the index finger of his other hand across the scratch-blurred area. "Shut up," he said irritably; the computer terminal had started beeping again. He reached over and three-fingered a group of keys, silencing the machine. "Excuse me," he said to McNihil. "I haven't done this in a while."

"Take your time." McNihil thrust his hands into his coat pockets. "As I said before, I'm not on the clock."

As he waited, the bishop rummaged through the nailed-up plastic shelves above the computer terminal, finally taking down a can of WD-40. The bishop sprayed the tip of his index finger, then started to rub away the accumulated dirt and grease with a not-much-cleaner rag.

Personal hygiene held no fascination for McNihil. He looked away, over to the terminal screen. The confessional and altar-rail images had been replaced by numbers. Percentage statements, in a column headed TRAN and another headed CON; as he watched, the numbers following the decimal points shifted, TRAN going up to fifty-three, CON dropping to forty-seven.

"That's the direct line from the College of Cardinals," said the bishop as he scrubbed his fingertip. "Well, except that anybody really can log on and vote. The church has gotten very democratic that way. You have to change with the times."

McNihil nodded toward the screen. "What's the big debate?"

"Oh, the transubstantiation versus consubstantiation thing." The bishop held his index finger close to his eyes, dabbing at it with the wet part of the rag. "It's been going on for a while."

"Yeah, I guess so. It was on the last time I was here. And that was years ago."

The bishop shrugged. "Well, the doctrine of the E-charist is a big issue. Personally, I think the consubstantialists are coming pretty connectin' close to being Protestants; I mean that's essentially the Lutheran doctrine of the Real Presence. To say that the body and blood of Christ are present 'in, with, and under' the electrons moving down the wires . . ." His voice had risen in anger, before he managed to calm himself. "I suppose you can see where I stand on the issue. I mean, it *has* to be transubstantiation. The electrons are changed *into* the holy substance, and the communicant is downloading the actual body and blood of Christ." The bishop waved the solvent-damp rag in his excitement. "If that's not the case, then really, it'd mean we were just connecting around here."

"That's what it would mean, all right," said McNihil.

A sulky cloud settled over the weighted landscape of the bishop's face. "I can tell that these things aren't important to you."

"Hey." McNihil pointed a thumb toward the computer terminal. "You were the one bitching about your job."

The bishop scrubbed even more determinedly at his fingertip. "I can't help it if I've started to believe." A dry streambed of tears grated in his voice. "It's an occupational hazard."

McNihil took pity on him. "Why don't you just read the code," he said softly. "That's all I came here for."

From the corner of his eye, McNihil saw the numbers disappear from the monitor screen; enough time had gone by with no clicks or taps, to bring the automatic screen-saver up. He had just a glimpse of the image, a skeletal form with wild eyes and streaming black hair, clothed in pennantlike rags of human skin, before the bishop's hand shot past him, hitting the monitor's power button. The image disappeared, replaced by dead blankness.

"You weren't supposed to see that," the bishop said stiffly. "I'd appreciate it if you didn't tell anyone."

What else McNihil had caught on the monitor screen had been a single word, in letters of fire. *Tlazoltéotl*. "What is it?"

The bishop drew back, holding the cross against his chest. When he spoke, he sounded abashed and sullen. "I didn't say *what* I've started to believe."

McNihil let it drop. He watched as the other man hunched over the little bit of metal.

After a few seconds, the bishop ran his fingertip across the minutely incised coding on the back of the crucifax. "Okay, I'm getting a read on this." The contact point at the end of the bishop's index finger shone like a sliver of broken glass. "The guy's name was . . . Trummel? Trabble?"

"Something like that."

Gazing up at the mottled ceiling, the bishop continued to sort out the info. "Pretty recently updated," he said. "The stats aren't too bad; received communion on a regular enough basis to get the volume discount. Just the standard five percent, though. That's a shame, kinda; with a little extra effort, this person could've gone up to the platinum Gen-U-Flex™ level, where you start getting the really good merchandise promotions." The bishop shot a hopeful glance over at McNihil. "The ID card's good at over ten thousand retail outlets in the central Gloss alone—"

"Don't bother with the pitch." McNihil held up a hand to ward off the other's flow of words. "My credit rating couldn't take the hit."

The bishop sighed and went back to deciphering the crucifax. "You can't blame a guy for trying," he mumbled. "Gotta keep the flock's numbers up. I mean, this poor bastard's not going to be at the rail anymore. You said he was . . . um . . . deceased?"

"Dead."

"I'll have to log a candle on for him. That's a freebie; we don't charge for that." The bishop's fingertip moved across the last of the incised code. "Now that's interesting . . ."

McNihil looked down at the hand and the cross, as though the tiny marks had been converted into something easily legible. "What's that?"

"This Trabble person . . ."

"Travelt, actually."

"He wasn't just an on-line communicant." The bishop peered curiously at the crucifax. "He actually came around here to see me, and received the sacraments directly. Now *that's* very unusual. Pretty old-fashioned, if you ask me; hardly anybody does that anymore." The bishop nodded toward one of the larger tomes on the shelves. "I actually had to look it up in the operating manual, to see how it's done—live and in person, I mean." A visible shiver ran across the man's flesh. "It was kind of creepy, you know? All that *touching*."

"Next time it happens," said McNihil, "put in for hazard

pay." He pointed to the cross in the bishop's hand. "Would that tell you what he talked about when he was here?"

"Naw . . ." The bishop shook his head. "There's not enough room for that kind of content, even if you overwrote the baptismal records. But—come to think of it—I might actually remember this guy. I mean, remember in my head." The hand without the cross stroked the bishop's stubbled chin. "I'm trying to recall what he looked like . . ."

McNihil dug another bill out of his wallet, one of the old kind with a still portrait of a famous dead person on it. "He didn't look anything like this, I suppose."

"You're right; he was younger." The bishop stuck the bill into a hidden pocket of his vestments. "I can see him plain as day now, though."

I bet, thought McNihil. "So what did he talk about? He must've come to see you for some reason. Some special reason."

"Of course." The bishop showed a yellow-toothed smile. "The only reason people would come to see someone like me would be because they're connected-up. Or more connected-up than usual."

"And that's what Travelt was?"

"Connected-up? Oh, yeah." The smile had gaps in it, through which the bishop's tongue showed like a wet lizard. "I was B.S.-ing you. Of course I remember the guy. Not just for the rarity of his visit here . . . but the *severity* of it. Severe on him, I mean; even before he got here. He looked like quivering hell." A slow shake of the head. "Or at least that's what he said he was afraid of."

"Really?" The poor bastard sounded like an even sorrier case than before. "Of going to hell?"

"No—" A damp glittering had collected around the rims of the bishop's eyes. "Of going *back* there."

"Right," said McNihil. *Like he would've known*—that was always the problem with these junior-exec types, leading their sheltered lives in their little corporate rabbit warrens. *They get a little experience,* thought McNihil, *and they figure it's the end of the world.* "Not even firsthand experience," he mused aloud. "The jerk was using a prowler to go out and get his stimulation for him. It's not like the Wedge ever saw him step inside its limits."

"Maybe his way of enjoying himself wasn't as safe as all that." The bishop spoke in a tone of mild reproof. "The man is—as you've said—no longer with us."

"Just goes to show," said McNihil. "Accidents will happen."

One of the disordered eyebrows rose in skepticism, creasing the bishop's forehead. "Would someone like you be here . . . if you really thought it was an accident?"

" 'It?' " McNihil's sharp gaze fastened on the man in front of him. "What 'it' do you mean?"

The bishop spread his hands apart, the cross dangling on its chain from his fingers. "Whatever happened. I wouldn't know—the ways of this world are not my concern. I'm paid to be concerned with matters of the soul."

"And that's what Travelt came and talked to you about? His soul?"

"Of course." The bishop studied the cross's swaying pendulum. "Like the way people would take their cars into the garage for repairs. They didn't do that if the machines were working fine. Same way with this poor fellow. Only I'm not sure his could be fixed."

"That's what you told him?"

The bishop nodded slowly.

"I thought," said McNihil, "it was different in your line of work. A matter of doctrine. That all things could be fixed. Washed clean." With his forefinger, McNihil gave the cross a gentle push, setting it in motion again. "Forgiven."

"Ah. That *used* to be doctrinal. But that was a long time

ago. Mankind has progressed since then, in so many ways. Including sin."

"What about guilt?"

The bishop pursed his lips, mulling over the question. "Actually," he said, "I think guilt's stayed pretty much the same since the beginning. There's never really been a lot of incentive to improve on it. Not a lot of market fluctuations there. Whereas with sin . . . people want to enjoy them-selves, don't they? They just never want to pay the price."

McNihil knew how that was. From professional—and personal—experience. "Was that this Travelt's problem?"

"Guilt and sin?" The bishop twirled the cross in a verti-cal loop. "Man, it looked like he was *covered* in it. Like he'd been skinny-dipping in the tar pits. Metaphorically, of course; the most you'd have been able to see with your eyes would've been the way the guy was sweating and shaking. You know that sick gray look people get just before they disconnect the life-support systems in the hospital, when there's no more reason to run up the electric bill? Only this poor bastard was still walking around." Another flip, and the bishop caught the cross in his fist. "But I could see the rest; I've got a little expertise in the line. That dark, sticky stuff was spread on his soul an inch thick and rancid."

Another thing that McNihil knew to be a fact. To his regret. *You sleep with the wrong kind of people*—he'd told him-self this before—*and there's no telling what you're going to wake up and find on yourself.* The corpse on the cubapt's floor hadn't learned that lesson until too late. Or, seen another way, the late Travelt had learned it and had checked out early, rather than deal with the consequences. Not having to walk around caked in sin and guilt . . . maybe the guy hadn't been so stupid after all.

"Did he talk about . . . anything specific?" The termi-nal had switched itself back on; the numbers on the screen tugged at the corner of McNihil's eyes. Tran or con, substance or accident; it didn't matter. The dead were still here in this world. The only difference between this Travelt and McNihil's wife was that he could still talk to her. Whereas Travelt's silence had to be picked apart, tweezed out of other people's memories. "Something that he'd done, or had been done to him?"

"He talked about having been someplace, and having seen some things; that he wished he hadn't gone there, and hadn't seen whatever it was." The bishop gave a little round-shouldered shrug, his own admission of guilt. "I suppose I should've asked him for the particulars, gotten him to let it out, tell me all about it. That probably would've made him feel better. The only problem is that it would've made me feel *worse*. I'm not interested in that sort of stuff." His gaze moved away from what was hidden inside his fist and over toward McNihil. "And I'm not paid to be, either."

"That makes two of us." McNihil felt his own minor remorse, the awareness of wasted time. "I only came here because I was mildly curious about this guy. But I'm not going to take the job."

"What job?"

"The one this guy's old bosses are leaning on me to take. They want me to find out what happened to him. Besides bad luck, that is."

For a moment, the bishop was silent. He laid the chain and cross over the flat of his palms, regarding it as though some reduced metallic pietà had been left in his care. "You're a wise man," he said finally. "You may not be a particularly nice one, but a certain degree of wisdom . . . you've got that."

McNihil lifted the object from the other's hands, letting the cross and the free end of the chain dangle from the other side of his fist. "Why do you say so?"

"You're better off," said the bishop, not getting involved with this one. Some dead are . . . *cleaner* than others. This

Travelt person . . . if he thought he was mired in sin, there's a reason for it. Some of the things he told me, before he realized I'd stopped listening . . . or that I was trying not to hear . . . they weren't pleasant kinds of things."

"Like what?" Obvious to McNihil that the bishop had been avoiding the question he'd asked before. Theology was fine enough, but it didn't provide any answers in this world. "Come on, tell me. That's what I paid for."

The bishop looked sulky. "You got enough for your money."

"Not quite," said McNihil. "And if I think I've got change coming back to me, believe me, you're not going to enjoy the process."

A lung-deflating sigh escaped from the other man. "All right. He talked about a woman—"

McNihil seized on those words. "Did he say what her name was?"

The bishop shook his head. "No. Because he was too frightened of her. He tried to, but he couldn't say her name out loud. That's why he was shaking so bad." The bishop let a sickly smile appear on his face. "Isn't that funny? In a way. Considering that she didn't even exist."

"How do you know that?"

"Not hard." The bishop barked a sharp laugh. "This Travelt guy was obviously losing it." His finger, still shining from the solvent, tapped the side of his head, close to the network of spider veins curving around his brow. "Up here. Where it counts. He was imagining things. Weird, bad stuff," said the bishop. "Stuff that just can't be. About this woman he was so afraid of . . . and other things." A shake of the head. "I don't get out much—I'm just too busy, taking care of my flock—but I can still tell when someone's undergoing a psychotic break with reality."

"You can, huh?" McNihil wished he could say the same

for himself. *Maybe,* he thought, *it's because I don't think it's such a bad thing.* He wouldn't see the world he did, the one that continously leaked out of his scalpeled eyes, if he'd been satisfied with the other one. The one that everybody else saw.

Darker thoughts connected with that notion. That he didn't want to get into right now, or any other time. Maybe the world he saw wasn't in his eyes, but was farther back, inside his head . . .

The bishop's voice pulled McNihil away from that cliff.

"Sure," said the bishop. "With the kinds of things this Travelt was raving on about, it wasn't hard. Like that woman he was so afraid of. Catch this: he said what made her so scary was that she was realer than he was."

McNihil heard that, and a sliver of soft ice threaded through his heart.

"He was afraid that he didn't even exist at all." This time, both the sickly smile and a shake of the head from the bishop. "Compared to her, that is. And then the loathsome gynophobic fantasies, all of his talk about contamination and disease. This Travelt guy might as well have been some nine-teenth-century French decadent, rhapsodizing about syphilis or something."

"Stigmata," murmured McNihil. "He talked about stig-mata, didn't he? Some kind of mark or sign . . ."

"Yeah, he did, actually. Something that wasn't just in his blood, but on his skin. Something that he'd caught from this woman, that she'd passed on to him like a black fun-gus . . ."

McNihil said nothing. He closed his eyes for a moment, and saw in that darkness a capital letter *V*, with serifs sharp as teeth, its slanting edges defined with a knife's-edge precision against dead pale flesh.

"What he said," continued the bishop, "was that he

couldn't even see himself—if he looked down at his body, or looked in the mirror. 'Cause he wasn't real anymore; all the realness had been drained out of him. All he could see was this mark she'd left upon him."

I know how that feels. McNihil opened his eyes, steadying himself against a faint current of stomach-roiling vertigo. An after-image of the black letter, as though burnt by some negative light, floated and ebbed from his vision of the small chamber. The woman's unseen presence, con- or transubstantiated, bled away as well.

"Know what else he told me? This is good—"

"I thought," said McNihil, "that you didn't listen to him."

The bishop shrugged. "I caught a few things."

McNihil dropped the cross and thin chain back into his pocket. "Thanks for your time."

"That's all right." The bishop followed him to the damp cement steps that led up to the street. "I shouldn't even have charged you. It was a pleasant break for me." He gestured toward the computer terminal. "From my usual routine."

The bishop caught McNihil's jacket sleeve, just as he was about to emerge into the nocturnal city. "You know," said the bishop, "it's not too late."

McNihil looked back at him. "For what?"

"For your confession. I've got the hang of it now. Of doing it in person, I mean." The bishop raised himself up, gazing deep into McNihil's eyes. "It'd be good for you."

"No, it wouldn't." McNihil shook his head. A chilling night wind sifted between the buildings' unlit shapes. "You're wrong. It's too late. It was too late a long time ago."

"I wonder . . ." The bishop had already started to draw back down the cellar steps; his form merged with the hole's shadows. "What you see . . ."

"When?" He knew he shouldn't ask, but didn't stop himself.

"When you look in the mirror," whispered the bishop. "What do you see?"

The figure disappeared down the steps. McNihil regarded the empty space for a moment, then turned and walked away.

SEVEN

THE ENTIRE ECONOMY OF THE DEAD

Tell me a story," said the professional child.

The man sitting by himself—in fact, the only other person on the train—looked up. It seemed to take a little while for him to focus on her, as though there was something wrong with his eyes.

"All right," said the man after a moment. "How about a Bible story?"

"That'd be fine." The professional child flounced the ruffy skirt of her party dress over her bare, red-chapped knees. She dangled her shiny black Mary Janes above the train's littered floor as she sat in the seat next to him. "Whatever you like." The man looked lonely and a little sad. *He needs,* the professional child thought, *what I have.* "Go ahead."

This is the story he told her.

" '¹AND IT CAME TO PASS,' " he said, " 'AS THEY JOURNEYED FROM THE EAST, THAT THEY FOUND A PLAIN IN THE LAND OF CALIFORNIA, AND THEY DWELT THERE.

" '²AND THEY CALLED IT THE LAND OF ORANGES, BECAUSE THAT FRUIT WAS OF PLENTITUDE THERE, AND FREE FOR THE PLUCKING AND EATING.' "

"You're making this up," said the professional child.

The man shook his head. "It's all true. '³AND SO PLENTEOUS WAS THE GOLDEN FRUIT, AND SO DIZZYING THE GOLDEN SUNSHINE, THAT THE PEOPLE SAID, "WHY SHOULDST NOT ALL THINGS BE AS FREE AS THESE? ESPECIALLY TO US, WHO ARE SO DESERVING. WHY SHOULDST WE PAY FOR THAT WHICH WE WANT?" ' "

"You're right." The child scowled darkly; she'd been stiffed a couple of times in her career. "People *always* say that."

" '⁴SO THE PEOPLE OF THE LAND OF ORANGES SENT OUT TO THE PEOPLES OF ALL THE OTHER LANDS, AND SAID UNTO THEM, "GIVE US THAT WHICH WE WANT, AND PUT IT ON OUR TAB."

" '⁵THEY SAID, "GIVE US, AND YOU SHALL HAVE OUR SACRED PROMISE THAT WE WILL PAY FOR ALL THESE THINGS. YOU CAN TRUST US." ' "

"Yeah, sure," said the professional child.

" '⁶AND SOON,' " continued the man on the train, " 'THE PEOPLE OF THE LAND OF ORANGES HAD PARKS AND LARGE HOUSES, WITH GARAGES OF MANY DOORS; AND THEY HAD BOAT HARBORS AND MULTI-LANE FREEWAYS AND FIBER–OPTIC CABLES ROOTED THROUGH THE EARTH, SO THAT THEY MIGHT CON-

VERSE WITH EACH OTHER AND ORDER MORE THINGS FROM ON-LINE CATALOGS.

" '7AND THEY BUILT WALLS AROUND THEIR HOUSES, AND GATES WITH TWENTY-FOUR-HOUR MANNED SECURITY, SO THAT THEY MIGHT NOT HAVE TO SEE ANYONE OTHER THAN THEMSELVES. AND THEY DID LOOK AT EACH OTHER, AND SMIRKED AND SAID, "ARE WE NOT EXCEEDINGLY FINE IN OUR EYES AND GOD'S EYES?" ' "

"Then what happened?"

" '8AND THEN THE PEOPLES OF THE OTHER LANDS CAME TO THE PEOPLE OF THE LAND OF ORANGES, AND THEY DIDST HAVE THE BILL IN THEIR HANDS, FOR ALL THE PARKS AND THE FINE BIG HOUSES AND THE BOAT HARBORS AND THE BOATS THEREIN.

" '9AND THE PEOPLE OF THE OTHER LANDS DIDST SAY, "THIS IS HOW MUCH YOU OWE, AND THIS IS WHEN YOU SAID YOU'D PAY UP."

" '10AND THE PEOPLE OF THE LAND OF ORANGES DIDST QUAKE BEHIND THEIR GATED WALLS, AND GREW ANGRY, NOT BECAUSE THEY COULD NOT PAY BUT BE-CAUSE THEY DID NOT *WANT* TO PAY.' " The man slowly shook his head, playacting a storyteller's weary disgust. " '11AND THE PEOPLE OF THE LAND OF OR-ANGES SAID TO THE PEOPLE OF THE OTHER LANDS, "WE WILL NOT PAY. WHY SHOULDST WE? WE ARE TOO FINE AND NOBLE AND TOO CONNECTING WON-DERFUL TO HAVE TO PAY A BILL LIKE THAT. YOU CANST TAKE YOUR BILL AND SHOVE IT." ' "

The professional child's brow creased. "Bas-tards."

" '12AND THE PEOPLE OF THE OTHER LANDS, WHO'D PAID FOR ALL THE PARKS AND HOUSES AND BOAT HARBORS, VERY CALMLY SAID, "ALL RIGHT.

HAVE IT YOUR WAY. BUT THERE WILL BE CONSE-
QUENCES."

" '13AND THE PEOPLE OF THE LAND OF ORANGES
LOOKED AT EACH OTHER AND SMIRKED SOME MORE,
AND SAID, "WHAT CONSEQUENCES CAN WE POSSIBLY
SUFFER? FOR IS NOT OUR GOD A GOD OF GREED, AND
ARE WE NOT HIS CHILDREN? HE'LL LOOK OUT FOR
US." AND THEY DIDST WIPE THEIR ASSES WITH THEIR
BONDS OF THEIR SACRED PROMISES.' "

"Yeah," said the professional child, "I think I
know the people you're talking about."

The man waited a moment before continuing, in
a lower, spookier voice. " '14BUT THE SKIES DIDST
DARKEN OVER THE LAND OF ORANGES, AND THE
EARTH GREW SOUR AND DIED, SENDING FORTH ONLY
DEAD THINGS.

" '15AND THE TIDES CEASED TO ROLL IN THE
HARBORS, AND THE SHIT AND WASTE FROM THE SEW-
ERS MIRED THE BOATS AMIDST THE DEAD AND ROT-
TING FISH.

" '16AND THE GATES RUSTED AND FROZE IN THE
WALLS AROUND THE FINE HOUSES, SEALING IN THE
PEOPLE OF THE LAND OF ORANGES. WHICH WAS NO
GREAT LOSS, FOR BY THEN THEY HAD BECOME DEAD
THINGS, LIVING—SORT OF—IN A DEAD PLACE.

" '17AND THE PEOPLE OF THE OTHER LANDS DIDST
SAY TO ONE ANOTHER, "THAT'S HOW IT GOES. THEY
BROUGHT IT ON THEMSELVES. WHEN YOU DON'T PAY,
YOU CAN'T PLAY."

" '18AND THE PEOPLE OF THE OTHER LANDS HAD
DEAD OF THEIR OWN AMONGST THEM, AND THEY
DIDST SAY, "NOW WE HAVE SOMEPLACE TO SEND
THEM."

" '19AND SO THEY DID.' "

NOIR   99

The man fell silent, eyes closed, head tilted back.

"Is that it?"

Raising one eyelid, the man glanced over at the professional child, then nodded.

"Well," she said, "it's not a *great* story. And I don't think it's *really* from the Bible. Is it?"

The man shrugged. "Depends upon whose Bible you're talking about."

"But it must mean something important to you, huh? Or otherwise you wouldn't have told it to me."

"That's true, at least."

"So?" The professional child smoothed her frilly skirt above her knees, and waited.

He didn't need any more prompting than that. The man shifted in the seat, reaching into the back pocket of his trousers for his wallet.

This sucks, thought McNihil as he gazed out the train's window. *I would rather in heaven be.* That just didn't seem to be an option these days.

Having that conversation with the Bishop of North America (and Central America by Proxy) must have put him in a religious frame of mind. So that making up Bible stories came easily. The little bit of time spent storytelling just now with the professional child had been marginally satisfying, in a melancholy way. McNihil and his wife, when she'd been alive, had never put in for a childbearing license, and now it was too late. Her ova had been harvested long ago and sold to pay off some tiny fraction of her debt load. So for him, a bit of child exposure, even from one whose eyes had been as ancient and cold as a DynaZauber exec's, had been worth it.

" '²⁰AND INTO THAT LAND—' " McNihil murmured another piece of the story to himself; there was no one to overhear him in the train. " 'TO CONVERSE WITH THE DEAD, THAT HE MIGHT LEARN OF

THEM THAT WHICH WOULD BE TO HIS PROFIT, NAY,
SURVIVAL; TO THAT REGION OF THE DEAD CAME A
STILL-LIVING MAN, WHO HAD COME THERE BEFORE
MANY TIMES ON SIMILAR ERRANDS. BUT IN THIS TIME,
THE LIVING MAN'S THOUGHTS WERE OF RELUCTANT
NATURE. SO THAT HE DID SAY TO HIMSELF, *"CHRIST
AL-CONNECTING-MIGHTY, I DON'T WANT TO BE DO-
ING THIS . . ."* ' "

But such petition, thought McNihil, *availeth not.*

Rattling on the poorly maintained tracks, the train made
slow progress across the blighted landscape. Slow and south-
ward, leaving the ill-defined outskirts of True Los Angeles
behind. There had been a time—McNihil had seen the
photos, watched the videos—when L.A. had merged seam-
lessly with the densely suburbanized zones below it, like a
corpse on the slab of God the Mad Doctor, a somewhat
living thing stitched together by arteriosclerotic freeways. All
flowers die eventually, though, even the ones that are already
toxic, and the black blooms wither and curl up on their black
stems.

McNihil looked out the window, his breath against the
glass, and saw ashes and the charred skeletons of buildings,
steel girders twisted by the heat of long-extinguished fires,
rows of square, empty eye sockets staring past fields of jewel-
like glittering broken glass. A grid of streets remained embossed on the deathscape, with the cracked emblems and
nonsense words of what had been backlit plastic signage on
tottering or spine-snapped poles, all transformed into an idiot language by having melted into one another. The logo of
a defunct international hamburger chain merged with the
trademark of what had been the West Coast's largest retail
purveyor of automobile tires, the resultant muddle sliding
into the blinded facade of an abandoned full-service Church-
&-Shop™, the combination seeming to promise seminutri-
tious grease and small plastic toys served as a holy sacrament

inside a steel-belted radial. Overall, the air looked and smelled—it seemed to seep through the solid glass and into McNihil's nostrils—as if the smoke from the ancient fires had never dissipated, the ocean winds no longer rolling over the petroleum-striped beaches, the clouds heavy and listless above the waves too sullen to crest. The air had yellowed and turned rancid, becoming some sort of breathable cheese, a substance accumulating on one's alveoli like the stuff found at the bottom of backed-up drains.

This was the one zone where McNihil's vision matched up perfectly with exterior hard reality. The black-and-white movies inside his eyes might just as well have leaked out and congealed, thick and heavy, on the dark landscape.

He turned away from the window at his side and glanced around the interior of the train. The perceived aspects of the world outside had permeated the train as well. Empty, the seats' torn vinyl extruded dirty-gray stuffing like infected tongues across the narrow floor's mounds of rubbish. Spray-can *placa,* even more stylized than the previous century's glory-days tags in the prescrub New York subways, flowed across walls, seats, windows, and the more permanent strata of trash, as though some judging angel had crashed a party gone badly wrong. McNihil couldn't read the scrawled, looping words; he'd always found third-generation Huichol slang in Cyrillic characters somewhat beyond him. *Mene mene tekel upharsin*—he wouldn't have been surprised if that was how it translated, given the nature of the territory they had entered. *Weighed in the balance,* thought McNihil glumly, *and tossed out.*

The meter-high graffiti included a psychotic drawing that didn't need to be translated. In rapidly shaded Day-Glo, the artist had sketched a malevolently grinning skull, complete with dangling bony vertebrae for a throat. Some minimal animation had even been done, if that term could be applied to a depiction of corpse pieces. Enough sulfurous

daylight slid in through the windows on the opposite side to
trigger the paint's remaining shutter-pixels, cycling the image through its program of one empty bone-orbit closing and
reopening in a leering wink. The skull's white forehead was
splintered open, with uprooted male genitalia thrust through
the chasm; a drop of bloodied semen sparkled and faded,
over and over, like a false and deceptive pearl.

McNihil didn't know, and didn't care, whether the skull
was the vanished artist's self-portrait or an iconic *homage* to
the passing landscape's ruling deity. He was going down to
see and to talk to his dead wife. Slumping lower in the seat,
he folded his arms across his chest, though there was no chill
in the air. On the contrary: the climate just south of L.A. was
an unvarying hell, unbroken by either grace or rain.

"Don't forget the mesolimbic dopamine system," said a
little voice right behind his ear.

He turned and saw no one. Which was all right with
McNihil; he preferred the occasional random auditory hallucination to sharing a train car with the low-level businessper-
sons encountered farther north along the Gloss's edge. Those
could creep him out the most; he hated watching them busy
in their seats, as they worked with the muscles and nerve
endings from their brows to their chins converted to inter-
faces for their built-in databases and spreadsheets. A trainful
of those types looked like a clinic for terminal Bell's palsy
victims, all of them winking and grimacing and twitching
away. Some of them, McNihil had always suspected, were
frauds, poor bastards who'd gotten downsized out of their
jobs but kept up their fronts regardless, going through endless
facial spasms to give the impression of productive labor.

Even that was better than seeing some of the graying
oldsters, tapping away on their antiquated laptops. Especially
the ones whose companies had made them have the Tiny
Biz-y Hands™ manual-abatement operation. The sight of
those particular poor bastards, with their squirrel-sized paws

sticking out from their shirtcuffs, infant-sized fingers skitter-ing across the hundreds of ideograms on combined English-Mandarin keyboards, always put a sour rock in McNihil's stomach.

The little voice spoke again: "If you correlate the info from the ventral tegmental area scans . . . implications are clear . . ."

This time, McNihil caught the source. Literally: his hand darted up and grabbed a fluttering black image just above his head. The holo'd piece of E-mail stayed trapped in his fist just as though it were made of something more physical than intersecting beams from the geosynchronous satellites over the Gloss.

He could tell it was a data-scrap, something too broken and damaged to live much longer, the minute strength ebb-ing away as it scrabbled at his palm. Not even addressed to him; he didn't pay for any accounts that covered a service area extending this far south. On a hunch, McNihil dug into his jacket pocket with his other hand and came up with the little cross on a chain that he'd shown the Bishop of North America. The E-mail scrap struggled harder in his fist, trying to reach the bit of cheap gold-toned metal.

The E-mail was Travelt's. It orbited the cross dangling from McNihil's hand, responding to some faint emanation of its dead addressee. The lack of any security encryption made him suspect that Travelt had written it to himself, a little personal-reminder memo. Of what?

Hard to say; the recorded voice had faded down to near-inaudibility. ". . . axons narrow . . . engine of addic-tion . . ." McNihil couldn't be sure of the squeaking words. ". . . the hand on the valve . . ."

There was no point in trying to figure it out. McNihil pushed open the window beside him, just far enough to fling the chain and the cross outside. The fading, crippled E-mail darted after it and was gone, vanished from sight like a fleck

of ash churned up by the iron wheels below. McNihil rolled
his head back against the seat and closed his eyes.

A few minutes later, he felt the train come to a stop, the
outmoded diesels up ahead wheezing and shuddering. In this
segment of the Gloss, on a local milk run, the Rail Amalgam
didn't put its shiny new or newish rolling stock, its sleek
maglevs and other high-speed bullets. Transit for visiting the
dead called for rolling antiques, bolted-together retrofits, rust
and grime that could be sent along the tracks more or less in
formation, the heavy ghosts of industrial society. Un-
manned, either by passengers or crew; a few black boxes had
been wired to the engines, the embedded piloting systems
linking up with whatever sensors and bar-code readers were
still operational along the right-of-way. That was enough for
the job; if any of the trains ceased functioning en route and
couldn't be fixed with more than a change of fuses or a
simple board-swap, it was bulldozed off the tracks and left as
a long parallel corpse, to decay into the underlying mulch of
corroded metal.

McNihil hoped that wasn't going to be the case right
now; he didn't want to get out and walk the rest of the way
to his destination. He could hear, rattling through the train's
loose-jointed steel bones, the various servo-mechanisms des-
ultorily futzing around with the engines, trying to get them
going again. Something clanked, metal on metal, one blow
after another; the image came to him of some articulated
iron arm, speckled with rust and oil spots, swinging a sledge-
hammer or a giant boilermaker's wrench against the dented
side of the ancient diesels, a last low-tech resort.

The clanging sounds continued as McNihil gazed out the
window. Ordinarily, he wouldn't have minded the prospect
of hoofing it the couple of hours it would take to get to his
dead wife. Even in a depressing territory like this, the notion
of seeing her again would have made the trek semibearable.
Those were other times, Jack, he told himself. Coming down

here before, he'd been on no other mission except seeing her, for no reason but to twist tighter the little knot of guilt that lay beneath his heart. If not pleasure, there was always a certain broken-tooth satisfaction to be gotten out of such a grim excursion, the confirming knowledge of just how much of a sonuvabitch one could be. And had been.

On the other side of the dust-mottled glass, a few slowly moving figures could be seen, going about their business in the rubble and ashes. The vaguely human shapes—they were so hunched over in their rags that it was difficult to make out their true forms—had devolved much farther down the scale than their beggarly counterparts in the cities elsewhere in the Gloss. The communard panhandlers and hustlers that McNihil usually encountered on his travels still had some detectable barrier between themselves and their surroundings, an envelope on one side of which was the however-loathsome definition of human, and on the other side was insentient matter. In this bleak territory, that border phenomenon had been erased: here, whatever looked and/or acted more-or-less human—usually less—did so as a point on a continuum that ran back down into the trash and rubble filling the streets and burnt-out building hulks. As if muck and sun-withered debris had become such a basic constituent of this part of the universe, the way hydrogen atoms abounded everywhere else, that it could have begun its own hobbled evolution, knitting together creatures from scraps of old, greasy fast-food wrappers and flaccid, discarded condoms. Instead of dead things, perhaps they were the yet-to-be-alive, lifting their soft faces from the rotting Eden they were to inherit, prepared for them by a God of Discards . . .

A sudden jolt snapped through the seat and into McNihil's spine; the train lumbered into motion, as though pulling itself from the mire that had trapped other great beasts. The scene outside the window began to slide farther

back along the rails. A small breath of gratitude eased from
beneath McNihil's breastbone. Another few moments and
the ragpicking shamblers, the bottom stratum of this zone's
animated dead, would have looked up and spotted his face.
They would have lifted their hollow-eyed gaze to his, then
nodded slowly. Saying without words: *Pass on, Traveler. As we
are, so shall you be.*

"How was your trip?" His dead wife looked up at him as
he walked through the door. "Was it all right getting here?"

From his shoulder, McNihil eased the strap of the bag
he'd brought with him. The train from the land of the nominally living to that of the officially dead had finally creaked
and wheezed into the local station, like a senile long-distance
runner clutching his chest and expiring as he collapses across
the finish line. The station, the same one at which McNihil
always disembarked when he visited his wife, was really just
the place where the tracks came together from different directions, including the no-longer-functioning ones that ran
into the east, into the center of the continent. Whatever
came out of here, the pretty boys and girls who were the
heartland gene pool's only viable export, arrived on foot. As
had McNihil at the place where his wife existed—the word
lived was too cruel a misnomer to be applied in her situation.

"It was okay. About like usual." He sat the bag down on
the kitchen table, a rickety construct of plywood sheeting
with reinforced fiberboard boxes for legs. As with most
things in this territory, it survived from day to day, caught
somewhere in the process of collapse and dissolution. The
table wobbled and bent under the slight weight of the shoulder bag; the nails—which McNihil himself had hammered
in—gave small, harsh cries as the loose joints twisted against
each other. "Nothing happened on the way, at least." He
turned a minimal smile in his dead wife's direction. "For me,
that makes it a nice trip."

She said nothing, but went on watching him with her

✗'d-out eyes. Empty, but not in the way that living persons' eyes so often were, when they had let their souls ratchet down into a state of pure mercantile hunger. *Hungry,* McNihil had told himself more than once, *is not her problem. Not anymore.* In that sense, she had an advantage over both the living and the other dead. He could console himself with the notion that he'd done that much for her, at least.

"I suppose you brought me stuff." She sat beside the table, in an only slightly less fragile chair. If she'd possessed more mass than was typical for the long-term, animated dead, the chair might have collapsed beneath her; as it was, she had no more effect on it than a ghost or living memory would have. "You always bring me these little things." In one hand, held near her face, a cigarette slowly drifted a gray trail through the dusty air. The pack had been one of the gifts McNihil had brought her the last time he'd come down here. She didn't smoke, not in the sense of drawing anything into her motionless lungs. But the spark and ash were reminders of her previous existence. *And of mine,* brooded McNihil. "I appreciate your thoughtfulness," his dead wife said.

He would've preferred it if she had screamed like some sudden banshee and buried a knife in his heart, one of physical metal to match the invisible one whose blade he felt turning there. But perhaps that was why, he knew, she didn't do any such thing. Besides not being her style, it would have made it all too easy—and over—for him. She still loved him enough to torture him.

Nodding slowly, McNihil zipped open the shoulder bag and started pulling its contents out onto the flimsy table. The items were all bright and shiny and new, things from the land of the living. They didn't have to be expensive, he knew, though sometimes he spent the money anyway, just as one of the milder forms of self-laceration available to him. Stuff that wasn't even anything his wife had cared for when she'd been alive:

- fast food in self-heating structural-foam containers, with full-motion figurines from this week's disnannie dancing on top;

- collect-the-set chocolate bars with the twenty-sixth and twenty-seventh installments of an updated Story of Job on the wrapper, the little 3-D panels filled with images of a multicar pileup on some anachronistic freeway and garishly bright blood pooling on the floor of a hospital triage room;

- postliterate romance novels with audio chips sighing and moaning in synch with the nearest ovulation cycle that the built-in hormone sensors could pick up.

Downscale consumer goods, effluvia from the cheap-'n'-nastiverse, glittering with an enticing pseudo-life. Which was already dying, even before the tiny microbatteries, lightsucks, and other power sources could be exhausted. McNihil looked at the bright things that he had carried down here, and saw them visibly fading, the little dancing figures hobbled in their *paso dobles* and quadrilles, slowing down and going inert in hunched-over postures, like a miniature gallery of terminal osteoporosis.

He gazed down into the illusory depth of the romance covers, like windows into a nobler, more sun-filled world, tilted ninety degrees and laid out flat. The optic traps caught sight of his irises and responded by deepening the images, the red-streaked oceans stretching out even farther to impossible sunsets, the great doors of the Regency ballrooms swinging open to reveal curve-swept grand staircases, high arched windows overlooking Capability Brown gardens silvered with perfect moonlight. Designed to entice: a part of McNihil wanted to dive into those soft vistas and fall gravityless through them forever. But even as he looked into them, the liveried, bewigged footmen holding back the brocade curtains were growing old and shriveled, their faces crepe-paper masks. The buccaneer oceans filmed over with toxic oil slicks, the slow waves washing anoxic, aborted creatures against the ships' rotted wood. Lovers gazed into each other's hollow eye sockets, yellowed skull-teeth visible through the papery skin of their withering faces. Their embraces had become huddling refuges from the chill winds sliding through broken glass and brownly corrupted palm fronds; their kisses had been delayed too long, and now could only be consummated in the skin-deep grave between their hearts.

McNihil's dead wife brushed a hand across the once-bright things he had brought her. "I don't really know why you do this, though." The cigarette in her other hand continued to burn on its own, maintaining its brief spark of life. "It must be sad for you. You come all this way, and you give me this stuff . . . and look." She pushed one of the fast-food containers with the tip of a thin finger. Its imbedded power sources had already run out of juice, leaving the cartoon images gray and drained of what little pseudo-life they'd had. A slow shake of the head: "That's what happens down here." McNihil's dead wife looked up at him. "That's what happened to me. Isn't it?"

He said nothing to contradict her, though technically she was wrong. The once bright and now fading bits of the other world—their life, or imitation of such, had still been in motion when McNihil had crossed the border of this territory. Whereas she'd been dead already when she'd been brought here, her lungs gutted out by viral mesothelioma to the point

where that other world's life-support machines—what a
laugh—hadn't been doing anything more than inflating, de-
flating, reinflating a cold flesh balloon with her empty-eyed
face attached.

"It didn't happen to you," lied McNihil. "You didn't
fade." The impulse hit him, to sweep the rapidly dulling
trash from the table with his forearm. "You're still beautiful."

She smiled indulgently. "In my way, I suppose." She put
the cigarette to her pale lips, though the smoke wasn't drawn
in, trickling slowly by her ashen cheek instead. "How does
the old poem have it? The Coleridge—is it 'Life-in-Death'
or 'Death-in-Life?' "

"I don't remember." Though in fact, he could hear
some of the lines being recited in his head. *Her lips were red,
her looks were free, / Her locks were yellow as gold: / Her skin was
white as leprosy, / The nightmare Life-in-Death was she, / Who
thicks man's blood with cold*. . . . If McNihil looked at her in
a hard way, without the blurring overlay of memory, that
was what she reminded him of. It wasn't pleasant; he preferred to let his mental vision go subtly out of focus, to turn
his head and see, from the corner of his eye, something closer
to the woman who was alive in the unforgotten past.

"You didn't come down here to discuss poetry. At least,
not this time." McNihil's dead wife leaned an elbow on the
wobbling table. Gray ashes drifted across the stricken lovers
on the romance novels. "You're in trouble, aren't you?"

That was how it was, dealing with the dead; they always
knew stuff. The virtue, the advantage of death; their vision
wasn't occluded, betrayed by simple things like memory,
dreams, hope. McNihil wasn't the first to discover that the
dead were wired into cold reality, in a way that the living
could never be.

The entire economy of the dead—the indeadted—and of
the dead territory in which they existed, depended on that
relationship. Which varied: there were high-functioning

corpses such as McNihil's wife, and low-level scrabblers such as the ones he had seen from the window of the train coming down here. A lot resulted from whatever shape the particular deceased was in when the reanimating transition was made. If some poor bastard had scoured out his neural pathways with various pharmaceuticals, reduced the cortex in his skull to a red sponge squeezed down to its last endorphins and catecholamines, then all the batteries and add-on sensors and motivational prods that could be retrofitted onto his chill-cased spinal column weren't going to make him into anything more than a shambling scrap-picker. The little scattered herd of unfortunates out along the tracks used their low-grade but effective skills to pluck out recyclable metals or anything else of possible value from the rubbish heaps that the garbage-laden trains dumped off twice a day. Cheaper to let the idiot dead scavenge and collect, in their slow, hunched way, than spend the money for automated scanning machinery to do the same thing.

Which proved that being in trouble was a relative thing. McNihil felt an old horror, familiar enough to be almost comfortable, deep at the floor of his gut, when he saw the pickers and scavengers going about their black-fingered rounds, like crows minus even a bird's intelligence. But they didn't seem to mind it. Rooting around for scraps of aluminum foil, the still-shiny tracings off busted circuit boards, probably didn't even bring in enough to service the interest on whatever debt load they had died carrying. "Died" in that other world, the one the officially living inhabited. So most of them—short of coming across some lucky find, maybe an ancient collectible Lone Ranger and Trigger lunch-box at the bottom of some unexplored slag-pile—were actually just scrabbling themselves deeper into debt, becoming more truly indeadted with every bent-spined raking of splintered fingernails across the mulching discards of the world they were no longer part of.

They could go like that for decades, McNihil knew. With no cellular regeneration, the scavengers would wear away their hands against the corrosive, sharp-edged trash, until they were poking through it with the stumps of their forearms, their backs permanently fused into perfect half-circles. And beyond: dismaying rumors circulated, of the torsos of unlucky deadtors scrubbed free of all limbs, chests dryly flayed to breastbones and spidery ribs, the exposed batteries draining down to the last feeble amperage fraction.

"You shouldn't think about these things," said McNihil's dead wife. She smiled; even when alive, before acquiring the skills that came with death, she'd been in the habit of reading his mind. "You're just spooking yourself."

"Sorry. Can't help it." Being in the territory of corpses made it difficult to put away the grim images. Of worse things yet, of poor bastards worn down to ragged skulls, trailing an umbilicus of batteries after them as they inched their way across the bleak landscape with little motions of their dirty-white jawbones. Digging out glittery bits of old gum wrappers with their eroded incisors, nudging like dung beetles their little wads of recyclable detritus to the redemption center at the zone's border, making another meaningless nick at the tab they'd accumulated in that other, pre-death life. Like Marley's ghost, dragging around a chain whose links were instead forged out of the enticing perishables of the cheap-'n'-nastiverse, bright junk like the stuff that McNihil had laid out on the table between himself and his wife.

"It's not so bad." The cigarette in her hand was half gone. "Don't blame yourself. It's the thought that counts."

She was correct about that as well. As with so many things. This was why they were still married. What death could not put asunder: he had never stopped thinking about her, in love and guilt, even long after it would've been better for him to have done so. Though there were advantages to the arrangement as well, to having her dead and communicating. Better than a Ouija board, for getting messages from the other side, he received the word face-to-face, rather than having to wonder if it came from his own imaginings.

"You're right," said McNihil. He had pulled the other chair out and sat down at the table, across from her. "I'm in trouble. More than usual."

"The usual . . . that's just what you bring on yourself." His dead wife nodded slowly, thoughtfully. "Just from your usual bad attitude. For more than that, other people are required."

Nothing he didn't already know. Even who the other people were: McNihil had gotten on the train and come down here to the territory of the dead, even though he had an existing job to take care of, a favor for an old friend. Because he needed to find out what the deal was with Harrisch and all the rest of that DynaZauber bunch. Plus the mystery of how Travelt the rising young corporate junior exec had become that empty-eyed clay gazing up at the ceiling. If all that hadn't been the most interesting thing in the world to McNihil before, it stood a good chance of going that way.

"I don't need analysis of my personal shortcomings right now." McNihil laid his forearms across the tabletop, leaning toward her, close enough to see into the little black ✖'s of her eyes, but not close enough for a kiss. "Tell me something else."

"If you want to know about the trouble you're in . . ." His dead wife gave a shrug. "It'd be simpler to just wait. You'll find out soon enough."

"Probably so. But I'd rather know right now."

"Why?" The same question she always asked, whenever her still-living husband came here, wanting to find out things. "Now . . . or then . . . what difference does it make?"

"You're forgetting." It was McNihil's turn to give a little indulgent smile. "Where I just came from, time still matters. One way or another. That's why they call it *timing*. These people I'm dealing with . . . I just don't want to be caught surprised by them."

She shook her head. "You poor thing. Someday . . . you'll be over all that."

The way she said it, gently, with pity and no malice, chilled the sweat on his skin. "Maybe so," said McNihil, after a moment. "But in the meantime . . . it's like I said. I've still got to take care of business."

"And like I said. You poor thing."

No reply from him; all McNihil had to do at this moment was wait. In a small dark room, in a house in dead territory, a declining construct that had been abandoned by the living a long time ago. Abandoned, then reinhabited, taken over by the dead. *Who take over everything,* thought McNihil, *eventually.* The prefab walls leaked formaldehyde, appropriately enough; the windows cracked beneath layers of dust; some archaic god of burials alone knew what was in the closets of the bedrooms down the hall. McNihil had been here before, sitting at this table in a kerosene lantern's pool of light; he had waited then as he waited now. What was the point in trying to hurry the dead?

His dead wife closed her eyes. The cigarette had burned down close to the backs of her fingers; McNihil leaned forward and plucked it away, then ground the stub out against the table leg beside him. She didn't appear to notice what he'd done, just as she wouldn't have noticed her dead flesh being singed by the small fire. There were already a couple of careless burn marks between her knuckles. As with the others inhabiting this territory, her sense of pain, the boundary between herself and the dead world around her, had dwindled almost to the point of nonexistence.

That was McNihil's own personal theory of how dead

knowledge, the knowingness of the dead, worked: they had given up the useless distinctions between themselves and any other thing, so they were open to all the information, raw and unfiltered, in the dead world and the living. A salvageable gum wrapper buried in street muck was as evident to their percept systems as the prick of a knifepoint against their cold skin. It was a characteristic of the dead, to be so well connected, to be wired into everything. Only the living maintained defenses and filters and immune systems, tried to unhook and disconnect themselves from the world; an attempt that was doomed to failure, inasmuch as they would all wind up as ashes or worm food eventually, or at least if they were lucky. But a brave and necessary attempt, regardless.

"They've been leaning on you," said McNihil's dead wife, "for a long time now." She spoke without opening her eyes, the cold, battery-juiced brain behind the bruised eye sockets tuned into frequencies faint and invisible as radio waves. "Putting the pressure on. For you to do something for them."

McNihil knew where she was getting that much from. *Right out of my head,* he thought. She'd been wired into there even before she'd died. Perhaps a little more tightly now; "leaning on you" was his language, not hers. That mirror-gazing effect was something to be expected when hanging out with the deceased.

"I know that." McNihil regarded the stubbed-out cigarette butt at his fingertips. "Just about everyone in the world seems to."

A scowl creased his dead wife's brow. "Something about a corpse?" She tilted her head, as though listening to a ghost's whisper. "A real one, I mean. Really dead."

"Yeah, and not going to move around anymore, either." McNihil tossed the cigarette butt onto the floor, with all the others scattered there. His wife's housekeeping, as he'd noticed before, had gone all to hell since her death. "Even if this Travelt guy—that's the corpse's name, by the way—even if he'd been in debt when he was croaked, they wouldn't have been able to power him up, get him walking and talking again." The finance companies and loan sharks monitored their debtors' health, even to the point of radio-tagging their vital signs with detector implants; that way, their post-mortem surgical teams could swoop in on someone who'd died with an account in arrears and splice in the thermal packs and batteries before the cortex decayed into unrecoverable mush. *Really and truly dead,* mused McNihil. Lucky bastard Travelt had died with money in the bank; lucky for him, too bad for Harrisch and the rest of his executive-suite cronies, who could've otherwise pumped Travelt's animated corpse for the answers as to how he'd died.

"Hard luck for you as well," said McNihil's dead wife.

"Yeah . . ." He nodded. "If they'd been able to get the info straight from the corpse's mouth, they wouldn't have had to come around and bother me. It's not as if I wanted to get dragged into this sorry-ass loop."

"Oh, no—" She opened her dark-filled eyes, gazing straight at him. "It's not because of the corpse. That wasn't the start of it all. They wanted you even *before* he died."

McNihil said nothing. He leaned back in the chair, letting his own brain silently pick away at what he'd just been told. This was something new, something he hadn't known or even suspected before.

"Why should you have known about it?" The dead woman continued her calm regard. "They wanted you, but they hadn't come round for you yet. But as soon as they had a reason to . . ."

"Not a reason." McNihil gave another slow nod. "You mean, an excuse."

His dead wife shrugged, bones visibly articulating beneath the surface of her skin. "Whatever."

It put a different light on things, he had to admit. If his

wife was right—and McNihil had no call to doubt her, and plenty for belief—then the implications were even deeper and spookier than before. If Harrisch and the rest of DynaZauber had been scheming on him, trying to find a way to drag him into its net, then Travelt's death was suspiciously convenient. *And not just the poor sonuvabitch's death,* thought McNihil. *Everything leading up to it.*

"Which would mean—" McNihil spoke his next thoughts aloud. "That they connected him over. Harrisch and his buddies at the company. They set Travelt up."

"Possibly."

He studied his dead wife, as though he could see the workings behind her eyes. "You don't know?"

"If I did," she said, "I'd tell you."

"Would you really?" McNihil brushed his hand across the cover of one of the romance novels on the table. "Considering . . . what it would mean . . ." The bare-chested adventurer, with flowing blond hair as long as that of the brunette temptress in his arms, had collapsed with her skeletal form across the oil-stained beach. The mingled, graying strands floated like seaweed in the tired waves. McNihil looked up at his wife. "Because if they set *him* up . . . one of their own . . ."

"They'd be just as happy to set you up." The idea didn't seem to have any emotional impact on her, one way or the other. "For whatever reasons they might have."

I knew, thought McNihil, *I didn't like that asshole.* The image of Harrisch's smiling face floated by on the screen inside his head. There'd been an instinctive aversion on his part toward the exec, more than McNihil usually felt when dealing with high-level corporate types. The one lying on the floor, looking up with empty eyes, was his notion of the only good executive type. Too bad that Harrisch didn't fit—at least, not yet—that terminal description as well. Loathing for the man had been the main reason that McNihil had turned down any job offer. He could've used the money, might even have enjoyed finding out how the late Travelt got stiffed, but without even reasoning out why, he'd let the rising of his stomach up into his throat tell him that he'd wanted nothing to do with the whole creepy setup.

And now, what his dead wife had just told him—that confirmed the wisdom of his initial reaction.

"You were right," she said. "From the beginning. Sometimes you are, you know. You don't need me to tell you everything."

"No . . . I suppose not." The business with Harrisch and the corpse, all of which he'd now been pressured into making his own business, faded from his thoughts for a moment. He studied his dead wife, looking at her with that same slow contemplation as when, in the middle of the night, back when she'd still been alive, he would raise himself up on one elbow in the bed they'd shared then, and in the muted darkness watch her sleeping. The rise of her breasts against the sheets, the draw and exhale at her slightly parted lips, the flutter of her dark eyelashes as some unshared dream traced her vision . . . that was all a long time ago. A long time, and another world away. Everything about her now was as still as the empty bed he looked back at every night, the one perpetual night, from the door of the room in which he tried to sleep.

Death hadn't been as hard on her, as far as looks were concerned, as it had been for the slowly decaying scavengers out in this territory's cold fields. The transition had perhaps leaned her down, lost her the few pounds she hadn't really needed to lose when alive; now she had both a fashion-model thinness and pallor, even to the dark, bruised-looking eye sockets. Her hair had been untouched by gray; it fell black as he remembered, past her shoulders, to that place along her back where he still had a tactile memory of his hand resting. Death, at least in the sense of physical beauty,

had done her some good; he knew she had a certain vanity
about that. She'd looked worse in the hospital, when she'd
been dying, making the change from one state of being to
another; that'd been the roughest, on both of them. And the
most corrosive of feeling: he might not have done what he'd
wound up doing, gotten into the betrayal mode so heavily.
That was where I connected up, thought McNihil as he gazed at
his dead wife.

"Don't be so hard on yourself." She extracted another
cigarette from the pack on the table. "You got something out
of it. And that's all that matters, isn't it?"

Moments like this, when she made little remarks so close
to the bone, he could almost hate her. The other side of the
guilt equation, the handle she had on his soul: he had prof-
ited by her death, in more ways than one. *She doesn't have to
remind me,* thought McNihil bitterly. That was what had
enabled him to make his place in the Collection Agency,
scrabble his way up the ranks of the asp-heads. It was a
competitive field, in which a career could stall out from
either a lack of guts or the right equipment. The agency itself
only paid for the essentials, thus keeping its basic operating
costs down, passing on the bulk of the royalties to its clients,
the artists and content creators. To get the plum assignments,
which was where the excitement was, and the resultant
bounties and bonuses—small, but they added up eventually—a hustling young asp-head had to trick himself out with
some expensive goodies, paid for from his own pocket.
There was a valve at the center of his head, the installation of
which hadn't come cheap.

And had been worth it; not all the pirate types that he'd
wound up dealing with had been candy-ass pushover types.
Some serious bad people got into copyright violation, theft
of intellectual property, on-wire counterfeiting and pass-
word-forgery scams, ID shadowing and third-party bucket
relays. Operations of that sort, whether it was a fly-by-night

anonymous remailer setting up shop in the New Guinea jungles or a Fortune 500 heavyweight trying to muscle in on just a little bit of a competitor's crypt'd-up patents, took substantial capital investments to get up and running. People like that, with that kind of money sunk into their illegal enterprises, and with the kind of payoff they were hoping for in mind, didn't enjoy the Collection Agency fouling up their plans. An asp-head, the visible embodiment of the agency, was in for a major—and final—ass-kicking if he couldn't take care of himself. Which happened sometimes, the result being a small box arriving at the agency headquarters, a box that leaked from the bottom and smelled like the dumpster behind a butcher shop by the time it got opened and the pieces identified for a proper burial. McNihil, just starting with the agency and totally green, had been in on the tail end of the raids on the last Guangzhou holdouts, deep inside the Guangdong FEZ in the Chinese mainland—data forgery, mastering and distribution facilities so entrenched that they had their own military, way beyond Beijing control. A lot of older asp-heads had gone home in crates before that had been wrapped up; McNihil owed at least part of his rise in the agency to the holes that had been shot through the ranks above him. Also his caution, and his more-than-willingness to keep his chops and equipment up-to-date. But that cost money.

"The good things in life always do," said the dead woman sitting across from him. "That's the difference between life and death. When you're the way I am . . . prices really don't matter anymore."

"How the hell should I know?" McNihil didn't feel like smiling back at her. "I'm not dead yet. I'm trying to avoid that."

"Because you're smart. Smarter than I was, at any rate." She contemplated the unlit cigarette in her hand. "Inasmuch as I trusted you."

Which she shouldn't have. *For both our sakes,* thought McNihil. He supposed he could've quit the Collection Agency, gotten some other job where the consequences for failure weren't quite so grim. Or if he had to stick it out as an asp-head, for whatever reasons he carried around in the dark rooms of his head and heart, he could've found some other way to finance the upward motion of his career there. Some other way besides spending the insurance payout that fell into his hands upon his wife's death. The payout that would have otherwise wiped off her indeadted status and bought her a nice, quiet resting place in the ground or a crematory urn.

"Oh, I would've wanted the cremation." His dead wife nodded as she reached for a book of matches. "Definitely. Even before finding out what I know now. About what happens after things die." She lit the cigarette. "It's so much cleaner."

It was more or less the same conversation they wound up having every time he came down here. Not so much because she wanted to talk about these things—from the beginning, she had displayed a casual acceptance about her transformed condition that had left him somewhat stunned and mystified, until he'd figured out why she was doing it. All the better to twist the knife inside him. Which was the same reason McNihil thought and talked about these things. As the ancient sage had said, *As long as you use a knife, there's still some love left.* It just depended on whether you used the knife on yourself or not.

That was the trouble with death and money combined. They could be either evil or innocuous on their own, but when they were wrapped up together, when they slept in the same coldly burning bed, that was when things got messy and weird.

"Connect this," said McNihil. "This isn't getting me anywhere." Some other time, when he wasn't being leaned on by Harrisch and his crew, he could dig the past up from

its unsilent grave, and dissect with his dead wife how he'd
screwed her over, spent the insurance payout on his asp-head
gear, and somehow never got far enough ahead on his Collection Agency salary and bonuses to pay off her living debts
and stick her ashes in that little jar she coveted for her final
residence. "Right now," he said aloud, "I've got other
things on my mind."

"Sure." His dead wife let the new cigarette burn, without bringing it to her pale lips. "You came here for advice.
Analysis of the situation you're in. People have been calling
on the dead for these services, for a long time now. Before,
though, they usually didn't get any answers."

"Lucky for them." A grim mood had descended upon
McNihil. It was easier to deal with guilt and the past than the
present situation. He knew where he was with the past.

"Didn't I tell you enough? You know more than when
you came here." His dead wife shrugged, cigarette held aloft.
"I can't figure out everything for you. Even if I could . . .
why should I?"

She dealt in fragments, he knew, fragmentary info, fragmentary answers. The scraps and pieces that came drifting on
hidden, subterranean currents into the dead territory. Proof
that she was on a much higher functioning level than the
scavengers he'd spotted so many times from the train windows. Her existence, this little bubble of ersatz bourgeois
comfort amidst the rubble and decay, was financed from her
earnings as an analyst of discarded data banks, medical
records, consumer surveys of products that had been taken
off the market decades ago, bins full of old credit-card receipts; all the informational flotsam that washed up on this
terminal shore. A couple of small-time research services, including one university sociology/ethnobiology department,
kept her and a few dead colleagues on minuscule retainers
and piece-work schedules. That brought in enough to pay
the interest on her debts and even chip away a little on the

principal amounts. At the rate she was going, sometime in the next century she might be able to keep her long-delayed appointment at the crematorium.

"Why should you?" An old question. "Maybe just because you love me. Still."

"Do I?" Her dark, empty eyes regarded him.

"Maybe." His turn to shrug. "You tell me."

Her gaze shifted to the spark at the tip of the cigarette. "That's one of the things I'm not ever going to tell you." A speck of ash touched her wrist, then drifted the rest of the way down to the table. "It'd be just too easy on you."

"Fine," said McNihil. "I'm way beyond needing anyone to be that kind. So why don't you just tell me instead, something about what I came down here to find out?"

"These people you're dealing with? What more do you need to know?" The smoke drew a smudged gray line beside her face. "You know enough to be cautious."

"I knew that *before* I came down here." He couldn't tell if she was jerking him around or not. Sometimes, from the random backwash of information into the dead territory, she extracted worthwhile answers; other times, not. The luck of the draw. "I could use something a little more practical. Something that would help save my ass."

"Is that all?" His dead wife smiled behind the cigarette. "Might be rather late for that. Like I said. They've been scheming on you for a while."

"Then I'll have to take my chances. I don't have anything to lose."

"Fine." She set the cigarette down on the edge of the table, inside a row of small burn marks. Unsmiling, she leaned toward him. "You want something more? Something you can use? I'll tell you right now. What you probably know already, because if you don't, you're too stupid to live." Her voice grated harsh, as though sand were caught in her corded throat. "It's not that guy Harrisch and the rest of those corporate types that you have to worry about. They're nothing. They've got their plans for you—there's something they want from you, something different from what they've said—but you might be able to handle that. You've got a chance. But where you're connected—and you are; you know that, don't you?—that's nothing much to do with them. It's what they want you to get involved in. That's the problem for you. Where they want you to go." She picked up the cigarette again and held it aloft. When she spoke again, it was in a quieter, scarier voice. "And who's waiting for you there."

It took a few moments before McNihil was able to ask the next question. "And who's that? Who's waiting?"

"Come on." His dead wife shook her head in mock exasperation. "You know perfectly well. The same thing that's always been your downfall. You're just one of those guys who's cursed by women. It wasn't just me that you have problems with. There's always some other woman that you have to deal with, that you *can't* deal with. One that decides your fate. And you know who it is."

"You mean . . ." McNihil frowned, trying to puzzle out her words. "There's one that's been tailing me around; a young one. I don't know why she's doing it. Is that the one you're talking about?"

"For Christ's connecting sake." Genuine anger flashed from his wife's deep-socketed eyes. "Stop messing around. You're wasting time you don't have. If you want to pull your ass out of the fire, you'd better get your mind straight. For once. I don't know anything about some 'young one.' " The anger darkened, as though transmuting for a moment into sexual jealousy, an emotion that even death hadn't managed to render out of her. "You idiot. God knows what you're imagining now." She managed an actual draw on the cigarette, pulling the smoke deep into her inert lungs, then exhaling a dragonish cloud. "You know who it is. The same one as before. The same one who screwed you over as badly as you did to me." The tobacco haze slowly dispersed in the airless room. "It's Verrity. It's always been her."

Rage beyond anger blossomed inside his heart, a fist shattering his breastbone from inside, as though some rapid feedback loop had taken her disdain and amplified it toward murder. As if the dead could be killed again—if so, he would have lunged across the table and seized her neck in his hands, pressed his thumbs against her throat until small bones had snapped like dry wood. It was how he knew she still hated him as much as she loved him—*She wouldn't have said that name to me, otherwise.*

"You're wrong." Whatever emotion was inside his dead wife, it had compressed itself into a coldly hardened gaze. "I'd say that name to you, no matter what. Because you know it's true."

The fury dwindled as quickly as it had sprung up at his core, leaving an ashen hollow there. McNihil opened his fists, laying his hands flat against the table to control their residual trembling. He nodded slowly.

"I know," he said. Defeated, for now if not forever. "Like you said . . . I've always known." Just who was waiting for him, in that place he'd been before. And didn't want to go to, ever again. "It's her. It's always been her."

EIGHT

MAYBE THE SKY EXPLODED

When the explosions hit the train, McNihil thought to himself, *I should've walked home.*

Loud enough that there were no longer words after the first reaction: the derailing charges made a hammer out of the air, ringing McNihil's lungs like soft percussion instruments. He found himself suspended, thrown loose from any mooring or balance as the passenger car tilted around him. His arms reached backward instinctively, hands level with his head, to catch the dizzily tumbling wall, to keep it from shattering his spine.

"Shit . . ." Spoken through clenched teeth, blood oozing salt from his bitten lower lip; McNihil was more irritated than afraid, even as one of the metal window surrounds struck him in the small of the back. Whatever breath had been left in his lungs was expelled in a last raw-throated semi-word. The catch holding the door between cars had disintegrated, the round-tipped metal claw twisting like a broken finger as the mating latch rotated and deformed; the door slid open with enough violence to splinter the passenger car's interior panels, sending soft daggers of foam-core insulation tumbling through the space. Through the doorway, as though it were a suddenly exposed video billboard, could be seen the dark outlines of the world outside, spinning on multiple axes. For a second, McNihil had the kinesthetic hallucination that the train was still, gravityless, and the landscape beyond had erupted into chaos.

A warm black velvet filled McNihil's sight; he blinked it away, and saw blurred light piercing the thin fabric. The light focused itself into stars; for a moment, he wondered how they had wound up scattered across the rubbish dunes of the dead territory through which he'd been traveling, heading back toward the inhabited zones of the Gloss—inhabited by the living—and his own tiny apartment therein. *Maybe the sky exploded,* he thought. And all the pieces had landed on the ground; that could account for it.

Gravity reasserted itself, along with his perception of it; he realized he was lying on his back now, with the open doorway of the baggage car above him. The view of the night stars was veiled by drifting smoke, which he supposed was connected to the acrid burning smell in his nostrils. One foot and leg were pinned by debris; he managed to kick himself loose without leaving more than tatters of cloth and a few square centimeters of bloodied skin behind.

Silence had replaced the explosion's shock wave; his own breath and pulse, and the hissing of something like steam, were all McNihil heard as he climbed toward the doorway above. The derailed train, or at least this section of it, had

landed at less than a ninety-degree displacement, leaving him
an off-vertical slope to claw his fingers into.

He managed to get his elbows up over what had been the
lower sill of the baggage car's sliding door. The bent metal
tracks cut into the flesh of McNihil's arms as he let himself
hang for a minute, catching his breath. Smoke and the burning smell hung low in the air, forming a thick knot at the
back of his throat as he breathed it in.

The salt of his own blood trickled into the corner of
McNihil's mouth. A billow of smoke, invisible in the darkness, stung his eyes; he wiped them clear against his shoulder,
then hoisted himself farther onto the doorway's tilted sill.
Another shove with his feet, and he toppled out and onto the
loose gravel lining the tracks below.

As soon as he'd managed to get to his knees, the sharp-
edged stones cutting through the stained and torn trousers,
he could hear the soft human sound of ragged breath and
preconscious moaning. He got to his feet and stumbled a few
meters alongside the overturned cars. His eyes had adjusted
well enough that he could see the starlight glistening off the
iron wheels, some of them still slowly turning, hubs thrust
higher than his head. Flakes of rust peeled off and drifted
snowlike into the spreading pools of oil; the glossy liquid
mirrored the stars and smoke as though it were polished
obsidian.

He found the source of the human noises. A female,
condition not good: she lay on her back, arms outstretched,
blind face and neck darkened with red that shone like ink in
the partial illumination. A piece of one of the broken cars, a
beam studded with rivets and twined cables, lay diagonally
across her breast, its weight crushing the ribs beneath the
grease-smeared leather of her jacket.

For a few moments longer, McNihil stood beside her,
letting his own breath and pulse slow, and whatever strength
he had left settle back into his limbs. *Shouldn't even bother,* he

told himself. He'd already figured out that, whoever she was, she was the one who'd been following him on the sly. Otherwise, she would've been inside the train's passenger car with him.

"Hey." McNihil knelt down, bending close to her red-webbed face. "You still with us?"

The young woman blinked, her eyes focused at some point past him; one pupil dilated large and black, the other small and trembling. "Connect you," she said. A blood-streaked bubble popped on her lower lip. "Goddamn . . . idiot . . ."

"Yeah, I'm charmed as well." He set his fingertips against the side of her throat, gauging her fluttering pulse. "You're in a bad way. You know that, don't you?"

She made no answer. Her eyes rolled back in their sockets, showing only white, as though the effort of answering him had knocked her out.

"She'll be all right." A voice came from behind McNihil. "Or maybe she won't. It doesn't really matter much, either way."

Still crouching beside her, McNihil turned his head and looked up at the figure standing only a few feet away. Though actually, not standing; he saw that now. More like hovering. A familiar face, with a too-familiar smile. "For Christ's sake," said McNihil, shaking his head in disgust. "What're you doing here?"

"Pretty much the same as you." Harrisch's voice was mockingly gentle. "Looking to make some kind of connection." He used the word in its nonslang form. "Aren't we all?"

McNihil already regretted at least one of his own words. The DZ exec was obviously on some kind of redeemer-image kick, without needing it pointed out to him. Harrisch, in his sharp Arma-Ni-Lite™ suit, stood with arms stretched straight out to the sides and ankles overlapped, fastened to a glistening white crucifix. Which in turn was mounted on a circle equally luminous; the top of his head, the tips of his palm-outward fingers, and the soles of his well-shod feet were just grazed by the circumference. Harrisch could just as well have been modeling one of the positions of da Vinci's measurement of man as parodying any ancient Nazarene.

"Like it?" Some of the silvery glow caught on the teeth in Harrisch's smile. "I hope you do."

"Yeah, it's great." The soft light had made its little internal adjustments to McNihil's vision; he could make out now the way in which the cross-imposed circle was suspended a few feet above the rubble-strewn ground. "Real impressive." Some kind of minor-league earth-moving equipment, with caterpillar treads and a bored DynaZauber employee at the levers, had crept out of the low hills. An articulated crane arm dangled the circle and its occupant on a length of heavy-linked chain. The operator had his name stitched above the DZ logo on his grease-stained jumpsuit's breast pocket; he nudged one of the control sticks, the chain clanked and retracted, lifting Harrisch another meter higher in the air. "But really," said McNihil, looking up at him. "You shouldn't have gone to the effort."

"It's no trouble." Even with his arms pinioned out, Harrisch managed a nonchalant shrug. "And . . . you know . . . I even rather like it."

I bet, thought McNihil. He nodded toward the cross and circle. "Your own creation?"

"This old thing?" Harrisch laughed. "I inherited it. Or let's say . . . the company did. Look." He turned his head, glancing up at the rim just above his head. "Can't you see the letters there?" His gaze darted back toward McNihil. "Stuff like this doesn't have a corporate emblem on it. It has *insignia.* There's a difference."

He saw what the exec was talking about. The letters *R*

and *A*, stylized in an *echt* Teutonic manner, intertwined with each other so their legs stuck out at broken forty-five degree angles; the result was halfway between a Manx triskelion and a deformed swastika.

"The Rail Amalgam," said McNihil. "What, they've been absorbed by DynaZauber? They're one of your corporate divisions now?"

"They wish." A sneer formed on Harrisch's face. "DZ wouldn't have them; we have our standards. Those people are all talk and no action. Strictly yesterday's news."

That might or might not be the case. Like most people in the Gloss—or at least those who weren't sunk too far into their own bleak, inner L.A.—McNihil heard various rumors about what was going on with their world's circular lifeline, the extended skein of rail lines reaching around the Pacific Ocean, from the old True Los Angeles core, up through where the urban metastasis thinned out in Alaska, across the fragile Bering Strait connections and down toward the Vladivostok financial centers and the transformed eastern edge of China, the little and now-aging dragons of Myanmar and Brunei, then back around the even more fragile and dangerous southern crossing, frozen tracks running across the floes and crevasses of the Ross Ice Shelf, in the shadows of the Transantarctic Mountains, and up the spine of South and Latin America, picking up *maquiladoristas* and boutique organic white-powder drugs before hitting the impacted Hispanic sprawl of Baja Los Angeles.

"Does that thing work?"

"You bet," said Harrisch. "Check it out." His middle finger pressed a button in the center of his palm, right where a rusted iron nail would have fit. The circle surrounding the cross grew brighter, sending hard-edged shadows, McNihil's included, from the spot. "You see it?" Harrisch looked up at the rim above his head. "Great, huh?"

What McNihil saw, as he stood before the elevated cross,

was the crawl of smaller, more intricate lights around the circle in which the DZ exec hung suspended. Blinking symbols and scurrying numbers, all tracking the progress of traffic—freight, people, whatever—along the greater circle of the Gloss's rail links. A kludge of whatever had existed before the advent of the *Noh*-flies, which had forced everything in the air to creep along the ground, and the new stuff that had been brought on-line—literally—to complete the loop.

A red dot blinked on a line horizontal with Harrisch's left knee. McNihil supposed that was the kink in the circuit that had been created by the train derailment, right here in the dead territory. Other red and yellow lights, all along the glowing circle, flickered at different rates and intensities. *Trouble all along the line,* figured McNihil. Which was to be expected; there was everything in the rail-transport system, from steam-powered cog-wheelers cranking through the thin-aired Andes, to sleek maglev bullet trains tearing through the flat, smoky guts of California. In some places parallel to each other; at the inevitable bottlenecks, track gauges of wildly differing dimensions were crammed into each other. Plus sabotage and other industrial/political squabbles, ice shifts near the poles, earthquakes anywhere along the edges of the ocean's submerged tectonic plates—given that degree of barely contained chaos, it was a miracle that the circle surrounding Harrisch didn't light up as fiercely red as a biblical wheel of fire.

Or maybe it had, one time; McNihil wondered if that was how Harrisch had inherited the circle and the cross. The old, powerful Rail Amalgam had been run by a high-*mysterioso* figure named l'Etatbrut . . . or that at least had been the rumor. If he'd existed at all, perhaps he'd been consumed, annihilated, turned to sifting ash by all the red alarm lights going on at once, his outflung hands gripping a rolling inferno of catastrophe data. If that hadn't been enough to burn the mythic l'Etatbrut to cinders, it still might have been a sufficient adrenaline rush to unplug his heart from the cage of his ribs.

"You'd better watch out," warned McNihil. "There are other people who might want to be hanging where you are."

The smile shifted to sneer again. "Such as?"

One word: "Ouroboros."

"Bullshit." Harrisch's sneer became uglier—McNihil wouldn't have thought that was possible—and tinged with an unhidable nervousness. "At least the Rail Amalgam exists . . . or it did. Ouroboros . . . there never was such a thing. That's all legend."

"Maybe," conceded McNihil. He had no way of knowing for sure. Maybe no one except those inside Ouroboros—if it existed at all—had that certainty. It was an entity wrapped inside darkness deeper than this night could ever have achieved. A true shadow corporation, summoned into being by the Rail Amalgam itself. The Gloss's great circle of a railway was put together into one operating unit by government confiscation of various independent railway systems; some of them didn't like that. Something called Ouroboros, taking on the symbology of the snake swallowing its own tail, supposedly represented the conspiratorial interests of those systems' now-dispossessed owners. In its nocturnal sphere, Ouroboros would have needed to operate on a much more concealed basis than the Rail Amalgam ever had. No wonder there was so much disagreement among the daylight world's police agencies and the underground's denizens as to whether Ouroboros was real or just some deeply spooky imagining.

Maybe that was what Travelt found out, thought McNihil. That was the other part of the legends and rumors circulating around Ouroboros like overlapping, partially legible scales. That the shadow corporation was the delivery service, the rail line, that serviced the unlit, steamy environs of the Wedge. The theory being that the amalgam's fascist purity made some things *streng verboten,* way off-limits. Not sex so much—like most fascist organizations, the Rail Amalgam was fueled by erotic tension—but the kind of sex that the Wedge and its occupants dealt in. The kind that a shadow corporation like Ouroboros would be only too happy to move along its underground tracks. *Underground* being, perhaps, both literal and metaphorical; if no one knew whether Ouroboros existed or not, then by logic, anyone or anything could be part of it. Which led the farthest-out conspiracy theoreticians to posit that the Rail Amalgam and Ouroboros were the same thing, their spheres of identity and operation coexistent with each other. When the Gloss's brownish-yellow sun was out, Ouroboros was reduced to a shade, a silhouette of the Rail Amalgam, a nothingness sliding across the ground. But when darkness fell, then it was the Amalgam that disappeared, and Ouroboros that became both invisible and omnipresent. *Like God,* thought McNihil. Or its opposite.

The area around the train's wreckage grew brighter, as though McNihil's unvoiced notion had been the cue for a theatrical dawn. He glanced over his shoulder and saw the bright, blue-white glare of generator-driven worklights flickering on, turning the tracks and displaced machinery into color-drained ghosts of themselves. Big shadows wavered into the darkness of the surrounding rubbish dunes; McNihil could see other figures, presumably fully alive, stationing themselves along the shattered metal. The sparks of an arc-welding torch hissed in the farther distance, accompanied by the deeper groans of heavy-equipment jacks being levered into place.

He turned and looked back up at the suspended figure. "I suppose it's your funeral," said McNihil. "If the Rail Amalgam comes back and wants its property returned, or if Ouroboros shows up and kicks your ass . . ." He shrugged. "Not my problem."

"Funerals?" Something amused Harrisch, enough for a
quick laugh. "You know, I'm not worried about them, either. There's a psychological advantage to taking a posture
like this." He rocked his head back against the cross on
which he was bound. "You figure, whatever's the worst that
can happen to you—three days later, they roll away the stone
and you're as good as new."

"As long as you're feeling that way . . ." McNihil titled
his head toward the unconscious girl on the ground. He
hadn't forgotten, even during the whole conversation with
Harrisch. "I'm a little concerned about her."

"Really?" The other man appeared both wondering and
somehow pleased. "I'm surprised. Doesn't seem to be your
style."

"I'm trying to cultivate a sympathetic attitude these
days."

"Is it working?"

"Not in your case," said McNihil.

Another muted groan, as though from the midst of trou-
bled sleep, sounded from the body laid out on the ground.
McNihil nodded toward the girl. "How about doing something for her?"

"I'm touched by your concern. That speaks of some
innate kindness in you that I wouldn't have otherwise suspected." Harrisch called over his shoulder to the DZ flunky
at the controls of the crane. "Get some medical attention for
this unfortunate person. Find out if she's going to live or die,
at least." He glanced again toward McNihil. "There's nothing you or I can do for her. Not right now. Why don't we
get out of the way? There's a few things I'd like to discuss
with you." With a nod of his head, Harrisch signaled to the
crane's operator, who kept his bored expression as he put the
equipment into gear.

McNihil followed alongside the crane, its caterpillar

treads moving parallel to the railroad tracks and the wreckage of the train. "I don't," he said, "feel much like talking now."

"Really?" The other's smile glistened in the worklights' bright radiation. "But there's so much we *need* to talk about."

McNihil rubbed his brow with the butt of one palm, smearing the blood from the minor wound. The sting nudged him back toward full consciousness; for a moment, from the effort of walking, he'd felt somewhat woozy. *It's not her,* the thought came to him, *that's having the bad dreams. It's me.* The train, turned over on its side, emitting ghostlike billows of smoke and the hisses of small creatures writhing in damnation, rolled past the corner of his vision as though it were the painted backdrop for some elaborate hallucination. The glare from the suspended worklights and the DynaZauber crews' welding torches bounced around inside McNihil's eyes like raw electricity converted to some kind of straight optical feed.

"Don't worry about the girl." As they continued alongside the steaming wreckage, Harrisch had the circled cross brought down closer to McNihil, the better to impart confidences. "I've got an emergency medical crew here on the scene. My people will do whatever's possible for her. And if there isn't anything that can be done . . ." He shrugged. "Then you needn't have wasted your time worrying."

"Thanks." The exec's presence repelled McNihil like a magnetic pole constructed of razor blazes. "I appreciate that."

The smile eased into place again. "All part of the job."

"Maybe you should look for another job."

"Ah." With mock ruefulness, Harrisch gave a slow shake of the head. "But I think I'm getting pretty good at this. And with the Rail Amalgam out of commission, who else is going to take care of the trains?"

McNihil glanced past the toppled cars. "You call this

'taking care'?" It'd been obvious to him, as soon as the other man had popped up in front of him like some kind of Kristallnacht jack-in-the-box, that Harrisch had been responsible for the derailing explosions. "No wonder I'm concerned about the girl."

"All minor and easily fixed. Readily assimilated into the overall plan." The crane moved past McNihil and started up one of the nearby rubbish dunes. "Come up here where you can get a better view."

As he followed the dangling exec out of the illuminated zone, McNihil's footsteps ground into shards of ancient circuit boards and the softer detritus of empty gum wrappers. At the hill's crest, he stopped and turned around, looking where the other's nod directed his attention.

"You see?" Harrisch's gaze swept across the vista. "All rubber—or might as well be." A smirk of self-satisfaction moved over Harrisch's leanly angled face. "We use the same SCARF weapons technology that the *Noh*-flies do, but in a noncatastrophic way. If you rein it in, it can be really quite benign."

He saw what Harrisch meant. From here, McNihil could see that the explosions hadn't ripped apart the railroad tracks. The rails themselves, where they weren't obscured by the toppled engine and cars, seemed like a demonstration of wave activity frozen at one moment in time. Ripples in the lines of rusted iron, the largest extending higher than any of the surrounding work crews, had turned the tracks into ribbons of vertical S-curves, tapering down into progressively smaller hillocks and bumps. Beyond the last car, the tracks smoothed back down into level, undisrupted parallel lines.

"Very clever." McNihil didn't care much, what exact techniques might have been used. He supposed that DynaZauber had found some way of ramping down the SCARF transmutation effects, the narrow-beamed quasi-alchemy that turned aircraft parts into metallic forms too soft

to function. That plus enough explosive charges to deform
the resulting elasticity, and they could have all the remediable
train crashes they wanted. "But you wouldn't have gone to
all the trouble of devising these methods, if you weren't
going to use them on a regular basis."

"Regular enough," conceded Harrisch. "It's not just an
issue of managing the corporation; you have to manage the
customers as well. Which in our case is the world. Or at least
the Gloss—not that there's any other part of the world that
matters. What some people at DynaZauber believe, is that if
it isn't L.A., it ain't shit. That language is a little more color-
ful than what I'd use. But the agreed-upon principle is the
same: the Pacific is the new Mediterranean. The omphalos,
the middle of the earth. It has been for a long time. The
great middle ocean, the navel, the solar plexus. Who cares
what goes on in Kansas or Ulan Bator? I mean, if there *is* a
Kansas or an Ulan Bator any longer."

"There'd have to be." McNihil watched the crews bashing away at the deformed rails. Under the worklights' glare,
the lengths of iron reddened as the welding torches and
SCARF invectors continued their assault. "All that flesh on
the streets comes from somewhere."

"As I said: who cares?" The expression on Harrisch's
face was all politeness and charm. "It comes from somewhere. So do cockroaches. But it doesn't ride these trains to
get here." He looked even more pleased with himself. "Kansas and Ulan Bator aren't on the schedule."

"Nobody is, if you keep taking out the tracks."

"That's how they learn to appreciate us." The smile remained, but Harrisch's gaze had hardened to simulated diamond. "The Rail Amalgam was too soft on them. We have
to put the squeeze on every once in a while. Remind the
paying public of all we do for them. How we make *their*
world possible. If we don't do that, they mistakenly assume
that the railroad, the great circle of transport around the rim,

is something fixed and eternal, that they can depend upon to be there always, like gravity keeping their feet glued to the earth."

"Silly bastards," said McNihil.

"Exactly." The other man pretended not to notice the sarcasm. "There was a time when they thought that about air travel. Or, to be more precise, they didn't think about it at all. But their unspoken assumption was wrong. As the world found out." The glint in Harrisch's eyes was one of scary earnestness. "How wrong they were—the *Noh*-flies showed them that. Which was, of course, a good thing. It's always best to find out the truth, no matter how painful."

"Or profitable."

"Oh, admitted." Harrisch smiled again. "DynaZauber gains thereby—and why shouldn't we? The truth, the new world, brought us into existence. Therefore, we're necessary. Therefore, the world should appreciate us, and all we do for it."

Past the overturned engine and cars, past the crews bashing away beneath the banks of worklights, past the dunelike heaps of rubble mottled with the embers of the dead scavengers' campfires, a thread of violet had seeped around the edges of the true hills to the east. McNihil was grateful for that vision, the little bit that his own night-filled eyes allowed him to see. It meant that eventually the night would be over in that other world and some form of day would roll across the earth. *At least for everybody else,* thought McNihil.

"So what do you want from everybody?" He glanced over at Harrisch hanging on the cross beside him. "A letter of thanks? A testimonial dinner?"

"Of course not." The smile faded a little. "Those kinds of things are always lies. Because they're made up of words, aren't they? And thus they would have to be lies, wouldn't they?"

"I don't know." McNihil shrugged. "You tell me."

"More words. When all that really counts is money." In the flares of light coming from the base of the rubbled hill, Harrisch's eyes looked ancient and cold. "It takes a lot of money, both officially and under the table, to keep everything rolling along. It costs a great deal to put things where they need to be. Real things, that is; but that's all that matters, finally." White-and-blue marbles of ice filled Harrisch's eye sockets. "All that cute blather people talked about a while back, about how the future would be nothing but little bits of information being zipped back and forth, the whole world on-line and freed of the constraints of gross materiality—that didn't come to pass. Atoms endure, Mr. McNihil; they have a tendency to do that. Solid things are built out of them. Whereas information is mainly lies. *Nacht und Nebel;* night and fog. So in that sense, it's not even information at all. Misinformation, disinformation; something like that. Therefore, it doesn't exist at all, for the most part."

What the hell. McNihil rubbed the dried blood on his forehead. He hadn't followed that at all. Or even why Harrisch had bothered laying it on him. Maybe when the sun came up, when the shadows of the hills would gradually shrink like detumescing male genitalia, maybe Harrisch would disappear as well, as though his dark image were constructed of the *Nacht* he spoke of, encasing the pale *Nebel* of his flesh, which would burn off with the day's first heat.

"You see," continued Harrisch, "it's important to concern ourselves with what's real. What's really real. Who was the wise man who said that reality is that which, when you stop believing in it, it's still there?"

"Beats the connect out of me." McNihil brushed his own dried blood from his fingertips as he glanced over at the other man. "I don't have the slightest idea what you're talking about."

"That's a shame. Because it really is important." The mad spark at the dark centers of Harrisch's eyes was as ice-cold as their surroundings. "I'm talking about how the world is constructed. Our world, Mr. McNihil, the one in which we exist, for good or ill."

Mainly the latter, thought McNihil.

"You know," continued Harrisch, "I share some sentiments with your little friend, back there on the ground. I know a lot about what she thinks and feels. She has the same coital phobia, the disgust and rage that come with all that sticky, messy wiring-up and networking. The erosion of one's sharply defined outlines, the loss of one's individuality, subsumed into the great puddinglike mass." He shook his head. "After all, I didn't become such as I am by having any great fondness for ego loss. But November—that's her name, I believe—she thinks the ocean is just sex. Whereas I . . ." The narrow face's expression darkened, generating its own shadows in its etched crevices. "I take a considerably wider view. A definition of greater compass. One that takes in all the world, and not just that smaller one bound by sweating skin and mucosal emissions."

"I either don't know what the connect you're talking about," said McNihil, "or else I just don't care." A glyph of ash had been smeared across the back of his hand, sometime during the extended, steel-crumpling crash; he rubbed it away with the ball of his other thumb. "Either way, it doesn't matter."

"Perhaps not, Mr. McNihil." The sharp gaze regarded him, as though he were some small creature suspended on needles. "Why don't you tell me what *does* matter to you, then."

"Look, uh, you have to understand something." McNihil pointed across the bleak landscape gradually forming out of darkness. "I made my living out in the field, working for the Collection Agency; I'm an operative, not an ideologue. People like you, you start going on about some big cosmic notions, and then I just want to go home and lie

down. Lick my wounds, crank up the music, wake up with
an empty bottle beside me. I don't have time or inclination
to listen to your theories about how the universe is stitched
together. Why don't you try giving me some kind of clue?
About why you wanted to talk to me so much. And this job
you're so hot for me to take on. About looking into what
happened to your boy Travelt." His bruises and bone-aches,
from being thrown around inside the toppled passenger car,
twinged as he looked at the exec. "I can't imagine you start
off all your appointments this way."

"Perhaps not." From above, Harrisch bestowed an indulgent smile. "But you have to admit that it got your attention."

"Right now, you could *have* my attention. In exchange
for aspirin and morphine." McNihil shifted his aching bones
inside his jacket. "And that was before the unscheduled
stop."

"You'll be on your way soon." The other man nodded
toward the work crews, farther back along the rails. Between
the sizzling sparks of the welding torches and the softer blue
of the anti-SCARF generators, the thin lengths of rust-
colored metal had been restored, straightened into level func-
tionality. "Our times together are brief, though I hope this
one will prove at least . . . memorable to you. Even after
your scars heal." A slight signal passed from Harrisch to the
dark-uniformed assistant at the crane's levers; the circle and
cross dipped hoveringly closer. "Tell me, Mr. McNihil.
What do you know about TIAC?"

" 'Kayak?' " Out of the blue; that puzzled him. "You
mean, like Eskimos used to paddle around in?"

"Bigger than that." Amused, Harrisch shook his head.
"It's an acronym. Tee . . . eye . . . ae . . . see. Any
idea what that is?"

"Not a one."

"You should," said Harrisch. "It has to do with your

new job. With the late Travelt. And a lot to do with what happened to him."

"Ah." *Could've guessed that much,* thought McNihil. "So I take it that this TIAC thing . . . it's got something to do with DynaZauber? Maybe it's a DZ project of some kind? That seems like the kind of code designation that you and your friends would be fond of."

"Very good," Harrisch nodded. "It's DynaZauber's baby, all right. And mine, in particular. I've been in charge of it for a long time. Exclusively; I don't have any other corporate responsibilities at the moment." A shrug. "Well, almost none."

"Really?" With one hand, McNihil gestured over toward the tracks. "What about all this rail stuff?"

"A little diversion, is all. I'll be handing it back to the exec who's actually in charge." Harrisch's smile widened. "Let's just say I borrowed it for a little while. Just to make a grand entrance."

"Whatever." McNihil felt more weary than amused. "So this TIAC thing. The letters. So what do they stand for?"

"Actually," said Harrisch, "you have no need to know. And in fact, perhaps it's just as well that you don't know." The smile disappeared. "All you really need to know is that it's something that belongs to us. To DynaZauber. And we don't like losing things that belong to us. Or having them taken."

"Really?" McNihil wasn't surprised by that. "How'd you lose it? Or to put it another way . . . who took it?"

"Those are very good questions." Harrisch turned his cold gaze around, like aiming a gun. "That's the reason we hired you, Mr. McNihil. To find out exactly that." The two black holes at the centers of his eyes were as deep and reflectionless as the surrounding night. "We figured—or I did, at least—that it would be the kind of thing you'd be very good at finding out. Somewhat perfect, actually."

"Why's that?"

"Simple." A few empty seconds passed while Harrisch regarded him. "Where it's lost, is someplace you've been. Someplace you know all about. Rather a specialized area of knowledge for you."

McNihil said nothing. He had a premonition of where this was all going.

"The Wedge."

He looked over at Harrisch. "You've been mis-informed," said McNihil. He kept his voice quiet and con-trolled. "I don't go there."

"Not anymore?"

"Ever."

"How interesting." One of Harrisch's eyebrows lifted in mock surprise. "My sources are very reliable. And they tell it differently. You had some big times in that little district. Famous times. People are still talking." The bad smile again. "You don't hear them, but they are."

McNihil felt his own anger stacking up inside himself. At this point, after those words, he didn't care if the other man had his corporate flunkies and thugs all around. *I'll unload on him,* swore McNihil, letting the hands dangling at his sides tense in fists. *I don't care what happens.* Not anymore . . .

"I seem to have upset you," said Harrisch smoothly. "My apologies."

"Don't bother." McNihil supposed that the vein he could sense pulsing at the corner of his brow was the dead giveaway about his emotional state. "You can go back and congratulate your sources. They've got it right this time."

Ancient history. It felt that way, like something engraved on rock-faced stelae on the mountainsides, the records of fallen empires. Though the only thing that had fallen was McNihil himself. A bad fall, the kind that you survive. *But I wish I hadn't,* he brooded. Another night, older and deeper than this one, folded around him.

The truth of the matter: any line McNihil handed out about not working as an asp-head anymore was pure shuck and jive. He knew the score; it was burned into not only his personnel file back at the Collection Agency, but into the file he carried around inside his head. The file marked both Learn to Forget and Not to Be Forgotten.

"You have to expect things like this." Harrisch's voice slid into his thoughts. "You have to expect that I'd know all about what happened. Back then."

"Big deal," growled McNihil. "So you know I didn't leave the agency voluntarily."

"That's one way of putting it. Another would be to say that they canned your ass."

"Whatever."

"Look at it this way." The exec's voice needled farther under McNihil's skin. "Forced out of one job, forced into another one—it's a wash. I'm giving you a golden opportunity."

He turned a heavy-lidded glare toward Harrisch. "To do what?"

"To finish what you started." The smile went lopsided as Harrisch tilted his head. "That's what you want, isn't it?"

McNihil went silent again. A few seconds ticked away before he spoke. Then, quietly: "How would you know what I want?"

"Come on," said Harrisch. He spread his unstigmatic hands apart. "It's human nature. You might not think I know anything about that, but I do." One hand lifted, as though in preparation for laying a benediction on McNihil. "More than you might imagine, as a matter of fact; it's kind of a speciality of mine. So when I say that you're still pissed about what happened to you—what went down in the Wedge—I'm pretty sure I'm right."

The man was right; that was the problem. McNihil coldly regarded the DZ exec. "Human nature," said Mc-

Nihil, "isn't the problem with the Wedge. It's the inhuman parts that screw people up. You think you're clued in on that as well?"

"Enough. Enough to know what happened to you." Harrisch's voice went monotone and level, a deliberately flattened recitation of facts. "You were the head of the Collection Agency team that was going to sort out the Wedge. That's how high up in the agency you were; you had total control over—and responsibility for—the operation."

"That's right." McNihil nodded. "I reported straight to the agency director. No levels, no organizational hierarchy, between me and the top."

"You even initiated the operation. It was your idea. So when things went wrong—and they did, badly—there was nobody to take the fall except you. Nobody to blame but yourself."

Also true. The Wedge, that amorphous zone of sexual license, existing everywhere and nowhere simultaneously, in the human mind and in flesh and somewhere in between—it was only to be expected that a place and a concept like that would become the home for other excesses, other crimes. If not against nature, then at least against property. Specifically, the kind that the Collection Agency was supposed to protect. Copyright infringement as sexual stimulation; that was to be expected as well. One perversion always led to another. Where Eros linked up with Thanatos; the fact that in the daylight world, the social universe outside the Wedge, that kind of screwing around led inevitably to one's death, or worse, only ratchetted the thrills up even further.

"All right," said McNihil. "That's all true. I took the fall . . . and I deserved to. If for no other reason than because I was the guy in charge. But I don't have any regrets about it. I'm sorry about the way it turned out, but I still believe we had to do it. We had to give it a shot."

" 'Sorry'?" That got a laugh from Harrisch. "*You're*

sorry? Hey, there were people who died in that little fiasco. I've seen the body count. Your fellow agents; some of them came back in bags, others didn't come back at all. No wonder your reputation went to shit inside the Collection Agency."

"They knew what they were getting into."

"Did they?" Harrisch peered closer at him. "Did you?"

"There were some . . . surprises," admitted McNihil. "Things we weren't expecting."

"I'll say." Nodding, Harrisch folded his arms across his chest. "There's one thing in particular you didn't expect. Or should I say 'someone'?"

He knew what Harrisch was going to say next, the name that would be spoken.

"You weren't expecting Verrity, were you?"

"No," said McNihil. "We weren't. We didn't know. We'd heard of her—at least I had—but nobody thought she was real. I thought she was just . . . legendary. Just the kind of myth that grows in places like the Wedge."

"So she took you by surprise." Harrisch's gaze was close to pitying. "When you found out she was real."

"That was . . . the last thing I expected."

"Not *just* real," corrected Harrisch. "More to it than that, wasn't there? More to her. Realer than real—at least inside the Wedge. And that's all that matters, isn't it? That's enough of a world for Verrity to be queen of. Enough of a world to kick your ass in."

"Not just mine." McNihil's turn for a grim smile. "You're the one who's complaining about someone having your valuable missing property."

"True." Harrisch nodded. "So you see—we do have something in common, you and I. A common enemy. Verrity has something of mine—something that belongs to DynaZauber—and she also has something of yours. Your past, a great big bloody piece of it. Which translates to your pride. Your self-respect."

"That's where you're wrong." McNihil shook his head. "I don't have any of those things. I never did. They're not important."

"So you say. But if that's the case—" The needle of Harrisch's gaze probed deeper. "Then why do you want revenge? Why do you want to get back at her so badly?"

For a few seconds, McNihil made no reply. Then: "Because. Like you said"—simply and quietly—"I just want to finish the job. The one that I started."

"And that's why you'll take this one," said Harrisch. "The one for us. Finding out what happened to Travelt. You could've gotten out of it; there are ways. A person like you would know how to just . . . disappear. Where you couldn't be found, even by the regular police. But you didn't."

"I didn't want to. I'm way too tired for that kind of shit." Another shake of the head, more ruefully intended. "Like the old lines go: better to die where you stand."

"Dying would be one of your easier options." Harrisch didn't appear impressed. "Easier than going up against Verrity again."

McNihil knew what the DZ exec was talking about. When the Collection Agency's operation into the Wedge had gone down, the operation he'd planned and overseen, he hadn't been there. In the Wedge—even the agents who'd died, the ones who'd taken the big hit, the one you didn't stand up from afterward; they hadn't gone into the Wedge, either. There was no need to . . . or at least that was how the reasoning had gone. Nothing made of human flesh went into that zone; that was what the prowlers were for. To go and fetch, like human-shaped dogs in artificial skins, the physical equivalent of the so-called intelligent agents that'd been created before the end of the century, those software entities programmed to scour the old on-line networks for desired info. Prowlers, on the other hand, were really real; they went out into the Wedge and brought back another kind of hot blue info, for the remote—and safe—consumption by their masters. The Collection Agency troops who ventured into the Wedge may have done so for reasons other than those of the zone's habitués—to extinguish rather than experience—but they did so using the same means. Not their flesh at risk, but their surrogates'; the Collection Agency's own little squad of purpose-built prowlers.

The agency's prowlers went into the Wedge, and found the hot blue zone wherever it faded from mental concept into physical reality; only sometimes, they went in and didn't come back out. A few did, and brought back death with them. The asp-heads who'd been working for the agency back then, the ones who'd volunteered for McNihil's clean-up-the-Wedge squad, wound up sticking their tongues into those wet red sockets . . . and had received a fatal communion in their bloodied saliva.

"But you knew—you found out—who was responsible." Harrisch's voice crept through all those old memories, as though he had some direct line into the skull that held them. "Didn't you?"

McNihil remained silent, knowing that there wasn't any answer required. The other man was way ahead of him. *He must've been rooting through the agency files,* thought McNihil. Or else DynaZauber itself had a direct line; maybe DZ had bought out the Collection Agency somehow, and was operating it as a wholly owned subsidiary, just as they were apparently doing now with the rail network. It could happen; DynaZauber was one of the big predators in the corporate world, and the Collection Agency was going through a headquarters shake-up, at least according to McNihil's own longtime contacts inside.

There was another possibility. *Maybe,* thought McNihil,

the information came from the other side. That was something to be considered: that DZ was forming its partnerships and strategic alliances from among the bad guys, the technically, legally bad guys. *Wouldn't be the first time*—McNihil dredged up a reference from ancient history. It'd be like some sort of Hitler-Stalin pact of the intellectual-property sphere, the collusion of entities that were supposed to be at each other's throats.

"Whatever." He turned away and looked across the rubbish-strewn landscape. His distaste for the conversation extended, permeating everything he saw before him like a bad smell. *This is what I get,* thought McNihil grimly. For getting involved—for *letting* himself get involved—with all this happy horseshit. Enough morning sunlight spilled over the distant mountains that the world's details were even more depressingly revealed to him. The scavenger dead were already out, creeping away from the ashes of their tiny, perfunctory campfires; the scrabbling, black-nailed hands had begun their owners' hunchbacked rituals of turning over each crumbling leaf of trash, looking for something, anything, that could be converted to the usual small profit. McNihil felt as if he had already joined their number.

Then again . . . maybe he wasn't the only one. He looked over at Harrisch, having suddenly realized something else. "You wouldn't be talking about Verrity," said McNihil, "unless she was important to you, too. If you've lost something . . . she must be the one who has it."

Hanging on the cross, Harrisch looked even more uncomfortable. "Well. We don't know that for sure."

"But that's what you suspect."

The exec shrugged That was answer enough.

"So what is it," said McNihil, "that she's got of yours? You must want it back awfully badly. Or otherwise you wouldn't be putting up with my shit."

"God, that's true enough." Harrisch rolled his eyes up

toward the sky, then sighed. "What we lost is one of our own. We lost Travelt."

"No, you didn't. We were all standing around looking at him, back there at his cubapt."

Harrisch shook his head impatiently. "That's what's *left* of him. The outside part. We lost the inside part of him. That's what we want back."

For a few seconds, McNihil mulled that over. "Why?" he asked at last. "What's so valuable about a junior exec? They're not that hard to replace. Promote one out of the copy room, you need one so badly."

"Look, pal. You don't need to know *why* we want him back. Maybe we're sentimental at DZ—"

That'll be the day, thought McNihil.

"All you need to know," continued Harrisch, "is what. And where. You go and do the rest."

Dream on, connector. "Just what inside part of Travelt do you think I should go looking for? The package I saw back there at the cubapt seemed just about ready to be picked apart."

"Shouldn't be all that difficult." Harrisch's irritation appeared to have simmered down. "For somebody of your talents and experience. Except that it's still walking around. Not in the Gloss per se. But in the Wedge."

McNihil wasn't surprised. "What you're talking about," he said, "is a prowler. You want me to go find the prowler that your little junior exec was using. Gone missing, has it?"

"That's right."

"So what?" McNihil had started to get a crick in his neck from looking up at the exec on the cross. "It probably didn't come wandering home, because there's no reason for it to do so. Its user is dead. Who's it going to come back and down to? The refrigerator?"

"We don't care if it downs to anybody—or anything." Harrisch was way past smiling anymore. "Matter of fact, we'd prefer if it didn't. If it just disappeared into the Wedge—if it disappeared off the face of the connecting *planet*—that'd be fine by us. But unfortunately, it's still out there somewhere. And it's causing us a little embarrassment."

"I don't see why. Prowlers are legal. Technically." McNihil reached up and rubbed the back of his aching neck. He wondered if this idiot's arranged train wreck had given him whiplash. "As long as you don't get caught doing something stupid with one. If you think it's bad for the DynaZauber corporate image that one of your junior execs got himself one—" *As if anybody cares.* "Hey." McNihil dropped his hand and shrugged. "Tell 'em you fired the guy's ass before he got into trouble."

"Travelt didn't 'get' himself a prowler. He was *given* it. By me."

"Ah." That didn't particularly surprise McNihil, either. "That was nice of you. Seems to have wound up getting the poor bastard killed, but what the heck. Does everybody at DZ get one? Must really play hell with the personnel department."

"It was a present," said Harrisch stiffly. "A bonus. A little token of my esteem. Travelt had done . . . particularly well on some of his assignments at DynaZauber."

"I bet."

"So he'd earned himself . . . a little something extra. And at the same time . . . he needed it." Harrisch made the words sound reasonable enough. "Travelt was a hard worker; perhaps a little too hard. Too serious. All work and no play. He needed something . . . for relaxing. Bringing a little . . . variety into his life. He was valuable enough that I didn't want him burning out on me too soon."

"Of course not," said McNihil. "Just soon enough." Nothing in the exec's spiel surprised him. *Why he had me check out the corpse*—so it would be obvious that prowler us-

age was involved. And even . . . approved of, as Harrisch
might say in that arch manner of his. *Because they're all doing
it.* All of Harrisch's flacks and flunkies, the various ranks of
business suits that had been hovering around there at the
cubapt—they'd all had that look about them, smug and conspiratorial, in on something good. Something better than
regular people ever had. It was the same look that baggies
and other chem'd-out types radiated, at least on the upslope
of their crash-and-burn biographies. They'd all had it . . .
except for Harrisch himself. He was on to something even
better. Control was the best drug, the spark better than anything that could be gotten out of a prowler's mouth.

"I didn't think . . . he could hurt himself with it." A
little actorly remorse slid across Harrisch's face. "For most
people . . . they're harmless."

"Sure they are. And for other people . . . they're even
profitable."

Harrisch drew his head back against the top of the cross.
"What do you mean?"

"Come on. Prowlers are manufactured by a DZ subsidiary. If nothing else, you got it at cost." *Cheap bastard,*
thought McNihil. "A box of chocolates would've run you
more."

"Maybe you're right," said Harrisch. "Maybe that's what
I should've done. But it's too late now. And besides . . .
we were sandbagged. Somebody connected with the prowler
that I gave to Travelt. Altered it, outside of its original speci-
fications. That's where the trouble comes from."

"How do you know that?"

"Perhaps if I gave you proof?" Harrisch's voice resumed
its usual oily ease. "Or at least some evidence. Then maybe
you'd give some proper consideration to what I've been trying to tell you."

"Sure." McNihil glanced up at the other man. "Lay it on
me." He didn't have very high hopes.

With a nod of his head, Harrisch signaled to an assistant lurking nearby, possibly the same flunky that had led McNihil to the dead man's cubapt; he couldn't tell any of them apart. The assistant walked over to McNihil and dug inside his jacket, finally extracting a couple of sheets of paper, which he deposited in McNihil's hand.

"What's all this?" The papers had the look and feel of inexpensive photocopies. McNihil unfolded them and turned them right side around. "Receipts? For what?"

"You can read," the assistant said sourly.

McNihil held the papers toward the advancing sunlight. Now he could make out the logo and words at the top of the first sheet of paper. "That's great." He shook his head; this, at least, he hadn't been expecting. The receipt was from the central L.A. branch of the Snake Medicine™ franchise. McNihil held the papers out at arm's length, not so much to read what was on them, as from some instinctive, deeply rooted aversion. *Cheesy sexual services,* he thought glumly. At the low end of the business, which was probably where the company made most of its profits. "What's this for? The little novelty items for the Christmas office party?" McNihil wondered if the Adder clomes at the SM clinic handled that sort of thing; streamers and other decorations, little party hats, all with some sort of grossly obscene motif. He didn't know; he'd never been inside one of the shops, or boutiques, or whatever they were called. A fragmentary image came into his thoughts, of Harrisch and his coterie of ass-kissing junior execs, bedecked with wobbling phallic headgear—at best—and blowing hideous flesh-colored noisemakers at each other. "You know . . . I wasn't aware that you and your bunch were such fun guys."

"We're not. Take a closer look."

McNihil saw now what the exec meant. This particular receipt was obviously for some kind of high-end merchandise; McNihil glanced at the dollar amount at the bottom of the right-hand column, and was impressed despite himself. "Was all this for you, or one of your friends?" He tried to hand the papers back to the assistant, but without success.

"Come on." Harrisch didn't rise to the bait. "Look at the address. Where the merchandise was delivered."

"Travelt's cubapt." It took less than a second for him to make the connection. "So this is for the prowler you gave to him."

"Correct. As you said, chocolates would've been more expensive. But that's not what I wanted you to see. Read the next page."

McNihil shuffled the two pieces of paper, bringing the second one up on top. This one also had the Snake Medicine™ franchise logo on top, and the same order reference number as the other paper. "What's all this?" The additional words and numbers didn't make any particular sense to him. "Am I supposed to know what this means?"

"I'll tell you," said Harrisch. "It's the catalog information for the modifications that were made on the prowler, before it was delivered to Travelt. Modifications I didn't order."

"What were they?"

"*That* . . . I don't know." A spark of anger flared up in the exec's voice again. "The numbers don't correspond to anything in the regular SM catalog. Or the secret one, which they don't even keep under the counter. The one they make available to just their top corporate customers."

"Like you."

"Like me," said Harrisch.

What the connect could it've been? wondered McNihil. Hard to imagine; the commercial clomes at the Snake Medicine™ clinics, the owner-operators fronting the business establishments, made a point of advertising their full range of services. That was their shtick, why they were all surgically altered into the idealized sleazy image from some old semiforgotten book, the doctor with the knife sharp enough to deliver whatever the customer wanted, sex-wise. From a simple stay-in-one-place tattoo, all the way to a Full Prince Charles job; you made the appointment with whatever Adder clome had set up shop in a low-rent storefront in your zone of the Gloss, and as long as you had the money for it, you could have your own little doorway into the Wedge carved into your body. The Snake Medicine™ clinics were even more legally tolerated than prowler usage, though the Adder clomes always tried to make it seem that they were operating right on the edge of the law, at least in part. McNihil had always figured that was just the usual faux rebellious ad spin on the clinics' regulated, safe-'n'-sane merchandise and services.

"Why not call them up?" McNihil lowered the sheets of paper in his hand. "Talk to the clome in charge. Ask him what these modifications were. If you're paying the bill, you've got a right to know."

"No can do." On the cross, Harrisch shook his head. "This item was paid for out of a corporate slush fund. If I initiate a billing-error inquiry, all hell breaks loose in the accounting department. Believe me, it's easier to go outside the loop, have somebody like you poke into the matter. Besides—I don't need to know exactly how this particular mess was created. I just need it cleaned up."

"Your lost property?"

"Exactly. The sooner it's back in my hands, the happier I'll be." Harrisch's ugly smile reappeared. "And when I'm happy . . . I make sure everybody else gets happy, too."

I'd be happy, thought McNihil, *if you'd get off my ass.* "You still haven't told me what this inside part of Travelt is, that you've lost."

"Travelt . . . knew things." Harrisch nodded, slowly and thoughtfully. "He'd have to have, he'd worked himself up in the corporation pretty well. He really knew the TIAC project inside and out. Close to being my right-hand man on it. As a matter of fact . . ." The exec shifted uncomfortably on the cross. "There were some things only Travelt was completely knowledgeable about."

"For somebody who wound up dead," remarked McNihil, "he sounds pretty smart. There's nothing like making yourself indispensable."

"True. He wasn't an idiot. As it turned out . . . neither was the prowler I gave him."

McNihil tilted his head, trying to catch an angle into the other man's eyes. "What do you mean?"

"Something happened," said Harrisch. "Between Travelt and the prowler. That we weren't expecting. It's always a very . . . *tight* relationship between a user and his prowler; intimate, you might say. And the one between Travelt and his prowler became more than tight; it apparently started to overlap. Big time. Instead of an essential separation between the two, a unity started to form. Transference occurred."

"That's what's supposed to happen." Something was hidden in the exec's gaze, that McNihil wasn't yet able to make out. "That's what a prowler is designed to do. It goes out and gets a certain kind of information and transfers it to the user in the form of memory."

"Sure—but that's a one-way street. The information goes from the prowler to the user. Not the other way around." Harrisch's voice went up a notch. "Something else happened with Travelt and his prowler. That's what the un-authorized modification must've been about. Something to make the overlap possible, to change the one-way street into a two-way. *The information went the other direction*—something from Travelt wound up inside the prowler's head."

Now McNihil got it. "The TIAC information. Whatever it was." The exec hadn't told him the details. "It trans-ferred over into the prowler. Right?"

"Exactly."

"Along with what else?"

"That's . . . hard to say." Harrisch's shoulders lifted, then fell. "It may be safer just to assume that *everything* crossed over, from Travelt's head to the prowler's. The whole personality structure, memories, ideas, information . . . the whole gestalt of Travelt got downed into the prowler."

"How do you know?"

"There've been . . . indications. Little bits and pieces showing up. Details about the TIAC project, personal things—all sorts of stuff. Stuff that shouldn't be turning up at all, especially if the person who had them in his head is deceased now. It's a leakage phenomenon. When other prowlers go into the Wedge, and they bring back things for their users to enjoy . . ." Harrisch inhaled deeply, then breathed out. "That's how I know. Because the other execs, the ones who also have prowlers, report these things to me. He's out there, all right."

"You mean," said McNihil, "the prowler is."

"It's the same thing." A fierce possessiveness tinged Harrisch's words. "The prowler I gave him has gone missing, and it's got Travelt inside. Or enough of him, at any rate. And enough of him is my property. DynaZauber property. Every detail about the TIAC project—that's ours. And I want it back."

McNihil looked away from the angry figure on the cross. He didn't know how much of Harrisch's story to believe. *And I don't care,* he thought. "Maybe you should climb down from there." He glanced back over to the elevated Harrisch. "And go looking for it yourself. Because I'm not going to."

Before Harrisch, face darkening, could say anything, one of the first-aid techs, in a green scrub uniform, showed up at the foot of the circle-enclosed cross. "Sorry to interrupt." The tech stripped latex gloves from his hands. "But I figured you'd want a report on that woman. The one from the crash, that you were having us take care of."

Harrisch's annoyance was visible in his furious expression. "What about her?"

"She's fine. Bruised and banged up, but nothing more than that." The first-aid tech wadded up the gloves and held them in one hand. "As a matter of fact, she's so fine she's gone."

"What're you talking about?"

The tech shrugged. "She took a powder. Got off the stretcher, unhooked the monitors, and went for a walk. Guess she didn't want to hang around." The tech started to head back toward the rail line. "Like I said, just thought you should know."

"That's how it is for me, too." McNihil looked up at the exec. "If the train's ready to roll, so am I."

"What about the job?" Harrisch looked like he was about to decrucify himself, to jump down from the apparatus and go face-to-face with the asp-head. "Now you know all about it. So you're ready to take it on, right?"

McNihil shook his head. "Sorry. The answer's the same as before. Not interested." He turned away and headed toward the train, set right once more on its tracks. The repair crews were wrapping up the last details.

The exec shouted after him. "Why the connect not?"

"I'm busy." McNihil stopped for a moment and glanced back over his shoulder. "I've already got a job to take care of."

PART TWO

Fred, understanding that he seemed a
bleak, sexless person to Harry, tried to
prove that Harry had him wrong. He
nudged Harry, man-to-man. "Like
that, Harry?" he asked.

"Like what?"

"The girl there."

"That's not a girl. That's a piece of
paper."

"Looks like a girl to *me*." Fred
Rosewater leered.

"Then you're easily fooled," said
Harry. "It's done with ink on a piece
of paper. That girl isn't lying there on
the counter. She's thousands of miles
away, doesn't even know we're alive. If
this was a real girl, all I'd have to do for
a living would be to stay home and cut
out pictures of big fish."

—KURT VONNEGUT, JR.

God Bless You, Mr. Rosewater

(Delacorte Press, New York, 1965)

NINE

THE NUMBERS WRITTEN IN HER PALM

As she was settling in, starting another vigil, somebody came round to remind November that she had bills coming due.

"You're always forgetting your friends," said the big dark shape. The man's face was hidden by shadow, but she knew what it looked like. "But your friends don't forget you."

Shit, thought November. *Sonuvabitch.* "Maybe you could just stop thinking about me for a while. Every now and then wouldn't hurt."

There was no way of getting past the guy, breaking out into the open street beyond; he filled up the alley's mouth like a fourth expanse of bricks, the cork in the bottle's neck. She'd stationed herself here with a pony bottle of Minnesota Evian and a pack of acetone-laced Gitanes, watching the

doorway of the building her quarry, McNihil, was slated for.
Her bruises from the train crash were slowly fading. In the
meantime, she didn't want to lose track of McNihil and the
bill-paying score he represented. *And now this,* she thought.
Thinking about the money she owed had summoned up
their walking embodiment of debt-load, heavy and nasty.

"How can we?" This one had a sense of humor. "You're
so connectin' cute."

November took a last harsh drag off the cigarette she'd
had going, reducing it to a stub. She bent down to throw it
through the gap between the man's hip and the alley wall,
tensing at the same time to dive through that narrow space
and hit the ground with a shoulder-first roll on the other
side.

"But not cute enough." The man's beefy fist seized onto
the collar of her jacket, lifting her up dangling in the air.
"Let's talk some more."

She let herself be nailed by his one hand up against the
damp bricks, her bootsoles inches from the needles and
patches strewn across the alley's floor. "Numbers are always
interesting," he said. "Let's take a look."

"You know what the numbers are." November tried to
convey an irritated, tolerance-stretched disgust; it was hard in
her present position. "You wouldn't be talking to me otherwise."

"Just want to make sure *you* know what they are." Still
holding her up with one hand, he grabbed her wrist with the
other. "Palm-reading time. Let's have the Gypsies tell your
fortune, sweetheart."

He twisted her arm around hard enough to get an involuntary squeak of pain out of her. *I bet you enjoyed that*—she
kept herself from speaking the words aloud. She knew better
than to try anything on him, the kind of stuff that worked so
well on her postcoital marks on the trains; not that it
wouldn't work just as well on him, dropping him paralyzed

on his back. But that the consequences, when he caught up with her again—and that was guaranteed—would be so much worse than letting him do what he wanted now. That was the problem with being in hock, she'd often reminded herself. It gave other people power over you, and not the enjoyable variety.

"So what do we have here?" He squeezed her trapped wrist, enough to make her fingers splay out trembling. "Your heart line . . . well, that's pretty much as to be expected, isn't it?" His small eyes glanced up to hers. "Kind of a narrow little scratch, that doesn't lead to much. And your life line . . ." He pressed his thumb into the middle of her palm. "That one doesn't look good at all."

"I'll do the worrying about that one."

"Oh, no; we all have to worry. Don't we?" The wide ball of his thumb rubbed sweat between her skin and his. "Because if something happened to you—then we'd be out quite a bit. We've invested a lot of money in you."

"Right." November managed to nod her head, scraping against the wall behind her. "And you've gotten it back. With interest."

"Not all of it. And not *enough* interest—not what you're down for at least, sweetheart." The man raised his thumb from her palm. "Let's add 'em up."

She said nothing, but watched as he turned her hand toward the light slicing down the alley. The invisible numbers, written in the cup of her palm, were visible to him as well. He had a master filter cut into his eyes—when he'd looked up at her, she'd been able to spot the dull silver worm at the far depth of his pupils. So he could read not only what was there in her hand, but in the hands of all those who'd signed themselves over to his sharkoid employers.

"Honey, you're *way* into us." He sucked his breath in between his teeth. "You taken a look at this lately? I knew we loved your ass, but I didn't think we loved it *this* much."

"I know what it says." The jacket's leather, drawn up by the man's hold, had gathered under her arms; November felt as if she were being softly crucified. "You don't have to make a big production number out of this."

He leaned his broad face close to hers. "Then you're the one who should be tap-dancing." His breath smelled like hydrogenated fat and Thai peppers. "Just as fast as you can."

Taking a step backward, he let go of her collar. The back of her head skidded down the wall, the friction enough to snap a match into flame. Her butt hit the ground, jamming her spine upward; it felt as if the topmost vertebrae had crunched against the inside curve of her skull.

She had no time to react; the man jerked her arm up by the wrist he still held. He reached down with his other hand and grabbed a fistful of her hair, rocking her head back.

"Look up here, cunt." The sweetheart rhetoric was over. "Up here where the numbers are."

Her throat was stretched so taut that she could barely whisper. "I see them . . ."

"Oh, take a *good* look. Because I don't think you know what they are at all. You must not have checked them very recently, that's for sure." He gave a quick rap with the back of her head against the wall. "Otherwise, you'd be a *lot* more scared than you are now."

"All right. All right; just give me a moment . . ." November knew the guy wasn't playing around now; it didn't matter whether he might be enjoying this part more than the cute stuff that'd preceded it. She gazed up at her hand, focusing on the numbers written in her palm, just below the little black ▶ symbol, just above the knuckled cuff of the thug's fist. The filter in her eyes rendered the numbers visible to her, the secret history of her accounts . . .

"Christ." The single appalled word escaped from her lips. She saw what he'd meant. And just as he'd predicted, she was afraid. "What happened?"

The numbers had always been in red; that meant nothing, just the way the filters made them appear, like legible, luminous blood. But at the bottom of one of the columns, the total blinked on and off, speeding ahead of her pulse. That meant a great deal. None of it good.

"Things can change on you. Really fast." He looked down at her with a mixture of pity and contempt. "The Djakarta quarterlies—*and* the peek-ahead from the Vladivostok exchanges—their output figures were way up. The *teneviki* put out a regulatory call, and the bank conglomerates jacked their prime rates. Get the picture?" He gave her arm a tug, not for pain, just for emphasis. "Your main account, the one in which you've been rolling over all the others—you didn't lock in the interest. You wanted that discount from going with an adjustable. That was stupid of you."

"It seemed like a good idea." November still felt a little dazed. The numbers kept on blinking, like intermittent stigmata. "At the time, it did."

"That was then. This is badly now. Bad for you, sweetheart." His voice had actually softened. "You got the picture, didn't you?" He brought her palm down nearer to her face. "We can call in our markers right now. We can foreclose on you. We can have your ass on toast, if that's what we want."

She looked up hopefully into his face. "Is it?"

A smile showed at one corner of his mouth. "That's a tempting offer, sweetheart, but not right now. I don't mix business with pleasure. And at this particular moment, my business is telling you what the score is."

"Please . . . you really don't have to." November hoped the guy wasn't about to go into details, all of which she was familiar enough with. She'd spent enough time down there, south of True Los Angeles, talking with the dead and indeadted, including McNihil's deceased wife, to know what happened to people who couldn't pay their bills. Especially the kind she'd run up; the loan sharks were always hardest on speculators and hustlers such as herself. Maybe out of some ruthless Darwinian motivation: weeding out the failures was how a tougher, faster species was bred into existence.

"Look," said November. Her thoughts had pulled together, enough that she could at least talk, even if she didn't know what hustling verbiage to use. "Maybe we can work something out . . ."

"I told you. I'm not interested in that right now."

"No, no—I mean some kind of, uh, financing arrangement." She could feel her brain kicking into overdrive; all she needed was some traction on this slippery ground. "You know I'm about to score here. Really. All I need is a little more time." The words started coming faster and faster. "It'd be a shame, I mean a shame for you people, if you had to write off my account, all that money down the toilet, just because you couldn't cut me a few extra days—"

"Don't sweat it." The man shook his thick-necked head in a combination of amusement and disgust. "We're not writing you off. You want some more time? Great, that's what I'm here for."

She drew back, eyeing him. "What's the catch?"

"What do you want it to be?"

November frowned in puzzlement. "I didn't follow that one . . ."

He used her trapped hand to pull her upright. "Like I said: whatever you want." He pushed her palm toward her face, almost touching her nose. "How do you like *these* numbers? Better?"

The red numbers were so close, she could just bring them into fuzzy focus. But that was enough for November to see that the baleful total wasn't blinking anymore.

"Does that do your heart good?" The man smiled at her from the other side of the hand in front of her face. "Think you can breathe now?"

"I don't get it . . ." The tips of her fingers felt numb, detached. "What did you do . . ."

"No big thing." The man let go of her wrist. "I just took care of your problems, that's all. Or let's say . . . they were already taken care of." He wiped her sweat off against the front of his coat. "You're a lucky girl. Today, at least."

They refinanced me, thought November. She moved her hand away, bringing the numbers sharper. Without needing any authorization from her; the sharks had that option, if they wanted to, when somebody's account went into the foreclosure zone.

"Look, I appreciate this . . ." November lowered her hand. "But I don't know if I can take any higher interest rate than what I had already. You're gonna be slicing my margins pretty tight . . ."

"I wouldn't know about *tight*. Like I said, I'm not interested in that." The man's heavy shoulders lifted in a noncommittal shrug. "Besides, you don't have anything to fret about. We haven't jacked up your rates. We're doing you a favor: your terms have been rolled back to what they were when you signed for the adjustable, and we've frozen 'em there. Plus we're cutting you an extension on the due date."

"What?" November stared at him in amazement. "Nobody does that."

"So what can I say. We're connectin' saints."

"No, you're not." She pressed her hands flat against the alley wall behind her. "I know that much."

"Well, maybe you're right about that." The man looked out at the empty street, then back toward her. "Maybe there is something we want in exchange." He brought his face close to hers, his exhaled breath as fiery as before. "For being so understanding of your problems."

She said nothing. Just waited, without moving.

"Don't fuck up." No smile, nothing but the black holes

of his eyes, capturing the tiny images of her face. "You got that? That's what we want. Don't connect up this one."

His voice, without shouting, had efficiently pinned her to the wall. *It's not about money,* realized November. *Or at least not about the money I owe them.* Something else was going on. Deep shit, with its own negative luminosity, like some dead and malignant sun.

She spoke at last. "I got it," said November.

"That's why you don't have to say thank you." The man stepped back from her. "It's not really necessary, is it? Strictly business, that's all."

That got a nod from her. "Strictly business."

"Maybe next time . . ." His smile floated lazily to the surface once more. "Maybe next time, we can talk about that *other* business. Between me and you."

"I don't think so." November regarded him coldly. "Like you said; you're not doing me any favors. So I don't have to be nice to you. So connect off."

He laughed, then turned and walked away, steering his wide bulk toward the alley's mouth.

When he was gone, November turned her gaze back toward the building she'd been watching. Her target, McNihil, would be arriving soon, she knew. She'd kept her vigil; all the time the loan sharks' man had been harassing her, she'd been able to keep a minimum eye on the building's doorway.

The connector didn't know how important he was. For a lot of reasons, and not just for her. She wondered, as she folded her arms across her breast and leaned back against the damp bricks, just what some of those other reasons might be.

McNihil leaned back into the padding of the taxicab's backseat and watched massive, vaguely Stalinist buildings slide by. For a moment, he wondered if he had actually overshot his destination and wound up in some entirely dif-

ferent segment of the Gloss, over on the Pacific's Asian
shores. He checked his watch; it hadn't adjusted for moving
into a new time zone, so he knew he was still on the West
Coast of the North American continent. Plus, he simply
hadn't been traveling long enough to have looped around the
Bering Strait and south toward Vladivostok. *I may be losing it
these days,* he thought, *but not that much.*

He figured this had to be around Sea-Tac, where the
international airport had been, back when the *Noh*-flies
hadn't taken up residence in the gray, endless clouds and
people could still take jetliners from one point to another on
the earth's surface. McNihil just hadn't been up this way for
a while—months, at least—and the rate of new construction
piling out of Seattle's core had gotten away from him. The
architecture, great brutal slabs and cubes of poured and up-
tilted ferroconcrete, was the manifested embodiment of the
lowering weather and the population's taste in bloodstream
additives. There was a certain smack grandeur, the conflu-
ence of De Quincey and Cobain, to such massive, raw vistas.
Places where one could be borne to the sepulchre in a crystal, soundproofed coffin by leering hallucinations of alliga-
tors, streets cleaved between towers to the frozen center of
the earth, the annihilation by scale of all that was puny and
human.

Settled in the cab's stained upholstery, McNihil let bleak
architectural musings seep from his thoughts. He took comfort in the knowledge that he was heading into the center of
the old city, that the business he'd come here to take care of
was located in a zone of comprehensible and familiar decay.

"Here?" The cabbie sounded incredulous. "This is
where you want off? You're kidding, right?"

The vehicle had come to a stop, after the push and pull
of the interstate feeder traffic. McNihil glanced out the window. "Doesn't look that risky to me." He'd seen worse
places. He lived in one.

"Of course not. It's just such a tourist trap." Disappointment filtered into the cabbie's voice, as well as expectation of a stiffed tip. "I took you for some kind of exec type."

"Yeah, there's that kind of aura about me. It's a curse." From his wallet, McNihil extracted his debit card and poised it at the slot of the reader mounted on the dividing panel. "What's the damages?"

A string of blue LED's blinked on beside the reader. "There's a hazard add-on." The cabbie didn't sound apologetic. "I don't usually bring people from the station out this way."

"Don't worry about it. I take it off my taxes." He ran the card through the slot, the reader taking a recorded bite from his only operational account. "And it's not even a scam." *Or not much of one,* thought McNihil.

The cabbie gave him a reappraising look. "Maybe you want me to stick around? For when you're ready to go back?"

McNihil shook his head. He'd gotten out and slammed the passenger door shut. "I'll take my chances."

Scanning the area, as the cab's engine noise faded down the narrow street, McNihil's gaze took in a withered park, a little urban pocket of dead greenery. Lack of sunshine hadn't killed it; the buildings surrounding it were ancient nineteenth- and twentieth-century constructs, nowhere near high enough to form a well-like canyon of steel and faux-marble facades. Another channel of light had been cut by a crashed 747, one of the first *Noh*-fly victims to have its unshielded cockpit electronics HERF'd out and rendered useless. The plane had gone down here as though, in its terminal arc, it had been trying to return to its vanished Boeing birthplace. It had almost made it; a few miles farther south and it would have slept in the factories of its ancestors.

McNihil passed under the skeletal shade of the airliner's tail section, like tripartite shark fins angled into the air. The

swath that the fuselage had dug through the city lay to the
west; he could see a wedge of ocean, framed by avalanched
brick rubble and twisted steel girders, at the bottom of the
city's slope. He picked his way over the denuded struts of
the wing lying tonguelike across the sidewalk and into the
cracked asphalt of the street. This close, he could see down
into the old subterranean levels of the city, the 747 having
torn a stratified hole the way a table knife would have parted
an anthill. Scuttling noises, the flicker of battery-operated
lights and peering eyes, revealed the presence of the hole's
occupants, charity-resistant scavengers making their homes
in the tunnels where tour groups had been led a long time
ago. Some of the cave dwellers who were still comfortable
with daylight had extended their realm up into the stripped
aircraft fuselage, stringing hammocks and clamber-nets between the rows of charred, rain-soaked seat remnants. Whatever baggage survived the crash had been looted and
converted into nominal curtain walls, barriers stitched together from business suits and lingerie, the aged rags all fluttering in the salt wind coming off the ocean. The empty
suitcases, broken-locked Samsonites and American Touris-
ters, a few shabby imitation Vuittons, had been strung up on
the surrounding power lines; they swung and banged like
giant castanets.

   As he passed by the nose-buried plane wreckage,
McNihil saw a cobbled-together gantry arm, corroded sewer
pipes hinged with telephone-pole bolts, swing up like an
improvised construction crane. Its blind head, guided by a
system of rope pulleys, jerked toward him.

   "This is an official panhandling station." An unamplified
voice traveled up a duct-taped hose, dangling in loops like
throat wattles from the gantry. A funnel was aimed toward
McNihil; the other end of the tube ran down into the hole.
"Charity expands the heart. Literally—the cardiovascular
benefits are immense, buddy."

"Yeah, I'm sure." With one hand, McNihil pushed aside the funnel. "Not today."

"We accept cash, but prefer wire debits." The gantry's head, steered by the ropes and pulleys, followed along beside him. "See the reader there? I'm sure you do. You look like a smart sonuvabitch. Just dash the ol' plastic down the groove, and reap the rewards in the world to come."

"Pie in the sky." McNihil could see the scam as well. The card reader was a fake, a slit mouth with either glue at the bottom or some kind of clamp trap, ready to be triggered by another, smaller line running down the gantry neck. No data conduit behind the red-dotted LED's; the ferrite-sheathed cables were as bogus as the hidden beggar's pitch. Anybody stupid and tenderhearted enough to fall for the gag would have his card snatched out of his hand, then disappeared back down into the dimly lit tunnel world; the gantry was strung with tensioned elastic, synthetic rubber sliced from the downed 747's landing gear and depolymerized to a taut and stretchy consistency. The panhandlers wouldn't have to do anything more than pop the restraining clutch in their grubby hands, to have the thin rectangular prize come flying their way. "I'm not falling for this one," said McNihil as he walked on.

"Don't be such a hard case." The talking funnel floated near his face. "God loves a cheerful giver."

"I don't."

"Come on—" The funnel's voice continued pleading. "Money is just information, a concept, infinitely replicable without generation loss. That's the way it is in this new world."

"Don't be a connecting idiot," said McNihil. "Wake up and smell the burning corpses of your dreams, pal."

"Watch it—" The voice coming through the tube turned huffy. "*Connecting* isn't a dirty word around here." A little shriller: "It's people like you, with your antiquated anti-

connectivity mind-sets, that are going to be dead meat someday! You just watch! Wait and see!"

Blah blah blah. McNihil wasn't surprised that the broken
airliner was a nest of pirasites, that aging-hippie combination
of *pirate* and *parasite,* with their warped premillennium notions about information, concepts—and concepts *about* concepts—being as real for them as the world outside their
shaggy, graying heads. The business he'd come up here to
take care of was with a copyright thief, but at least one who
was doing it for money, rather than from some outdated
crackpot ideology. That was the kind of thing that ticked
him off even more than simple, straightforward larceny.

It was just like these 'net-twit types as well, to have a bug
up their collective ass about what'd become the popular usage of the verb *connect.* These idiots had never gotten it
through their soft skulls that the only ones who really believed connecting was an unalloyed good thing were people
who had something to sell and rapists, two categories that
weren't that far apart in this world.

McNihil took a knife from his coat pocket, flicked its
small blade open, reached over, and sliced through one of the
thick black rubber bands. It sounded a pizzicato viola note as
it snapped loose, followed by a twanging chorus, a chain
reaction all the way down the length of the gantry. The
articulated device swooped out of control, hinge pins squeal-
ing as the eyeless head jerked up toward the gray-clouded
sky. The violent motion ripped loose the phony card reader;
it went spinning in a high arc across the street.

McNihil was impressed in spite of himself. With a certain
childlike, pure delight in random destruction—*You never grow
too old,* he thought, *for this kind of stuff*—he watched as the
gantry went wild, raking its terminal claw in the airliner's
row of broken-out passenger-section windows. The gantry
end snagged in the window hole closest to the raised tail,
with enough force to snap loose a few critical bolts and

struts. The dead plane shivered and began to disintegrate, the
remains of its laminated exterior peeling away like shed
snakeskin, the structural elements wrenching loose from one
another. The urban scavengers who had been making their
homes in the fuselage were revealed as their sheltering curtain rags were torn away, the network of spun ropes snapping
and whipping in air. A Brueghelian scene tilted in the midst
of the city, of compressed, interwoven sleep and copulation,
chemical ingestion and little meals prepared on tinder-fed
campfires. Tilted to briefly vertical, the awake and sleeping
inhabitants, in narcotized or other dreams, tumbled down
the fuselage's central aisle as the hooked gantry swung the
other direction, upsetting the wreckage's fragile balance.
Their screams and surprised shouts echoed off the surrounding buildings.

   With a metallic groan, the downed 747's spine snapped,
the rusted cylinder folding in the middle at a ninety-degree
angle. Rag-ensembled bodies dropped to the ground below,
the fortunate ones being able to shake their dazed heads and
scramble to their feet before more debris fell upon them.
McNihil had prudently backed away, retreating to the littered sidewalk on the other side of the street. From there, he
watched as the broken fuselage now arced sideways, the motion uprooting the nose section from its grave in the tunnels.
The operators of the panhandling gantry could be seen behind the cockpit's shattered windows; a gray-bearded face
displayed terror as the figure desperately clung to the useless
levers and ropes.

   The L-shaped wreckage finished its sideways roll, coming
to rest in the middle of the empty street. Creaking metal
sounded in basso, accompanied by the smaller, bell-like notes
of rivets and bolts clattering through the struts, as the 747
continued to disintegrate in slower motion. The inhabitants,
those who were still alive and relatively uninjured, stood in
the clouds of billowing dust, commenting upon the loss of

their home with emotions that ranged from hysteria to fatalistic amusement.

McNihil checked his watch. The unplanned destruction
of the pirasite colony had been entertaining in its way, but a
distraction from what he'd come here for. He was already a
few minutes late for his appointment, and there were still
some details he had to take care of before meeting up with
the guy. He shielded his eyes from the dust and partial sunlight, scanning across the street-level fronts of the surrounding buildings. *There we go,* thought McNihil; he had spotted
what he was looking for. Leaving the wreckage behind him,
he strode toward a small transient hotel a block away.

"I'm going to be needing a room in a little while." The
jittering neon outside read End Zone Hotel; the place had a
pro football motif, yellowing posters of numbered and hel-
meted players on the walls, from a time when there'd been
those kinds of teams anywhere in the Gloss. Now the words
seemed to have taken on a different meaning: the hotel's
lobby looked like one of hell's waiting lounges, for those
damned from sheer inertia. *Not even half-devils,* thought
McNihil. *Quarter- or eighth-devils, at the most.* God probably
couldn't be bothered to hate them. "I'll pay for it now." He
dropped old-fashioned cash into the battered chrome drawer
extruded toward him.

"Then it's your room right now, buddy." Behind the
overlapping layers of steel grilles, the desk clerk roused himself long enough to pull the drawer back and count the
money. "Hour rate works out the same as the day rate. You
only get a break if you stay a week or longer." One yellow-
tinged eye regarded him with suspicion. "You don't look like
you're going to be around that long."

McNihil glanced over his shoulder at the humpbacked
upholstered chairs and sag-spined sofas, Salvation Army cast-
offs, that furnished the lobby. The furniture's occupants had
assumed the same coloration, the exact tone of dirty-gray

putty he knew would be edging the clouded windows upstairs. The chairs and the nominal people in them looked as if
they were made of the same substance, as though the sweaty
cushions had been caught in the act of giving birth to blank-
faced human beings, or the seated figures, legs and crutches
sprawled in front of them, were slowly devolving into last
century's seating arrangements. McNihil glanced back at the
desk clerk. "You got that one right."

"Want the key now or when you head back here?"

"It can wait." McNihil pulled several items out of pockets and deposited them in the tray. "But I need you to hold
on to some of my stuff for a while."

The desk clerk pulled the drawer onto his side of the
counter and looked at the objects. "You gotta be kidding,
mister." The biggest and heaviest of them was the black
shape of his tannhäuser. "We don't get involved in that kind
of trouble."

McNihil slid more cash under the bottom edge of the
grille.

Nodding, the desk clerk tucked the money into his shirt
pocket. "Now we do."

"Good." McNihil pushed himself back from the
counter. "Take care of everything and see how much better
you feel." He put his wallet away slowly, making sure the
clerk could see the other bills' corners sticking out of it.
"Later on."

As McNihil was heading out of the End Zone Hotel's
lobby, he glanced over again at the figures slumped in the
decaying sofa and upholstered chairs. A half-dozen of them,
still looking vaguely human, tundra for spiders to begin laying their gray nets over. A bigger web had already been spun:
sustenance checks had obviously been pooled, so that a
multi-apertured I.V. dispenser could be rented. The surgical-
steel box sat on the lobby's threadbare carpet, at the base of a
chrome tree with clear, fluid-filled bags hanging from its

short branches. An octopus network of tubes ran from the unit's central control mechanism to the hypodermics of the connectees, the needles taped down to the arms of the ones fortunate enough to still have usable veins there; other lines snaked up trouser legs or were fastened onto necks like long, skinny, reverse-flow vampires. The most decrepit of the figures had the line trailing into his open fly, as though the sharp metal and polyethylene tube were his final lover, searching for any place where his blood still flowed.

From the other tube, the big one of the television mounted on a plywood shelf in the lobby's upper corner, mumbling junkie dialogue seeped out. McNihil stopped for a moment and glanced up at the screen. On it was the popular hypo opera *He's Never Early, He's Always Late*; transactions involving little folded slips of paper and glassine envelopes were going on among the professionally disreputable-looking actors. A long time ago, back when he'd still been working as an asp-head, McNihil had done some heavy copyright defense for the show's producers, laying into a Thai cable start-up that had tried to clone the central concept without paying royalties. He was glad to see that the show was still running, though he'd never been able to figure out the charm of it. For the decaying, knocked-out figures sprawled around the lobby, it must have brought back memories of their younger days. As he watched, needle-tip penetrated flesh on the screen; blood flowered up a calibrated cylinder. He turned his head, hearing the steel box click and hum; the thin hoses trembled. The gray faces turned grayer and half-lidded eyes unfocused as the synchronized hit, triggered by a data wire plugged into the back of the TV, rolled up their brainstems.

The show, McNihil knew, prided itself on authenticity, or enough of a simulation of it to get the ratings. On the screen, at the other end of the cable, the actors probably weren't chipping at the same low-grade opiate as this audience—AFTRA regs usually insisted on blissful fentanyl—but it certainly wasn't sterile Ringer's solution being shot up. *That's entertainment,* thought McNihil as he headed for the door.

Outside the transient hotel, he found himself thinking of the last dead—really dead—person he'd seen. Which had been the one named Travelt, lying with blank eyes on the carpeted floor of a cubapt farther south on the circle. A little movie with no action unrolled behind his eyes, on the smaller screen of memory. That poor bastard would've been exactly the kind of fool to imagine that there was some sort of low-rent glamor to that sad congregation in the hotel lobby, that his sheltered exec life had kept him from all sorts of dark fun. Imagining things like that, and then acting upon them, was what had most likely left Travelt staring up at the ceiling, his breath all clotted blood in his throat. Which was just a little too late to acknowledge the hard lesson he'd been taught.

Unencumbered by the tools he'd left with the desk clerk, McNihil headed toward the movie theater off the little urban park. By now, the dead 747 had finished collapsing, its disjointed wreckage strewn across the grassless raw earth and the surrounding streets. The destructive work that the *Noh*-flies had begun was complete; the city's dispossessed who'd made temporary shelter from the fuselage now stood around or scrabbled with their black-clawed hands to drag their meager property from it.

"Hey! That's the sonuvabitch! That's the guy!" A voice called after McNihil as he passed by. "He fuckin' did it!"

He recognized the voice as that of the panhandling gantry's operator, now undistorted by the tube-and-funnel arrangement. The face behind the beard was cave-pallid from what had probably been years down in the buried nose section of the airliner. Even this zone's diminished sunlight was enough to force the red eyes into teary, squinty blinking. A dirt-encrusted hand pointed an accusing finger toward McNihil.

Soon there were a dozen or so ragged figures trailing after him on the sidewalk. He stopped and turned around to face their bearded leader.

"Look," said McNihil. "Too bad about what happened. But I've got business to take care of. And you're cramping my action."

"Screw that." The one with the beard hunched over troll-like, as though his confinement in the airliner had permanently bent his spine. "You owe us, man." A grimy paw, the flesh-and-dirt equivalent of the articulated gantry, extended toward McNihil. The crowd behind the bearded figure emitted a mumbling, angry chorus. "Pay up. Card or cash."

A familiar adrenaline ticked through McNihil's bloodstream, as measured and evocative as that produced by the machine back in the hotel lobby. Part of him could sit back inside his skull as his hands grabbed the front of the other man's shirt, gathering the tattered cloth into his fists, then lifting the other into the air. The line of McNihil's white knuckles pressed up beneath the bearded figure's collarbone.

"I tried to tell you." McNihil turned and slammed the man's spine against the nearest building wall. "I'm busy. And I don't like being harassed for small change."

Pinned between McNihil's doubled fists and the wall, the bearded figure did a spastic butterfly dance.

"I knocked your squat down because I don't *like* you." McNihil leaned his weight into the other man's chest, hard enough to make a pink tongue protrude through the beard. "I *meant* to do it," he lied. "And I wasn't *nearly* as pissed off then as I am now."

"Urrf." Mottled patches appeared on what little of the bearded man's face was visible. "Agk."

The others, who had been following behind, had now

backed off a few meters. Their faces showed that they hadn't been prepared for the violence level to go up another notch.

"Now I'm going to put you down. And then I'm going to walk in one direction, and you're going to walk in another. Got me?"

Above McNihil's fists, the bearded figure nodded.

Wiping the backs of his hands against his trousers, McNihil watched the squatters scurry away. In the distance, back at the block-long park, fires had broken out in the 747's disassembled wreckage, from overturned camp stoves and the few bits of electrical wire shorting out. Black smoke coiled toward the sky as McNihil turned and headed once more toward the movie theater.

What a putz, thought November. She had watched the whole bit, from her vantage point in a shadowed alley. From here she had been able to see her target, the former asp-head, come striding onto the scene, heading for what he was probably telling everyone was a business appointment. *Right*—she nodded to herself—*same business as before.*

The little knot of homeless—more homeless now—were making their way back to the smoldering plane debris. November turned her head, letting the shuffling figures fade from her attention. She hadn't come here, stationed herself to wait for McNihil's arrival, on their behalf. They couldn't pay her tab, they couldn't even get her close to making the monthly nut that kept the breath in her lungs. Inside her fist, the sweat-damp skin of her palm itched; she could feel the red numbers crawling across her life line, red numbers that she didn't want to open her hand to look at. She was the only one who could see them, and right now she didn't need to. Not after that last encounter with her finance company's representative.

Her gaze swung across the narrow city streets and the boarded-up or burnt-out storefronts. And back to the figure

of McNihil, disappearing into a little fly-by-night movie
house without a glance behind himself.

Hard to believe this guy had ever had any cop moves at
all. November shook her head, reflecting on the teeth of the
slow gears, the inexorable machinery of time. *They get old,*
she thought, *they lose it.* That was probably a big reason she'd
put herself on a short leash, become a fast-forward. When
she couldn't cut it, when the numbers in her hand pulsed
down to zero and the minuses beyond, it'd be a quick end.
She wanted to avoid having that happen just yet, though.

A ticket stub from the little rat-hole theater was in the
pocket of her jacket; she'd already been in and discreetly
checked that McNihil's "business" was there, scrunched
down in a center-row seat and watching some stupid cartoon
with a tub of butteroid popcorn in his lap. McNihil was
running late, in risk of blowing the connection he'd come
here to make. But he'd have to be late, considering the mess
he'd made in the streets.

Real subtle. November sighed, feeling sorry for the poor
old bastard. Why not just show up in town and blow up the
whole place, like some old vintage Schwarzenegger flick?
She smiled at one corner of her mouth, thinking maybe that
was the real reason McNihil had gone to the movies, in hope
of picking up a few destructive tips.

She didn't feel like following him into the theater. She
knew that he'd be out soon enough, with his "business" in
tow.

With the red, invisible numbers ticking down inside her
palm, November leaned back against the alley wall and
waited.

TEN

BRAIN CELLS IMPLODING INTO
SOME TERRITORY OF OPIATED BLISS
OR GUNS, WOMEN, AND ANGST

All *right*," said the business. His hand rooted around in the grease and unpopped kernels at the popcorn tub's bottom. "This is a good part. I really wanted to see it again."

From the next seat over, McNihil glanced up at the screen. This month's disnannie, all bright cartoon colors and state-of-the-art CGI, was playing. A week ago, it'd been fresh and coming over the wires to the upscale movie houses. Now its earnings had already dropped off enough for it to be printed out on old-fashioned film reels and dumped at flea-pits like this. There hadn't even been a marquee or a pretense of a ticket window outside, but just an old woman on a folding chair, a debit-card reader and a cashbox on her *schmatta*'d lap.

"What's it about?" McNihil pushed away the popcorn tub that the pimply kid extended toward him.

"Beats me." The kid shrugged. "I never pay attention to that story stuff."

The kid was in his early twenties; that was what McNihil pegged him at. All skinny arms and legs, folded up in the seat with his knees against the one in front of him, looking like a whooping-crane carcass dressed in T-shirt and faded jeans. The reflection of the movie images made bright, shifting rectangles out of his glasses.

"It's the visuals," said the kid. "You just gotta go with that." His hand operated by itself, feeding more fluffy shrapnel into his mouth. "That's all that's important."

"Really? How can you tell?" In places like this, the standards were always shoddy. McNihil pointed to the wedge of light, filled with dust motes, above their heads. "They've got their projector element canted backward. Look at that keystoning on the screen."

"Huh?" The kid bent forward, spine arched, squinting through his glasses. "What're you talking about?"

"You can't see it? The image is wider across the top than the bottom. That's why everybody looks like some kind of hydrocephalic."

"Aww . . ." A moan of disappointment escaped from the folded scarecrow figure. He hadn't been able to see the aberration until it'd been pointed out to him, but now he wouldn't be able to keep from seeing it. "That sucks." He glanced toward the simple plywood door behind him. "I oughta get my money back."

Like there's a chance of that. McNihil let his gaze travel around the theater, such as it was. In the dark, smelling of sweat and urine and spilled wet sugar, the screen's soft radiance fell on just a few scattered faces. And some of those were asleep, or looked so narcotized that if the film had broken and nothing but white light had filled their blank eyes, they wouldn't have protested. They'd probably just have thought it was their own brain cells imploding into some territory of opiated bliss. McNihil looked back at the kid. "Don't sweat it."

The eyes behind the lenses were glaring at him with real hatred. "You're a pretty smart guy, aren't you?"

McNihil shrugged. "On occasion."

"Smart enough to figure out why I wanted you to meet me here? At the movies?"

A song had started coming out of the theater's rinky-dink speakers, mounted on the walls with cables dangling. McNihil glanced up at the misshapen screen image, remembering now that this month's disnannie was a cartoon adaptation of the ancient black-and-white film *The Lodger,* transformed into something called *Jackie Upstairs.* A teenage Ripper was serenading a fogbound period London from his boardinghouse window, while a trio of cutely animated viscera—Kidney, Liver, and Uterus—danced and wisecracked around him.

"Beats me," said McNihil. He looked back over at the kid. "If you feel like telling me, go ahead."

"Because . . ." The kid leaned across the armrest between the seats. A yellow fleck of popcorn kernel hung on his lower lip. "I figured you might not be on the level, mister. Maybe you're not a book collector at all. Maybe you're a copyright thug. What do they call 'em? A snake-head."

"Asp-head," corrected McNihil. "It's one of those bilingual confusions. Deutsch-lish, German and American muddled together. *Asp* from the English, *kopf* the German for head. So you get *asp-head*; it's what they call a back-formation, from the name of the old twentieth-century organization ASCAP. They were the ones who used to round up the money for composers and musicians, until the Collection Agency came together from the old software protection and

copyright defense outfits, so there was just one rights author-
ity for all intellectual-property forms."

The kid goggled at him in distaste. "Did I ask you for
some connectin' historical lecture?"

"No . . ." McNihil shook his head. "You didn't. But
you figured asp-heads, or whatever you want to call them,
don't go to the movies?"

"Connect if I know. But they carry lotsa big clunkin'
metal around with 'em. Guns and stuff. 'Cause they're *bad*."
The kid couldn't keep an excited gleam from appearing in
his eyes. "They like to hurt people."

"Do they?" McNihil put away his smile. "I better watch
out for them, then."

"But you don't have to. Not here. At the movies." The
kid displayed horsey teeth. "You can't get into the movies,
even in a crummy place like this, without walking through
the metal detectors. Everything past the front door's got a
detection grid wired around it. If you'd walked in carrying a
gun, man, every alarm in the place would've gone off."

"Really?" McNihil let his own eyes go wide and round.
"Gosh."

The kid's expression darkened. "Maybe if they didn't
have to spend so much on security procedures, places like
this could get better projection equipment."

"Naw . . ." McNihil shook his head. "They're probably just cheap-ass bastards in general." A shrug. "I'm older
than you. I don't have expectations about people anymore."

" 'Older.' " The kid nodded appraisingly. "Yeah, an old
guy like you . . . I figured you'd be the kind who'd be
interested in this kind of stuff." He shifted in the broken-
hinged theater seat, so he could dig a chip out of his jeans
pocket. "Not my kind of thing, but it should be right up
your alley."

"What the hell's this?" McNihil took the featureless gray

square from the kid and examined it between his thumb and forefinger. "I thought we were talking about bookscans."

"Scans? Are you kidding?" The kid sneered at him. "You think I'm gonna walk around with prima facie evidence of copyright violation in my pockets? You're out of your mind."

"I thought you weren't worried about asp-heads. And all sorts of other bad things."

The song on the movie's soundtrack had ended. The animated uterus, specked with bright cartoon blood, was perched on the young hero's shoulder, dispensing its feminine wisdom.

"Not," said the kid. "I'm just *careful*." He tilted his back toward the doors. "That's another reason for wanting to do the deal in a place with metal detectors. This way, somebody like you—if you were an asp-head or some other kind of uptight intellectual-property freak—you can't read out what's there on the merchandise." The kid smiled even bigger. "You couldn't get the hardware you need in here. The readers and outside lines."

"Huh." McNihil smiled and nodded in appreciation. "Pretty clever." *You poor bastard.* It took some effort to keep his pity for the kid from showing through. The little schmuck wouldn't know what hit him—except that McNihil would make sure he did. "So what am I supposed to do with this?" McNihil held up the chip. The ghost light from the projector beam made it sparkle like a blank postage stamp. "What good is it to me?"

The kid's smile oozed self-satisfaction. "Plenty. If you want those scans of those old Turbiner titles, complete with cover art—" The kid nodded toward the chip in McNihil's hand. "That's how you get 'em."

Another scene popped up inside McNihil's head, a little private show, blanking out for a moment the images up in front of the theater's seats. McNihil could see the book cov-

ers the kid meant, all perfect retro, the color version of
McNihil's own black-and-white world. Guns, women, and
angst. It all seemed like home to him.

Those books, the words in them, all sadly out of
print—that was the merchandise the kid was peddling.
Stolen merchandise. McNihil carefully maintained his pulse
and blood pressure at a normal level.

"Look." The kid leaned over and took the chip back
from McNihil. "Here's all you have to do," he said with
elaborate faux patience. "You take this, you go home, you
pry off the back of your phone—it's easy, there's just a little
thumbplate there—you take out the regulation bellchip
you'll see there, you pop this baby in its place. You don't
need to know anything about how it works." The kid had a
superior smirk, the attitude that the young and hip always
took toward the old and out-of-it. "Then you'll be able to
dial right into a nice little on-line database down in Lima.
They're good people; they got a real commitment to information being free."

McNihil knew the site the kid was talking about. What
the kid didn't know was that it was an entrapment front
maintained by the Collection Agency.

The kid handed the chip back to McNihil. "That's all
there is to it."

"I don't quite see it . . ." McNihil studied the chip,
turning it back and forth. "I thought you were being so
careful and all. About asp-heads and bad stuff like that." He
held the chip up between himself and the kid. "Now, if you
sell this to me . . . if I give you money for it, an exchange
of legal currency for merchandise, and I put it in my
pocket . . ." His words were meant to give the kid every
conceivable out, every incentive for backing away from the
deal. Not that McNihil figured the kid would; he just didn't
want to have what was about to happen on whatever remained of his own conscience. "Aren't you violating Alex

Turbiner's copyrights? They're his books. The writing and all."

"No, man . . ." The kid laughed and shook his head. "Don't you get it? I'm not selling you any *words*. I'm selling you a key." He nodded toward the chip. "There's no pirated, copyrighted material on there." He left the popcorn tub so he could raise his open hands. "There's no pirated shit on me, period. Nobody's gonna bust me and trophy me out, just for selling you a phone number. Little bit of trunk-line access code, some block-switching jive . . . that's all you're buying from me." The chip made black squares in the center of the kid's glasses. "If the copyright sonsabitches want to send their asp-heads down to Peru, let 'em. That's the Lima bunch's lookout. It's no skin off *my* ass." A sneering shake of the head. "Besides, even if you were with the asp-heads, I'd be long gone from here by the time you got through to the data. There's a delay routine built into that puppy. Forty-eight hours from firing it up, you get your goods, all those crappy old books. You wanna read that shit, it's up to you. Whatever you want. You just gotta wait a little bit. That's the deal."

McNihil felt even older and sadder. He could hardly believe it, the whole song and dance the kid was going through. Whole generations of freelance pirates must have come and gone, risen up and been scythed down, and left no one to clue the poor child in. McNihil hadn't heard that spiel about selling a key in decades, since he'd first started working as an asp-head. *And that bit about a forty-eight-hour delay,* he thought. That had never worked. It didn't keep someone like this punk off the hook, either legally or in hard practice. It wouldn't keep the trophy knives away from him. McNihil felt like a killing priest, as though he should lay his cupped palm against the kid's spotty brow and give him the absolution that idiots earned.

He thinks he's so clever. That was the sad part. The kid was doing it, illegally trading in copyrighted material, because he wanted to see if he could do it and get away with it. There wasn't even that much of a profit to be made, relative to the time and effort the kid had put into this little project. The ego rewards would've been the big thing for him, if he were to get away with it. And the scary risk factor, the adrenaline crawl that came with scooting up close to the edge, sailing past the asp-heads' teeth. However the kid had come into possession of the scanned-in Turbiner books—there were always tiny low-level transactions that even the asp-heads couldn't keep track of—if he'd just kept his head down, kept them to himself or traded them with other little scurrying rats, he'd probably have gotten away with that much. The risk, the exciting part, was in going commercial, in putting out a carefully worded hook ad on the lines, looking for a buyer. Looking for a cash exchange. A fatal error, like something from a great old fantasy novel, where the character puts on the ring or the Tarnhelm or the cloak of subtler appearance, and becomes invisible to everybody, everything . . . except the cold annihilating scan that he would otherwise have never been seen by. This kid had raised his head—more than once, less than half a dozen times—and been sighted. He'd gotten a customer with a wallet stuffed with money, every bill of which had a grinning skull where a dead president should be.

"All right," said McNihil. "It's a deal." He slipped the chip into his jacket pocket, the left outside one where his bag of tricks was built into the lining.

"Uh-uh." The kid waggled one of his long, large-knuckled fingers at him. "Not so fast. You gotta pay. Remember that part?"

McNihil smiled. "What if I just rip you off for it?" He was giving the kid one more chance. *Must be getting sentimental in my old age,* he thought.

The kid shrugged, unconcerned. "I phone down to

Lima, have 'em yank the base. Forty-eight hours from now, you make your call and there ain't squat to down. All you got is one ugly cuff link."

Little things were working away, which the kid didn't even know about. McNihil could feel them in his pocket; not in any ordinary tactile sense, but just by knowing. Like ants crawling on a lump of sugar, but so much smaller; it only took seconds for the chip to be engulfed by the swarming, programmed micro-organics, and then just a bit more time for them to link up into their structured layers of membrane.

"You're the clever one." McNihil gave a nod. "You've got this one all figured out." He reached into his hip pocket for his wallet, being careful not to jostle the still-fragile activity in his coat. "If there'd been more guys like you a while back, the asp-heads and all that crowd wouldn't have gotten very far. You could've been the Lenin of an information-access revolution."

"Connect that. I'm an independent operator. I look out for my own ass."

"Yeah, I can tell." The micro-organics had finished linking up with each other across the chip's surface. McNihil could sense a low-level electrical charge seeping out of his pocket. "Dealing with you has been a real education."

"It's not over yet." One bony-knuckled hand with grease-shiny fingers extended toward McNihil. "You still gotta pay."

The wallet held only the cash that had been prepared for this transaction; McNihil hadn't wanted to contaminate any of his own walking-around money. He extracted the bills, folded them in one hand, then laid the wad on the kid's palm. "Don't spend it all on popcorn."

"I might." The kid didn't even bother to count it. As McNihil had figured, the dollar amount wasn't important to him. The cash was his own green trophy. "Fun talking to you, old man. You taking off now?"

Angry shouts, crowd noises, fell from the speakers on the theater's walls. McNihil turned and looked at the screen again. A mob of cartoon Londoners—fishmongers, cockney pearlies, comical bulb-hatted bobbies—were chasing the tragically misunderstood teenage Ripper through the fogbound streets. The massed chorus number told of how the townspeople's own sexual frustrations kept them from accepting poor Jack's attempts at finding love.

McNihil shook his head. "I think I'll stick around for a bit."

In the kid's hand, the folded cash had already been activated. Nothing that the kid could sense, but McNihil knew it had happened. When he'd signed on as an asp-head, so long ago, he'd had the skin temperature of his hands surgically lowered—microscopic heat dissipaters, inert threads of directional-flow fibers, ran back through the centers of his forearms. The disadvantage was that up north, any farther around the top of the circle than here in Seattle, or down around the ice floes of the bottom curve, his metacarpals stiffened and ached like sonsabitches. The advantage—the reason for the modification—was that McNihil could hand an evidentiary prop like the treated money to somebody without triggering the heat-release chemicals that the bills had been impregnated with. By now, the kid's hands, wherever they fell in the cash's 98.6°-centered range, had sent the self-dispersive substances all the way past his elbows. The stuff went so deep into the pores that it couldn't be washed off with acetone. Deeper, even; enough seconds had passed for it to have reached the bones. McNihil could haul the kid's skeleton in and put it under the flickering UV's—he'd done that to others, back in the old days—and he'd still be able to prove the kid had taken the money. The bait, the hook, the trap. The kid didn't know it, but he'd already been stamped with the Cain mark of his sin.

McNihil pointed to the screen. "I want to see how this comes out."

"It's a pretty good one." The kid had tucked the money into his jeans pocket. "I liked last month's better, though. Something about oppressed workers of the world . . ."

"The Communist Manifesto," said McNihil. He hadn't bothered to go see it.

"Yeah—there were all these little chains with big-eyed faces, dancing and singing around the guys in the factories. It was cool."

Pulling himself up in the theater seat, McNihil moved one foot to the side, a measured distance closer to the kid's feet. Not enough to touch, but to knock over the half-finished soft drink that McNihil had spotted there when he'd sat down. The paper cup spilled its contents, complete with half-melted ice cubes, across the already-sticky floor.

"Was that yours?" McNihil pulled his foot back, as the kid looked down at the mess. "Sorry—I'll get you another one. I was heading out to the lobby for a minute, anyway. I'll be right back."

While McNihil was in the men's room—the tiled floor was nearly as sticky as in the theater proper—the micro-organics finished their job in his pocket. The last item on their programmed agenda was to form a tympanum a few molecules away from the pirate chip's surface, stiffen, then reverse magnetic polarity rapidly and repeatedly enough to sound a tiny, bell-like note, soft and high enough that only the nerve implant in an asp-head's inner ear could pick it up. That was the only signal that McNihil needed. It meant that the clever little creatures had finished breaking down the chip's code, the enveloping membrane had run it through a fast-forward simulation of two days' worth of time, and matched the resulting access key with the checksum already written in the micro-organics' cores. There was no need to call anywhere in Peru; McNihil's pocket held enough of the world to hang the kid in.

At the snack bar, which wasn't more than a narrow sheet of plywood laid across folding metal sawhorses, he picked up a couple of drinks. The bored-looking girl behind the improvised counter hardly seemed to notice as McNihil took from his other pocket a gelatin capsule, snapped it in two, and poured the white powder into one of the cups. There were no other customers waiting behind him; with a plastic straw, he stirred the contents so that the powder was dispersed and invisible.

"Here you go." Setting himself back down in the theater, McNihil handed the drink to the kid. The one he hadn't messed with he kept for himself.

"Thanks, man. I'm dying here." The kid had finished the last of the popcorn, and had thrown the empty tub into the strata of litter on the theater's floor. "They put too much salt on this stuff. I guess that's so you'll spend more money on drinks, huh?"

You are a clever bastard—McNihil kept his reply silent. He figured the ironic intent would be lost on the kid, anyway. From the corner of his eye, he could see the cartoon figures on the screen, teenage Jack and the one London whore who'd always loved and believed in him, singing a treacly duet. Jack's cartoon knife glittered like a narrow mirror, as McNihil watched the kid tilt the cup to his mouth.

Nothing for the kid to taste, nothing wrong to detect. The powder was inert, not even as close to living as the programmed micro-organics in McNihil's coat pocket. From being dispersed through the drink, the powder had been activated, re-formed into a gel, and settled at the bottom of the cup, waiting for its next trigger.

"You know," mused the kid, "that one last month, with them Communist guys—those people were right. Even if they were cartoons. Everything should be free."

McNihil set his own drink down on the theater's sticky
floor. "It should, huh?"

"Yeah . . ." The kid nodded slowly, on to something.
"Because it all *wants* to be free."

"Does it?"

"Sure. You know . . . like the way information wants
to be free."

"Information wants to be free, huh?" McNihil didn't
wait for an answer. "Well, here's some info you can have for
nothing." He swung his fist in a hard, flat arc, landing it
straight to the kid's nose, which exploded in a bright flower
of blood.

He caught the kid's drink before it could spill. The kid
had both hands to his face, red leaking between his fingers.
McNihil leaned forward, grabbing the T-shirt collar in one
hand, bringing the plastic cup up to the kid's face with the
other. The Tanaka hydro-gel with which he'd doped the
kid's drink was keyed to McNihil's parasympathetic system;
the gel would respond to a shift in certain physical indicators,
blood pressure and adrenaline level being chief among them.
McNihil had been carefully keeping his emotions under control—he had worked so long as an asp-head that it was easy
for him—but now he'd let them go. Pumped them up, just
by letting the pure loathing he had for copyright infringers
come boiling out of the little box he kept inside his skull.

The gel came alive as though it were part of him. He
knocked the kid's bloodied hands aside, as the stuff inside the
cup swelled with explosive speed.

There was no time for the kid to react with anything
more than the eyes going wide behind the glasses, his mouth
taking in a quick gasp of air. His last one, for a while at least;
the hydro-gel shot up from the bottom of the cup, spraying
the remaining liquid and ice across the kid's face. It trickled
from his ears and down the tendons of his neck as the gel
swarmed over all the human skin it was programmed to find.

The gel expanded from its compression state, soaking up the spilled drink and moisture from the air, transforming itself into a sticky mass larger than the kid's head.

McNihil leaned back from the scene he was watching. Dispassionately now; once the hydro-gel had been triggered by his worked-up emotional state, there was no need to maintain it. He let his anger subside, pulling his blood pressure back down with it.

The kid's scrawny hands were still clawing at the transparent gel enveloping his head, all the way to the back of his skull. It had flowed onto his hands and down onto his wrists, welding them to the suffocating mass. The kid's mouth was still gaping open; the gel trembled with his scream, but let no sound through.

A few of the other scattered theater patrons had roused themselves and looked over at what was going on. They watched in silence, either unconcerned or grateful that it wasn't happening to them.

Past the kid's mired fingers, the face that could be seen through the wavering, inch-thick layer of hydro-gel had turned red, as though even more blood were about to start seeping out of the kid's pores. McNihil knew what came next, the red turning to black, the lungs laboring for breath that couldn't penetrate the clear mask, anoxia and death. The heart stopping, and then the delicate cells of the brain collapsing into each other like fruits forgotten and rotting in a refrigerator bin—but faster. McNihil didn't want that; he wanted the kid alive for at least a while longer. Trophying out a brain-dead corpse yielded unsatisfactory results.

McNihil reached over and grabbed the kid by the neck, his own fingertips sinking partway into the hydro-gel. He didn't have to worry about it fastening onto his own skin; the gel had already locked onto the kid's sweat and wasn't interested in any other human touch now. Something reduced to less than human stared out of the panicking eyes under the gel; the kid's consciousness had been devoured by animal fright. The scent of warmer liquid rose in the theater's dark air as the kid's urine soaked down his jeans leg and mixed with the spilled drink on the floor.

With his other hand, McNihil poked his way through the kid's hands, caught by the gel. A crooked fingertip was enough to tear open a small breathing hole, right above the kid's flattened nostrils; the gel had stiffened enough that it wouldn't flow to refill the little gap. McNihil flicked the dollop of bloodstained matter away from his fingernail; it landed like soft crystal on the back of the next row's seat, then dribbled snotlike downward.

"Let's go, pal." McNihil hauled the kid upright and dragged him toward the theater aisle. "We've got more business to take care of. I think you know what kind."

A whinnying noise, sheer terror, came from the kid's exposed nasopharynx. That, and the eyes that had managed to open even wider beneath the hydro-gel, was eloquent enough.

The girl behind the improvised snack bar cast a bored gaze at McNihil as he dragged the kid through the lobby and out onto the street. If she hadn't seen it before in reality, she'd seen it over the wire, and that was close enough.

Strangled, muffled noises continued to be emitted from McNihil's human parcel as he hit the sidewalk outside the theater. The kid's urine-damp legs thrashed, heels against the cracked cement. McNihil wished he had torn a slightly smaller hole in the gel; the kid was getting just a bit too much oxygen into his lungs.

In the world outside the theater, time had rolled into its own dark hours. McNihil could see a trace of the dwindling sunset tingeing the petroleum-mottled ocean to the west; the ancient buildings of the city's center were folding into deeper shadows. Human silhouettes wavered across the empty storefronts and up the alley walls; the bare-dirt park had

become one bonfire, the uprooted 747 a skeletal carcass in
the middle of the flames, like some sacrificial totem of a
forgotten age.

The scene didn't look good to McNihil. There was a
much bigger crowd in the streets than when he had gone
into the little fly-by-night theater. *Riot time,* he judged. The
crowd was feeding the fire leaping above their heads; ragged
figures hauled scraps of lumber and other fuel, broken furniture and commercial fixtures from the unoccupied buildings
surrounding the area, and threw them in with a bright swirl
of sparks and cinders. The roar of the fire gave the mob's
instigators something to shout over, to bring their voices to
the properly impassioned hoarseness. McNihil spotted the
bearded figure who'd operated the panhandling gantry, now
standing on an overturned trash dumpsker, upraised fists
shaking with every word.

McNihil quickly debated whether he should go back to
the End Zone Hotel, where he'd left his gun and tools, all
that ponderous metal that would've set off the theater's security devices, or head to the train station with the stifled,
struggling kid in tow. He decided against the latter; with this
kind of civil disturbance in progress, every cabbie had probably—and wisely—fled to the outskirts of town. It'd be a long
walk to the station, especially with an untrophied kid slung
over his shoulder.

The crowd gave no attention to anyone dragging a gel-
bound captive down the sidewalk. McNihil kept close to the
buildings, but was still jostled by newcomers streaming into
the action zone. The fire mounting at the center laid a shifting orange glow over the sweating faces, the sparks dancing
in their overstimulated eyes.

In the hotel lobby, the television audience spread out on
the sagging couch and upholstered chairs hadn't stirred. The
program's addicts and hustlers were still going through their
paces, copping and geezing, while the tubed-together view-

ers received their sympathetic hits. Whatever glow of the
outside flames landed on their gray faces, it wasn't enough to
ignite their interest.

"I'll take my room key now." McNihil had dragged the
kid up to the lobby desk. He dropped him onto the floor and
pinned him with a foot to his spine, so he wouldn't try
running away. "Any'll do."

"You're fuckin' crazy." The desk clerk looked aghast
behind the heavy mesh screen. His face was radiant with
sweat and he had a fire extinguisher cradled in his arms, as
though the mob outside were about to burst through the
lobby doors. "Get the connect outta here."

The metal drawer beneath the grille pushed against
McNihil's stomach. He looked down and saw the familiar
comforting shape of his tannhäuser and the pack of asp-head
tools he'd previously deposited with the clerk. McNihil
scooped them up, dropping the gun into his free coat pocket
and holding the tools in one hand. "I still need a room. I
paid for one, remember?"

"Aw, Christ . . ." The clerk got the sick, dismayed
look that comes with the realization that one has just handed
a high-caliber weapon over to another person. He hurriedly
pulled money out of a cashbox, shoved it into the drawer and
back toward McNihil. "Look, there's a refund. Now just get
moving, pal. I don't want you around here."

"Can't." McNihil shook his head in a show of regret.
"Still got a little business to finish up." He spread the pack of
tools open on the narrow shelf in front of the grille. On a
bed of cushioned black leather lay a row of shining surgical
instruments, their polished steel and honed cutting edges
touched with the fire mounting outside the End Zone Hotel. "I would've preferred a little privacy for this part—hey,
he probably would—" McNihil nodded toward the struggling figure under his foot. "But if you want it to all happen
right out here in the open . . ." McNihil shrugged and

picked up the scalpel with the biggest blade. "I've worked under worse conditions."

The desk clerk looked even more panicked than before. His stare shot past McNihil, to the lobby's door and windows. None of the crowd had noticed that McNihil was inside the hotel. But it wouldn't be long before they did.

"All right, all right." The clerk hurriedly snagged a key off the board behind him and shot it out in the drawer. "Do it, and then just get out of here, for God's sake. Please—"

McNihil rolled up his tools and picked up the key. "Thanks," he said as he dragged the kid away from the counter.

The elevator, an antique cage, was out of commission; the kid's head bounced against each stair as McNihil hauled him two floors up.

He slammed the hotel room's door shut and turned the lock; leaving the kid squirming in the middle of the floor, McNihil pulled up the dirt-smeared window and looked out. The bonfire permeating the skeletal 747 had grown larger, the flames leaping as high as the surrounding rooftops. The crowd had grown larger as well, having gone well beyond the critical-mass point; McNihil could see the eddies and ripples running through the closely pressed bodies. At the edges of the open space, the street levels of the empty buildings had been broken into, with flames and smoke pouring out of the shattered windows and plywood barriers.

Get to work, McNihil told himself. Fortunately, this part always went fast. Other asp-heads had always admired his speed with the knives.

McNihil knelt down with his tool pack. He rolled the kid facedown, turning the gel-encased head to one side so the exposed nostrils could still draw in some breath; the kid's lungs weren't superfluous yet. An agonized scream managed to pierce the clear mask, coming out as a muffled, distant wail, as McNihil jabbed the first sharp-edged tool into the vertebrae between the kid's shoulder blades. Using anesthetics had never been part of an asp-head's job description; he had a few bee-sting syringes and quick-dispersion epidermals in the pack, and had used them on occasion, but there was no present need. The shouts and excited cries coming through the window drowned out whatever noises the kid would make.

Blood had started soaking into the T-shirt, as though the white fabric had been wounded rather than cut. McNihil grabbed the edges on either side of the knife and tore the shirt to either side, exposing the kid's skinny torso. There was no need to look as he reached over to the pack for more of the glittering tools; years of practice in the field had put his hands on autopilot.

From kneeling, he raised himself onto his haunches, to keep the pooling blood from getting on his trousers. The wet red seeped through the worn carpet and beneath the soles of McNihil's shoes. He balanced himself with one hand against the kid's bare shoulder, leaning over the torso and guiding the tools as they worked. At one time, when he'd first started out as an asp-head, McNihil had dispensed with any of the autonomic surgical tools, preferring to do everything manually—he'd wanted to get the feel of cracking bone and neatly shearing flesh right into his hands. But, just as the older asp-heads had warned him, he'd started getting twinges of carpal tunnel syndrome in his wrists, and he'd gone to using the clever little machines.

At the back of the kid's neck, the retractor device had expanded itself crabwise, flaring the gristle and muscle sheathing the spinal column. The miniature plow of the auto-incision knife had worked its way down toward the kid's waist, steered by a few correcting taps of McNihil's fingers and the machine's internal terrain-recognition program. Following behind came the mantislike bone saw, stopping in position over each vertebra and mapping the projected depth and angle of its blade with quick ultrasound pulses. The saw needed a confirm signal before each cut; McNihil checked the grid on a handheld monitor before thumbing the proceed button; a fine spray of blood and bone dust drifted up as the tiny whirling blade descended.

As the devices inched their way farther apart, from nape to buttock, they set up a focused irradiation field, keeping the incision free of contamination. From micropore nozzles in the metal, a yellowish haze of nitromersol spread over the violated flesh, the mercuric compound acting as a backup disinfectant. Even if there hadn't been a personal element in the favor McNihil was doing, asp-head professionalism would have ensured a neat, antiseptic job.

He glanced up at the room's open window. Flames higher, shouts louder; glass shattered and rained across the mob-filled streets—McNihil could see, in his mind's eye, the razorlike fragments nicking the oblivious, upturned faces. The people below would be lapping their own blood as it trickled into the corners of their mouths. Which would, he knew, only make them thirstier for someone else's. His, mainly.

"Let's wrap it up." McNihil spoke aloud, as though the surgical devices were not only clever but sentient. He'd had this set a long time; they were almost to the status of pets, cared for and maintained. As if it could sense the controlled urgency in his voice, the tractor knife gave a last surge, opening up the kid's back to the base of the spine. The kid had lost all consciousness, as McNihil had expected; there was a limit to what fear could keep awake, before pain temporarily annihilated it. For McNihil, that was just as well; the last segments of the procedure were tricky and delicate enough that he didn't need the body quivering and jerking around.

He'd already brought out and inserted another pair of retractors like the first, up by the kid's head. The second one, positioned halfway down the back, pushed its curved claws outward, exposing not just the spine but the viscera clustered below the ribs. Those were of no importance now; the kid had no further use for them. McNihil picked up the auto-incision knife and set it aside, so the last retractor could settle into place and force the bleeding flesh apart.

In a few more seconds, the bone saw had finished its work; McNihil removed it as well. The spider-clawed feet penetrated the blood-soaked carpet as the bright opticals and other sensors faded to empty black.

From the pack of tools, McNihil's quick hand extracted an inert polymer ring. One pull telescoped it into a flexible tube, open at one end, a tapered bulletlike seal at the other, the whole thing longer than the kid's split torso. The retractors and saw had exposed the protective meninges encasing the spinal cord, the bundled nerves running through the core of the kid's torso. The machines went to work again, slicing through the dura mater, then the tangled arachnoid layer beneath. Using their finest, tweezerlike implements, the retractors peeled back the fragile pia mater, revealing raw and naked nerve tissue. With one of the smaller, nonautomated knives, McNihil made a series of cuts, freeing the spine from its elongated nest. He lifted and compressed the blood-specked sacral plexus and slipped it into the open end of the polymer tube. Cutting with one hand and drawing the ring opening up with the other, in less than a minute he had the tender spinal material encased in the tube. The ring rested against the back of the kid's neck; McNihil pulled the tab inside, releasing another hydro-gel inside the tube. This one had a mesh structure woven into the substance; as it expanded and protectively encased the spine, oxygenated microfilaments formed a temporary life-support for the human tissue. The tube's outside shell turned stiffer and harder, responding to the gel's precisely calibrated lowering of temperature. McNihil knew he had a few hours, just time enough to get the trophy to where it needed to be.

The cerebral matter was the last that had to be taken care of. A judgment call for McNihil: he could either do a quick-and-dirty extraction, pulling the entire brain out of the skull and packing it with him, or he could take the time to let the cleverest of his tools pare away the unnecessary segments. The easiest and fastest would have been to just lop off the kid's head guillotine-style and wrap it in a freezer pack, carry it out of here like a bowling ball in a bag—he'd done that before, in situations less time-pressured than this. It was considered bad form in asp-head circles, though; the microsurgery that was needed to reattach the brain portion to the top of the spine was a lot of work for the agency techs—McNihil still had enough favors to call in that he could get it done, but he didn't want to deplete his account. Plus, the results were never as good, trophy-wise, as an original, unsevered connection. *I may be getting old,* thought McNihil, *but I've still got pride issues to deal with*.

He shifted his position closer to the kid's head. The tiny hotel room's carpet was now soaked from wall to wall with blood, the sagging bed and battered chest of drawers like islands in a red sea. "Damn," said McNihil aloud; he'd brushed his knee too close to the kid's shoulder and gotten a smear on his trousers leg. He hated spending the money for dry cleaners. He reached over and grabbed another pair of tools from his pack.

With a few quick blows from a calibrated chisel, he split the skull open like a thick-shelled egg; the scalp tore from nape to brow, revealing the soft matter beneath. Between the two red, empty hemispheres of bone, McNihil set the big spider—that was what the asp-heads themselves called the device—and let it go to work.

McNihil stood up, knees creaking, and went over to the room's window. The smell of burning architecture filled the night air. Now he wished he'd given the panhandling gantry a donation; his hopes of coming in here, doing the job, and getting back out with no big excitement had evaporated. Just getting out, with his baggage and trophy intact, was going to be something of a problem. The mob had improvised torches from the fire crackling through the 747 carcass; with all of the unoccupied buildings already lit, the action had spread to the others. McNihil turned from the window and inhaled, trying to detect whether the End Zone Hotel had become part of the action.

He glanced down at the prostrate form on the redly shining carpet. The spider was halfway through its procedures; the steel refrigerant needles had plunged through the brain, their course determined by the device's initial mapping scan. The drop in temperature and simultaneous oxygen delivery from the fibers radiating out from the probes would prevent any gross cellular decay. The second, more detailed scan was under way—McNihil could tell from the pattern of LED's flashing across the spider's mirrorlike carapace. As he watched, the small lights blinked out; the articulated knives lowered from the device's underside and began carving into the soft, wet tissue beneath.

Wedges of cortex, neatly sliced as though by a butcher's knife, were expelled from the gaping skull, landing on either side, trembling and seeping into the blood-soaked carpet. From a storage bin in the spider's thorax, delicate claws plucked out tiny cylindrical memory shunts, each with a self-branching data capacity. The little claws, precise as a watchmaker's screwdrivers, tapped the shunts into place, soft-welding them to the brain's neurons and synapses.

Another few minutes crept past, as the spider device continued its surgery. The hotel room was a relatively sterile and quiet environment, compared to the battlefield situations for which the technology had originally been devised. The aspheads had made their own adaptations to it; they weren't interested in stabilizing soldiers with head wounds as much as getting trophies reduced down to a convenient traveling size.

The twin piles of discarded brain matter had grown to mounds a couple of inches high, pinkly weeping blood. The core of the subject's memory and personality, all that had made the kid the punk he was, had been reduced to an oblate sphere the size of a tennis ball. Almost all of the brain stem had been cut away; there was no longer any need for the stilled and equally discardable organs to be regulated. The connection between what was left of the cortex, studded with the shunts and a few other implanted devices, and the tube-encased spine, was pristine and inviolate. McNihil reached into the skull with one hand and lifted the cortical essence; with his other, he took from the pack another gel-filled casing and enveloped the exposed tissue with it. He flipped the activation tab and, as the gel inflated to protect the carved-down brain, sealed the casing to the longer tube.

On the hotel room's wet floor were the remains of the kid, the gross, unbreathing matter of torso and limbs, the face still sheathed in the first gel that McNihil had used on him, back in the theater. Turned to one side, the kid's face had a blank, empty gaze, mouth open but silent, as though the tongue were somehow trying to taste blood through the clear barrier. Whatever low-wattage spark had existed behind the dulling eyes had been caught in a jar like some bright, fluttering insect. Dead meat wasn't trophy material; asp-heads brought back to their clients something a little livelier.

McNihil returned his scattered tools to their slots in the pack, folded it, and stood up. He wiped the pack off against the wall, leaving a long red hieroglyph across an ancient pattern of faded roses. He slipped it into his jacket pocket. Turning and reaching for the trophy container he'd left propped against the front of the dresser—with the spherical casing sealed to the tube, the result looked like a fatter version of a drum major's baton—McNihil saw smoke laced with sparks rising past the window. The temperature in the room had gone up a few degrees, the heat penetrating from the floors below; much hotter, and the blood soaked into the carpet would begin to boil.

He didn't bother saying good-bye to the corpse. Some asp-heads, he knew, were in the habit of leaving behind some indication of a mess like this being the result of an agency hit—some went so far as to sign their names and ID numbers with the point of a scalpel on the dead flesh—but McNihil had never seen the need for that. Anybody who couldn't tell what had gone on from the evidence, the hydro-gel mask and the laid-open spinal column, was beyond educating.

Smoke, thick and black, rolled down the hallway outside the door. McNihil had drenched his jacket sleeve in the room's tiny efficiency sink; arm raised, he held the wet cloth against his face, his eyes stinging as he made his way down the corridor.

From the landing one flight down, he could see into the lobby of the End Zone Hotel. The mob with its primitive torches had shattered the street-level windows and ripped the door from its hinges. A shrill, clanging alarm sounded above the voices and battering clamor. An iron bar had been used to tear the grille from above the counter; the desk clerk had either fled or been trampled beneath the crowd's feet. The tethered junkies in front of the lobby's wall-mounted television hadn't bothered to move; through the obscuring smoke, the slumped figures on the sofa and upholstered chairs could still be seen, watching the dead screen or languidly rolling their heavy-lidded gazes toward the riot with equal interest. One of the chairs had already caught fire, the edges of the yellow-stained upholstery crawling with a charred red line, gray smoke billowing around the comatose figure sprawled there. The black hook-ups to the metal drug device writhed snakelike in the heat.

"There!" A voice split the laden air. The vocal cords emitting the words sounded raw with shouting and smoke inhalation. "There he is!"

McNihil recognized the voice as his recently acquired nemesis, the bearded operator of the panhandling gantry. With the encased trophy tucked under one arm, McNihil peered across his other forearm and managed to spot the mob's leader through the thickening haze. In the face blackened with soot, the red-rimmed eyes glared with a fierce delight; the burning buildings and the excited mob were all to the bearded figure's liking.

Torches and improvised weapons aloft, the mob surged up the bottom of the open staircase. McNihil backed up a few steps as he dug into his coat pocket, past the folded tool kit, for the hand-filling tannhäuser. He brought it out; barely having to aim, he fired into the center of the welling crowd below.

The gantry operator had the sense not to lead the charge; McNihil saw the bearded figure being toppled backward by the crowd momentarily retreating under the impact of the broken-chested corpse at their head. His fall had sent the gantry operator sprawling across the lobby's floor, shoulders bumping up against the base of the desk clerk's counter, the impact enough to knock the torch from his hand. He was still conscious; a shake of the head, and the gantry operator managed to refocus his gaze toward the top of the stairs. His eyes widened at what he saw.

This time, McNihil aimed. Above the heads of the crowd, toward one specific target—not from any hopes of improving the present situation, but just from the personal conviction that people shouldn't be given extra chances to make trouble. He pulled the trigger and saw, through the smoke filling the lobby, a bright red flower substitute itself for the bearded face. The gantry operator's body rolled shuddering onto its side.

Won't hold 'em, figured McNihil. He'd been in crowd situations before; he knew that it would only be a few seconds before whatever panic and good sense that the tannhäuser's shot had instilled would be overcome by the mob's bloodlust. Seeing two of their number blown away was like gasoline thrown on the already-existing flames. Tucking the elongated trophy container tighter under his arm, McNihil turned and sprinted down the corridor, away from the stairs and the shouting below.

A well-placed kick broke open one of the room doors. Any occupants of the hotel had either fled or joined the mob below. The tiny space's window, bright and hot with the flames in the street, was jammed tight. McNihil shattered the glass with the butt of the tannhäuser, then used its muzzle to knock away the remaining shards. He climbed out with the trophy container, onto the rusting metal grid of the fire escape.

The irony of the term wasn't lost on him, as McNihil scanned the scene beneath. Enough of the surrounding buildings' contents had been dragged out and thrown onto the fire for it to have spilled from the central open space—the downed and uprooted 747 was by now a twisted, blackened skeleton—and across the streets. One major branch of the fire had rolled right up against the walls of the hotel; the bottom section of the rickety framework on which McNihil stood was engulfed in flames. The heat traveled up the metal and scorched the palm of his hand, as he tried to look past the roiling smoke.

No way down, at least not that he could see here; at the same time, McNihil could hear the sound of the mob, their adrenaline courage revved up again, filling the End Zone Hotel's darkened interior.

The rusting iron creaked and swayed, bolts pulling loose from the building's side, as McNihil reached and drew down the narrow ladder above his head. Climbing one-handed, with the gun tucked against the trophy container, he headed toward the roof.

ELEVEN

A DAMP CARNIVAL OF BILLOWING FOAM
AND SLIPPERY HUMAN SKIN

Too fucked-up to stay out of trouble, thought November. *Too valuable to let suffer the consequences.* From an alley tucked safely away from the flames, but close enough to feel the heat rolling in waves across her breast and face, she watched the action over at the End Zone Hotel. She wondered what would be the best moment to go over and save that poor bastard McNihil's ass.

The mob rampaging around in the open space had made it easier for her to tail him and his incapacitated business, from the movie theater over to where McNihil would complete the job. All the excitement, the crowds and shouts and mounting flames, had obviously distracted McNihil, kept him from doing even the most cursory scan to see who

might be following him. She'd watched him dragging along
the skinny kid that he'd come up here to meet, the contact's
face swallowed by that hydro-gel glop asp-heads were always
so fond of—November admitted it had its uses, but she preferred more direct and obviously violent methods. What was
going to happen next to the kid, she'd already known; asp-
heads weren't exactly reticent about publicizing the consequences for copyright infringement. Too bad for the kid
trying to peddle those old books—but that was what you got
for being a wiseass.

For McNihil as well, it was going to be too bad; he
didn't know what he was getting into. November shifted her
position in the alley, going a little closer to its mouth in order
to peer toward the lobby of the hotel. The bottom floor of
the hotel building was engulfed in flame by now; the crowd
with the torches, who'd been so hot for McNihil's blood,
had streamed back outside, leaving their dead and wounded
to cook. *Maybe I've waited a little too long,* thought November.
She'd been pretty sure that McNihil would be able to take
care of himself, but that might have been an overly optimistic
prediction, given the present situation. The windows of the
hotel's next floor up had blown out from the heat, raining
glass shards on the people below. It wouldn't be long before
the whole building was on fire, from top to bottom. If
McNihil was still in there when that happened, her own
scheming would take a considerable setback.

November stepped out of the alley, easing her way
through the crowd. The mass adrenaline peak had been a few
minutes ago; the smell of that hormone-laden sweat hung in
the air as an invisible stratum just below the smoke. A certain
fatigue level had set in, the result of all the incendiary excitement. The central fire, with the skeleton of the ancient airliner warping and blackening, had begun to die down into
ashes and smoldering embers. Most of the crowd had gone
into spectator mode, the upraised torches either nothing but

charred wood or a few red tongues and brighter sparks, drawn horizontal by the night wind that had sprung up. Necks craned, faces turned in all directions around the totem 747; the gazes took in the surrounding wreckage with pleased smiles, the hard satisfaction of vandalism taken to its limits.

Keeping silent, November rapidly worked her way closer to the burning hotel, shoving her way past the crowd's backs, knocking away without difficulty the hands of either sex that tried to clutch at her. She lost sight of the hotel until she had reached the curb right in front of it. The rest of the onlookers, pushed away by the heat of the flames, were watching with varying degrees of amusement what was happening in the building's lobby. The ceiling had started to break up, raining plaster fragments and chunks of wooden beams onto the space below. A few human remnants, dark scarecrow figures, were visible in a semicircle of blazing furniture; it was hard to tell if they had been asphyxiated or were just narcotized to their own ongoing deaths. One, wrapped in flames, had dropped forward onto his hands and knees; under the rolling smoke and sparks, he crawled laboriously, dragging a melting black hose and a toppled-over I.V.-drip device along with him. The burning man's progress was the main topic of discussion in the crowd; November heard bets being placed behind her. Before the figure reached the hotel's hinge-smashed door, he fell over onto his side, curling into a fetal position, hissing bones revealed beneath his cracked flesh. When the figure had been still a few seconds, November heard the various wagers being collected.

By then, she had already started to move away from the front of the End Zone Hotel. She had spotted what she was looking for, what she had hoped she would see. What the others in the crowd hadn't noticed: another figure, above their heads and closer to the building's corner, climbing up the rickety fire escape. McNihil had completed his business, obviously; she could see that he had an asp-head's trophy container—a thick, roundheaded tube—clutched tight by one arm against his ribs. With his free hand, he was pulling himself up the creaking, snapping iron construction, the smoke from the flames below obscuring him in its heavy coils. As November watched, head tilted back, a section of the fire escape pulled loose from the building's exterior wall; loose bricks and bits of rusted metal tumbled into the fire at the hotel's base, sending up a flurry of sparks that surrounded McNihil like luminous wasps. McNihil's distant figure hooked one arm into the nearest strut as the grid beneath his feet gave way, dangling as though it were a slotted trapdoor; McNihil clung to the swaying metal, still grasping hard the elongated container.

Another sound, rapid and bass-driven, sounded from past the surrounding buildings. A cursing groan arose from the mob, the multiplex organism aware that its fun was at an end. Not from any city police—a zone like this was redlined by the various rental forces—but from the fire department of the Gloss's Seattle division: the first of the 'copters, flying low to avoid the stinging attentions of the *Noh*-flies, appeared above the buildings' roofs or through the gaps in the low skyline. The black shapes, like armored angels, swooped in close to the still-burning 747, the outstretched nozzle arms dispensing swiftly expanding, smothering foam. The roar of the flames was replaced by a steamlike hiss as the soft wave of the extinguishing agent flowed through the central open space and into the streets around it.

That wasn't going to help McNihil any, judged November. The FD 'copters weren't going to hurry to put out the buildings that were already ablaze. In these old sectors of the cities on the Pacific Rim, it was standard practice to incorporate arson into the various urban-redevelopment plans, like forest fires clearing the way for new growth. A second line of airborne equipment had descended into the area beyond the burning buildings, using the foam and other chemicals to keep the flames from spreading toward more valuable real estate.

All of which left McNihil stranded on the side of the End Zone Hotel, with the fire rapidly advancing through the structure's interior, blowing out the windows with each level it consumed. November could see McNihil on the swaying fire escape, desperately reaching one-handed for the metal struts just beyond his grasp.

Behind her, another party atmosphere had set into the crowd; the incendiary rage had transmuted into a giddy frivolity, a damp carnival of billowing foam and slippery human skin. The smell of wet wood and other debris, floating on the soft whiteness as though it were a slow-motion sea, mingled with pheromone-laden sweat. The streets that had been on fire a minute ago had been turned by the angels' whup-whup-whupping above into a bed of earth-clinging clouds. A bed fit for general copulation; the scarred flesh of the squatters, the unshelled homeless, the urban gutter tribes, all looked like engraved pearls of every shade from sunless white to African aubergine, as limb tangled with limb, orifices were born and created, sealing lubricant tight upon any possible protuberance, blood-warm or steel-cold. A panting, industrious silence replaced the cries that had echoed off the buildings only a few minutes ago.

That's all right for them, thought November. *What about my plans?* The slippery environment was obviously fun for the crowd, taking their minds off the interrupted torching of the city, but it was making McNihil's situation even more precarious than before. November had a clearer view of him, now that the crowd had spread from vertical to largely horizontal. The foam had been blown outward by the downdraft from the 'copters' blades; enough of it had landed on the fire escape to slicken the fragile metal. McNihil's grip on the creaking strut had become even more of a desperate struggle;

November noted with some satisfaction that he'd still held on to the elongated trophy container, instead of letting it fall to the street below.

She weighed her options. Even though she already knew what she was going to do; she moved away from the front of the hotel, the lobby behind the shattered windows mainly ashes now, interspersed with charred corpses. The fire was still traveling upward through the building's floors; even if McNihil managed to hang on to the fire escape outside, he'd either be fatally burnt or in the skin-graft ward of a hospital for so long that his usefulness to her would be zero. He was her door—though he didn't know it yet—into the whole business with Harrisch and the dead Travelt, so he had to be preserved awhile longer. Once she had walked through that door and gotten to the other side, then it would be just as well if he was off the scene, crisped or in a box, it didn't matter which. But until then . . .

Stepping over the writhing bodies, a vision came to November unbidden, of the strictures of form and identity dissolving, the prisoning matter of the city's heart reverting to some premammalian coitus. *The way,* she thought, *that fish and things that swim around in the ocean do it.* Enough cheap black leather, rags and ancient thrift-store finery, jointed crutches and small sharp-pointed weapons, had been shed that skin could be sluiced to some infantile purity by the liquefying foam. The distinction between one body and another was erased, the membrane between the body's interior and the soft outside world forgotten; she almost envied them. Or it. November supposed it was the oncoming tide of the future, humans finally having gotten tired of bones and jobs to do. She just hadn't reached that stage yet.

Thinking diminished her attention for a moment, just long enough for a hand to snare her ankle. She fell, hands quickly bracing and catching herself against the white-smeared curb. November rolled onto her back, seeing some

wide-eyed, happily grinning face. Which received the heel
of her boot at the bridge of his nose; the bare-chested figure
toppled backward unconscious and was subsumed into the
general mass.

For a moment longer, she couldn't get up; the foamed
street was too slick for her scrabbling hands to get a purchase
on. Other hands, without specific intent, clutched at her,
limbs and shining torsos pressing at all sides. A breath-stop-
ping panic rose in her, flooding out all thoughts but of escape. A generalized terror, the sense of her own boundaries
melting away, the result a horrifying *connectedness;* this was
what she had run from all her life. Even her brief moments
of coition aboard the circle's trains, with the glittery-eyed
businessmen in the private spaces between cars—no linkage
in those encounters, but instead a sharper sense of the alien,
the penetration of the other. The pharmaceuticals she slid
beneath the resealable patch of her skin; those packets were
always laced with enough amphetamine to render the division between herself and the world as sharp as a razor, even
while her higher brain functions were opiated down to lust.

Twisting onto her side, November reached past the wet
forms around her and managed to grab the sidewalk's curb;
black ashes slid beneath her fingertips as she clawed her nails
into the cracked cement. The foam clutched at her like some
reluctantly yielding amniotic fluid; she slowly managed to
push herself, shoulders-first, against the base of one of the
building's walls. Her legs curled beneath her in a belated fetal
posture, the ankles of her boots just out of reach of the
conjoined organism in the streets.

Bracing herself against the smoke-stained bricks, November got to her feet. Her breath returned to her lungs.
Time had come to a halt, the line between one second and
the next as meaningless as any other division; she had no idea
how long she'd been out there. She tilted her head back,
wiping a white residue from her eyes, wondering if the dis-

tant McNihil was still alive. The figure on the tilting fire
escape was there, holding on to both the trophy container
and the creaking iron structure. As she watched, another pair
of the heavy fastening bolts worked their way free, dropping
to the sidewalk a couple of meters away from her. The fire
escape, continuing its slow disintegration, peeled its higher
sections farther from the building.

The flames and smoke billowing from the shattered windows, close enough to singe McNihil's trouser legs, indicated
that there would still be no path up through the hotel. One
building over, an empty storefront had been touched less by
the fire; past the boards and torn-aside plywood barriers, the
street-level interior held a few smoldering display counters
and shelving units. November kicked one obstructing board
loose, then ducked her head beneath the next one up and
pushed her way inside.

A long sprint up the building's dark stairwell had brought
November to the rooftop. An easy leap landed her on hands
and knees, on top of the hotel. The peeling sheets of roofing
material felt hot against her palms.

At the rooftop's edge, she could look out across the
foam-drenched street, the extinguished wreckage of the
downed airliner rising from the white sea like the empty-
eyed ghost of some forgotten technology.

"McNihil!" Clutching the edge of the roof's low parapet, she leaned out above the swaying fire escape. "Look up
here!" she called again.

His hold on the fire escape was several stories below; it
took a moment for McNihil to realize where the voice was
coming from. Without loosening his grip, he tilted his head
back and gazed upward. "Who the hell are you?" His face
was set hard with suspicion.

"Right now, I'm your best friend." *Distrustful bastard,*
thought November. Her eyes stung with the smoke rolling

up the side of the building. "Hang on, and I'll get you out of there."

"The connect you will." Below, McNihil looked around, as though there might be some alternate route off the fire escape. A gout of flame, larger than any before, burst through the shattered window nearest him.

"For Christ's sake," said November disgustedly. "Don't be an idiot." She turned away from the parapet—he wasn't going anywhere, she knew—and scanned the rooftop for something she could use. A thick black cable, an outmoded video or power feed, dangled from a wooden crossbeam at the roof's center. November reached up and pulled it loose, wrapping a coil several meters long between her hand and bent elbow.

The cable was long enough to lower a doubled length, knotted into a loop at its end, down to McNihil. "Here's the deal," shouted November over the roof's edge. "Grab it and I'll brace. You can walk yourself up here."

Wind from the fire-department 'copters blew into November's face and rippled the steaming puddle of water that had collected around her bootsoles, the runoff from her foam-wet clothes. If the FD crews were aware of her and McNihil on the burning hotel, they made no sign of it. The 'copters banked and swooped away, toward a couple of flaring hotspots at the open space's perimeter.

She could see McNihil looking over his shoulder, down to the street, as though he was gauging the impact his body would have on the ones below, mired in their dissolving white blanket. Not enough there to safely break his fall; November wondered if the people in the street would even notice when he hit, or whether his hard death would trigger some massive, longed-for climax through the interlinked organism they had created.

McNihil looked at the black cable dangling near him, then back up at her. "Why're you doing this?"

"I'm a public-spirited citizen." November shook her head in disbelief. "What the connect does it matter?"

"Yeah, right." McNihil made no attempt to grab the cable. "And you just happen to know my name."

It'd been the first time she'd spoken his name aloud, when she had called to him from over the parapet. Though she had thought McNihil's name enough times inside her head. November had realized it'd been a mistake, as soon as the three syllables had escaped her lips; she couldn't bring them back, but she'd been hoping that, given his current circumstances, the significance would've zipped right by him. That she knew who he was, when he was supposed to be going about his asp-head business all incognito.

"All right," said November. So it hadn't gotten past him. "I want to talk to you. Is that okay? There's some things we need to discuss, you and I."

"People who want to talk to me, they can make an appointment." McNihil seemed unperturbed by the grinding metal joints and swaying of the fire escape. "You know my name, you should have my phone number, too."

"I do. But this is personal." She was lying her ass off, but the situation called for improv. "Face-to-face." The last thing she'd wanted was to talk to the guy, at least right now. "Without anybody listening in."

McNihil, arm hooked around the fire escape strut, managed a disdainful laugh. "People who want to go private with me, I've found that they rarely have my best interests at heart."

That exasperated her even further. "What the hell's that supposed to mean?" November's hands shoved against the edges of the parapet. "If I wanted something bad to happen to you, I'd just leave you where you are. In a couple of minutes, you're going to be fried anyway—and you're arguing with me? Jeez." And asp-heads were supposed to be so connecting smart. "Grab the wire, goddamn it."

November figured that it wasn't her that convinced him, as much as a sudden rush of flame from the window, large and close enough to singe McNihil's sleeve. The force of it rocked him back against the angled corner of the ladder, the entire vertical length of the fire escape going through a lurching wave. A couple more bolts popped out from the bricks and fell through the smoke to the street below. McNihil let go of the strut on which he'd had a one-handed grip, and seized the dangling black cable beside him.

"You want to talk?" McNihil shouted up to her. "Then pull, already."

The fire escape collapsed, shearing away from the burning hotel, before November had completely braced herself. McNihil's weight, suddenly unsupported, slammed her hard against the parapet, the doubled cable cutting deep into her palms. She dropped to her knees, to keep from being yanked over the edge of the rooftop. The raised section was just low enough for her to see over, with one shoulder dug into it. The fire escape, shedding pieces of metal as it went, angled above the streets, the loosened joints shifting and breaking apart. In an agony of high-pitched rust, what was left of the structure, its base still fastened to the bottom level of the End Zone Hotel, fell across the copulating bodies in the street. With a shudder that moved outward in concentric rings, the composite organism reacted as November had seen other pale flesh react, stung by the lash. If the extinguishing foam was now flecked with blood, shining black in the night's partial spectrum, then a small, painful price had been paid for the orgasmic groan that welled up simultaneously from a thousand throats and a single one.

She paid no attention to that sound; she'd heard it before, if not on quite so large a scale. November, leaning back from the cable tourniqueting both her hands, had managed to get to her feet. The different angle allowed her to see the figure at the other end of the tether, McNihil swinging in a wide arc outward from the building.

"Grab it with both hands, you jerk!" November shouted to him. "You're going to fall!"

McNihil clung stubbornly to the trophy container, its tapered shape pivoting with momentum in his grasp. He reached the apogee of his horizontal arc and came back into the wall, turning so that he landed with both feet in classic rappel position. As November watched, he struggled to pull the trophy container across his bowed chest, until its smaller end had snagged inside the front of his jacket. He shoved the object downward, releasing his grip on it only when the point protruded from his shirt's bottom hem. The tube was held diagonally across his torso, the larger, bulbous end hard against one side of his face.

"All right!" McNihil's shout went past November and into the empty sky. "Hold on!"

He worked himself up the hotel's wall, hand over hand on the taut cable. As he approached, November let herself slowly sit back on the rooftop's tarry surface, her legs locked against the parapet. In the gunsight V of her crotch, McNihil appeared, convulsively snagging first one arm, then the other, onto the low rise at the building's edge. The trophy container impeded his being able to kick a leg up onto the parapet; he had to take one hand from the cable and pull the tube out from his shirt, then throw it with a heavy clatter on the roof. With one more heave, he landed sprawling on top of November. The weight knocked the cable loose from her hands, setting it free and slithering over the roof's edge. She heard, but didn't see, its impact on the mingled crowd below, the lighter stroke producing the sigh that a lover's kiss might evoke.

"Pardon me." McNihil rolled off her and got to his feet. He strode over and picked up the trophy container, giving it a quick once-over to make sure that it hadn't been damaged.

He seemed satisfied by the inspection. His gaze moved back to her. "Thanks."

"Any time." November pushed herself onto her elbows, then closed and drew up her legs. It had been one of the more strenuous encounters she'd had, in which she'd wound up in more or less this same position. She stood upright, taking a look at her hands. They ached, fingers curling, from the grip she'd had on the cable. She forced her palm open wide, and could see the red numbers there, the ticking away of her accounts. The amount of hours she'd already wasted on this guy irritated her. There wasn't that much time left now.

"So you want to talk to me, huh?" A few feet away, McNihil wasn't even looking at her. He was examining the trophy container again, knocking a few smudges of soot from the object, checking that the seal between the head and the elongated body hadn't been violated. He smiled when he looked back around at her. "I bet you do."

The blow from the back of his hand took November by surprise; she was cursing herself in fury even before she landed sprawling on her back. Before she could pick herself up, one of her outflung wrists was pinned against the rooftop by the sole of McNihil's shoe. Her vision cleared, and she found herself looking into a black hole inches away from her face. Behind the hole was the familiar shape of a high-caliber weapon, and behind that, McNihil's outstretched arm pointing down at her. Behind that was his face, no longer smiling.

Never underestimate these old bastards, vowed November. Now she'd have to find some way to maneuver around him. "What'd you do that for?" she asked. "Fine way to treat somebody who just saved your ass."

"It's how I treat people who follow me around." The gun looked like some unmoving geological outcropping in McNihil's fist. "And who don't do a very good job of it."

"What're you talking about?"

"Sweetheart, I have blown away people just for coming on all dumb with me." McNihil could have leaned forward and tapped the gun's muzzle against her brow. "Figure it out. We're standing on top of a burning hotel, someplace nobody gives a rat's ass what happens to it. I can walk off here easily enough. But if the scavengers tomorrow go rooting around through the ashes and they find your bones with a hole drilled through the skull, do you really think anyone will care?"

She said nothing. Her pinned arm was beginning to ache from the pressure of McNihil's shoe.

"What's your name?"

No need for lying. "November."

"Good enough. There's so little poetry in our lives now-adays." McNihil shook his head. "Most of the time, it's just scrabbling around and pointless subterfuge. Like your tailing me. Like your hanging around whenever I was having my little meetings with Harrisch and his pack of execs."

Shit, thought November. She'd been operating under the impression that she'd pulled that one off, that he hadn't a clue about her keeping tabs, at least up until that engineered train crash. She wondered how much else he knew. The dismaying prospect came to her that he could be completely ahead of her. That he might've known that she would be here waiting for him.

At that moment, an invisible fingertip, with ice under the nail, touched her heart. November looked up at him, with a new understanding and even a degree of admiration. There was a good reason to be afraid of people like him.

"Okay," she said. The rooftop was uncomfortably warm beneath her, the tarry surface liquefying and seeping into her jacket. "But I already told you—we need to talk. And if I hadn't been following you . . ." She nodded toward the parapet. "You'd be all over the street by now."

In his other hand, McNihil held the trophy container like a staff of office. Smoke billowed behind him, from holes torn in the hotel's structure. "Talk about what?"

She didn't see any need to lie about this, either. "Harrisch, of course. All that stuff he's leaning on you about. It's not what you think it is."

McNihil laughed. "As if I care. Since he can lean on me all he wants, and I'm still not having anything to do with it."

There were also good reasons for feeling sorry for him. *He still doesn't know,* thought November. The trap had just about closed tight around him, and he still didn't feel its teeth.

Which was just as well for her, she figured. One way or another, she was going to move in on his action. The more connected he wound up, the easier it would be.

"You know," said McNihil, peering at her, "I can see the gears turning around inside your head. You've got a nice cold attitude, young lady. Most people, their brains stop when they're staring into something like this." McNihil tilted the gun a fraction of an inch, letting it catch bright points of light from the flames licking past the roof's edge. "You could've been an asp-head. But there haven't been a lot of openings posted by the agency lately. That's kind of a shame."

It's because you're ancient history. She kept her reply silent. *You and all the others.* The reasons for the asp-heads' existence—if there had ever been any—were long gone. Somebody like McNihil could blow away a scamming punk, put his spine and cut-down brain in a long metal jar; big deal. Who needed that anymore? It was what pissed her off about all her own scheming and plotting against McNihil. *They should've just come to me first,* November brooded. *Harrisch and his little pack.* If they'd done that, instead of thinking they could get some line on their dead colleague by using some old, burnt-out asp-head, they would've been off and rolling by now. She could've finished the job, found out what they wanted to know—*Hell,* she thought, *I'm already more up-to-speed on what happened to Travelt than this guy could ever be*—and pumped the numbers in her palm back up to where they should be. But no, it was never that simple. The standard complaint of freelancers such as herself: you not only had to *do* the job, you had to *get* the job first.

"I wear no man's collar," said November. "Except for pleasure, and then only on a time-limited basis. What I mean is that I prefer to be an independent operator."

"That's ridiculous." McNihil took his shoe away from her wrist. "When you work for the Collection Agency, you get full medical and dental coverage." He took a step back. "It's the benefits, not the salary, that's important."

November sat up, massaging the blood back into her hand. "I don't worry about things like that."

"You should." He kept the gun aimed at her, though his grip had relaxed slightly. "Believe it or not, someday you'll be as old as me."

"No, I won't." If the numbers blinking from her palm got much lower, she wouldn't have to worry about even getting into her thirties, let alone through them.

"Whatever." He let her stand up, the gun lowered in his hand. "But as I said before. If you want to talk to me, punch in the number. People who walk in on me while I'm doing business are likely to get hurt."

"I don't mind." November showed him a three-quarter profile, her gaze emitted from the corners of her eyes. "That could be fun, actually." She stepped closer to him. "Like you also said . . . I'm young. Flexible, as it were."

This time, McNihil made no reply.

It's too easy, thought November. It was *always* too easy. She wasn't used to an encounter of this nature, with its familiar accelerating ramp-up and its foreordained conclusion, happening out in the open. But the smoke folding above their heads gave a comforting claustrophiliac illusion, the heat from the burning hotel beneath them completing the sense of giant machinery rushing toward an endlessly receding destination. There were even syringes and pads underfoot, debris left from the tenants who'd preferred to ingest in the stars' cold view. If she closed her eyes, November could feel the world narrowing in around her shoulders, the corset or casket of desire, as she moved past McNihil's gun and inside the perimeter of his defenses. Close enough to sense the human temperature of his body, close enough to bring the awareness of her body—she knew—into his machinelike percept systems.

November stood next to him, her narrow hip against the front of his thigh, the curve of one small breast deformed by the pressure against his torso. She looked up into McNihil's face, then stood on tiptoe, reaching her hand to caress the corner of his brow, the soft touch of her fingers brushing the side of his head. Just as she had done so many times before, with other men, in other places that had collapsed down to the nonspace held between her body and his.

She wanted to punish him, just a little bit. For being such a smartass, for holding an ugly gun in her face, for standing on her wrist; that still ached somewhat. But mainly to show him that he should pay serious attention to her. She let the localized magnetic-resonance pulse travel through one arm and into her palm, a paralyzing spark leaping from between her heart and life lines and into the sonuvabitch's skull . . .

For a moment, the clouds of roiling smoke parted, enough to let her see the cold points of light in the dark sky. If that's what they were; in another moment, she wondered if she might be gazing into the blackness at the center of McNihil's eyes.

Then she realized she was lying flat on her back once more, the fire-heated rooftop beneath her spine. Bits and pieces of the world slotted together again, replacing the blank daze inside her head.

November realized that her arm, the one with which she had reached up to McNihil's face, was numb and trembling; the first pinpricks of sensation had started. They felt as if they were happening to a piece of meat disconnected to her body. She managed to raise her head—the rooftop tilted dizzyingly—and could see her cupped palm, the one without the red numbers written there. A burn mark had been seared into the flesh, as though she had laid hold of a high-voltage cable; the pain from the wound had begun working its way up her stunned arm.

She lifted her gaze from the marked hand to McNihil, standing nearly a meter away from her. The shock must have been powerful enough to launch her through the air, like a crumpled tissue he'd discarded.

"Don't try that one again." McNihil had put away the gun. He smiled. "I'm wired, shielded, and all zipped up against your kind of action."

No shit, thought November. With her still-functioning hand, she rubbed the corner of her brow, feeling a massive traumatic headache coming on. That kind of subcranial block, with a feedback and amplification circuit built in, wasn't standard asp-head issue; he must have paid for that with his own money, somewhere along the line. Worse, she hadn't known that McNihil had it, when she'd been operating under the assumption that she had him down cold, all his little details. Now, there was no telling what kind of stuff he had.

That was the kind of surprise for which she had no liking. *I'm screwed.* All her calculations were meaningless now. And at the same time, she was too far into this situation to abandon it and start over somewhere else. The red numbers in her palm would scroll down to zero before she had a chance of scoring another paying gig. If she had been look-

ing into the centers of McNihil's eyes, there weren't any stars
there; nothing but empty black, the unknown. For better or
worse, her fate was welded to his.

A liquid shiver traced down the center of her spine, as
though some central element of her self were being dissected
by an asp-head's clever little knives. A sex twinge, the feeling
of things beyond her control, opened below her gut. If she
hadn't been worried about sheer survival, she could almost
have been grateful to him.

"Gotta run." Carrying the trophy container in one hand
like an oversized scepter, McNihil moved toward the farther
edge of the rooftop. "But like I said. You want to talk? Give
me a call."

November watched as he leapt easily over to the adjacent
building. Then he was gone. For a while longer, November
stayed where she was, regarding the flames and smoke rising
on all sides.

A little too long.

When the rooftop gave way, a section collapsing beneath
her as quick as a sprung trap, she found herself falling into
smoke and flames. And then she wasn't falling, and she could
only marvel—for a few seconds, before she lost consciousness—at how much it truly hurt.

TWELVE

AMYGDALIC SHUNT OR THUS EVER TO VIOLATORS OF COPYRIGHT

Even after he washed up, he smelled of fire and smoke and burnt things. McNihil came out of the bathroom, into a sonic ambience of vintage Haitink conducting Mahler, the acoustics of the old abandoned Amsterdam Concertgebouw cranked up loud enough to be heard through his whole apartment. He took the towel from across his shoulders and rubbed his gray-flecked hair dry as the contralto came on.

O Röschen roth!
Der Mensch liegt in größer Noth!
Der Mensch liegt in größer Pein!
Je lieber möcht' ich im Himmel sein . . .

Little red rose, thought McNihil. He always agreed with the singer, about preferring to be in heaven. A goal he had come close to achieving, when he'd been out there taking care of business. Like most asp-heads, or at least the ones who weren't born cold-blooded, McNihil had an amygdalic shunt microsurgeried into his brain, a tiny shutoff valve triggered by the adrenaline levels in his system; when the juices got high enough, fear became an abstract concept. Even the contemplation of his own death—he'd had time to consider it while he'd been hanging on that disintegrating fire escape—seemed like no more than an assemblage of words, something he'd read about in a book. It worked better than a straight hormonal tamp-down; the adrenal fluids kept the body revved and fast-reacting, while the head contents lived up to the agents' collective nickname.

"Knock knock," said the door. The sound got only a slight irritated reaction from McNihil.

When he'd moved into this place, forking over the rent and deposits and key money from one of his last bonus checks from the agency, he'd taken his Swiss Army knife to the workings of the hallway security system, trying to dismantle the annoying visitor-announcement protocols, so that if somebody came to see him, on business or pleasure, he'd hear the sound of actual human knuckles on reinforced simulated-woodgrain fiberboard. He'd been defeated, though; the circuits kept repairing themselves, usually while he was out of town on an extended assignment. McNihil would come home, sometimes bleeding and with the crap almost literally beaten out of him—not every piece of business had gone as easily as this last one had—and would find that the circuits had healed over, soft boards and severed wires seeking each other out and knitting themselves back together again. Though usually in some increasingly crippled manner, the announcement sounds devolving through an entire programmed auditory repertoire after McNihil's attempts at a

permanent silence. He and the system had worked their way
through lisping trombones, Everett Dirksenoid kazoos, and
splintering glass that shouted in Provençal French before arriving at a compromise: the system remained functional,
McNihil put away his miniature tools, and the circuits announced visitors with a realistic-enough simulation of
knuckles on wood. McNihil no longer cared beyond that
point.

"Knock knock," said the door again. Leaving the towel
draped around his neck, McNihil pulled the door open.

A delivery, the one he'd been expecting; McNihil tipped
the kid, an agency intern he vaguely recognized, and carried
the long package back to the flat's living area. The package's
contents had weighed more when he'd been hauling them
around, freshly harvested, inside his old trophy container. A
note had been tagged on the wrappings, signed by the
agency's head prep tech.

Nice job, McN. Haven't lost your touch. Keep cutting. R.

He placed the package on the flat glass kidney of the
Noguchi knockoff coffee table. For a moment, McNihil idly
wondered if he should tie a red ribbon around the package's
middle; it was, after all, intended to be something of a gift. A
favor, something nice done for a person he admired—the
other red ribbons, the shining wet ones that had pooled
around the vivisected body, counted for nothing against that
sentiment. He finally decided to omit any fancy wrappings,
to just leave the completed trophy adorned in its plain, mat-
ter-of-fact agency routing-and-shipping labels. The person
for whom it was intended went in, McNihil knew, for that
kind of procedural detail. It was something left over from
when the guy had still been working and writing, cranking
out his trashy and sublime thrillers, and always on the lookout for real-life bits he could stick in to establish an air of
authenticity.

McNihil had a row of those books himself, in a temperature-and-humidity-controlled shelf unit. Thinking about them, about the chapters and sentences and carefully strung-together words on the pages, put McNihil in a good mood. Or as good a one as he could be in, considering the aches and bruises he'd garnered while bringing this trophy back from the city farther north on the rim. When he'd first gotten back here and stripped off his smoke-ridden, blood-stained clothes, he'd examined himself in the bathroom mirror and had seen the rickety fire escape's imprint from his chest to his chafed-raw ankle. *I'm getting too old for this,* he'd told himself. *Way too old.* Like those characters in the books; McNihil had found out—eventually—what it was like to be tired and more than a little burnt-out, yet still handing people's asses back to them. Like that smart-ass little number up there on the roof of the enflamed End Zone Hotel; he'd seen her eyes go wide when he'd come right back at her, knocking her off-balance in more ways than one. That was the part of his condition that felt as good for him as it did for the fictional old bastards in the yellowing pulp novels; he'd *enjoyed* that.

> *O glaube: du wardst nicht umsonst geboren!*
> *Hast nicht umsonst gelebt, gelitten!*

"Yeah, right." He spoke aloud his rejoinder to the soprano. Though he didn't feel cynical at all, not this time, as he finished buttoning his shirt, the cloth dragging across that of the bandages he'd plastered across his ribs. "And I'll live forever, too." As it was, he knew he was doing better than that November person. If she was still alive at all; when he'd gotten home, he'd phoned one of his remaining friends at the Collection Agency and asked for some kind of readout on her. The agency's database already had her logged as being in a hospital burn ward, in one of those sterile-nutrient chambers where the most badly crisped wound up. From long practice, McNihil found it easy to stop thinking about things like that. He pulled on his jacket, picked up the package from the table, and headed for the door.

Still in a good mood, package tucked under his arm like a furled umbrella, when he got to Turbiner's place. Of the old, yellowing paperbacks on McNihil's preserving bookshelf, just under a fifth of them had been written by Alex Turbiner. Who was still alive, though his schlock-o literary career had ended a couple of decades ago; the old guy's color was gray around the edges rather than that browning tinge that low-quality paper developed from time and oxygen. Still alive, which meant that his copyrights were one-hundred-percent enforceable, and a mean bastard, which meant that he'd get a kick out of the present McNihil was about to lay on him. But then, all writers were mean bastards. *Must come with the territory,* McNihil figured. And approved.

"Anybody home?" McNihil leaned his thumb against the call button beneath a grille of rusted metal. Or what artfully appeared to be rust, made to look that way from the beginning. "Got something for you."

He stepped back and looked up the building's facade of perpetually crumbling cement and broken windows interspersed with the ones that people actually lived behind. Turbiner had moved in here during his peak earning years, paying cash outright for a stationary unit; being a freelancer, he never had to put up with that cube-shuffling business that the big corporations put their employees through. The building was a ruin, but deliberately and fashionably so, designed during one of the severer deconstructionist, *nostalgie de la boue* crazes, when everybody who could afford it wanted to reside in something that looked like an arson-bait crack house.

"Sounds like that evil McNihil." The speaker grille crackled and spit, just enough, without ever cutting out completely. The old man's voice would have sounded like a frayed wire even without the additional effects. "Come on up."

McNihil carried his package down a corridor lined with broken plaster and nondenominational graffiti, chosen for its aesthetics rather than turf-staking capabilities. At one time—McNihil could remember it—there had been programmed mechanical rats scuttling up and down the hallways, even a Mumbling Junkie™ mannequin in the urine-scented stairwell, but the building's residents had finally voted to stop paying for those decorative services. The rats had kept flipping over on their backs and scrabbling their feet in the air in an unrealistic way, and the partially animated addict had begun declaiming Yeats in a Shakespearean actor's voice; old, poorly erased programming had risen up from the mannequin's circuits, like dreams of a former life. To be confronted by a rag-bag, needle-tracked scarecrow expostulating about widening gyres and Bethlehem-ward slouches was considered a bit much by the more fastidious of the building's residents. There were limits.

The Mahler Second was on Turbiner's stereo as well, as an example of the universe's secret, synchronistic workings. Or not: McNihil had just started his up when he'd phoned Turbiner, to tell the old man that he was coming over. Turbiner might've heard it in the background, behind McNihil's voice, and decided he wanted to hear Emmy Loose or Beverly Sills or any of the other celestial voices, long dead and gone, still audible on the ancient recordings. The sopranos and the contraltos and the big, booming choruses stepped through the even more ancient words of the Klopstock ode, and none of them ever died.

Aufersteh'n . . .

"Good to see you." Turbiner turned down the volume as his visitor pushed the door shut behind himself. "How ya been keepin'?"

McNihil nodded slowly. " 'You will rise again . . .' "

"Huh?" Over the tops of his trifocal lenses, Turbiner peered at him with age-clouded eyes. "Oh, yeah; right." He glanced toward the nearest loudspeaker, listened for a moment, then translated the next line to be sung. " 'You will rise again, my dust, after a short repose . . .' " When Turbiner shrugged, he looked shambling and diminished, like the most moth-eaten bear in the zoo, the one the keepers debated about—whether it would be a kindness to put him down. "Well, maybe that's true. Old Gustav M. would know better than I would. For the time being, at least."

The massed voices, whispering now, surrounded McNihil as he followed Turbiner into the cluttered lair. The flat's space had grown so tight with the old writer's possessions—mainly boxes of books and stacked rows of CD's, tapes, datachips, even some antiquated vinyl—that McNihil had to hold the package vertical against himself, to keep from knocking anything over.

Turbiner's housekeeping had gone all to shit after his wife had died, ten years back or thereabouts. McNihil remembered her as elegant and sarcastic, and not overly given to sweating the small details like dust, but still with enough ingrained female instincts to keep the disorder somewhat at bay.

Thinking about dead wives, while McNihil stood in the middle of this heavily past-filled space, took his good mood down a few degrees. Guilt had a way of doing that. Turbiner had loved his wife (*And didn't I love mine?* thought McNihil glumly), enough to scrape close to the bone a couple of his savings and investment accounts, all to pay off whatever debts she'd had when she died. Thus buying her a quiet grave, free from the reanimating forays of the bill collectors.

Aufersteh'n, my ass—right now, lyrics about the desirability of resurrection weren't striking McNihil the right way. His wife, when she had died . . . he hadn't done as well by her as old Turbiner had. Though he'd meant to, and there

was still a chance; it still might happen. Guilt could be
bought off. All it took was enough money. More money
now than before; he hadn't been keeping up with even the
interest payments on his wife's debts. The numbers kept
ticking upward, compounding like hammer blows, one after
another. It would take a lot to pay it all off now, to set his
dead wife sleeping in the ground along with the late Mrs.
Turbiner, dreaming the endless, empty dreams of the really
and truly dead. *And I'm good as retired now,* thought McNihil.
To come up with that kind of money, he'd have to find some
way of going back full-time with the Collection Agency,
plus hustle up every kind of on-the-side gig he could manage. Instead of doing little favors for old writers that nobody
read anymore.

"I'll make some coffee." Turbiner was already in the flat's
kitchen area, on the other side of the counter, rinsing a glass
pot out at the sink. "That okay by you?"

"Sure." Horizontal slices of sunlight fell across McNihil's
face, from the barely opened blinds at one side of the flat. "I
wasn't planning on hanging around very long." He held up
the package. "Like I said on the phone, I just wanted to drop
something off for you."

"Yeah, so I see." Turbiner fiddled with the coffeemaker's
pieces, rinsing them off and putting them back together,
watching his hands at work rather than glancing back at
McNihil. "It's amazing, the kinds of things people walk
around on the streets with, these days." The old man turned
a thin smile toward his visitor. "What a world we live in."

McNihil sat on the couch, moving aside a stack of papers
and cascading books to make room for himself. He started
taking apart the package's wrappings, figuring that it would
take Turbiner a while to get around to it. That was one of the
ways you could tell when somebody was really old. *Or older
than me,* thought McNihil. They all acted as if they had
forever to do things, rather than a rapidly diminishing re-

mainder of time. He wondered if it was just wishful thinking on Turbiner's part.

"So what is it you got there?" Gurgling and hissing noises came from the kitchen area; Turbiner had come back around to the flat's larger open space. "Anything cool?"

The old man knew what was inside the package; it wasn't a secret. Turbiner himself had been the one to tell McNihil about what was going on in the Gloss a little farther to the north, about the kid ripping off his old copyrights, selling them to the collectors' market that still existed for that sort of thing. McNihil would've despised those sorts of people, even if he'd never worked for the agency. How could you be into something, into it enough that you wanted all you could get of it, and not want to pay for it? Really pay, not in terms of paying lots of money for it, but just making sure that the money went to the right person. The person who'd created it. Written it, composed it, sung it . . . whatever.

True bastardliness, McNihil had always figured, lay with people—and he'd encountered more than a few of them—who'd shell out nearly the same amount or even more to a pirate, some copyright rip-off specialist, rather than see the same money or even less go to the rightful creator. He'd had a lot of time recently to think about stuff like that, and had started to formulate a general theory of evil, pieced together from those things that he'd just instinctively gotten pissed off about before. The way he saw it now, there were certain people who loved the art—the music, the books, the pictures, whatever it might be—but who actively hated the creators of the same. Hated them from envy, jealousy, spite—from just that gnawing, infuriating sense that the creators could do something they couldn't, could make something happen on a page or a canvas or with the sequence of one pitched sound after another. The basic criminal mentality says to itself, *Why should that person have something that I don't have? Where's the justice, the fairness, in that?* And thus thievery and vandalism are justified, not only by the brain, but deep in the outraged heart of anyone who can't get over the notion that he's not the center of the universe.

So they don't steal things—McNihil had thought this before—*just so they can have them.* That would be too simple. When he'd been working for the agency, he'd encountered too many idiots who could've easily paid for their stolen desirables. They stole to prove that they could steal, that they had the right to steal. And to punish anyone, particularly the creators, all those smug writers and musicians and artists, all those busy, talented hands and mouths and brains, the possessors of which swaggered around as if God loved them more than those who burned with a righteous envy. To steal from the creators was an act of justified vengeance; it showed them that they couldn't get away with that infuriating shit. It proved that the books and the music and the paintings and everything else really belonged to the thieves, that it was all theirs by right; in some strange way, the thieves and not the creators had brought it all into being. So it wasn't really thievery at all, then, was it? It was the returning of stolen property to its rightful owners. Or such was the belief of the thieves, written upon the cracked tablets of their souls.

"Here's your coffee."

McNihil heard the voice behind him, and glanced over his shoulder. He saw Turbiner shoving aside a stack of papers on a low table and setting down a nominally washed mug; steam rose from its glistening black contents. Turbiner straightened up somewhat creakily, and headed back into the kitchen area.

"Thanks," said McNihil. His attention dropped back into present time, into this shuttered space. He'd stopped halfway through unwrapping the package he'd brought for the old man, and had been sightlessly gazing at the crammed bookshelves on the other side of the flat. They stretched from floor to ceiling, running the whole extent of the flat's longest unbroken wall, and were stuffed with old paperbacks and a few hardbounds. Some of them were Turbiner's own books, the ones he'd written, including various translations; the rest were the ones that other people had written, that Turbiner had read along the way, that bit by bit he'd constructed the world inside his head from.

Not a particularly nice world, but one that McNihil was comfortable living in. It'd become real for him when he'd had the work done on his eyes, as though the contents of Turbiner's head and books had seeped out into the larger universe and taken it over. Or maybe it'd been the real world all along, the one that Turbiner and all the writers like him had seen in its true lineaments, and the surgery had merely been an extraction, the removal of some kind of invisible cataracts that had prevented it from being seen in all its dark, annihilating beauty.

He and Turbiner had talked about this before. A little flashback unreeled through McNihil's brain:

"You see, that's the way it is, when you're talking about noir." Turbiner had been kicking back with the single malt, an inch of Bruichladdich with a stable polymer ice-cube substitute drifting in the glass. *"It's a literature of anxiety. Somebody's always getting screwed over."*

The word had been floating around in the room, cold and false as the imitation ice. It had come up in the general course of conversation, while McNihil had been slouched down in the armchair opposite the couch, his own nervous system slightly buzzed from the effects of the same bottle that Turbiner had opened. McNihil hadn't cared where the word came from ultimately, and hadn't supposed that Turbiner cared, either. French intellectuals talking about lowbrow American culture, ages ago, ancient black-and-white movies filled with shadows, garish paperback cover art that seemed equally devoted to guns, lip-dangling cigarettes, and off-the-shoulder cleav-

age—no one cared anymore. Not about the word itself, which had gotten applied to so many things that it now meant—according to Turbiner—nothing at all.

"You see, that's where the later variations, especially in the movies, that's where they all went wrong." Turbiner had gotten into full lubricated lecture mode. "They mistook the images, the look of some old Billy Wilder masterpiece, and they thought that was the only thing that mattered. Really, it was only the people still cranking out books—like me—that had any fucking notion." He had taken another swallow, hard enough to rock his head back; from where he sat, McNihil had been able to watch the alcohol rolling down the other man's tendon-corded neck. "Any fucking notion at all, about what the essence, the soul of noir was all about." The words themselves had been drunk; no wonder the old writer loved them. "The look, all that darkness and shadow, all those trite rain-slick streets—that was the least of it. That had nothing to do with it."

McNihil had ingested enough alcohol to make his own eyelids feel like lead-weighted curtains. He'd looked out from underneath them at the old man. "So what was it, then?"

"Oh . . . it's betrayal." Turbiner had taken his glass down to the last brown remnant. "That's what it's always been. That's what makes it so realistic, even when it's the most dreamlike and shabby, when it looks like it's happening on some other planet. The one we lost and can't even remember, but we can see it when we close our eyes . . ."

The flashback was interrupted as McNihil, on autopilot, took a sip of the coffee that had been set down in front of him. It tasted like hot acid on his tongue, pulling him back into real time. Not unpleasantly so, or at least not unexpectedly.

Listening to the old man, McNihil knew he'd been speaking the truth. It came from somebody who'd loved his dead wife enough to put her in the ground for good, debt-free and gone. Or perhaps she was ashes in a jar, tucked somewhere in the general clutter of Turbiner's flat; either way, it didn't matter. The words about betrayal ran knifelike through somebody who'd loved just as much, but hadn't kept the same faith with the dead.

And the old man had known that, too. McNihil had never spoken to Turbiner about his own domestic affairs, but still, there it was somehow. Maybe from somebody else in the Collection Agency, another asp-head; Turbiner had been having his copyrights protected by the standard means for so long, there were bound to be other operatives with whom he was on a friendly basis. So for Turbiner to be talking about betrayal and things like that . . . McNihil had to admit, the old man had never claimed to be any kind of a nice guy.

"So what've we got here?" Turbiner had sat down in the plush chair with his own cup. He nodded toward the partially unwrapped package. "Not big enough for an automatic rifle, at least not a good one."

McNihil ignored the comment. He knew the old man was going to dig the present; if nothing else, it would complete the set Turbiner already had.

"Check it out," said McNihil. He pulled off the rest of the wrappings, balled them up in his fist, and tossed them onto the rubble-strewn floor. An elongated black leatherette case was revealed on the low table; the standard agency presentation job, nothing too fancy—the little metal hinges and clasp were just a cut above cheap and flimsy—but good enough. "A little something for you."

"How sweet." Turbiner leaned forward and drew the box around toward himself. "Ah." He nodded in appreciation as he looked over the contents. "Very, *very* nice."

"I figured, the way you've got your system set up, you'd need about twelve feet." McNihil took another sip of coffee. "Think that'll do you?"

"Perfect." Turbiner's voice went down into a pleased murmur, his grayed eyes glazing in happy anticipation. "It'll be perfect."

McNihil watched as the old man lifted out the presentation box's main contents, letting the snakelike object lie dangling across his level palms. It even glistened in a proper
herpetoid fashion, the decorative polyethylene sheathing put
on by the agency's techs shimmering with a subtle faceted
pattern.

The scale finish was on the outside; what was on the
inside was actual human spinal tissue, the last living remains
of McNihil's visit to the city farther north in the Gloss. That
was what he'd brought back from the End Zone Hotel, that
he'd returned with, safely tucked inside the regulation asp-
head trophy container. He'd been worried about it on the
trip back, what with all the knocking about it'd gotten,
when he'd been scrambling up and then clinging to that
disintegrating fire escape. And then the fire itself, up on top
of the burning transient hotel, the tarry roof smoking and
bubbling beneath him and that would-be severe female
who'd rescued him. With all that heat—including the lethal
radiation from the young woman's eyes, when she'd finally
caught on that McNihil wasn't the gratitude-ridden
type—the spinal and cerebral matter he'd scooped out of the
pirate kid's carcass might have been cooked inside the long
tube he'd been carrying. *Stupid broad,* thought McNihil, seeing her tough-cookie little face pop up on his mental screen
for a moment. She'd saved his ass and kept the trophy intact;
the techs, when McNihil had finally dropped it off at the
agency, had told him it was in fine shape, nothing to worry
about. And what had she gotten out of it, whoever she was?
Nada. By this time, McNihil had stopped wondering
whether she'd even try to get in touch with him again. If
anything, she was probably too embarrassed by an old connect like him having gotten the drop on her. *And so easily,
too;* that thought came to him with a certain measure of
satisfaction.

"Absolutely perfect." Turbiner's voice held the same

bright emotion. Still holding the present across his palms, he
looked up at McNihil. "I've wanted this for a long time."
He glanced over at the rack of stereo equipment, then back
again. "Finally, man; you're not really optimized until the
cables all match."

Or match close enough; McNihil knew, and was sure the
old man knew as well, that there'd be no way that the long,
dangling object, with the snakey texture and the gold-plated
tips at each end, could perfectly match what he already had
in his system. But it was certainly the next best thing.

There was already human spinal tissue in Turbiner's music setup, two long stretches of it running from his hyper-
tweaked power amp, one of the last of the classic Moffatt
lithium-flux designs, and out to the big square mirror-im-
aged Dahlquist DQ-10's. Each speaker cable had the same
glistening snakeskin finish—they looked, in fact, like two
swollen anacondas forming horizontal S's across the threadbare Afghan carpet that was the bottom layer beneath all the
other strata of books and sloppily stacked papers. The
agency's trophies had been bulkier back when Turbiner had
been presented with those; the techs hadn't quite gotten
down the miniaturization for the cables' life-support and
oxygen-delivery processes, all the silent workings that kept
the encased tissue alive.

McNihil figured that those archaic cables must be at least
twenty, twenty-five years old; they still had the big grape-
fruit-sized bulge close to the amp ends, where the scooped-
out cerebral matter was lodged in its own thermo-insulated
padding. He remembered dropping off to other clients cables
and similar trophies, back when he'd first started working for
the agency. Nowadays, the techs had come closer to perfect-
ing their microsurgical crafts; the new cable was narrower—it
could've slid through the circle formed by McNihil's thumb
and forefinger—and the same diameter from end to end,
minus the smaller connector spades at the very tips. The new

cable held just as much of the brain of a pirate—in this case, the kid that McNihil had worked over up north—only condensed and stripped of any unnecessary synapses and neurons, and dispersed evenly rather than bunched up in one unsightly lump.

Thus ever to violators of copyright, thought McNihil as he watched the other man admiring the trophy. This was the part of the job, when he'd still been working for the agency, that he'd always enjoyed the most.

"The only way it could be better . . ." Turbiner held the cable up higher, squinting one eye as though examining the object through a magnifying glass. "The only way it could *possibly* be improved"—his glance and a sly smile darted in McNihil's direction—"is if the first two guys, and then this one, had been triplets. A three-way identical match, boom-boom-boom with the genetics. Wouldn't that be a hot-rod rig?"

"To end all rigs," agreed McNihil. He was starting to get a contact high, partially enhanced by the caffeine, from Turbiner's obvious enjoyment of the gift. The crack about what would've been the perfect rig, the ultimate cable setup for a hard-core music lover's stereo, wasn't meant as criticism, McNihil knew. How likely was it that a set of identical triplets would get into copyright piracy? Not if they had one person's smarts amongst themselves. Turbiner had lucked out as it was, back when the Folichman twins had glommed onto some of his old titles, and had then made the mistake of thinking nobody would catch them if they scanned the yellowing pages, encrypted the digitized results, and offered them for sale through a Djakarta phone-bank front operation that hadn't been any smarter than they were. Turbiner's copyrights hadn't been the only ones infringed, but he'd been near the top of the agency's list for trophy handout when the hammer had come down on the pirate operation. Plus McNihil had been the agent in charge, so he could pull

a few strings, make sure that the top goodies went to his
personal heroes. He'd already met Turbiner, at one of the
agency's semiannual PR-banquet functions, and had been
into the old guy's books—when he'd been able to find
them—for some time before that. McNihil had assembled
nearly a complete set of Turbiner's backlist, had gotten him
to inscribe and sign them, the whole trip; that was when
he'd found out about Turbiner's significant music fixation,
particularly in regard to the equipment angle. That also being
the moment McNihil had decided on scoring the ultimate
upgrade for the old writer, something to put the final cherry
gloss on his antique, perfectly preserved stereo setup.

Which was what pirates, copyright violators, were good
for. If they could be said to be good for anything. Trophies;
the final, tangible, and fitting result of the draconian enforce-
ment of the laws protecting the ownership of creative content and intellectual property. If there were assholes out there
stupid enough to attempt violating copyright—and there always were; the Collection Agency would never go out of
business—then asp-heads like McNihil had no compunctions
about putting the points of their field scalpels into the hinges
and locks of the pirates' skulls. The consequences of screwing
around were so well-known—the agency put a lot of effort
into its various public-information programs, cluing in the
world on how the system's sharp-edged gears meshed—that
most asp-heads, McNihil included, figured their prey were
into some sort of self-destruction imperative, sure and certain
suicide by means of the law's swift, implacable enforcers.
What else could it be? If any asp-heads had ever had pangs of
conscience about the bloody nature of their work—McNihil
himself had always slept well enough at night—then the notion that the agency's operatives were giving the pirates not
only what they deserved, but what they wanted as well,
should have been enough to ease those feelings.

"Look," said Turbiner. "I've *got* to hook this up right

now. I can't wait." He had coiled the trophy cable into a loop around one hand; with the other, he knocked back the last of the coffee in his cup. He stood and moved toward the equipment rack against the wall. "Sorry to drop out of the conversation . . . but you know how it is."

McNihil shrugged. "Knock yourself out."

He watched as Turbiner powered down his stereo gear and pulled the rack out far enough to reach the connections behind. The old man knelt down, already oblivious to anyone else's presence in the flat, and began unhooking the ordinary, non-trophy cable running from the amp to the massive, refrigerator-shaped subwoofer sitting between the two DQ-10's. The recording of the Mahler Second had come to an end some time ago—it had been turned down so low that McNihil had barely been conscious of the silence becoming complete inside the flat. In absolute quiet, a combination of the flat's double glazing and the acoustic interference waves pulsed out from around the windowsills, Turbiner busily unhooked from a monochannel power amp the two gold-plated spades of the cable running to the subwoofer cabinet. Beneath the cable's clear plastic sheath were the smaller diameter wires of ordinary six-nines copper, insulated black and red, signal and ground; no human tissue involved. Disdain for the non-trophy cable was already showing on Turbiner's creviced face as he popped loose the spades at the other end.

"There we go." Just as swiftly, Turbiner worked the screwdriver to tighten down the amp's and subwoofer's connectors onto the new cable. He stood up, slipping the screwdriver into his shirt pocket, then brushing his hands off. "Thus we approach audio nirvana." Turbiner pushed the rack back into place—he had left the curve of the trophy out in front, a thin ribbon snaking across the carpet—then commenced the intricate sequence of powering up all the equipment in the proper order. A fiery glow came from inside the ranks of NOS Sovtek 65512's, the dome-headed vacuum tubes lined up across the tops of the amps like combustible soldiers. "This oughta be good."

Turbiner didn't bother putting in a new disc, but just started up the Mahler Second from the beginning. He settled back in the sweet-spot chair, its leather and underlying padding molded to his frame from long hours of listening. The upholstery was still sighing as the invisible cellos and basses, long distant in space and time, dug into the opening bars.

For a few seconds, the music bore down like all the gears of the world grinding to a halt, the vast machinery of the cosmos snagging upon God's trapped hand. *De profundis* outrage, the garments of the angels rippling into the time-stilled fabric of the universe.

"That sounds pretty nice," said McNihil.

Turbiner made no reply. His crepe-paperish eyelids had lowered, leaving a narrow slit of unfocused vision beneath. In furious concentration, he leaned slightly forward, tension clicking into some deeper, slower state of existence. He looked like a desert turtle going into hibernation, all bodily functions shutting down, except for the tingle of nerves from his cochlea. His ears, everything beyond the stiff cartilage of his pinnae, were the youngest part of his body; McNihil knew that the old man had had cochlear implants put in about a decade ago. All in the service of the music, his only surviving love.

It'll be a while, McNihil told himself, *before the old guy resurfaces*. He'd been here before, when Turbiner had gone off into the zone of vibrating air molecules. Pushing himself up from the couch, McNihil wandered back into the flat's kitchen area. He opened the cupboard over the sink, took out the half-empty bottle of Bruichladdich, and poured himself a shot.

The music washed into the kitchen like a hammering

tide. Leaning against the counter and taking a sip, McNihil could see the brown spots on the other man's skull, lipofuscin deposits underneath the thinning silver hair. Alcohol on top of caffeine added another glow to McNihil's mood. It didn't matter—not really—that the new cable, the one with the would-be pirate kid's brain essence smeared inside, was a bit of a shuck. It brought such obvious pleasure to the old guy; where was the harm?

Of the shuckness of the agency's trophies, McNihil was something of an expert. When he'd still been with the agency full-time, he'd been rotated out of the field for a while, back into the offices and a design team working on revamping and updating all the stuff that went out the doors. (He remembered thumbing the *yes* button during one feedback session, registering his professional opinion on the exact spooky snakeskin finish that graced the cable now running between Turbiner's amp and subwoofer. McNihil felt a little proprietary surge whenever he spotted those glistening scales.) When he'd been on that duty, itching to get back outside and connect up lowlife copyright infringers, the Collection Agency's top brass had decided on a full-out review of its signature gear, the trophies themselves. McNihil had ended up wading through an entire history of the desired objects, complete with a sideshow memo presentation, an art gallery of vengeful matter.

Just looking at the cable forming an extended *S* across the flat's carpet—the gift that McNihil had braved fire and heights to procure for the old man—the history of the Collection Agency's compensation for larcenous copyright infringement turned slowly inside his head. Like a prismatic hologram, entire to itself and outside the flow of linear time that had produced it; the narrative didn't need to be gone over by McNihil, not again, for him to know its detail and sequence:

- When it was first determined that death was the appropriate punishment for copyright infringement, the reasoning went more or less along these lines:

- The world had changed, in both the theory and the practice of its economy, to one in which people made their livings—put roofs over their heads and the heads of their children, bread in their and their children's mouths—from intellectual property. *Ideas* and/or *design* and/or *content*—whatever word, name, label one wanted to use—if that was the most important thing in the world, that which determined whether you ate or starved—

- Then why would it not be defended? How could the *ownership* of it *not* be important? The same rule of survival applied to big international corporations, to midlevel localized players and entrepreneurs, to scrabbling, scribbling little content creators, writers in their basement offices and musicians in their one-man-band back-bedroom studios and red-eyed videomakers slamming between cuts on their desktop editing rigs, all of them turning their brains inside out, turning the tiniest neutral sparks into words and images, encoded, intelligible, transmittable-to-someone-else thoughts. If they were going to have something to sell, they had to own it—it being the product of their minds and creativity—in the first place.

- And no utopian notions, no weird 'net-twit theorizing, propagandizing, self-serving merchandising of predictions, no half-baked amalgam of late-sixties Summer of Love and Handouts, Diggerish free food in the Panhandle of Golden Gate Park, and Stalinist collectivization, lining up the kulaks and shooting them 'cause they're in the way of the new world order, nothing had been able to change that. The laws of economics were as immutable as those of physics; once the fringy out-there stuff was dismissed, it still remained that if one flapped one's arms and jumped off the roof, one landed on one's butt.

• The arm-flapping maneuvers, the attempts to get around reality, had all burnt out and been discarded, one by one. The "gift-based" economy had been a hippie dream, nice for exchanging information of no value, worthless itself for selling and buying anything *worth* buying and selling.

• Salvation hadn't come from advertising revenues, either. The notion of giving away intellectual content, everything on the wire for nothing, like old reruns of *Gilligan's Island,* all paid for by the companies sticking their ads all over the monitor screen—that had eventually evaporated like spit on an unventilated power supply as well. There had been no need for anything like ad-stripping programs, going right back to the classic forerunner Privnet IFF, peeling the advertisements off like soggy stick-'em stamps and dropping them into whatever electronic wastebasket caught unseen, never-seen, never-should've-bothered bits and bytes. The evolution of the human brain had taken care of the situation. A filter is like an immune system, and *vice versa;* it hadn't been too long before a benign mental cataract had been determined to exist, one that spread memelike through the species. Ad-blindness, linked to the refresh rates on visual display units. Any pitch other than hard copy in the real world never made it past the optic nerve.

- If stuff was worth buying and selling—not just hard physical stuff, but intellectual property as well—then it was worth stealing, too. *Thieves are always with us,* as the mercantile bible might have warned of, but not blessed. For a while, the inchoate, not-yet-coalesced Internet had fostered the kind of informational darkness in which thieves prospered. The so-called anonymous remailing services pleaded an ideological agenda and served as a front for criminals and vandals. The first and most famous, anon.penet.fi, folded in 1996, its spine broken by Finnish court orders. The rest were hunted down and exterminated off the wires—it took a while—on the simple legal principle and mechanism that receiving stolen goods was as much a crime as the theft that produced them. That was what being a *fence* was all about: there was essentially no difference between a sleazoid pawnshop trafficking in hot, wire-dangling car stereos and an on-line service receiving a stolen, copyrighted piece, whether it was a song digitized into an audio file or a book with all its words OCR'd into zeroes and ones, then stripping off the transmission data that would identify the thief and routing the result to a prearranged buyer. It wasn't just in the hypothesized merchant's bible that facilitating theft was considered as much a crime as the theft itself. *Christ,* McNihil had thought before, *you could find that much in the Koran.* And in the hearts and minds of decent people everywhere—which was why:

- Nobody really objected to the severe nature of the system, the Collection Agency and its attendant asp-heads, that was eventually set in place to take care of the remaining copyright infringers. (Nobody, that was, except the most foolishly tenderhearted and the irredeemably ideology-ridden, who persisted in confusing intellectual-property issues with censorship and limiting access to information.) A hard world, and getting harder; no sympathy went to a clown who interfered with somebody trying to make an honest buck. When to steal from someone was not to take some expendable, frivolous trinket off them, a van Gogh off the dining-room wall of some bloated plutocrat; but rather to lift some hard-pressed hustling sonuvabitch's means of survival, the only way he had of turning the contents of his head into the filling of his stomach; when to steal from someone was the same as to murder them—then nobody cried when, through law and custom, executing thieves became the wholly proper thing to do.

- With all intellectual property merchandised or archieved on the wires, and accessible with a few keystrokes—it became obviously necessary to find a way to take thieves, copyright infringers, off-line for good. When survival is at stake, no second chances are allowed. Which was why, even back before the last century had ticked over into this one, a general maxim had gone the rounds:

- **There's a hardware solution to intellectual-property theft. It's called a .357 magnum.** No better way for taking pirates off-line. Permanently. Properly applied to the head of any copyright-infringing little bastard, this works.

- Once death was accepted as public policy—murder as the answer to murder, the solution to people who had problems with respecting copyright—then it had just been a matter of properly implementing it. To get the most out of it.

"This sounds great," said Turbiner. He had pulled himself up from his Mahler-driven, wordless meditations. He turned and looked back toward the flat's kitchen area. "It was worth the wait, man."

"Glad you like it." McNihil splashed a little more scotch into the glass on the counter; he knew Turbiner wouldn't mind that he'd helped himself. "I'll let the techs know, back at the agency, that it met with your approval."

Actually, it *did* sound better. McNihil had known there would be an improvement, but hadn't been quite prepared for this order of magnitude. The bass coming out of the subwoofer was deep and clean, with no cheap-'n'-fuzzy boom-box reverb; the drum strokes hammering out from the back of the invisible orchestra were as tight as the heads on the timpani themselves. The old guy had had a good setup before, but now McNihil could sense the actual physical structure of the Amsterdam Concertgebouw responding in synch to the music, a nearly subliminal tremble coming up through the floorboards and into the soles of his shoes.

Pretty good for a shuck, thought McNihil. Which it was:

- For death to be effective public policy, it must be *public.* If the message to be gotten across is, *Connect around with someone else's copyrights and you die,* an emotionally resonant depiction of that truth had to be created.

- Witnessing the death of intellectual-property pirates—taping and broadcasting the various raids and apprehensions, getting the videocam lenses in close for the spattering blood, the wide-eyed look in some jerk's eyes as the cold circle at the front of some large-caliber tannhäuser was set against the bridge of his nose, his stare going cross-eyed as he watched the trigger being slowly pulled back—that worked at the beginning. High ratings and message through-put, audience retention up above the ninetieth percentile.

- Then the drop-off, wire share falling along with the novelty factor; after the first dozen or so punks have their brains removed out the backs of their skulls, after a few good raids on rogue Chinese factories, with the new, improved Smart-Enuff® bombs sniffing out illicit CD-ROM's and then scattering polycarbonate and body parts with equal facility; after everybody had *seen* stuff like that, the message migrated to the subconscious level of people's minds, instead of staying up top where the Collection Agency and its clients wanted it.

- Plus there was the suicide factor involved. Various jerks, operating out of the same tired ideological agenda and hippie wish-fulfillment dream, who wanted to martyr themselves for the muddled and not-very-well-thought-out cause of "free" information; or the terminally and personally screwed-up, who saw the Collection Agency's asp-heads as a neat and public way of bringing about their own demise—either way, the threat of death was in fact the *promise* of death for enough people to be a continuing trouble. Even if minor, it was still something that needed to be dealt with; the agency dealt in absolutes, its net tight enough to allow no one to wriggle through.

• This called for a certain amount of rethinking on the Collection Agency's part. Did death *necessarily* = punishment? The main problem with death as a negative motivational factor was that it was over too quickly, and not always painfully enough.

• Obviously, what was needed was to stretch death out in time, take it from a point to an extended process. *And* pump up the pain and humiliation factors.

Thus, thought McNihil, *the creation of the trophy system.* It worked even better.

THIRTEEN

A FLUTTERING MOTH IN THE
DEVIL'S COIN-PURSE

Here." McNihil had poured a shot for his host; standing beside the sweet-spot chair, he handed the glass to Turbiner. "Maybe this'll heighten the effect even more."

"Thanks." The old man took the glass and sipped, then nodded in appreciation. He kept his gaze aimed straight ahead, at the place between the two main speakers. "You hear that?" He nodded toward the unseen orchestra. "You clean up the bass, the midrange sorts itself out, too. Just less audible crap in general."

McNihil placed himself back on the couch, careful not to spill his own refilled glass. From there, he could watch as the other man let himself be drawn back under the music's engulfing tide. They were already at the third movement, *In ruhig fließender Bewegung*. Warmed by the scotch, McNihil listened, admiring the way the new cable brought the subterranean rumble of the basses into the flat. Admiring, despite what he knew of the nature of such trophies:

- The vindictive principle largely determined how the Collection Agency structured its compensation protocols. If someone stole from one of their clients—stole by way of infringing, pirating the client's copyright-protected material—then the agency saw the pirate's entire person as being essentially in forfeit to the client. If the client had a right to demand the pirate's death, then why not the pirate's life as well? The pirate as a living entity? And more to the purpose of providing an object lesson to anyone thinking about ripping off one of the agency's clients—as a suffering entity as well.

- Thus, an important evolution in the nature of trophies came about. At the beginning, when physical death was required—*absolute* physical death, with no parts surviving—trophies took form in less satisfying, less temporally extended ways. McNihil had read about these; they were slightly before his time in the agency—

- One author of romance novels, living somewhere in the English Cotswolds with a posse of beloved felines, had the three on-wire and unauthorized purveyors of her old books delivered to her in the form of canned, vitamin-enhanced cat food, suitably minced and labeled, the bones powdered and stirred in for the extra calcium essential to a healthy animal's diet;

- A mystery writer in New York City, still maintaining his rooftop garden long after the depopulation of the buildings around him, had a CD-ROM packager—who'd been running a sideline of distributing out-of-print titles for which he hadn't bothered to pay any royalties—delivered to him in the form of three sacks of bone meal and fertilizer. The roses did very well that year and the next.

- The beginning of the shuckness was in examples such as these. A chopped-up human being was justice, but not necessarily nutrition; the cans with the late pirates' scowling faces on the label had to have extra soy and fish-farm protein mixed in. Same with the fertilizer, only there the human portion didn't even hit the fifty-percent mark. As with so many things in life, it was the thought that counted. And the deaths.

- The same principle applied when it was determined that the agency's trophies, for maximum educational and moral value, should be living and not just dead things. In the cables lacing up Alex Turbiner's stereo system, there was actual human cerebral tissue, the essential parts of the larcenous brains of those who'd thought it would be either fun or profitable to rip off an old, forgotten scribbler like him. Conceptually attached to the cables, the old ones he'd already had and the new slimmed-down subwoofer cable that McNihil had just delivered to him, was a lot of audio-nerd gabble about the superiority of soft-'n'-wet neural-based technology for high-end sound systems, coherent full-spectrum wave delivery, optimized impedance matching, the transfer function be-

tween synapses quicker than that through the crystalline structure of metal conductors, et cetera, et
cetera, yadda yadda yadda.

• Only . . . that was bull. The Collection Agency
knew it; everybody who worked for the agency,
the administrators and accountants, the techs and
asp-heads out in the fields, they all knew the basic
shuckness of it. At the center of the cerebral tissue
inside Turbiner's cables, running through it like the
digestive tract of a mosquito surrounded by its
minute insect brain, was a core of thin-film cryo-
insulated stabilized quasi-liquid silver. The precious metal—made even more so by the expensive
high tech that had transformed it—had the con-
ductive qualities of ordinary silver, enhanced by
the mercurylike room-temperature flow and lack
of crystalline-structure inhibitory factors. That was
why the cables sounded so good, rolled out bass
like the shoes of God, made the percussion section's tubular bells ring like skinny angels. The
brain matter scooped from the skulls of copyright
infringers had nothing to do—in truth—with the
sound the cables made possible, though the
agency's claim was that it did.

• The brain matter, the still-living remnant of the
various pirates, was there for one purpose. To suffer.

McNihil set down his glass and pushed himself up from
the depths of the couch. He walked over to the stereo-equip-
ment rack, being careful not to get in between Turbiner and
the full impact of the music. Kneeling down beside the new
cable's boalike curve, he dug another piece of asp-head

equipment from his jacket pocket, something no bigger than
a handheld calculator with a few dangling gold-tipped wires.
As the third movement of the Mahler hammered and
steamed around him, McNihil inserted the thin metal probes
into the matching sockets toward one end of the cable.

The device in his hand was a readout meter for the neural activity encapsulated in agency trophies. When the techs
skinned down an apprehended pirate, reducing the brain to
its essentials, the biggest part of what remained was the basic
personality structure and an ongoing situational awareness.
The person was still inside the object, alive and conscious.
The techs also grafted on to the stripped sensory receptors a
minimal interface structure, just enough for the canned
scraps of a human being to know what had happened to it.
When the techs finished up their jobs, they left the sym-
bolic-manipulation subset of the personality intact, the
brain's language-formation centers still working.

On the face of the meter, a pair of red LED's pulsed on,
matching those on the cable's surface, and signaling that the
cerebral material inside the cable was up and running. On
very rare occasions, a strokelike condition was spontaneously
triggered, rapidly reducing the soft tissue connectors to a
jellied pulp oozing out of the sheath's porous wrap like
grayed-out strawberry jam. When that happened, there was
nothing to do but pull out the trophy and throw it back in its
presentation box, return it to the agency labs for the techs to
slice out the valuable electronics for recycling. Sad but true:
the little bastard would have, in a case like that, escaped the
grim immortality that his crimes had earned him. He'd be
well and truly, one-hundred-percent dead, the collapsed
brain matter fit only for tossing down the garbage chute to
join the rest of his previously discarded body.

This guy's doing just fine, noted McNihil, as he glanced at
the numbers displayed below the hot red dots on the meter.
The kid, the business that he'd gone north in the Gloss to

take care of, was still there in the cable hooked up to Turbiner's subwoofer. Or all that mattered of the kid was there. McNihil wondered if the agency's techs had left enough memory circuits for the kid's bottled personality to have a sensory recall of his last moments as a functioning, walking-around human being: the smell of the run-down theater's stale popcorn, the quick and clammy flood of the hydro-gel across his face, the rush of panicky adrenaline as he'd struggled for a gulp of shut-off oxygen. He supposed there might be a memory flash floating around in there, of McNihil's extended fingers poking an airway for the kid to breathe through, and then of his hands picking up the futilely struggling body and dragging it out of the theater. That, plus the kid's awareness of his crime, what he'd done to get worked over and reduced this thoroughly, was all that was required, a sad little biography boiled down to its essential, remorseful parts.

McNihil held the meter up to his ear. The little wafer-thin speaker inside was just loud enough for him to pick up, without intruding on Turbiner's enjoyment of the louder music, the verbalized outpouring from the soul inside the cable.

i'm sorry i'm sorry i'm sorry please please please please let me out out outoutoutout dark and cold and wet and stings sorry sorry sorry pleeeeeeeease

At times like this, McNihil felt like Mr. Scratch in the ancient black-and-white film *All That Money Can Buy,* with old Walter Huston back in 1941, radiating his evil, bright-eyed smile, the visual counterpart to all that creepy Bernard Herrmann soundtrack music. At least in the movie, sinners had to be tempted by a spooky Simone Simon to wind up as a fluttering moth in the devil's coin-purse. Nowadays, in this modern world, all it took was one's own stupidity, the kind above the neck rather than in the groin. McNihil took the meter an inch away from his ear, reducing the scrabbling, wailing voice to a distant, indecipherable noise, as though it were no more than RFI static on the dangling wires. All around the rim, and farther beyond, there were similar little voices, shouting inside their small damnations:

- Which was the point. A dead trophy did not have the moral and instructive impact of a living one. *Living* in the sense of there being the essence of the pirate, the skinned-down soul of the copyright infringer, that bit of brain tissue that held the larcenous personality, embodied in some common household appliance, its functions enhanced by the correct employment of what had once been a human being:

- Toasters were a popular trophy item. There was always a waiting list at the agency headquarters, clients who had put their names down, in case some fool messed with their copyrights. A great sense of satisfaction came with owning a little chrome-and-plastic box with a dial on the side for how dark you wanted the slices to come out—*and* a little chunk of cerebral matter wired onto the circuit board, making sure that the bread achieved the perfect state of golden crispness.

- Vacuum cleaners and in-sink garbage-disposal units—those were desired as well. The pleasure there came from the sense of someone who had stolen from you now being reduced to sucking up cat hair and miscellaneous lint from the carpet, or, whenever the switch on the kitchen wall was flicked, sluicing the unidentifiable, mold-covered soft objects from the fridge down the plumbing gullet wired to the pirate's brain tissue. *You want something of mine? Try this. Don't choke, now* . . .

• Other popular items: wall clocks, train sets for the kids, pocket appointment books with little built-in calculators (the recipients of those trophies had to be extra careful to keep fresh batteries in them, or the canned brain tissue would go off and start to smell funny), a new and improved version of the classic "Drinking Bird" toy . . . the variations were endless, dependent only upon the number of copyright infringers who got nabbed by the Collection Agency.

• Which were, understandably, fewer and fewer. Which was the point of such draconian measures. This was standard policing procedure, going back to and beyond the hard-core, take-no-prisoners attitude of the old, pre-reform LAPD. Plenty of people connected with the agency, McNihil included, believed the notion went back to the actual, nonmythologized frontier of the American West—or even farther, to the first societies to domesticate and herd animals.

• The principle being that if the valuable property was widely dispersed—as with cattle across grazing land, or intellectual property digitized on the wire—and therefore easier to steal, the antitheft forces had to amp up the *consequences* for theft: death to rustlers and horse thieves, trophy-ization for copyright infringers.

• Draconian measures have something of a life of their own. Plus, the Collection Agency had its own public-relations wing, to make sure that the fate of trophies was broadcast as widely as possible, to make sure that anyone contemplating a little info-larceny would know what would happen to them if they got caught. If you wanted to spend the rest of your life—*a long* life—as a toaster, it could be arranged.

- A certain immortality could be achieved, though nothing that anyone would want. Self-destruction has its seductive elements, but this was something else again. Purged of the grosser elements of the human body, the essential brain tissue, and the consciousness and personality locked inside the soft wiring, could last decades, perhaps centuries—only a few of the earliest trophies had crapped out in the field. The agency's packaging, the cellular life-support technology contained in the cable sheathing and the little sealed boxes inside the toasters, was designed for low maintenance and an indefinite run.

- Thus, into the economy inside people's heads, that private assessment of potential risks and benefits, the element of *catastrophic price* was introduced. Price beyond death, beyond the notions of desirability for even the terminally self-destructive.

- Nobel prizes in economics had been handed out in the twentieth century for deep thinkers who'd figured out with charts and graphs what cops had known for millennia: people, weighing a course of action, factor in the consequences of success or failure as well as the chances. Amp-up the negative

consequences high enough, and you can scare a lot
of little bastards from connecting around.

- In that sense, the Collection Agency dealt in sanctioned terrorism. The agency didn't have a problem with that.

I don't have a problem with that, McNihil told himself. He
pulled the probe tips loose from the cable's readout sockets,
wrapped the wires around the meter, and dropped it back
into his pocket. Glancing over his shoulder at Turbiner, he
saw the old man still absorbed by the music, the third movement dancing ominously to its close. Turbiner looked
drowned, as though the audible tide had taken him down to
its depths, the strands of his silver hair drifting like seaweed.
Those are pearls that were his eyes—McNihil stood up but
didn't move away from the equipment rack and its glowing
power tubes, as though cautious of breaking the spell.

All through the Gloss, in their scrappy or plush flats or
other living-spaces, old writers like Alex Turbiner, and composers and musicians, artists and programmers, symbolic
manipulators all—they were listening to their bloodily enhanced stereos or dropping slices of bread into their silently
screaming toasters, maybe not even thinking about the little
thieves canned inside. It didn't matter. It also didn't matter
whether the writers and others, including Turbiner sitting
here, knew as well what a shuck the trophies were. If they
knew that the cerebral material, the boiled-down residue of
pirates, really didn't improve the sound any, really didn't
make the toast come out any closer to a perfect golden
brown . . . so what? In an imperfect world, it was not just
the thought that counted, but the consequences as well.

Turbiner raised his eyelids a bare fraction of an inch and
glanced over as McNihil sat back down on the couch. "You
enjoying this?" One eyebrow lifted slightly higher. "You

must be." Turbiner held his glass up in a toast. "My thanks are hereby extended to you. And my congratulations."

"You're welcome. My pleasure." McNihil had drained his glass; he let it dangle at the tips of his fingers. The alcohol had slowed his thought processes; it took a moment for the puzzled frown to draw across his face. "Congratulations for what? Just doing my job . . ."

"I thought you weren't working anymore. That you were on the outs with the agency."

"Somewhat." McNihil shrugged. "But I can still do a favor for my friends."

Turbiner picked up the remote control from the arm of the chair and thumbed the *mute* button. The music vanished between one chord and the next, all harmonic progression left unresolved. "Doing favors for people . . . that's a nice thing." Silence had filled the flat again, the contrast making Turbiner's voice seem louder than before. "You know, in my world . . . that one I used to write about . . . there are no favors. Nobody does favors for other people."

"I guess we're lucky," said McNihil. "That we don't live there." He rubbed his thumb across the rim of the empty glass. "We live in this one. Or at least some of the time we do."

"Maybe that's the way it is." Turbiner gave a judicious nod. He looked like a shabby owl dressed in thrift-store feathers. "Some of the time."

The silence thickened, more oppressive than the music could ever have been. Time, stabbed by alcohol, had congealed in the spaces of the flat.

"Well." McNihil tried to shake himself free, by leaning forward and setting the glass down on the low table. "I'm glad you like the . . . present." It had taken him a few seconds to think of the right word. "Maybe I should be taking off."

"Not just yet. Stick around for a moment or two."

Turbiner's words were clipped and precise, as businesslike as the sharp gaze studying his guest. "I wanted to ask you a couple questions. About the . . . present."

"Like what?"

Turbiner shifted in the chair, redirecting himself in McNihil's direction rather than to the point between the main loudspeakers. "The fellow you got this from. The donor, as it might be put." Turbiner's voice sounded unusually loud and distinct, as though he were setting each word down in a row of numbered stones. "He was ripping me off, wasn't he? My copyrights, my old thriller titles, that is. He had some kind of scam going."

"What're you talking about? You know that." McNihil's puzzlement deepened. "You were the one who told me about it." That was true: he remembered getting the call from Turbiner a couple of weeks ago. He tried smiling. "Are you starting to forget things?"

"Maybe I am." The voice held no hesitancy, but was still loud and forceful. "Because I don't remember telling you anything about some guy like this."

A few seconds slid by, the flat's silence weighing upon McNihil's shoulders. "You know . . . perhaps I really should leave now." He felt uncomfortably sober, the scotch doing nothing more than souring the contents of his gut. "I'm not sure where this is headed."

"Sit down. It'll all be over soon."

Something's going on—he felt stupid, even reaching a conclusion that obvious. At the same time, a degree of tension ebbed out of his muscles, a fatalistic relaxation taking over. So many times, he'd been the agent of enclosure, his own voice the click of the lock snapping shut, the last thing somebody heard with any degree of freedom at all. Autonomy fled, control begun; now he was going to find out what that felt like.

"What's the deal?" A last measure of resistance was summoned up. "What's with the weird questions?"

"I just want to make sure." Turbiner's shoulders lifted in a shrug. "About the details."

"Like what?"

"Like your claim that this person—the one you rolled over, the one whose head is inside this cable you just brought me—that this guy was ripping me off. Violating my copyrights."

"That's not a claim," said McNihil. "It's the truth."

Turbiner nodded. "And your knowledge of this copyright infringement is based on . . . what? What I'm supposed to have told you?"

For a moment, McNihil studied the empty glass on the table, then looked back over at the other man. "You're saying you didn't tell me?"

"No. I'm just saying you can't *prove* I told you anything like that."

"Well, yeah . . ." That was true as well. "I'm not in the habit of recording phone calls from my friends."

"Maybe you should be more careful about that."

Another shrug. "Or maybe about my friends."

"Now that's something—" Turbiner gave an approximation of a smile. "You can't be too careful about."

"I've got a feeling that it's a little late for this kind of advice." The feeling was actually a certainty, like a rock in McNihil's stomach. "So why would I need to prove anything at all? About what you told me?" He picked up the glass from the table, remembered that it was empty, and set it back down. "This kid was ripping you off. He told me so himself. He was bragging about it."

"What a foolish young man." Turbiner glanced over at the cable running to the subwoofer, then slowly shook his head. "He must not've actually read those titles he was stealing from me. That's the problem with those collector and dealer mentalities." He looked back around at McNihil. "If they ever bothered to read the stuff—especially the old noir classics—they'd know that's how you get into trouble. By not clamming up when you've got the chance. You let your mouth run on, you can talk yourself into the grave." He nodded toward the snakelike cable. "Or worse."

"Yeah, well, he wasn't the smartest one I ever encountered."

"I suppose not," said Turbiner. "I don't suppose you bothered recording your little encounter with him, either. Even though that's standard agency procedure, isn't it?"

McNihil made no reply. *I should have*—instead of doing the job on the cheap, trying to economize on the nonessentials. When he'd still been working for the agency, even the smallest field assignments he'd gone on had been secretly—and expensively—bugged and taped. Some of them, his prize hits, had even been converted by the agency into training videos, instructional adjuncts for getting new hires up to speed on the asp-head way of doing business. But recording cost money, especially with all the masking and counterfeed-suppression technology that had to be added on, to make sure that the pirates, with their funky but effective hair-trigger alarm systems, didn't catch on to the fact that they were being taped in all their hard-evidence glory. Money that an effectively retired asp-head, doing a favor, might not want to tap into his own pocket to shell out.

"All right," said McNihil finally. "I didn't record you, and I didn't record the kid I worked over. What does it matter? As long as he was stealing from you, as long as he was violating your copyrights, his ass was mine."

This time, it was Turbiner who kept silent. He shifted in the chair so he could dig his wallet from his back pocket. Flipping the wallet open, he extracted a PDA card; its tiny display panel illuminated when he pressed the top right corner between his thumb and forefinger. With the edge of his nail, Turbiner scrolled down through the listed data.

"You've seen this before." Turbiner had found the entry he'd been looking for; he extended the card toward McNihil. "Standard issue, right?"

Most writers that McNihil had dealt with, or the composers or other creative types, had something similar with which they kept track of their copyrights. He'd had this one in his hand on previous occasions, when he'd been checking Turbiner's records against the agency's central database. He glanced at the little screen, tilting it away from the light sifting in through the flat's window blinds. "So what am I supposed to be looking for?"

"Bottom of the file. Most recent entry."

A name that McNihil didn't recognize. "Who's Kyle Wyvitz?"

"That's the name," said Turbiner, "of the kid whose brain is in that cable you just brought me." The words had been spoken softly, no added emphasis required. "Your latest trophy job."

"Ah." He could just about see it all now; the relaxation in McNihil's bones and muscles was echoed by a similar expansion in time, the appreciable gulf between one second and the next. Just as the would-be pirate kid's senses must have gone into slow motion as soon as the snaring hydro-gel had leapt up from the plastic cup; the way the small animal in the triggered leg-hold trap must have been able to study every tooth of the metal jaw slicing down toward its pelt and flesh. "And why . . . just *why* . . . would his name be here in your copyright tracking?" As if he couldn't figure it out, already. "What's that mean?"

"Other than that you're totally screwed?" Turbiner sounded almost sympathetic, as though he were in fact sorry to see the trap snapping shut. "But you know that already, don't you?"

"I know all sorts of things. Some of them I just learned." He looked at Turbiner, as though seeing him for the first time, unoccluded. In the flat's musicless silence, McNihil could almost hear the blood singing in his own veins. "I'm just interested in these particular details, that's all."

"You can work it out." Turbiner shrugged. "It's all there. I keep very accurate records—you know that. Just read the listing."

He hardly needed to; nothing on the little screen of the card came as a surprise to him. Not now. McNihil scrolled across the tiny words and numbers, the black marks like legible flyspecks beneath his fingernail. Beside the kid's name was a coded list of properties, old thriller copyrights of Turbiner's early writing days; McNihil was familiar enough with the account at the agency to recognize them without using the hyperkeys. He knew which titles matched up with the numbers: they were all the ones that the Wyvitz kid had been peddling.

McNihil drew his fingertip to the end of the line. The date for the licensing of the copyrights was barely forty-eight hours ago, the day that he'd gone up north on the rim to take care of this business. To do this favor for Turbiner. There was even a time stamp for the transaction: exactly when he'd been sitting in the theater with the kid.

They were watching me, thought McNihil. "They" being the ones Turbiner had been working with, cooperating on setting up this little sharp-toothed trap. McNihil already had a good idea who they were.

"The kid didn't know." McNihil looked up from the card and its info. "Did he? You used him."

A moment passed before Turbiner gave another nod. "Somebody did." He reached over to take the card from McNihil. "I wasn't in on that part."

"I'll just bet," said McNihil, "that the timing is exactly right on this one." He laid the card in Turbiner's outstretched hand. "A short-term licensing of your copyrights—what, ninety days?"

Turbiner shook his head. "Thirty. I don't like to let go of them for too long." He opened his wallet and tucked the card back inside. "If I can help it."

"And it was all set up to go through with the push of a button, I imagine. Soon as they saw how the deal was going to go down with the kid."

A nod this time. "They got it on tape." The wallet returned to Turbiner's hip pocket. "I've seen it. You know, you really should've checked around for surveillance gear. Even before you walked in there."

"Well, I guess I didn't know." McNihil leaned back against the couch's upholstery. "I didn't know what I was walking into. I thought I did. But I was wrong."

"You were wrong." Turbiner's agreement was a simple stating of fact, uninflected by emotion.

"Because if your records there are correct—"

"They are," said Turbiner. "Unfortunately."

"Then that means I murdered the kid." He could feel his heart opening up, as though to some perfect, damnable grace. *So this is what it feels like,* thought McNihil. *Absolutely.* He could almost understand how people got into it, enjoyed the element of control being stripped away from themselves. *At least you know where you stand.* It might be rock bottom, but it was certain. In this world—he supposed it was in fact, had been all along, the kind of world that Turbiner and the ones like him had always written about—there was a certain comfort in that knowledge. "And I thought," said McNihil with the barest fragment of a smile, "that I was doing you a favor. Something I didn't have to do, but just because I wanted it that way. *Por nada*—or maybe just because I liked your books."

"Actually, you did do me a favor." Turbiner picked up his own glass and then set it, empty now, beside the other one on the low table. "I got paid for the rights. Not by the kid, of course; as you said, he didn't know what the hell was going on. He got used as much as you did. But the people who set the whole deal up—they had to pay me."

"Not just for the rights, though. They paid you for keeping quiet. At least until I was through getting connected over."

"But you're not through," said Turbiner. "There's more to come. Once somebody is in your position, there's *always* more to come."

McNihil didn't need to be reminded about that. Even though there was still a part of the Wyvitz kid living, the cortical matter imbedded in the trophy cable, the little wanna-be pirate was legally dead. Or illegally, as the case now seemed to be. If the kid had had the rights to the old Turbiner titles licensed over to him—even if the kid hadn't been aware that he had the rights, even if he mistakenly believed he was a thief and was bragging about it—then carving him up for the desired bits wasn't a sanctioned agency operation. It was as much murder as if McNihil had gone out on the street and put the muzzle of his tannhäuser against the brow of the first person he ran into, and pulled the trigger.

Real bad news for someone like him; fine distinctions like this made the difference between being an asp-head and an asshole, someone who'd stuck his foot so far into it that there'd be no extraction short of sawing it off at the hip.

"You know . . . I was ready to leave a while ago." McNihil pushed himself up from the couch. "Now I'm way ready." Whatever buzz had been imparted by the alcohol had burned out of his system; a cold sobriety, cheerless as a gray post-insomnia dawn, crept through his veins. "It's been . . . *interesting* talking to you. I don't think we'll be doing it again anytime soon."

"I can understand that." Turbiner nodded slowly. "This sort of thing is pretty corrosive on friendly relations."

No shit, thought McNihil. There were other things he wanted to ask the man, things he could've said to him. But now there wasn't time. By the sheer force of will, whether it left him one-legged or not, he'd managed to get both himself and the surrounding universe started up again; McNihil could even sense his heart speeding up, as adrenaline trickled into its fibers. Which meant that if he started running, the things pursuing him would kick into high gear as well.

How much of the actual substance of time was left to him, he didn't know. McNihil supposed he'd find out soon enough.

"Take care of yourself." Halfway between the flat's living area and the front door, McNihil stood and gave a nod toward the other man. "You'll have to. After this, I won't be doing it for you." He buttoned his jacket, as though in expectation of the chill winds he'd find outside. "I'm gone."

"Don't leave just yet." Another voice spoke, from the mouth of the unlit corridor that ran to the back of the flat. "As a matter of fact, we'll really have to insist on your staying."

It was the voice he'd been expecting to hear. McNihil brought his gaze up from the figure in the sweet-spot chair. "Harrisch . . ." He nodded slowly. "Why am I not surprised?"

Still seated, Turbiner glanced back over his shoulder. "Should I take a walk?"

"Why bother?" Bearing his unpleasant knife-blade smile, the exec sauntered out into the living area. "You've been so helpful already; I'm sure you won't be in the way. Besides—" Harrisch gave a shrug. "You live here, after all."

McNihil heard the front door open; he turned and saw other corporate types, a pair of them, come in. Not execs like Harrisch and the ones who'd been there that other time, standing around the late Travelt's wide-eyed corpse. But thugs, refrigerator-sized and similarly intelligenced. They came to a halt, forming a wall with cheap suits and badly knotted neckties between McNihil and the exit. Small sullen eyes below bullet-headed brows fastened onto him and waited.

"Well . . . I'm not going to connect around." McNihil looked over at the smiling exec. "If I were carrying, it'd be different. But I left the tannhäuser at home." He tilted his head toward the others, now standing with their arms folded across their bulky chests. "So you don't need to drop the weight on me."

"No . . ." Harrisch made a show of considering the remark. "I don't *need* to . . ."

The thuggish types moved in and proceeded to take McNihil apart. Nothing fancy, sheer muscle and knuckle; knees to the kidneys, sweat-smelling forearms thick and corrugated as tree trunks, hard enough across the face to screw his neck around, a panoramic quick flash of the flat and its inhabitants as the one holding him up let go at last.

He could almost admire their professionalism. *Control,* came a fragmented thought inside McNihil's head; spread out on his back, he gazed up at the flat's conduit-laced ceiling. He was waiting for the blood to fade out of his vision, as though the hallucinated spinning he sensed could draw it away from his eyes. They'd hurt him just enough to make their point—or Harrisch's—but not so bad that he wouldn't be able to function again.

Which was Harrisch's point. The exec leaned over McNihil, looking down at him. "That was for being rude. The last time we got together." Harrisch let his smile fade, his voice dropping to serious as well. "When I offer somebody a job, I expect that person to give it a lot of thought. And not just lip off to me."

One of the company thugs gave McNihil a kick in the

ribs. He could recognize the nature of the boot, its steel toe
reinforced with a lump of depleted uranium; the guy would
have to be big to walk around in footwear like that. The
impact was enough to shock the contents of McNihil's gut
into his throat, but he managed to hold down the sour rush.
Rolling onto his side, he spat a red wad of saliva and a broken
tooth fragment out onto the floor.

"And then—" Harrisch squatted down and looked him
straight in the eye. "I expect him to *take* the job."

McNihil shook the last anesthetic fog out of his head.
The bruises sang up along his nervous system, but he could
string his thoughts together again. "It's going to be hard
. . . for me to get much work done for you . . ." His
mouth had filled with blood again; he swallowed thick salt.
"If I'm up on murder charges."

"Don't worry about that. I'll take care of your legal
problems. You won't even have to think about them."

That was what he'd expected the deal to be. If Harrisch
and his crew of corporate lawyers couldn't get him off entirely, they could delay it long enough for him to die of old
age. Or at least long enough for him to figure out some other
escape plan.

"You know where we are." Harrisch stood up, holding
the thin smile over him again. "We'll expect you bright and
early."

McNihil closed his eyes and listened to the heavy tread of
the pair who'd worked him over, heading toward the door
and pulling it open for their boss. The door closed behind
them and the flat was silent; another moment, and the stereo
started up again. The chorus sang once more of resurrection,
but he didn't believe them.

"What I'm not completely sure about . . ." McNihil
spoke slowly, tasting the trickle of blood down his throat.
"Is why you." He raised one swollen eyelid and brought

Turbiner into focus. "Why should you help connect me over."

In the sweet-spot chair, Turbiner dangled the remote control in one hand. "No special reason." He gazed toward the invisible orchestra between the speakers, rather than at McNihil. "Or just the usual ones. They made me an offer. I needed the money. I'm not getting a lot of reprints; nobody's really interested in old books these days." He shrugged. "You know how it is. You gotta make your copyrights valuable one way or another."

McNihil lifted himself painfully into a sitting position on the floor. He wiped red onto his palm from his chin. The strange thing was that he couldn't even manage to hate the guy.

At the door, McNihil stopped as he laid his hand on the metal knob. "You know . . ." He looked back over his shoulder. "This is why nobody reads your old books . . ."

Slouching in the chair, Turbiner raised his head. "Why's that?"

"It's that *noir* thing." McNihil pulled the door open, letting the darkness of the corridor outside stretch out before him. "People don't have to go into your books for that world anymore. Now they live in it all the time."

After a moment, Turbiner slowly nodded, then turned back to the music.

McNihil stepped out into the corridor and silence. But only for a moment; then he turned and walked back into Turbiner's flat.

Silence became total, the music over, when McNihil reached behind the stereo equipment and ripped the new trophy cable loose.

"Now that's just connecting petty," said Turbiner, disgusted. "That's just vindictive."

"That's right, pal." McNihil rolled the cable up into a

tight coil and stuck it in his jacket pocket. He didn't feel any better for having done it, but he didn't feel any worse.

"You know . . . that really does belong to me." The old writer followed him to the door. "It's from the violation of my copyrights. *My* books."

"Yeah?" McNihil halted; he glanced over his shoulder at the other man. "Your books, huh? And what would somebody like me do to you right about now, in one of your books? Tell me that."

Turbiner didn't have an answer. Or did, but didn't want to say it.

"Believe me," said McNihil. "You're getting off lucky." *Luckier than me.* He pushed the door open and walked out, trying not to limp too much.

PART THREE

Der Hölle Rache kocht in meinem
Herzen,
Tod und Verzweiflung flammet um
mich her! . . .
Zertrümmert sei'n auf ewig all Bande
der Natur . . .

Hell's revenge boils in my heart,
Death and Despair blaze all around me! . . .
Let all ties of Nature be forever broken . . .

—The Queen of the Night's Aria,
from *Die Zauberflöte*
by WOLFGANG AMADEUS MOZART,
libretto by
EMANUEL SCHIKANEDER

(1791)

FOURTEEN

A MOVIE VISION OF GLAMOUR AND LUST

fl re you sure this is where you want to be?"

"That's funny." McNihil found that funny, because the place looked like a doctor's office. A real one, the way doctors' offices looked in the movies stitched inside his eyes. He could've used a doctor, even though forty-eight hours or more—hard to tell in the perpetual night McNihil saw—had passed since Harrisch's thugs had handed his ass to him. He'd spent the time since that occasion lying on top of the narrow bed in his unkempt apartment, in the same clothes he'd been wearing then and was wearing now. Every once in a while, he'd gotten up and headed down the hallway to the bathroom, he'd had to lean his arm and forehead against the wall above the toilet to remain standing. His urine had gradually faded from the color of cabernet to a light rosé. Even now, his bones and a good deal of his bruise-darkened flesh still ached; it'd been a big accomplishment to even try shaving before venturing out and coming to this place.

There was another reason he found the question funny. "Somebody else," said McNihil, "asked me that exact same question, just a few minutes ago."

"Really?" The man sitting on the other side of the desk wasn't a doctor, not a real one; not even an imitation of a fake one. He was just an Adder clome, the commercial cloned replica of the maybe-fictional character that was always found running one of these Snake Medicine™ franchises. For his costume, the Adder clome wore a doctor's white examining-room coat and had a prop stethoscope tucked in the breast pocket. The brow of his hatchetlike face, the surgical embodiment of the corporate image, was encircled by a headband with that mysterious metal disk on it, which always indicated somebody was a doctor in the old movies. "Who was it?" the Adder clome asked.

"You're not really interested . . ."

"No," said the Adder clome. "But tell me anyway."

"It was a woman," said McNihil. "In a bar." He didn't need to tell what kind of a bar it'd been. He wasn't sure, himself. He'd let himself fall so far beneath the opacity of his vision, into the world leaking out of his eyes, that any details from the other world had been completely obscured. There wasn't any less pain to feel that way, but it seemed more appropriate, at least. He could exist as a beat-up operative on a cracked leatherette barstool, downing a shot and a chaser, in a place with beer spilled on the floor and neon flickering like ionic discharge in the mirror behind the nameless bottles. "Ironic discharge," he said.

"What's that?"

"Nothing," said McNihil. "A misfire in the brain. Some of the connections are still loose." The woman in the bar had

offered to tighten them for him. Or a similar service. She'd
sat down on the stool next to his, so close that he'd been able
to tell the difference between her flesh and his, through the
thin layers of his trousers and her skirt. Which was all right; it
fit in perfectly with the world he saw, that he preferred to
see. McNihil had brought his gaze up from the depths of his
glass and looked over at her. What he'd seen had made him
both remember and forget the cube bunny that had so briefly
visited his shabby apartment. The woman had been the ultimate barfly, a movie vision of glamour and lust, like the
dream of what nameless women in a dive bar should look
like. Complete with luminous golden hair in a soft curve
along one side of her face, à la Veronica Lake. But with a
radiation as bemusedly intelligent as Lizabeth Scott, giving a
hard time to Humphrey Bogart in the '47 classic *Dead Reck-
oning*. Her gaze, the unhidden part of it that McNihil had
been able to see, was colder than his dead wife's.

"You have to watch out for ones like that," said the
Adder clome. "It'd be better if they wanted money. Then
you could deal with them. But all they want is trouble."

McNihil couldn't tell if he'd spoken anything else aloud.
About the woman or the bar. But then, the man on the
other side of the desk, sitting beneath nonsensical framed
diplomas—he was supposed to know. It was his business to
know things like that. If someone possessed bad longings,
kundalinic warps, guiltily sweating desires, this was the place
to have them read out. As though the non-doctor could
spread one's heart open on his palms and decipher the
quivering lines that spelled out life and destiny.

"That must be why she came my way." McNihil leaned
back in the office's smaller chair, lacing his fingers together
across his stomach. "She figured I had enough to spare."

"Why did you come here?"

McNihil didn't answer. He was wishing himself back in
the bar, preferring it to this place, with its smells of disinfec-

tant-swabbed chrome and blood-soaked cloths thrown in the plastic bags marked For Biological Waste Only. Which was what he felt like at the moment, but he was trying to maintain.

The ultimate barfly, the woman with the cold dead gaze, had asked him the same thing. To which he'd replied, *I've got an appointment nearby. Just killing time till then.* Her hand had smelled of nicotine and lust as she'd touched him, stroking the side of his neck as she'd leaned toward him. *Is that,* she'd asked, *all that you want to kill?*

"I asked you a question." The Adder clome's voice tapped at McNihil's ear. "We're not going to get very far if you don't tell me."

McNihil pulled his darkened gaze away from memory and toward the white-coated figure. "You know already," he said. "Why I'm here. Harrisch told me to come and see you."

"Oh, well . . . sure." The Adder clome shrugged. "I've done a lot of work for Harrisch over the years. Him and the rest of his pals over there at DynaZauber. Regular customers. Anything they want, from one of those silly little iris tattoos on a secretary's ankle, to a Full Prince Charles job, we're happy to provide. We've got a corporate account set up and everything."

"I bet you do."

"Standard business practice." Leaning back in his leather-clad swivel chair, the Adder clome made a cage of his elongated fingers. "There's a certain natural . . . shall we say? . . . *interface* between their operations and mine."

" 'Natural,' " said McNihil, "isn't the word I would've used."

"Already with the sarcasm." A slow shake of the head. "And we hardly know each other."

"I know you well enough." Slouched in the smaller chair, McNihil gestured at the office's confines, at the ersatz

medical diplomas and the regrettably accurate photographs of
procedures and results. "I've been inside a Snake Medicine™
franchise before You Adders are all alike."

"From one reptile to another, then." The white-coated
figure's gaze sharpened, stripped of a layer of civility. "I
suppose an asp-head such as yourself has a certain . . . au-
thority in these matters. You should already know, then, that
if we're all alike, it's because we're *supposed* to be that way.
There are standards we have to maintain that come right
down from the SM headquarters itself. Not just hygiene re-
quirements and surgical quotas and the advertisements we
run on the shellbacks—all that stuff." Whatever nerve had
been struck was wired to simmering grievances. The Adder
clome's voice tightened to a rasp. "The only reason I'm
taking the time to meet with you at all is because
DynaZauber bought out a fifty-one-percent share in the SM
holding company. Now that Harrisch is on our board of
directors, all of the franchisees have got his boot on their
necks. We either produce or the head office's goons will
come out and strip the signs off the building."

"I'm bleeding for you." McNihil was past taking consola-
tion in other people's miseries. "So we're working for the
same guy. Do I look overjoyed about it?"

The Adder clome moodily pushed a blunted scalpel
around on the desk. "All right; so Harrisch sent you here.
And I'm supposed to talk to you. About what?"

"Beats me," said McNihil. "I wasn't provided with an
agenda for the meeting."

"What's the job you're doing for Harrisch? Maybe that'd
help, if I knew that." The Adder clome picked up the metal
instrument and pointed it toward McNihil. "You at least
know that much, don't you?"

"I'm looking for something . . ."

"Everybody who comes in here says that. One way or
another."

"Something that belongs to Harrisch. Or to DynaZauber." McNihil saw a triangular section of his own face reflected in the scalpel's blade. "There doesn't seem to be much of a distinction between those two anymore." The polished metal made his face look just as bright and hard. "But it's something he lost. Or it got lost for him. And he wants it back."

"Oh?" The Adder clome showed no sign of doubting him. "Mr. Harrisch does, indeed, set great store at not losing . . . things. Just what kind of thing are we talking about?"

McNihil shook his head. "You don't need to know."

"Now that," said the Adder clome, "is very much like Harrisch. Rather a private individual. Where did this certain item get lost?"

"That's why I'm talking to you." McNihil tilted his head back, a gesture indicating the office's door and the nocturnal world beyond the Snake Medicine™ franchise. "It's out there in the Wedge. That's where it got lost."

"Ah." An understanding nod. "Lots of things get lost there. That's where things go to get lost. Badly lost. You know what I mean."

For a moment, McNihil wondered if that was some kind of personal comment. How much would some Adder clome, a scrabbling sexual-services franchisee, know about what had happened years ago? Not much, maybe even nothing at all, unless their mutual employer had filled him in.

"I'm a little surprised, though," continued the Adder clome. "I wouldn't have thought Harrisch would be hanging around that particular zone. Either in person, or by proxy. So to speak."

"Knock it off." Irritation filtered through McNihil's voice. "I don't need all the cute stuff from you."

"Doesn't cost anything extra." The Adder clome had a creepy nonsmile that he could easily have picked up at the DZ executive suites. "I throw it in as a bonus, as part of my operating-table-side manner. You might as well try to enjoy it; like a lot of things in this world, there's no escaping."

"That's why I don't live in this world." The faces in the framed photos regarded McNihil with a blank absence of envy. "Or at least I try not to."

"I thought that was the case." Leaning across the desk, the Adder clome studied McNihil's eyes as though they were soft, inanimate objects. "When you're in the business like I am—the surgical business—there's little signs, indicators that professionals can pick up on." He sat back in his chair. "You must've had it done a while back."

"How can you tell?"

"The work's too good. You can hardly see the stitches around the corneas." The Adder clome sighted through his tangent fingertips. "The only problem is the one you already know about. This world is what you can't escape from. It always comes seeping back into your little private existence."

McNihil had said as much to the cube bunny not too long ago. *So it must be true,* he thought now. Or true enough—he'd had that proved to him at the last place he'd been before walking into the SM clinic with Harrisch's card tucked in his jacket pocket.

"That woman," said McNihil. "At the watering hole down the block. Sitting on the barstool next to me." The whole dimly lit space had been empty except for the two of them, as she'd leaned her cigarette breath and decaying-rose scent toward him—she'd been proof enough. Even in that black-and-white gloom, with the shadows leaking out of McNihil's eyes and stacking up in the bar's corners like strata of negative ghosts, the ultimate barfly's unsunned flesh had glowed with pale mycologic fire. But not all her flesh; some of it had been cut away and replaced, probably right here at this SM franchise, perhaps with the scalpel with which the Adder clome idly played. An oval window, in that space bounded by her throat and her naked shoulders, the bottom edge touching the first swell of her breasts; a soft window, made of some bio-mimetic polymer that was so expensive it got weighed out by the microgram like all the better or at least more effective drugs. McNihil had seen the price sheets on that kind of thing; the woman's elective surgery hadn't come cheap. She was either seriously in hock or rich enough to enjoy trolling around the Wedge's blurred circumference.

"Yeah, that's one of mine." The Adder clome nodded when McNihil reached that part of the description. "I've done a lot of work on her." He smiled. "She loves it."

"I could've guessed that much." McNihil had known, as he'd looked at the woman in the bar, his gaze moving away from her dead empty eyes, down to the window above her breasts, that if he'd touched that transparent substance, it would've felt as warm and soft as real flesh. That if he'd closed his eyes, his hand at least might've been fooled. But he didn't close his eyes. McNihil had left them open, and had seen, like smooth white coral under the slow rising and falling of a blood-temperature ocean, the woman's bones. Faintly luminous, laced with fine red threads: manubrium, clavicle, trachea, and farther behind, deeper in that soft ocean, the herpetoid segments of her spine.

Or would you rather be somewhere else? The next thing the woman in the bar said to him, with a turn of her head and a lowering of her dark lashes over the cold emptiness of her gaze, so that the message being radiated in a tight beam at him was made even clearer.

McNihil hadn't replied, but had gone on looking into the depths of her exposed body. To where the elegant, blackened engraving had turned her bones into fragile scrimshaw. The black, swirling lines were only slightly wavered by the flesh substitute's gelatinous layers. Rococo motifs, thorned rose stems and sickly fin-de-siècle lilies twined to frame a motto written in an antique Teutonic font.

I RUNNE TO DEATH, AND DEATH MEETS ME AS FAST

He'd let himself be drawn closer to her, so that he could bring his lips close to her ear.

" 'And all my pleasures,' " he'd whispered, " 'are like yesterday.' "

The remembered darkness of the bar ebbed a little, as the Adder clome's voice cracked the thin eggshell of McNihil's thoughts. "Quoting John Donne to barflies—" The voice was brittle with sarcasm. "There's a wasted effort."

"Is it?" McNihil looked up. "It's always worked really well for me."

"Gotten you this far." With one finger, the Adder clome balanced the scalpel against the desktop. "I suppose that's a good thing." The scalpel dug into the already marked-up wood. "You should've picked up on that number at the bar. She's not the kind that needs a lot of sweet talk. Some of my other clients have told me that she's a real experience. The kind that leaves marks. Inside your skull."

"Sounds great. But I'm working right now." McNihil felt like knocking the scalpel skittering across the desk. "Maybe some other time."

"And that's why you came here. Not to reminisce about the chances you've let fall out of your hands. So get on with it." The Adder clome used the scalpel as a pointer again. "Ask me a question, why don't you?"

"All right," said McNihil quietly. "Why did Harrisch tell me to come here?"

"I told you already. I don't know." The Adder clome scratched the side of his face with the blade's point, leaving a white mark on the skin. "Obviously, it wasn't to get information from me. You know too much already."

"What's 'too much'?"

"More than I know," said the Adder clome. "That's too much. You haven't even told me the name of this person.

The one who lost Harrisch's precious whatever-it-is. Or what happened to him."

"He's dead. And his name was Travelt."

"Ah." The doctor admired his reflection in the scalpel. "Now it becomes a little clearer. I do believe I remember something about a certain Travelt; one of Harrisch's associates, a junior exec over at DynaZauber. Right?"

McNihil nodded. "You've got that one."

"I did a little job for this Travelt—"

"He came in here?"

"No," said the Adder clome. "I don't think I ever set eyes on the man. No, I did something *for* him. A commission on his behalf, a business gift ordered up by another party. By Harrisch, in fact."

"You put together the prowler." That made sense to McNihil. "That Harrisch and the other DZ execs gave to Travelt."

"That's right. Though I don't know how much anyone else at DynaZauber had to do with it." The Adder clome gave a shrug. "It all seemed like Harrisch's little project. A personal thing. Harrisch is, as you might've already noticed, a hands-on kind of executive."

"That's him, all right." McNihil regarded the other man with a flat, level gaze. "But you're not telling me anything I don't already know."

"Well. There you go." Another false smile floated up on the narrowly angled face. "You see? It's just like I told you. You know too much already. Or if not enough—that's not my problem. You're the one who's supposed to be finding out things. That's your job, isn't it? What Harrisch is paying you for. Why should I make it any easier for you? Even if I could." The smile curdled into a sneer. "I don't think that's what Harrisch is paying *me* for, why he's underwriting our time together—"

"He's paying you? For this?"

"Of course. He's a businessman who understands a fellow businessman's problems, the need for a little cash flow.
There was a transfer of funds—nothing too big; nothing I
can retire on—before you came over here. For unnamed
services to be performed for a certain individual named
McNihil." The Adder clome rolled the blunt scalpel between his palms. "That's you, right? You told me as much.
So what is it you'd like me to do for you?"

McNihil looked at the man with welling distaste.
"There's nothing you can do for me."

"Oh, I think otherwise." The Adder clome's voice took
on a steel edge, as though by some transference of essence
from the surgical tool. "You're underestimating the range of
services we provide in this establishment." Even his eyes glittered as brightly. "Maybe it's been a while since you've paid
one of our franchises a visit. There's all the old classics . . .
and some new ones."

The Adder clome's spiel washed up against McNihil, like
the waves of a polluted ocean.

"Frankly," said the Adder clome, "you look rather unmarked to me. For somebody who's had all your, shall we
say, life experiences. You're a blank slate. But that was always
the word in old-fashioned tattoo parlors, sailor. We can do so
much more for you now. Just in terms of your skin. We can
put your biography on your flesh, in as many animated chapters as you'd like—so you could read yourself in the mirror, if
you wanted to. Everybody's favorite book. Wouldn't that be
nice?"

"Not particularly." McNihil glared back at the other
man. "There are plenty of parts I'm still trying to forget."

"Then we'll make shit up for you. Whatever you want.
The rise and fall of the Roman Empire, in detail so fine
you'll need a microscope to shave. Actually, I've done that
before; more than once. It's more popular than you might
think among the extreme crowd, especially some of the later

chapters where the decadence gets way rotten and shiny. Who was the empress who regretted that she only had three altars at which she could receive libations for the gods?"

"Theodora," said McNihil, unamused. "Sixth century A.D. The wife of Justinian, in Constantinople. A lot of people think it was Messalina, the wife of the earlier Claudius, but they're wrong. It was Theodora."

"Very good." The Adder clome nodded, impressed. "You have a historical sense. That's pretty uncommon these days. Most people I see in here think that the world started with their first orgasm."

No, thought McNihil. *They're wrong. That's when it ends.* He could hear the gates of Eden clanging shut, never to reopen.

"Or maybe," continued the Adder clome, "you'd prefer not wearing history on your body. Keep it all up here." One finger tapped the side of his head. "Perhaps you'd prefer something a little more purely fictional. All of *In a Budding Grove*—or something shorter? *Les Fleurs du mal;* that's a popular choice. Or perhaps something more esoteric." The Adder clome's voice shrilled higher and tighter. "*The Tragical History of McNihil, and How His Wife Died, Kind Of.* That might be one you'd find entertaining."

McNihil's heart slowed with the weight of the murderous impulse it carried. "That's good," he said slowly. "Harrisch must've told you an awful lot about me. You know . . . I'm almost flattered. By all the attention."

"You're not, actually—I know that much, too—but never mind." The Adder clome's words were still sharp-edged. "You're more of a private person. We can accommodate that in our services as well. We could do you up with all sorts of advanced materials. Inks that would appear only under certain light spectra, or that would phase-change into visibility at certain times of the day . . . or hours of the night. Whatever suits you best. We could insert pixel devices in your skin, with their own little batteries and programming, that would flicker at staggered subliminal rates just right, so that only the filters in your eyes would be able to decipher them. Now that should be right up your alley. Harrisch told me about how you like to see things that other people don't."

"If you saw what I'm seeing now," said McNihil, "you wouldn't be flattered."

The Adder clome didn't appear to have heard him. "Something more elaborate?" The mocking sales pitch rolled on. "Something that moves? Animation is easy for this kind of thing. You could have the empresses Messalina and Theodora getting it in every orifice, full-motion rock 'n' roll with digitized close-ups and a soundtrack with adjustable gain and auto-muting, for when you get tired of all the moans and groans. You could have the Bayeux tapestry marching down your spine, if you wanted, done in early Chuck Jones style. Whatever you want." The Adder clome gestured expansively. "Perhaps you want something for people to remember you by. Something that rubs off on them, like the smell of your sweat. We can do that. Your tattoos don't have to just stay on your own body, not anymore."

"So I've heard."

"Then you've heard right," said the Adder clome. "We can put an imprint cloning function in the design itself, hard or soft."

That last detail was new to McNihil. "What's the difference?"

"Hard is, anybody you sleep with—anybody you go skin-to-skin with—they walk away with a permanent transfer of your tattoo onto them. Permanent, at least, until they come to someone like me to take it off. Different with the soft ones; those fade on their own, on whatever schedule you have me set. Something for the ladies . . . or the boys. Or whatever. Your choice. Though that's not the end of the

possible variations. Your chosen design, whatever you have
us embed in your skin, could pass from your body to your
lover's, leaving your skin a blank slate again. And that other
person could pass it on to a third, like a message on a slip of
paper, going from hand to hand, body to body. A black
ghost, molecule-thin, traveling the world. Perhaps with a
little alteration with each exchange, a little play on Newton's
third law of thermodynamics and its application to information theory. So that when it comes back to you, eventually,
you don't recognize it and you do, all at the same time."

"I've already seen ones like that," said McNihil. In bars
like the one he'd left a little while ago, establishments that
served as the floating front doors, entrance points into the
Wedge. A dimly lit vestibule into that darker world, inhabited by its own retinue of circling regulars, like low-rent
cosmic debris unable to escape the gravity tug of a sweat-
smelling black hole. Too fascinated by what was down inside
there, that they couldn't slip off the barstools and push open
the yieldingly padded doors and walk out into the pitying
sunlight; too scared by the same, too scared to take the pink
dive in their own fragile flesh and find out what was at the
bottom. "It was a sacred heart of Jesus—at least that must've
been what it started out as." McNihil could see it in his
memory, on the biceps of some informant the Collection
Agency had been working with a long time ago. "The guy
told me it'd had a 'Mom' banner unfurled below. But when
it came back to him—hard to say how many other bodies it'd
swum across—it wasn't a heart crowned with thorns anymore, it was a kidney wrapped in an extension cord, and the
banner had become a three-word testimonial for hemorrhoid
suppositories."

"That guy was luckier than most." The Adder clome
laughed. "I've seen worse."

A few more bad examples floated across the screen of
McNihil's memory. Not all of them had been warmed by

blood; the morgue technicians at the Collection Agency had always complained of one of the risks in handling corpses taken from anywhere near the Wedge, the cold remains of those who'd dabbled in that lifestyle. *Death-style,* corrected McNihil. The techs took all the latex-gloved precautions possible, to keep any traveling tattoos with still-active battery charges from swarming off the decorated stiffs and onto their own hands and forearms.

Something even less substantial, the memory of rumor: he'd also heard that some of the morgue techs, inclined by their profession to ghoulish enthusiasms, had found ways of coaxing the tattoos, like flat black spiders, into big autopsy specimen jars, the kind with lids that screwed down tight. There was supposedly a storage room in the Collection Agency headquarters' basement, with shelves lined full of the jars, the thin-film images of the harvested tattoos slowly turning and writhing in their half-lives. A glass library of heavy neo-primitivist abstract designs, Sea Dayak and Maori, and traditionalist hearts and flowers and the mournful Rock of Ages, withering like plucked blossoms, black and fragile . . .

"Though somehow," said the Adder clome, "I don't think you came here for a tattoo. Of any kind. You're not the type that wants to achieve even that much immortality."

"So why did I come here?" McNihil left his hands flat upon the arms of the chair. "You seem to know so much more than I do."

"Why don't you go back to Harrisch and ask him? He gave you the job." Another shrug from the Adder clome. "He should tell you what it is he wants. Or . . . maybe he already did. Maybe he showed you."

What Harrisch had shown him; that was something else that came up in memory, from someplace just under the surface, where it had been cruising like a patient shark. A shark with a capital letter *V* upturned for its mouth, teeth black instead of glistening white, the angled point and serifs sharp enough to cut flesh. *My flesh,* brooded McNihil. The same way the dead Travelt's flesh had been sliced. Sliced and marked. . . .

"No," said McNihil. "Forget Harrisch for a moment. Let's go on raking over what you like to talk about. You and these complicated tattoos that you do here at the clinic. Your specialty, I take it."

"Like I said. We do all sorts of things here." The Adder clome leaned down, putting his hand on one of the desk's drawer handles. "I could give you a brochure and a price list, if you wanted."

"These tattoos . . . the traveling ones. That go from person to person. You do them just on human skin, or do you do them on prowlers as well?"

The Adder clome straightened back up in his chair. "I do them on both. Real or fake, human or prowler; it's basically the same technique."

"So if it was the right kind of tattoo, a human could pick one up from a prowler. The image, whatever it was, could pass from a prowler's skin and migrate over to a human's."

"No." The Adder clome smiled tolerantly and shook his head. "It doesn't work that way. Same technique, different materials; just because a prowler *looks* like a human being, that doesn't mean it's made out of the same stuff. You can't use the same inks and pixel embeds, the same programming and energy sources. You use the human stuff on a prowler, it'll just fall off like carbon dust, make a nice little mess on the clinic floor. On human skin, prowler tattoo materials go septic; they die and rot off like some kind of dermatitis or leprosy. A traveling tattoo has a basic self-preservation instinct wired into it, down at the molecular level. It looks for a suitable environment to migrate to, a place where it can go on living, in its own way. So a human tattoo wouldn't even be tempted to cross over to a prowler, and vice versa. Like

two different species; you can't just cut and paste from one to
the other."

"I didn't think you could," said McNihil. "I thought
that was the way it worked." He leaned forward, hands
against his side of the desk. "So tell me——" His voice stayed
level and drained of emotion. "What was the tattoo you put
on Travelt?"

"I didn't." The Adder clome spoke without hesitation.
"I've got a pretty fair recollection of that client. And he
never stepped into this clinic. I really never saw him at all.
Harrisch ordered up the prowler for him, and when it was
ready, we sent it on to the address we'd been given. And
there weren't any tattoos on it, either. I remember that
much."

"So why was there a tattoo—a big one—on Travelt's
body, when Harrisch showed it to me?"

"The guy must've wanted one." The Adder clome
looked unimpressed. "Plenty of places where he could've
gotten one put on. Could've gotten it at some other Snake
Medicine™ franchise, for that matter. He didn't have to
come here to get something like that."

"You're right. I bet Travelt didn't come here." McNihil
leaned farther across the desk. "But I also think you know
where that tattoo came from." One hand shot forward and
grabbed the front of the Adder clome's shirt, bunching the
thin fabric into the center of McNihil's fist. McNihil drew
his arm back, dragging the Adder clome across the top of the
desk. "And how he got it, who gave it to him—the whole
thing."

"What—what're you talking about?" The Adder clome
struggled like a gaffed fish. "I don't know anything—"

"Now you're really pissing me off." McNihil lifted his
white-knuckled fist up against the Adder clome's chin, rocking back the terrified face. "Tell me. What was the tattoo?
What did it look like?"

"You're crazy—" Papers and a cup full of pens scattered across the floor, as the Adder clome's arms flailed out to the sides. He gasped for breath. "You—you're out of your mind—"

"I've been told that before," said McNihil. "And that was before your pal Harrisch started leaning on me. So now you should be really scared about what I might do." The chair fell back as McNihil stood up, dragging the other man flopping the rest of the way across the desk. "You should've been scared *before* you started jerking me around."

The Adder clome's hands scrabbled futilely at the knee pressing him to the office's floor. "I don't—I don't know anything about the tattoo—"

"I'll give you a hint." McNihil still had his fist tight beneath the Adder clome's throat; with cold precision, he lifted his other one and brought it hard across the side of the man's head. "Does that work for you?" He wiped the spattered dots of red from his knuckles, onto the lapels of the white coat. "It's a memory thing, isn't it?"

"All right . . . all right . . ." Both of the Adder clome's hands had seized onto McNihil's wrists, holding fast as though to keep from drowning. "I'll tell you . . ." A red bubble swelled and burst at his lower lip. "It was a letter . . ."

"That's right," said McNihil. With the ball of his thumb, he smeared the blood across the Adder clome's chin. There was enough to have written the letter on the man's face, if he'd wanted. "A great big letter."

"*V,*" said the Adder clome. "It was the letter *V*." He gasped and swallowed, the hard labor of his lungs slowing. The panic in his eyes went down a notch, as though he'd surmised that McNihil wasn't actually going to kill him. "Done in a rather . . . ornate style . . ."

"You don't have to describe it." McNihil shifted his crouching weight back, easing up on the other man. "I've

seen it. I just wanted to know whether you had." He un-
clenched his fist; the back of the Adder clome's head
thumped against the clinic office's floor. "And if you didn't
put it there on Travelt—and I believe that part, all
right—then it would follow that you're in thicker with Harrisch than either you or he would like me to know about."

"That's it," the Adder clome said hurriedly. He nodded
as he propped himself up on his elbows. "Harrisch showed
the tattoo to me—"

"Where? When?"

A trace of the ebbing panic showed again in the other
man's eyes. "He . . . he didn't actually show me. Harrisch
told me about the tattoo, what it looked like . . ."

"Bullshit." McNihil backhanded the Adder clome, hard
enough to snap his head to the side and push his shoulders up
against the angle of the wall. "If you were in so tight with
Harrisch, you wouldn't have hesitated to tell me. You don't
do much to avoid self-promotion." McNihil stood up, looking down at the Adder clome. A tooth in the other man's
mouth had cut one of McNihil's knuckles; he wiped the
saliva and blood against his trousers. "So there must be somebody else you're in with. Somebody you wouldn't want
me—or Harrisch—to know about."

"I don't know what you're talking about." A sullen defi-
ance tightened the Adder clome's discolored face. He
hunched himself into a sitting position, back to the office's
wall. "I've got a nice little business going here." He rubbed
his palm against his swelling lip. "Why would I want to get
involved with anybody else?" He managed a ghastly, red-
specked smile. "I've got enough troubles already."

"Not as many as you will have," said McNihil, "if you
don't come straight with me." He fell silent for a moment, a
few seconds that stretched on through the hands of the clock
on the wall and returned to fill the space between one heartbeat and the next. It had happened before, usually in con-

nection with some surge of adrenaline in his bloodstream,
like that produced by taking the Adder clome to the floor.
Suddenly, McNihil had the sense of the world he saw, the
black-and-white vision capsuled in his eyes, having become
realer than real, truer than the dull world beneath the
perceptual overlay. The opaque film, the net of bits and
pieces from ancient thriller movies, deepened as McNihil
stood in the middle of the Adder clome's office; he could
feel it stretching out past the door and beyond the clinic's
walls, a tide of bleak, rich images flooding through the streets
and lapping up against the shadowed buildings. *No,* he told
himself. *It's the other way around.* An ebbing tide, a false ocean
being drained; the world he no longer cared to see was
swirling down into a subterranean reservoir of lies, as the real
world emerged with a few wet strands of seaweed clinging to
the rocks.

If they had eyes to see, thought McNihil. He was almost
convinced that anyone could have looked out of the window
at this moment, and seen this darkly perfect world. *But
they're still blinded.* Real time had ended somewhere in the
early 1940s; this other stuff, the shoddy substance of the
cheap-'n'-nastiverse that people so foolishly believed in . . .
what did it matter? McNihil felt as though his hand had
poked through a curtain made of some flimsy synthetic fabric and had found coarse wool and smooth cotton beneath,
the stitchery of God's tailor shop.

"Are . . . are you all right?"

McNihil didn't open his eyes so much as let his interior
sight shift focus, from the gelling world outside to the clinic
office's rummaged interior. He saw the Adder clome looking up from where he crouched on the floor; the expression
on the man's face showed he was wondering whether
McNihil was about to flip out even more violently, or
whether he was connected-up enough that a quick escape
was possible.

"I'm fine." McNihil reached down and, as reassuringly as possible, took the Adder clome's hand, pulling him upright. The vision he'd been granted was already fading, leaving him with a certain exhausted peace. "Don't worry about it." He stood the Adder clome up in front of himself and patted him gently on the cheek. "But I'd like to think that we understand each other better now. That's important."

"Oh . . ." The Adder clome rubbed his throat, where McNihil's fist had been jammed. "Oh, yeah. Right." He quickly nodded. "Yeah, we understand each other."

"Because what I'm getting from you—" McNihil held a single finger in front of the other man's eyes. "Is that you really do know more than you've been letting on. To either me or Harrisch. Now . . . Harrisch isn't here. Right? So we don't have to worry about him for the moment. About what he thinks. And you don't have to worry about me getting you in trouble with him. I don't work that way. Besides . . ." He let his own smile show. "What would there be in it for me? Better we should let our little . . . understanding remain a secret. Right?"

The Adder clome didn't look any less scared because of McNihil's soothing tone, as he gave another fast nod. "Sure—"

"Good." Even with the adrenaline leaching out of his bloodstream, the world McNihil saw still seemed real, or at least real enough to work with. "So why don't we start by you telling me exactly how you know what some dead guy's tattoo looked like. Where—or maybe who—you got that info from."

Silence. Another fear shifted behind the Adder clome's eyes.

"But I know that already," said McNihil. "You found out from her. From Verrity." McNihil tilted his head, studying the figure in front of him. "Naturally, you would—because you're working with her. And that's what you don't want Harrisch to know."

"If DynaZauber hadn't put the screws on," the Adder clome said sullenly, "I wouldn't have had to go with her. But DZ's cut the margins so tight—"

"You don't have to explain it to me." McNihil shrugged. "Either I understand already, or I don't care. All the same to me. Besides . . . I don't really think it's a money issue. People get involved with Verrity for other reasons besides profit. That'd be too rational. Verrity deals with the irrational side of things."

"True enough," said the Adder clome. "I wish . . . I'd known that sooner."

McNihil could hear the bitterness of regret in the other man's voice; it touched a string tuned to the same pitch inside himself. "I know how you feel. I found out too late, myself. That's the problem with self-destructive behavior. All the benefits are front-loaded; the bad shit comes after." He brushed a dark speck of dirt from the shoulder of the Adder clome's white coat. "But getting back to specifics," he said. "This is why you were connecting around with me, isn't it? All that talk of figuring out why Harrisch sent me here in the first place, and then your little list of services and products—that was all just stalling for time. Right? You were hoping maybe I'd get so tired and disgusted that I'd just go away. Without getting what Harrisch had already ordered up."

"You're so sure about that." The Adder clome had regained some of his composure. After dabbing away a trace of blood below his mouth, he smoothed his jacket's lapels. "If that's the case, why don't you tell me what Harrisch wanted you to get from me. Or maybe you don't really know."

"Oh, I know well enough. I know what Harrisch is pushing for. What he's been pushing for all along." McNihil felt a cold rock form and harden in his chest. "That's what the real job is. Harrisch knows that the only way to find out what happened to Travelt—what happened to Travelt's prowler—is for somebody to go where the prowler went. Down in the Wedge."

The Adder clome's gaze shifted away nervously, then inched back toward McNihil. "That's right," he said. "Harrisch wants you to do the pink dive. He wants you to go down there, in your own body. Your own flesh. Not by way of some proxy; not with a prowler bringing back the information to you." The Adder clome's voice went low and intense, as he laid a hand on McNihil's arm. "*This* is what you'd use." The hand squeezed tight through the sleeve. "Nothing between you and the Wedge."

McNihil didn't push away the other man's grip. "That's not a very inviting prospect."

"Some people—some of my customers—would love to do it. If they weren't afraid."

"They've got good reason to be."

Inside the office of the Snake Medicine™ clinic, the air temperature seemed to drop a few degrees, as though from a night breeze too soft to be felt. McNihil's skin prickled at the sound of his own words, the skin of his arm contracting tighter beneath the Adder clome's hand. *Good reason . . .* He and the Adder clome knew what that was. Death, mainly, and not in a particularly pleasant way. McNihil's colleagues at the Collection Agency, the ones who'd been part of the operation years back against Verrity, weren't the only ones who'd gotten chewed up by the Wedge's seductive teeth. There were still bloodied bits and pieces washing up on the shore of McNihil's memory, if not his conscience.

The Adder clome dropped his hand. "You're right, though." He nodded slowly. "That's what Harrisch has wanted all along. Or at least since Travelt was found dead.

How else is he going to find out what happened? Or get back his . . . property."

"More that than the other," said McNihil wryly. "Harrisch couldn't give a rat's ass about what happened to Travelt. Something of his got lost, and he wants it back. That's all. And he thinks I can go get it for him."

"But not without my help. Not without what he paid me to do for you."

One more thing I know. McNihil regarded the Adder clome for a moment longer. "There was something else . . . about Travelt's tattoo. It wasn't just a letter *V.* There was a banner with a word, some kind of a name in it." McNihil tilted his head to one side, watching the other man. "*Tlazoltéotl.* You know what that means?"

The Adder clome returned a gaze somewhere between suspicion and offense. "Maybe . . . there are some things you shouldn't try to investigate."

The clome's response brought back a memory. Of a room even darker than this one, with himself and one other in it. McNihil had gone to the Bishop of North America and Central America by Proxy, asking questions and getting not much in the way of answers. The word *Tlazoltéotl* had turned up there as well, on the screen of the bishop's monitor. With the same attitude on the part of the bishop as McNihil had caught just now from the Adder clome. Like some religion, it seemed to him, with observances both shame-filled and fiercely devout.

"I don't have a choice," said McNihil. "About whether I investigate or not. I have a call."

That hit the mark. He saw the resentment behind the Adder clome's eyes shift to grudging acceptance. "Maybe you do. I'm not the one who'd decide about that."

"And who would be? Tlazoltéotl?"

The Adder clome was silent for a few seconds. Then his words were soft, almost a whisper. "You're a lucky man,

McNihil. More than you know. You'll come out on the other side of your questions . . . or you won't. Either way, things will be different for you."

"I already knew that," said McNihil. "But you still haven't told me what the word means."

"Don't worry." The Adder clome smiled. "Where you're going, you're likely to find out."

"All right." McNihil knew there weren't any more answers here. "Get out your knives."

FIFTEEN

COLD-EYED FINANCIAL TRIAGE NURSES

The burn ward at the hospital smelled of disinfectant and the pumping cylinders of sterile machines. *I wonder what it smells like to him,* thought Harrisch, watching the asp-head walk down the white corridor toward him. In that world that McNihil walked around in, saw all around himself, the deep monochromatics of old and forgotten movies layered over the bright, shiny, and uninteresting real world . . . Harrisch supposed the hospital odors might be translated to simple carbolic acid and iodine and hot, soapy water. The new stuff, most of which was manufactured in some DZ subsidiary factory, worked almost as well.

"You tracked me down," said Harrisch, smiling as the other man approached. "See? I knew you still had it."

"I'm not in the habit of losing things." McNihil looked
tired, his face stiff and puffy, as though from bad sleep and an
alcohol-toxic liver. "Unlike some people."

Harrisch felt his own brain stall, unable to produce even
a minimal retort. The hospital's whispering silence and industrial atmosphere oppressed him; he would rather have
met up with McNihil anywhere but a place like this.
McNihil's suggestion; it struck Harrisch as being typical of
the gloomy bastard. Corporations like DynaZauber, and the
execs in the boardrooms, couldn't afford to be as dark and
antilife as some twisted little independent operator with a
history and agenda of self-defeat. *It's a Darwinian thing,* Harrisch figured. Only the corporations and the execs who
embraced life, swallowing it whole in their sharklike, all-
devouring mouths, survived in this world. Any other one, he
wasn't interested in.

"You look like hell," said Harrisch.

"That's how I feel, pretty much." McNihil prodded the
side of his face with one fingertip, like a sculptor testing the
consistency of wet clay. "I thought maybe around here, I
could bribe a nurse and score a little relief. Maybe a little
morphine or fentanyl. Even paraldehyde would take the edge
off."

"You gotta be kidding." With a quick laugh, Harrisch
shook his head. "You're talking ancient history. Nobody
makes that stuff anymore. There's no money in it." The DZ
pharmaceutical division worked full shifts every quarter, tag-
ging different atoms on their old formulas, generating new
patentables one step ahead of the knockoff communes down
in Belize. "And morphine," he mused aloud. "*Jeez . . .*"
Years ago, routine shots from the commercial rent-a-spy
satellites had passed across Harrisch's desk. Sand and airborne
rust drifted through the withered Afghani and Southeast
Asian opium fields, the dry poppy stalks victims of Sahara-
like desertification and market-demand shifts profounder

than any changes in global weather patterns. "You'll have to update your habits, if that's what you're into."

"I've found a new kick." Rainwater dripped from the bottom of McNihil's coat; a few clear drops clung to his waxy face. "Over at that little establishment you sent me to."

"Ah." Harrisch nodded, a degree of satisfaction cutting the unease the hospital evoked in him. "You've been talking to the good doctor. You must have found him to be . . . helpful."

"Very."

Harrisch leaned forward, examining the other man's face more closely. "You know," he said after a moment, "I was hoping for rather better results than this. I can still see you. I mean . . . if I look away from you . . ." He shifted his gaze to the corridor wall as if to demonstrate, then looked back toward McNihil. "Then I've still got a clear picture of you in my mind. That's not how it's supposed to work."

"We're not done yet." McNihil rubbed the side of his face; he looked like somebody just risen from the dentist's chair, flesh numbed by Novocain. Harrisch wondered if the guy was feeling any pain at all, or whether that had been all talk for sympathy. "Your doctor just got started," said McNihil. "There's a time gap between the first setup and the final stages. Just enough time, actually, for me to take care of a little business. Like coming over here to talk to you."

"What's there to talk about? You know what your job is."

"True enough." McNihil gave a slight nod. "But maybe we need to talk about payment."

You poor stupid bastard—Harrisch tried to keep pity out of his own gaze. For people to get paid, they had to be alive after the job was done. He hadn't even bothered filling out a pretty-cash voucher on McNihil's account.

"No need to worry," said Harrisch. "You'll be taken care of."

He didn't expect a smile from McNihil, and he didn't get one. "Let's go in here and talk." McNihil pushed open the door to one of the burn ward's intensive-care chambers.

"You know . . . I don't find this a good working atmosphere." Harrisch had let himself be shepherded into the cramped space, as though the other man's suggestion had held some inarguable force. As the door sealed shut behind them, he'd started to find it hard to breathe the filtered air, his lungs binding from some deep atavistic dread. "Maybe we could find someplace else . . . like down in the cafeteria or something . . ."

"Don't let it get to you." In the room's semidarkness, McNihil stood right behind him, voice whispering almost directly into his ear. "Somebody getting traumatically connected-up is just a natural part of life. It's no big deal."

"Easy for you to say." Harrisch felt nausea moving around in his guts like a wet rat. The sonuvabitch probably wasn't even aware of the burn-ward chamber, experiencing it, in anything close to its dismal reality. In that other world inside McNihil's eyes, the whole hospital probably looked like some benign and comforting environment, with white-suited doctors with stethoscopes dangling around their necks, nurses with air-pillow shoes and wing-starched hats, all trotting around dispensing their healing mercies. *He doesn't see,* thought Harrisch with a sudden rush of envy. The medical technicians in their full moon-suit antibiocontamination gear, square faceplates tinted dark and unidentifiable, moving around a factory with anesthetized bodies for workstations, shadowed by the similarly masked insurance agents and HMO accountants with their key-membrane clipboards and expenditure-review videocams, whispering on tight-link headsets with the cold-eyed financial triage nurses monitoring the taxi-meter gauges on the respirators and other clicking, sighing pieces of life-support equipment—the corridors were so thick with the cash-cure-or-kill types that it was amazing that the reality-blind McNihil could even make his way past them.

And what did he see on the other side of the transparent infection barrier? Some old-fashioned hospital bed, probably, with a crank at the footboard and a paper chart with a hand-drawn red line, a jagged little mountain range, hanging from a hook. And in the bed, something else from those crappy old movies that nobody watched anymore, a human form wrapped up head-to-toe in white bandages like a mummy, desexed, depersonalized, even somewhat funny-looking, a joke thing . . .

"This her?" McNihil nodded toward whatever it was he did see.

Involuntarily, as though his own head were fastened to a gently tugged wire, Harrisch looked at the living and mechanical aggregate on the other side of the barrier. Just enough of the human part's charred flesh showed, glistening with an antiseptic nurturant gel, to start Harrisch's stomach climbing into his throat.

"You know something?" He turned toward McNihil standing beside him. "You're a sick puppy. In your own unique way. You don't even know this stupid broad—not really—and this is where you want to have a little meeting." Harrisch shook his head. "Why? Is this the kind of thing you enjoy? Maybe you just like making people uncomfortable."

"I know her well enough," said McNihil, in a voice as emotionless as his in-progress face. "Or let's say I know enough about her. She told me her name was November; I suppose she picked that out herself. Something she probably thought suited her image. That's all I really needed to know. The rest I could figure out."

"Like what?" From the corner of his eye, Harrisch could still see the breathing human form inside the machines. "What did you figure out?"

"That she was your backup system. In case I didn't work

out." With his thumb, McNihil pointed to the unconscious figure. "She would've taken on your little job, the Travelt thing, if you hadn't been able to push me into doing it."

"But I did." Harrisch didn't feel like smiling, but dredged one up, regardless. "Or let's say you did. You saw reason. An offer like the one I made to you isn't anything to sneer at, these days." The smile became genuine as he regarded the other man's stiffened features. "Now you're just about ready to go. So I don't really need a backup anymore, do I?"

"Guess not." McNihil glanced toward the narcotized woman. "So this one's expendable."

"Expendable enough. It's not like there's a shortage of fast-forwards. We keep a list over at DZ, of people like her on call, for various little jobs that come up. It's a short list, with names failling off it all the time—let's face it, hers is just about to be scratched." Harrisch tilted his head toward the transparent barrier, still trying to avoid the sight beyond it. "Too bad, because she was right at the top. She'd worked her way up. First to be tapped. But we get new names. New volunteers. Wanna-be freelancers. It must be an attractive type of business. There's the basic fast-forward rush that comes with drawing on your future—I've never tried it—plus you get to run around and do violent things."

McNihil nodded. "That's a kick right there."

You'd know, thought Harrisch. "Plus," he said, "there's always the added bonus of engineering your own self-destruction."

"Maybe." McNihil glanced over at him. "But I don't think she's enjoying that part right now."

"Nobody ever does. Suicide is one of the best drugs, from a mercantile standpoint. All the pleasure is in the anticipation, and none in the realization. Regret and payment are simultaneous, but by then it's already too late."

"You've put some thinking into this." McNihil raised an

eyebrow, slowly, as though mechanically cranking it into place. "Business philosophy, over there at DZ headquarters?" An equally stiff smile lifted one corner of his mouth. "The essence of TIAC—right?"

"Very good. You've been doing your research," said Harrisch approvingly. "I was hoping you would. Maybe it'll improve your chances."

"I doubt it."

"So who were you talking to about TIAC?"

"Come on," said McNihil. "You sent me there to talk to the guy. Over at the Snake Medicine™ clinic. Your pet Adder clome. He's kind of a chatty guy, when you get to know him."

"Good." Harrisch gave a single nod. "I figured the two of you would hit it off. You both . . . have some things in common." He let his own smile widen. "Don't you think?"

"Connect you." McNihil's voice grated deep in his throat. "Even if we did . . . I'd rather be twins with somebody like that, then have to admit being in the same species with you and the rest of your DZ exec crowd. He told me all about TIAC. More than you'd probably care for me to know."

"Hey . . ." Wounded, Harrisch spread his open hands apart. "Did I hide anything from you? About TIAC or anything else? You could come down to my office and live in my file cabinet, root through my personal hard disk like a pig after truffles, for all I care. And you still wouldn't find out anything more about TIAC than I'd already told you. So it stands for 'turd in a can'; so it's a formulation of the ultimate capitalist drive, to always deliver less than what the customer believes he's paying for. So what?" Harrisch could hear his voice tensing with a righteous indignation. "That's what people like me are *supposed* to do. In the marketplace, at least, rape is the natural order of things. And remarkably popular, too, on both sides of the exchange. People hand over their money, their lives, to DynaZauber or any other corporation, they know what they're getting. They *want* to get connected; the customers are always bottoms looking to get topped, the harder and bloodier, the better. That's the dirty little secret that corporations know. The successful ones, that is."

"Whatever." McNihil shook his head in disgust. "I'm not doubting it."

"Fine. Because it's true. You might as well get used to it." A thrill of vindictive triumph flashed up from Harrisch's knotted gut. One hand's gesture took in both the burnt woman and the standing asp-head. "That's what people like you work for, whether you like it or not. At least *she* didn't walk around suffering from these boring guilt pangs—"

"Guilt's hardly what I feel."

"Good for you. So welcome back to the real world. The one in which you do what people like me tell you to do."

McNihil gazed at him through slitted eyes, the lids puffy from the first injections. "I've never left," he said in a low, taut voice. "Maybe I see a different world—I don't make any secret about that—but the reason I like it is that over here, where I am, I see things the way they really are. I see *you* the way you really are." He visibly swallowed the spit that had gathered under his tongue. "That's the way it is with dreaming. It's not dreaming at all. It's the real world."

"Then wake up." Harrisch leaned his gaze close into the other man's, almost touching the surgically hardened skin of McNihil's face. He tilted his head toward the transparent barrier. "Like you're always saying. And smell the burning corpses of your dreams. Like *she* has. Whatever dreams she's having, they're closer to the way things are in the real world than what's inside your head."

He watched as McNihil silently turned away and looked at the burnt woman. After a few moments, McNihil spoke. "How much longer does she have?"

"If your eyes hadn't been so connected with," said Harrisch contemptuously, "you could read the meters." He pointed toward the red numbers counting down on the life-support machines, though he knew McNihil couldn't see them. "This November person's drawing down the last of her accounts. She was pretty close to tapped out when she came in here, when the ambulances zipped her in from that hotel-in-flames where you left her. That's the way it is in her line of work: she was betting the farm on getting this job away from you, or on you blowing it so bad that we'd have to give it to her afterward. So she could clean up whatever mess you'd left and have herself a nice, fat payday. Which would've taken her out of the red, cleared off everything she'd tapped against her own future, and left her with num-bers written in black. A *lot* of numbers."

McNihil glanced over at him. "It's worth that much to you? Even if she'd been the one taking care of the job, instead of me?"

"Sure." Harrisch nodded. "What can I say? Maybe we're just sentimental types over at DynaZauber. Corporations are heirs to that old military mind-set, now that there are no armies anymore: we take care of our dead, we don't just leave their corpses out on the battlefield." He knew he was talking bullshit—McNihil probably knew it as well—but it didn't matter. The asp-head was already on track, wired into his fate, by this point; there were just a few details to be nailed down before McNihil would be on his way, diving pinkly down into the Wedge. "We would've been happy to pay good money—to anyone—for the results we want."

"You've got a corpse already," said McNihil. "If that was all that was on your mind, you could've buried Travelt and gone on with your business. Your TIAC business. Except it's not just TIAC anymore, is it?"

"What're you talking about?"

"Come on." McNihil's shoulder brushed against the contamination barrier, sending ripples through the transpar-

ent membrane. "Like I said before. That little Adder clome
at the Snake Medicine™ clinic that you sent me over to
see—he's a real talkative sort. More than you might even
have expected. He told me all sorts of interesting things."

A new sense of unease percolated through Harrisch's
remaining nausea. "Like what?"

"It's not TIAC now. Your canned turd is ancient history." Something less than a smile turned the corner of
McNihil's mouth. "A whole other acronym. A little more
exotic-sounding. Almost oriental . . . but not quite the
same. TOAW—with a *W* on the end. Right?"

The unease flashed to anger, like a match on spilled gasoline. "You're not supposed to know about that."

"You wanted me to find out stuff." McNihil glared
straight back at him. "You can't complain now, just because
I'm doing the job you wanted me to do. If you want the lid
taken off the box, you'd better be happy with what somebody else finds in there."

"TOAW," said Harrisch with teeth-gritted fury, "is not
any of your business."

"It wasn't any of your little Adder clome's business, either. But he knew about it."

"I'll take care of him later." *Connecting sonuvabitch*—Harrisch didn't know exactly to whom he was refer-
ring, inside his head. The clench in his gut tightened, a
response to the specter of losing control over the situation.
"He's my problem, not yours. Plus . . ." His brain finally
dropped into gear, producing the right line to take. "Let's
face it. The guy was lying to you. He's deranged; it's probably one of the inevitable hazards of the business he's in.
Somebody like that, with the kind of work he does—there's
no way he wouldn't wind up nuts. Inventing stuff to tell
people like you. It's all crap. TOAW—there's no such thing.
Not really."

"Sure. That's why that blue vein on your forehead is

about to break open." McNihil emitted a quick, harsh laugh. "Then again, if you're going to work yourself into a stroke, you're in the right place for it. Want me to call a nurse in here?"

Harrisch ignored the other man. For the time being; his thoughts had sped up, sorting themselves out, in regard to what McNihil had just told him. If some sort of leak had sprung open, in the form of that nonstop blabber over at the Snake Medicine™ clinic, then that would have to be shut down, and soon. When he got back to the DZ offices, he'd have to arrange for a damage-control team, a crew of silent heavies, to make their way to the clinic; whatever was left after their operation, including the Adder clome, would be in pieces small enough to be swept up with a dustpan and broom. No big loss, especially to the DynaZauber bottom line; the division would have another SM clinic—with an Adder who could keep his lips zipped—up and running in a matter of days. The customers would hardly be inconvenienced. *Connect 'em anyway,* thought Harrisch. The lag time between a bunch of perverts' desires and fulfillment of the same was not a big issue for him.

Though what would also have to be determined—Harrisch saw it now—would be where the Adder clome had gotten his information. The TOAW operation files were locked down tight inside DynaZauber, with only a few of Harrisch's most-trusted subordinates having even the most rudimentary access. *If one of them has been talking,* vowed Harrisch, *his ass is mine.* Or the researchers down at the DZ neurology labs—it could've been a white-coat directly on the payroll, even though they were all supposedly laced up with various secrecy and nondivulgence agreements. Some of the top researchers, the ones with the most TOAW pieces inside their heads, had death-pact employment contracts—the DZ human-resources department had paid plenty for the constitutional-rights waivers on those—or somewhat

grislier surgical-extraction modules already wired into their
skulls. Unauthorized talk would bring about tissue-loss results ranging from idiocy to corpsehood. For somebody in
the labs to have spilled, the person would have to be either
suicidal—not impossible; long-term TOAW work tended to
corrode morale among even the most blithely scientific—or
high-pressured by outside forces. *One of our competitors? Inside
or out?*—Harrisch kept a short list inside his head of enemies
belonging to other corporations, rivals in the various DZ
branches, and divisions not directly under his control or ade-
quately in liege to him. Any one of those names could be
seducing or leaning on the TOAW technicians; if somebody
inside DZ, they could've learned the techniques from watching Harrisch himself, the way he'd cracked McNihil. Harrisch supposed that was something of a personal tribute, but
it still meant ferreting out the parties responsible and elimi-
nating them, one way or another, either shipping them off to
the Kamchatka regional office or laying them in the ground
with bloodied lilies clenched in their teeth.

Anyway, decided Harrisch, *it doesn't matter right now.* That
was all housekeeping stuff, things that would have to be
cleaned up later. The nausea ebbed lower in his gut, like a
brown sea's low tide, when he considered just how well
things were going. If a hospital's human charcoal ward wasn't
his favorite place for a conference, so what? McNihil
wouldn't even have wanted to come here to talk if he
weren't caught on this particular hook, too tight to wriggle
free.

"You're hosed," said Harrisch aloud. He enjoyed saying
it. "Those burning corpses should just about be cinders by
now." The seizure of corporate poetry in his soul overrode
any doubts about whether the asp-head still dreamed or not.
"You connecting jerk." Fierce adrenaline was as good as any
white-powder pharmaceutical. "I could've met up with you
in the boneyard, if that was what you wanted, and it still

wouldn't have changed anything." These psychological-war-fare ploys were useless, at least when they were directed at him. "I don't care what you know about TOAW. If you know anything at all."

"Simmer down," said McNihil. He glanced over his shoulder toward the room's door. "You'll have the hospital security up here in a minute."

"Who cares?" The seizure had morphed into a spasm of self-congratulatory elation. The feeling returned, the one he'd had when he'd seen McNihil bruised and bleeding on the floor of that old writer's place. Absolute control, the future on rails, speeding directly into the embrace of his heart. *What God feels,* thought Harrisch as he closed his eyes. *When He's rolling dice at some infinite Vegas.* One of the arch-angels could've handed Harrisch a free drink then, with his life written on the little paper parasol sticking out of it, and he wouldn't have been surprised. "I can deal with them, the same way I've dealt with you." He wondered vaguely if it was possible to get drunk off repeated hits of adrenaline. If so, it was happening to him; Harrisch felt the same giddiness and lack of regard for whatever happened next. Whatever he might say to this poor sorry bastard standing next to him . . . it didn't matter. *Because I've already won,* thought Harrisch. Pleasure beyond smugness filled his body, like the bub-bling light of the transfigured saints. And—almost as nice—the other man had lost. McNihil not only didn't see the way things were in the real world—the asp-head was effectively blinded by his cut-up-and-stitched eyes, with their optical load of crappy old movie sets and shadowy light-ing—but he was blind as well to what had happened to himself. He'd been connected over, poisoned and contami-nated—*And he doesn't even know it,* thought Harrisch with complete satisfaction. McNihil had embraced blindness as a way of life; the real world wasn't good and darkly poetic enough for him. He had to have something else, see some other world more to his liking, with retro Warner Bros. shadows and—even more retro—tough-outside, tragic-inside women, just as if those had ever existed anywhere at all except in the movies. That was what he'd wanted, and so now he'd have no reason to complain about the consequences of his own self-generated ignorance, the chosen way of life turned to one of death. "You just don't know . . ."

McNihil studied him coldly. "Know what?"

"Never mind." Harrisch shook his head, letting his rhapsodic interior monologue fade away. "You'll find out soon enough. That's your job, isn't it? Finding out things. You should be grateful I've given you this opportunity, to do what you're so good at."

"Yeah, right." Beneath McNihil's hardened features, the now-vestigial muscles shifted, subtly indicating disdain. "You still didn't answer my question."

"My apologies," said Harrisch, still feeling amused. "Perhaps I didn't appreciate your burning thirst for knowledge. There's so much you want to know, isn't there? What question was it, that I haven't satisfied your mind about?"

"What I asked," growled McNihil, "was how much time does she have? November . . . how much longer before they pull the plug?"

" 'Pull the plug'? You can see something like that?" Harrisch laughed. "I thought maybe you'd just have some notion of a nurse or an orderly, maybe even a doctor, coming in here and holding a pillow over her face, just to put her out of her misery. As for how long it's going to be before that happens . . ." He glanced again at the numbers running down on the machines' various gauges and dials, visible on the other side of the contamination barrier. What little money remained in November's accounts was leaking away as though from a slashed wrist. The image came to Harrisch's mind of the numbers in November's palm, the stigmata of all fast-forwards, zipping by so fast that they blurred into a red, illegible smear, seeping through the bandages and dripping onto the floor beneath the chrome-barred bed. "Let's just say . . . a ballpark figure . . . that the next time you've got a chance to come by here, when you've finished your job, whatever bed you can see will be empty. Or there'll be some other mummy wrapped in gauze lying in it. That's what you see right now, isn't it? Well, it'll be the same package pretty much—people are always falling into the flames—but it'll be different contents inside. What's left of this one will've been crumbled up and sluiced down the drain by that time."

He watched McNihil silently regarding the human figure hidden beneath the gurgling machines. The stiffened angles of the other man's face made it impossible to read whatever thoughts might be working through McNihil's skull.

"I'll make you an offer." A few seconds had passed before McNihil had turned back toward him. "A deal."

"You're hardly in any kind of negotiation position."

"This one isn't negotiable," said McNihil, voice flat and inexpressive as his face. "You won't have any problem with it, though." He gestured toward the burnt woman. "I'll go her bill."

Harrisch stared at the asp-head. "What're you talking about?"

"You heard me. Call up the hospital's accounting department. Or have one of your little minions do it. I'll put up the cash for November's therapeutic procedures here. Anything the doctors figure she needs—I'll pay for it."

"With what?" Harrisch barked an incredulous laugh. "You don't have that kind of money, either. We're talking about major tissue replacement here. Major, nothing; *total* is more like it. At least as far as skin goes—she doesn't have a lot left. Even you should be able to see that. The DNA sample coding, the substrate matrices, accelerated regenerative foster-maps, all that epidermal plate-farming—and that's just to get the raw materials ready. After that comes all the surgery, the grafting, the stitching, the stitch-ablation work, the laser spackling, the blood-vessel resassignments, the neural patterning . . . let me tell you, it's not just some simple tuck-and-roll upholstery job that's involved with somebody in her condition."

"You seem to know an awful lot about the subject."

"Connect, yeah." Harrisch gave a slight shrug. "DynaZauber's medical-products division makes most of the disposables, the active gels and the tissue-replication forms, that are used in burn wards like this. *When* they're used—and we're talking about a big 'when.' We also crank out the billing software for those procedures, so I know what they cost. Your pockets aren't that deep."

McNihil spoke without looking over at him. "What about yours?"

"What do you mean?"

"You heard me." McNihil swung his flat gaze around. "There's a bonus involved, isn't there? For this job I'm doing for you. You can't just let me off the hook; you have to pay me as well."

"True." Harrisch nodded. "Technically, you're still on the Collection Agency's list of operatives. So compensation has to be according to the agency's fee schedule. So okay, you'll get paid for it. Big deal."

"It is," said McNihil. "Big. I already checked into it. This job—matter of fact, anything to do with the Wedge and with Verrity—it's on the Collection Agency's red list. Those are the hot tickets; hot in the sense that the agency would rather not pick them up at all. They'd rather have them forgotten, instead of people like you poking into them and risking more embarrassment for everybody concerned. So the agency's going to charge you a premium—a nice big fat one—on this job. And according to the last labor agreement between the agency and its operatives, ninety percent of that premium comes from the contracting party—that's you, or DynaZauber, at least—and goes straight to me. When I complete the job."

"*If* you complete the job."

"Ah." One of McNihil's eyebrows creaked upward. "That's not how you talked when you were first pushing me to take this on. Back there at Travelt's cubapt. That was when you were so confident about me being able to pull this off. Remember?"

"I remember fine," Harrisch said grudgingly. "But anything can happen. Anything bad. You're the right man for the job, but Verrity handed your ass to you before. She can do it again. My hiring you is just a matter of playing the percentages; there's no sure thing in this universe."

"The hospital knows that, too." With a tilt of his head, McNihil indicated the chamber's doorway and the brightly lit corridor beyond. "That's another thing I checked on my way in here. They're into speculative ventures, at least on a limited basis. Kind of a gambling mentality—for a twenty-five-percent surcharge on all fees and services, they'll do the full job on November here, the grafts and skinwork, the blood and neural microsurgery hookups, everything. A brand-new skin, shining like a baby's—that's a pretty good deal for her. Maybe they'll give her the dead bits, the ashes in a jar, to keep on her mantelpiece at home." He managed a brittle laugh. "Snakes get to shed their skins—so I've heard; I don't know from personal experience—so why shouldn't people? They need it so much more—don't you think?"

What the connect . . . Harrisch gazed at the other man, as the pieces fell into place. Slowly, because he couldn't believe it. "Let me see if I've got this right," he said. "You want to pay for this person's skin grafts and all the rest of the stuff they can do for her in this place, and you want to take it out of the bonus for the job you're doing for me? That's it?"

McNihil nodded.

"You've gotta be crazy." Harrisch stared at him in amazement. *How could anyone be so connecting stupid?* "You realize what that would mean?"

"Of course," said McNihil, voice calm. "It means that when I'm done with this job for you, there won't be a lot of cash going into my pocket because of it. The money will already have been spent here at the hospital, on this November person's skin grafts and therapy."

"That's what happens, all right . . . *if you pull it off.*" A fierce glee seized Harrisch, as the implications unfolded to him. "You'll have *everything* riding on this, McNihil. Because as soon as I sign over the bonus payment to the hospital, and they accept it and do their work on spec, then your ass is mine. Totally—way more than it is already." He had difficulty restraining the triumphant emotions compressing the breath from his lungs. "Because from that moment, you'll be in debt to me—"

"To DynaZauber, actually."

"Whatever," said Harrisch impatiently. "Believe me, your fate'll be in my hands and nobody else's. I'll have your file *welded* to my desk. Because of my deep personal interest in you, pal. Either way that it goes with you on this job, whether you track down and return our missing property or whether you slam straight into Verrity again and she takes you apart like a cheap watch—either way, I've got you. Succeed or fail, I'll get my money's worth out of you."

"Then I guess," said McNihil with a cool absence of emotion, "that I better succeed. Just to keep you off my ass."

Like there's any chance of that, thought Harrisch as he took his tight-cell phone out of his coat pocket. The poor bastard just didn't know. "Yeah." He spoke after dialing. "I'm going to need a contract notary up here. Immediately."

He'd left a couple of assistants sitting in the car, over in the hospital's multileveled parking garage. Within minutes, the elevator doors at the end of the corridor slid open, and the DZ flunkies had crowded into the burn-ward chamber. "You won't be able to say you didn't know what you were doing." Harrisch watched as the new document, a three-way agreement between the asp-head, DynaZauber, and the hospital, was recorded and sealed. "This is as close to full disclosure as it gets." Or as it needed to; he figured that McNihil would find out soon enough how thoroughly he'd been connected. That in fact and potential there had never been any way for him to win. *All he could do,* thought Harrisch with satisfaction, *was make things worse for himself.* He'd seen people engineer their own defeats before—the late Travelt was a perfect example of that—but never to such a complete degree as this. It was like watching someone screw down the lid of his coffin from the inside.

As soon as the contract was registered, the numbers on the financial-status monitor gauges changed, scrambling up into the high digits of temporary solvency. On the other side of the transparent contamination barrier, the readouts flicked from red to green, indicating a surgical Go condition. The almost-subliminal murmur of the pumps and tube-connected machines went up in tempo and pitch, getting ready for long-delayed action; from the corner of his eye, Harrisch could see the burnt woman's body contract, the large muscles tightening with the first unconscious rush of injected adrenaline, then relaxing as better and more expensive opiates ticked up in synch. Submerged in junkie oblivion, she awaited the knife. Harrisch heard the prep carts approaching, their black wheels rattling on the outside corridor's hard and glossy floor.

"That's fine." McNihil spoke first. He turned away from the contamination barrier and its dreaming captive. "I'd love to stand here and talk with you some more. But I've got work to do."

Harrisch stepped, letting the other man slide in front of him, toward the door. The two flunkies had already retreated out into the brighter light; they watched in silence as the asp-head strode past them.

"Good luck," called Harrisch. His raised voice trembled small waves on the vertical barrier. "You'll need it."

McNihil's hardened face glanced back at him. "No, I won't," he said. He turned and continued walking toward the elevators.

SIXTEEN

THE SMILE OF THE ULTIMATE BARFLY

You're back." The woman smiled at him. "I kind of expected you would be."

The smile of the ultimate barfly was part of the establishment's furniture, as much as the dim lights reflected in the mirror behind the bottles, as much as the long-enclosed air that crawled in and out of McNihil's throat. "Where else could I go?" His thumb sank into faux leather as he pulled out a stool and sat next to her. "This is the only game in town."

She laughed, holding up a glass with ice cubes rattling like polished bones, their round square curves melting into brown alcohol. "You got that right, pal."

McNihil sipped at the drink that had been placed in front

of him, without his needing to ask. Bad scotch, as though from the well of indifferent souls, trickled near his heart. In the mirror, flecked with dust and something more deliberate, he could see himself and the bar's space, both endless and claustrophobic. The black-and-white world in his eyes had set up tight and hard, shutting out anything more recent. *No future,* thought McNihil, *for me.* The obliging deity of the universe he saw had heard that decision, made even before he'd gone into the hospital and formalized it in front of the burnt November, floating at the altar like a charred brides-maid, tubes and oxygenated hoses trailing like the ribbons of a bouquet crushed to what was left of her small breasts. That particular god had heard and had obliged far beyond what the stingy, nonexistent object of the Bishop of North Amer-ica's worship would've given: McNihil's present as well as his future had been extinguished, leaving just this dark past, both threatening and oddly comfortable. *Just what I always wanted* . . .

The barfly nudged his shoulder with her bare arm. "I wonder," she said softly, her mouth close to his ear, "just what game you're talking about."

He drew his finger through the small puddle that had been jostled from his glass. "There's all kinds . . . aren't there?"

"No." She took his hand—the darkly shining polish of her fingernails caught sparks from the mirror—and brought it to her mouth. "There's only one." Gazing up at him through her eyelashes, she licked the smoky drop of alcohol from his fingertip. "You know that."

McNihil let his hand stay caught in both of hers, like a small animal too stupid to run away, even as the trap was folding around it. His eyes had adjusted to the bar's shadows enough that he had been able to catch a glimpse inside the woman's mouth, past the diminished-spectrum red of her lipstick and white, unsharpened teeth. He'd seen the scars along the surface of her tongue, the minute roughened and healed abrasions, as though from needles that had been held in a match flame. McNihil had seen the same marks before, and often. But the last time had been in the mouth of a corpse, lying on the floor of a lux cubapt, as he'd knelt on the deep-pile carpet to make his quick, disinterested examination. Scars indicating prowler usage, the wet flesh, all muscle and sensors inserted pluglike into the socket of that other mouth, that face like a mask opening and fused to knowledge.

Face like mine, thought McNihil; if he'd taken his hand away from the woman's, he could've touched his own inert flesh, skin yielding just slightly more than the bone beneath. On the way from the hospital to this bar, he'd stopped in at the Snake Medicine™ clinic and finished up the antitherapeutic course, the needles and tiny knives, that made his face the unmemorable equivalent of a prowler's. "There you go," the Adder clome had said, sorting out his bloodied tools into their chrome trays. "The full job, on DZ's tab—you don't owe me a nickel. I'll send the bill to Harrisch." The Adder clome had glanced over his white-coated shoulder, and had smiled with satisfaction at his work. "Just as well somebody else is paying," he'd said. "The way you are now, I could never track you down for my money."

In the bar's dark spaces, McNihil drew back, bringing the woman beside him into focus. He wondered just what she saw, if anything, when she looked at him. His gaze shifted to one side, from long automatic habit, looking for some bright, shiny surface that would give him a glimpse of that other world, the one he'd gladly vacated. The bartender had left a knife beside a halved lemon; in the glistening metal, McNihil saw the same image reflected as in the mirror. A face visible as long as you were looking straight at it, but that as soon as you glanced away, dropped out of memory like a stone beneath the surface of unrippled water. *I've*

eliminated myself, thought McNihil. Without regret; he
would've paid for himself, if he'd had to. *Should've done it a
long time ago. . . .*

"Honey," said the barfly, reading his thoughts, "you
look fine to me. Better than fine. Anyway—I wouldn't have
remembered what you looked like, no matter what happens.
In this world, memory's deadweight. We can do without it."
One of her hands stroked the back of his. "Real memory,
that is. And the other kind . . . we send out for it."

That word *we* was another stroke, lighter and more chilling; McNihil felt his skin tighten along his arms. In the bar's
enclosed silence, his hearing sharpened, attuned to his breath
and the woman's. And beyond that, to the previously unde-
tectable signals of other human presences. *Or close enough to
human,* he thought. He felt like someone exploring a cave
deep inside the earth, the little beam of his attention sweeping across cold stalactites and water-smoothed rock, miles
removed from any living thing, his own clouded breath the
only sign of warmth and motion—and then suddenly, the
explorer is aware of a thousand unseen eyes in the darkness,
all watching him.

McNihil turned on the leatherette-padded stool and
looked back across the bar. He'd gotten the impression before, somehow, that the place was empty, as though he'd
managed to slide in after some hypothetical closing hour,
with just himself and the barfly keeping the faith. Though he
knew that nothing ever really closed in this timeless zone; the
flickering neon wrote its partial hieroglyphics on the streets'
wet obsidian through all the motion of clocks without hands.
The doors were never locked; the dismal happy hour never
ended. The ghostlike bartender, impeccable in his
nonperceived state, set them up without even being asked,
leaving the drinks and the faint smell of a damp bar-towel
drawn across the overlapped circles of the previous round. It
was like the Platonic ideal of a drinking hole, someplace

different from where you lived, but with no one to intrude upon the slow march and collapse of your thoughts.

Now, though, he saw the others. That McNihil hadn't seen before; he leaned his elbow on the edge of the bar and let the fit of the cave-explorer analogy settle across the floor and walls of the establishment. Birds rather than bats, though; they sat hunched forward, hands folded around their own stingily nursed drinks, silent and watchful as crows under storm-clouding skies. *Watching me,* realized McNihil; the collective gaze emerging from the bar's shadows pressed against him like a slow tide, hours away from receding.

"They knew, too." The barfly leaned close to McNihil's ear and whispered. "That you'd be back. Or maybe they were just hoping you would be."

He realized that now as well. That expectancy was what put so much tonnage into the dark figures' watching. *Waiting for me*—another handless clock was shared out amongst them, its numbers slowly pecked away. In a place like this, time was that dead substance consumed but never extinguished.

"All right." McNihil turned toward the woman sitting beside him. "What do they think I'm going to do?"

"What did you come here to do?"

"I came here . . ." He had to think about that. Not because he didn't know. But because it would be easier to say something else. *I came in here for a drink*—that'd be good. And true in its own way. Because that was the other option, that always existed in this world, the one that had leaked out of his eyes and taken tactile as well as optical form. You watched those old movies, those black-and-white visions of the past, truer than history, and it was always noticeable how alcohol ran through and beneath every scene, like an underground river. Those people always had the option of drinking their problems away, or engineering their own dooms in an even more convincing and final way by fishing with their tongues for the key that lay at the glass's bottom—*Why shouldn't I?* He'd always wanted to live in and not just see this world; maybe that was how to do it. *Dive in and drown.*

McNihil set his own half-empty glass back on the bar, without having touched it to his lips. It was an option, all right—just one he didn't have at the moment. "I'm working," he said simply. "Believe it or not." He waited for some scornful reaction from the barfly, but didn't get one. "I've got a job to do. That's what I came in here for."

"Everybody here is working." She held her glass up like a crystalline trophy. "In our own way. We all have our little . . . *jobs* to do. That's why we're here."

He had come a little closer to understanding, or admitting to himself what he already knew. "Of course," said McNihil. "You're all prowlers."

A silence fell over the bar, as though all the oxygen had been sucked out through some hidden mechanism to the night's vacuum beyond. He could feel the gaze of the shadowed figures at the tables sharpening, penetrating and judging him even more thoroughly.

"That's right, sweetheart." The barfly gave McNihil a smile of alcohol-blurred delight. "You've come to the right place. This is where *you* belong—you know that, don't you?"

"I know." *That's why I didn't see them before,* he told himself. *I didn't see them because I couldn't.* He hadn't been ready to; but now he was. He brought his hand to the side of his face, prodding the skin. Either the anesthetics he'd received at the Snake Medicine™ clinic hadn't worn off yet, or the dulling of sensation was a permanent effect of the little Adder clome's work on him. "That's funny," he murmured aloud. "I thought my senses were supposed to get sharper . . ."

"Don't worry about it," said the barfly. "That's only for *real* prowlers. Not a phony like you."

"I'm not fooling anyone?"

"You don't have to. You never did." She reached up and placed a gentle, disturbing fingertip where McNihil had dropped his hand. "You could've come here in your own face, the one you gave up, and nothing bad would've happened to you."

He laughed. "I find that hard to believe."

"Well . . ." The barfly gave a shrug of her bare shoulders. "Maybe nothing *different* would've happened to you. From what was already going to happen."

"Don't tell me," said McNihil. "You'll spoil the fun." He looked away from the woman, back toward the space leading to the diamond-padded door. Though his eyes had fully adjusted to the darkness, he couldn't make the watching faces become any clearer, any more sharply focused than they already had been. *She's right,* he thought. *I'm not really one of them. Not yet.* He supposed if the Adder clome had had some way of transforming his entire being, from human to something-like-human, his percept systems would've been completely altered as well. But just having his face worked on, the minimum hallucination and anti-gestalting cues surgically implanted—that apparently wasn't enough. Even though the clome hadn't touched McNihil's eyes with all the clinic's bright scalpels and wetly glistening hypodermics—he'd forbidden that, staying awake through the entire procedure to make sure that the black-and-white world wasn't nicked and leached out of his eye sockets—something had happened to his vision. A change; the making visible of the previously unseen. *Like ghosts dipped in glue and flour,* he thought. If somebody had invented black wheat—the odd notion struck him that maybe bread the color of ink was what they ate in this world he'd entered through the bar's tightly sealed doors.

"I wouldn't want to do that." The woman's dark red fingernails clicked like insect shells against her glass. "Fun's

our whole reason for being. That's why God put us here."
She smiled, lazily and sure. "Isn't it?"

"Some god did." McNihil caught sight of himself in the
mirror behind the stacked bottles. He could make out his
own face, all right, perhaps even clearer than before. *Before I
even went to the clinic in the first place.* He nodded slowly.
"Now I understand."

"Understand what, honey?"

"What I've become. What I was always trying to become." McNihil picked up his own glass and used it to point
toward the mirror. "An extra. Like in the old movies. That
real world I was always trying to crawl into. Because it was
real." He glanced over at the woman beside him. "You see
them and you don't see them—the extras, I mean. They
exist in that world, they're even necessary—but you don't
remember them. Just like prowlers that way; there's nothing
in their faces to snag onto normal people's memories."

"*Our* faces," said the woman. "And yours."

"Exactly. And that's just what I always wanted." The
words were fervent in McNihil's mouth. "To be there—to
be here—and to exist and watch and maybe even have a few
lines to speak. You know; to tell a real person which way to
Fourth and Main, to maybe even light a cigarette for a real
woman, the one the movie's about . . ." He closed his eyes,
imagining all he'd spoken of. "That'd be all right."

"I don't smoke," the barfly said drily. "Otherwise I'd let
you light my cigarette. If that's what you'd get off on."

McNihil stayed silent, knowing he shouldn't have said
anything at all. *Not about this, at least*—it was too close to
some other dark place, a little unentered room inside himself.
He folded both hands around the almost-empty glass, and
thought about his dead wife. Thinking without words; just
the image of her face. Which was not just snagged, but
stitched with iron threads, to his own memory.

"Like I said before . . ." The barfly stroked the back of

McNihil's neck with her cold fingertips. "It's nothing you have to worry about. Everything's going to happen just the way it was meant to." She used one nail to draw a knifelike incision, just short of opening the skin at the top of his spine. "And that'll be fun. *Loads* of it. I promise you."

He lifted his head, raising the glass at the same time and using the watered dregs in it to sluice away the vision of his dead wife's face. The lock on the door of the little room inside him remained keyless. "Great," said McNihil. The single drink, combined with some percolating residue of the Adder clome's injections and his own self-generated toxins, turned a different key in a different lock. A doorway through which he knew he was going to step, though he already knew what was on the other side. The glass splintered into shards in his fist as he slammed it back onto the bar. "Let's get going."

"Oh," said the barfly in a voice only half-tinged with sarcasm. "I *love* a man who knows what he wants." Her hand seized his once again. Tight around his wrist; tight enough to force apart his fingers. The bits of glass dropped like dice, altered to transparency and razor edges, around his elbow. The barfly leaned forward, blond hair trailing through the pool of melting liquid; a red drop fell from McNihil's wounded palm, diffusing into blurred pink. She caught the next one on the tip of her scarred tongue; the blood glistened her lipstick as she kissed the center of his hand.

"I know, all right . . ."

"Like I said—you came to the right place." In a predator crouch, the ultimate barfly looked up at him through her lashes. The red looked like black, smeared on her chin. "I can do a lot for you, baby."

McNihil nodded, letting the key turn another click farther in his heart. "I bet you can."

The mirror of her eyes held him. "We've been waiting for you," she whispered. "We've been waiting for you . . .

for a *long* time." She used the back of his hand to wipe away the blood below her lip. "It'll be worth it."

Something between fear and disgust pushed McNihil's gaze away from hers; something in which those terms no longer had a negative connotation. He just didn't want to see that appetite in her eyes, in case it was a reflection from his own. McNihil looked across the bar, across the perceived but still-hidden figures in the shadows. He could discern them well enough that he could see both male and female prowlers returning his own scrutiny. *That's what they're made to do,* he reminded himself. *Just like me.* What he'd been before, and what he'd become once again—there really wasn't that much difference between a prowler and an asp-head. They went out looking for something, the sensory treasure they'd been programmed to sniff out, and they brought it back to their masters. *Just like me,* he thought once more. Answers rather than thrills, Harrisch's lost property rather than a collection of scars and tattoos that crawled over one's skin like the black-clawed shadows of sea creatures—no difference at all, it now seemed to him.

He squeezed his fist tighter, the blood oozing wetly between his fingers. He gazed at the trickle running down his wrist like spilled ink, wondering if he'd achieved some evolutionary apotheosis by combining asp-head with prowler. *Either the zenith,* thought McNihil, *or the nadir*—it was something else that didn't matter. Further proof that everything evolved, or at least changed, one way or another. He wondered if Harrisch, if anybody over at DynaZauber, knew about this. The world of the prowlers, the subterritory of the Wedge, might be getting out of their control faster than they knew. Maybe Travelt hadn't been the first to have undergone that transference effect, the shifting of his human nature into the mask-faced, artificial receptacles. It didn't appear that the late junior exec had been the last.

"I'm glad," said McNihil, looking over again at the

woman next to him. "That you've been waiting for me." All irony had been drained from his words. "It's nice to be wanted."

"We're not the only ones." The other's presence was so close and unfolding that a perfume of body-temperature latex and soft industrial resins had drifted in the air between them. "There's somebody else waiting." The barfly both kissed and whispered into his ear. "*She's* waiting, too."

McNihil didn't need to ask her. There was only one possibility. "I'm ready," he said. The glass had been drained and then shattered; what more was left? "Let's go."

"You first." The woman looked straight into his eyes, the way someone about to plunge into a dark, still lake would. "You know how . . ."

He hesitated only a second. Then brought his hand along the side of her head, the blood from his palm seeping lines through her blond hair. He pulled her even closer and kissed her.

The woman drew back suddenly, her gaze turned to both wonder and almost frightened concern. "Your heart's stopped." She had placed her own hand against his chest, as though helping him to keep his balance in the gap between her barstool and his. "I can't feel it beating . . ."

"Don't worry about it." He couldn't keep himself away from her. "Not important," said McNihil, pulling the woman harder toward himself and his mouth.

It took a moment for the inside contact to be completed. McNihil could hear behind himself the silence of the bar's shadows and the prowlers' mingled, expectant breathing. *Just what they want*—there was time only for that thought fragment, before the spark hit.

He'd felt the woman's tiny scars with the tip of his own tongue, like deciphering a wet braille that chaptered down her throat. If he'd known how to read it, a biography in stitched flesh or a warning:

Abandon all hope

Blue lightning sizzled the insides of his eyelids, like the frayed curtains of his apartment bursting into flame.

Ye who enter here

Image rather than words filled his head, a newspaper photo of an electric-chair execution a long time ago, where flames had burst from underneath the cloth mask as soon as the switch had been thrown. In a sliced-apart microsecond, he wondered if he looked as well as felt like that, his skull wrapped in the incendiary halo of a martyred saint, fire-laced smoke rising to the bar's low ceiling.

"You gave me . . . too much . . ." Talking like one of the spidered-together junkies in the lobby of the End Zone Hotel; he'd felt, been dimly aware through the rush of sensation and memory data, the woman grabbing the front of his shirt to keep him from toppling off the barstool. McNihil's tongue felt burnt and swollen, as though he'd licked it across the terminals of a live battery. "That was . . . too big a hit . . ."

Other hands grasped him under the shoulders, lowering him to the bar's floor. Far away, in the anteroom of the world he'd just left, he'd heard chairs toppling over as the seizure had snapped his muscles tight, and more than one of the watching prowlers running forward to catch him.

They laid him out corpselike, the back of his hand flopped against the stool's chrome leg. He gazed up, still able to discern a fragment of real time through all the hurtling images that had risen into his eyes from the woman's kiss.

"I should've known . . ." McNihil couldn't tell if he'd managed to mumble the words aloud. "I should've known it was you . . ."

"That's all right," said Verrity. Her blood-streaked hair tumbled over her bare shoulder as she looked down at him. "You did know."

"I had the strangest dream," said the burnt woman. Or formerly burnt woman; that part hadn't been in her dream, but had been real. *I nearly died,* thought November with a calm lack of emotion. A good deal of the peace that passeth understanding—at least for right now, in her case—came from the medication she was still on. She recognized that icy-warm feeling, all sharp edges reduced to fuzzy nubs, that came from a skin-pouch trickling its magic into her veins. "I was floating . . ."

"Not a dream," said one of the med technicians, leaning over the arm he and the others were working on. "You were in the tank. Remember?" He looked up from his 'scope and micro-waldo'd needles, and smiled and winked at her. "You didn't look so good then. *Now* you're looking fine, fine, fine."

November rolled her head back onto the hospital's paper-covered pillow. She'd caught a glimpse of herself in the chrome flank of one of the machines—different machines than the ones she remembered from before, less scary—and had seen that she'd lost most of her close-cropped black hair. A little soft fuzz was starting to show on her patch-work scalp. *As long as they're doing all this work,* she mused, *I should've asked for a makeover.* They could've given her a cascade of shimmering Botticelli-red hair down to her butt; anything. She'd heard about the money that was making it all possible. . . .

"Tell us about your dream." One of the other white-suited technicians spoke without taking his gaze from his fiber-optic eyepiece. "Passes the time. We're going to be here awhile."

She raised her other arm, the one they'd already finished. *Does look nice*—the skin on it was all new, soft and white as a Caucasian baby's. Since genetically it was her own skin, cooked up in the hospital's tissue labs for grafting, it would have to be. With a fentanyl-induced smile on her face, No-

vember admired the craftsmanship; the stitches only showed
if she imagined them. And when she opened her eyes wider,
raising her new eyelids, the stitches faded entirely from sight.

"What I dreamed . . ." She laid the finished arm back
down upon the snowy white bedsheet. "*While* I was floating
. . . I know the difference . . . I dreamed I was falling . . ."

"Yeah, like we pulled the drain plug on you or something." The med technicians exchanged buddy-ish grins
with each other. "So you'd run down the pipes, all the way
from here on the twentieth floor."

"That's not it . . . I wasn't even here at all . . ." She
hauled the pieces of the dream out of recent memory; they
were already falling apart, as though the touch of her reborn
fingertips were enough to reduce them to sugary dust. "First
I was back at the hotel . . . you know, where I got burnt so
bad . . ."

"Do tell." The technicians continued with their work,
stretching the freshly grafted skin and laser-polishing the
joins between sections down to nothing. "How utterly fascinating."

She didn't mind their gentle teasing. More than the casing of her material form had been renewed by the surgery
and all the other expensive therapies. *It's the drugs,* she reminded herself. But maybe something else as well: there had
been a moment when the anesthetics had thinned out in her
nervous system's receptor sites, when the nurses had been
switching her from one I.V.-drip regimen to another, and
the pain had rolled over her like a train screaming its heated
engine apart, pulling her bones and sinews to tatters with it.
And I didn't even get mad—the way she would've before.
She'd lain there, wide-eyed and gasping for breath, waiting as
patiently as possible for the next batch of opiates to hammer
her into diminished consciousness. That was the beginning
of some kind of wisdom, she'd supposed. Or maybe some

other part of her, inside the baby-new skin she'd been given,
had gotten older. It amounted to the same thing.

"And I was falling there . . ." November went on recounting her dream. "Through the flames and all the beams
and stuff breaking away . . . so I guess I was just remembering that part . . ." She couldn't be sure; when the burning hotel's roof had given way beneath her, she'd struck her
head on a rusted iron girder that had seemed to come leaping
up at her from the churning interior. Things had been
mostly blank after that, a well-erased tape, until the med
techs had removed her from the sustaining bath in which
she'd been floating. That had been just like being born all
over again, and present time starting up once more. "And
then . . . and then . . ."

"Then what, honey?"

The next part was harder to figure out, to pull away from
the surrounding blackness inside her head. *Because I wasn't
remembering,* November told herself. Not dreaming, either—she realized that she had been seeing something that
was happening right now.

"I saw somebody else falling . . ." Into some other
darkness, some other flames. Flames that burned but consumed not—or if they did, consumed something other than
flesh for tinder. Flames that ran cold inside one's veins, rather
than with heat. "It was . . . him . . ."

The technicians exchanged glances with each other, their
latex-sheathed hands stilled for a moment upon her arm.
One of them looked over at her. "Who's that?"

"You know . . ." She didn't want to say his name
aloud. She didn't know why, whether it had become sacred
or just personal. "The guy . . . who paid for all this . . ."

The med tech smiled. "Your secret admirer."

"No . . . I don't think so . . ." A paper-shuffler from
the hospital's accounting department had come by the burn
ward, to explain to her the financial arrangements that had

been made—but she still didn't understand. She knew how close she had come to the bottom of her accounts; the last thought when she'd fallen through the roof of the burning hotel had been, *How the hell am I going to pay for this?* Knowing that there was no way in any hell she'd be able to, that when her money was drained away, the burn ward's sterile tank would be as well, its softly charred contents flushed down some convenient drain. And one fragmentary thought beyond that, just the hope that whatever she hit on the way down would be enough to kill her fast and clean, so the money or the lack of it wouldn't even be an issue.

That McNihil the asp-head was picking up the tab for her was clear enough—but not why he was doing it. Just a nice guy? It didn't seem in his repertoire of tunes, from what she'd been able, before the burning fall, to find out about him. And she was sure that he wasn't interested in her in any kind of physical/sexual way. He had that thing going for his dead wife, way beyond mere necrophilia. That was something November couldn't crack, only envy. Though there was some comfort in knowing that McNihil couldn't have cracked it, either, even if he'd wanted to.

She thought some more about the puzzle, while the med techs bent over their work. Whim? *He always has reasons for what he does*—they might not be good reasons, but they existed. November idly wondered what they might be, and if she'd eventually find out, when they let her go from the hospital. In the meantime, she decided not to think about the falling dream, to play it back when she closed her eyes. With the anesthetics' help, she could will perfect black clouds for sleeping, whenever she wanted.

"There you go."

November opened her eyes, lifting her head a bit on the pillow so she could see the technicians. "You're done?"

The technicians laughed, like chiming bells. "Don't be silly," said the main one. "There's a lot more to do. It'll be a while yet before you're out of here and heading home." He and the others started packing up their tools, generating more tiny metal-on-metal sounds. "But don't worry about it, sweetie. Everything's paid for, already. You know that."

"Sure . . ." She watched them wheeling their shining cart out of the burn-ward chamber. They'd be back tomorrow, November supposed. She went back to thinking about her strange dream.

First her falling—but that was just remembering—and then McNihil's . . . but falling where? She had an idea about that, but she didn't want to pursue it down into the scarier darknesses. There had been something strange about his face, too, even though she had still been able to recognize him somehow. Not so much different as just . . . erased. She had an idea of what that meant as well. *They got to him,* thought November glumly. Harrisch and that pack of his over at DynaZauber—she'd picked up on enough of their plans for the asp-head, their plans beyond just getting him to take the Travelt job, that she could tell he'd wound up pretty well connected over. *Poor bastard . . .*

The way she felt now, even beyond the sweet drugs slow-rolling from vein to spine and back out again, she would've been sorry for him. Even if he hadn't picked up the tab for the skin grafts and all the other bodily reconstruction she was undergoing. *You've gotten soft,* she chided herself. *Just as well your fast-forward days are over . . .*

She'd already decided that. *You don't get a chance like this very often.* A whole new skin, a new life, maybe even a new town—if she could find some place beyond the Gloss, or at least a part of the constantly metastasizing city that was sufficiently different from the rest. Everything that had happened to her . . . it really was like being reborn, out of the wet womb and into the hands of doctors. Even the tumbling, vertiginous passage through fire; if she beat up the metaphor a little, she could make it fit some pre-uterine notion of sexual passion, heated and consuming and all the rest. *My own?* wondered November. If so, it was

• the first time that meant anything, really, and

• some weird sign that she had given birth to herself.

Another decision, not to think about any of that, now or ever. *Too weird, actually*—she closed her eyes, letting the drowsy weight of her shorn head sink into the pillow. The lights of the chamber dimmed in response, pushing her back toward sleep.

Before that could happen, November's eyes flicked open again. She could feel a little tingling sensation returning to her arm, the one that the med techs had been working on. She pushed herself up on her other elbow, raising her newly reconstructed wrist and turning the tender flesh of her palm toward her gaze.

She didn't know what she'd see there. What they'd left from before, if there had been anything left from that other life, that other body and world she'd lived in. The stigmata of her own autocrucifixion—*If you can birth yourself, why not death yourself as well?* But in this case at least, the nails had been pulled out, letting her drop to the muddy ground at the foot of the cross.

The little black symbol was still there, but changed from ⏩ to ⏹. But that was all that showed; now her palm was empty of numbers.

There might've been a red zero, if the surgeons and the med techs had left the fast-forward implants under the skin of her hand. All her accounts, her debts and credits, taken to nothing, canceled out and put back to the beginning. If a newborn baby—a real one—had a number in its little pudgy, wrinkled mitt, that's what it would've been.

Take it as a sign, November told herself. An anti-sign, a

true zero, an absence as important as anything that could've shown there. For all she knew, the number was still on her hand. She didn't know how deep the fast-forward implants ran in the flesh; she'd been connected out of her mind when she'd had that little job done. The med techs could've left it there as a souvenir. *Maybe it's my eyes now,* thought November, *that're different.* There had been some work done on them, she knew; they'd been pretty badly damaged by the flames. The tiny knives and needles might've taken out the wolf filters that had let her see the numbers in her hand, the ups and downs of her razoring career, the cliff's-edge dancing before the fall . . .

Or maybe, she thought, *I just don't need to see them anymore.* That was why the numbers were gone. Both she and the world had changed. When you were in the zero, the grace of the zero, you didn't need to look at your accounts to know how well you were doing.

She let that notion drift away, joining the others in the darkness past her fingertips as she lay back down. It was easy to. The techs had put a long-term pouch under her ribs; the device had a photoelectric cell wired into its outermost membrane, and it responded to the dimming of the light with a little surging pulse of drowsy endorphins. November floated on the wave, to a point on the warm, gelatinous ocean inside her, where she could see the last part of the dream she'd had.

That was the strangest part. She spread her hands out on the cool, sterile bedsheet at her sides, her new fingertips counting every fine thread. The man she'd watched falling in her dream, that she'd known was the asp-head McNihil despite his not having a face anymore—in the last part of the dream, he *did* have a face. But it wasn't his. And he wasn't falling, but had landed, not on the ground or in the wreckage of the burning hotel's lobby—but in an ocean different from the one in which she floated and dreamed. A thick, heavy ocean, without waves but only slow ripples across its expanse when something, a human form, fell and struck its surface; the water was so ponderous that it didn't even splash, but slowly hollowed under the man's weight and parted, drawing him beneath the shimmering membrane . . .

Of course, thought November. She felt so stupid for not realizing it before. The heavy ocean in her dream was the sterile tank of the burn-ward chamber, which she herself had been floating in, her ashes and blackened bits slowly dissolving, before McNihil had paid her tab. Things—the real and unreal, the remembered and envisioned—always got jumbled up in dreams. That was why she wasn't surprised when she finally worked out whose face it'd been, when the falling man had hit the gelatinous sea.

It'd been Harrisch. She recognized him even without his usual sharky smile, even with the furious rage that his darkened features had shown. *Nothing,* November told herself. *Doesn't mean anything* . . .

Her eyes were already closed; behind them, she stepped through the rooms inside her head, shutting the rest of the doors and sealing in the sleep that was already there.

SEVENTEEN

TAKING A CHANCE ON LOVE

Did you like that?" The woman's voice sounded far away. "Then here's another."

McNihil looked up from where he lay paralyzed on the floor of the bar. From this angle, he didn't have tunnel vision so much as something like an optical elevator shaft, a dark elongated space stretching up to whatever night sky existed above. His mouth tasted the way blown-out fuses smell, electrical and singed metallic; beyond his spastically clawing fingertips were the shoes of some of the prowlers who had gotten up from the little tables and come over to watch. He was just vaguely aware of the humanlike figures standing at the fuzzed limits of his sight.

Smiling, the ultimate barfly looked down at McNihil;

her blond hair tumbled alongside her face like slowly unfolding staircases of gold. She knelt beside him, her face
shifting in and out of focus as McNihil's eyes, feeling loose
and wobbly in their sockets, tried to adjust. Although he
knew that she was as she'd been before, and no longer transformed into the one he'd caught that single glimpse of. That
vision had already faded, the image of Verrity disappearing
back into the darkness behind the woman's eyes.

He had never seen Verrity before. He wasn't sure what it
meant that he'd been allowed to now.

The barfly's kiss descended on him as though he were
pinned at the bottom of the shaft, and all this world's softly
grinding machinery were about to crush him into a new
state of being. *Or non,* thought McNihil as he felt the
woman's lips press against his own. He was still connected-
up from the first kiss; his tongue had wedged inside his
mouth like a small animal convulsed in its dying.

"Here you go, sweetheart." The barfly's words brushed
her lips against his; she inhaled whatever deranged molecules
were released in his breath. "A little maintenance dose. Just
something to top you up."

The kiss had unknotted his tongue, enough that McNihil
could speak. "I could've . . ." It was like sorting out words
onto a tray, assembling them from the fragments left inside
his head. "Done without . . ."

"Sure . . ." The barfly stroked his sweating brow. "But
what fun would that be? Think of all you'd miss."

Right now, it didn't seem as though he were missing
anything at all. The first kiss, the slip of the tongue, had
sparked and made contact in a big way, an explosion from
the roof of his mouth to the cellar doors of his throat. The
inrush of the memory load—what every prowler bestowed as
its personal homecoming gift—had been what had laid him
out on the floor.

No wonder, a distant part of McNihil thought, *it knocked*

out that little wimp Travelt. Stuff like this would flatten anybody. Though he figured—one brain cell slowly hooking up
with another—that what he'd just gotten was stronger than
the usual. The barfly—or somebody—must've cooked up a
sampler for him, of all that could be found down in the
Wedge, in that world she and the other prowlers walked
around in on a regular basis. The images and other sensory
data were just beginning to decompress and sort themselves
out along his scalded neurons:

- A black-ink tattoo, a two-dimensional face whose
  carbon pixels pulled the mouth open into a silent
  howl of fury, as it crept across a woman's naked
  back (*Whose?* wondered McNihil);

- On the woman's flesh, between the small bumps of
  her spine and the angle of her right shoulder blade,
  a bubble of skin rose, as though blistered by some
  laser-tight application of heat; the bubble grew
  wide as a man's hand, a perfect glossy hemisphere
  tinged with pinkish blood; the thin membrane
  shimmered like a frog's pale throat, an artificial
  tympanum driven by a faint sound growing louder;

- Loud enough that McNihil could decipher the
  words it spoke, synch'd to the flat motions of the
  tattooed face's open mouth; the bubble sang, in a
  woman's crooning alto voice; the song was a
  down-tempo bluesy rendition of the old standard
  Taking a Chance on Love, the pitch-bending rubato
  husky as though the nonexistent vocal cords were
  writhed in blue cigarette smoke;

- That song the echo-warped, trance-mix soundtrack to the next vision and the ones after that; the

lyrics devolved into melismatic Latin, then San-
skrit, then the nonverbal cries of human-faced animals in love with the moon and the slow shiver of
their self-lubricating convulsions;

• The voice went on singing even after the bubble of
skin snapped into pink-edged rags, burst by the
woman turning over on an antique divan of acidic
green, the watered silk darkening as the blood
seeped from the now-hidden tattoo; the song was
inside McNihil's head, his own palate trembling in
sympathetic vibration as the woman smiled with
drowsy lust and reached up for him;

• *You see?* said the ultimate barfly, wrapping her naked arms around him, her blond hair tangling
across his sweat-bright face; *I knew you'd like it
here* . . .

"I'd really . . . rather not . . ." McNihil pressed his
hands flat against the floor of the bar. His singed tongue
scraped painfully against his teeth as he spoke. "I've got . . .
work to do . . ."

"Oh, I know you do, sweetheart." Outside of the kiss-
induced visions, the barfly was untinged by any reddening
wounds. "I'm just trying to help you along."

"You should let him go. . . ." Another voice spoke,
male and flattened monotonic. "Verrity's waiting for
him . . ."

McNihil shifted the wobbly focus of his gaze, and made
out one of the other prowlers standing next to the barfly.
The face could've been his own, or nothing at all; the same
thing, he supposed.

"That's right," said McNihil. The paralysis had started to
ebb, leaving his large muscles jittering as though in elec-

troshock aftermath. All that shivering made him feel cold, as
though drained of his own blood. "Listen to that guy . . ."

The male prowler spoke again. "You're just connecting
around with him."

"Shut up," said the barfly, more amused than angry. "I
know what I'm doing." She nudged McNihil with her shoe.
The pointed toe of the vampy five-inch-heeled number was
almost sharp enough to penetrate his ribs. "You don't have
any complaints, do you, pal?"

"The hell I don't." McNihil had managed to roll over
onto his side; he felt his own weight pressing against the
tannhäuser inside his jacket. He gathered and spat an evil-
tasting substance out of his mouth, the residue of the kiss's
transmission of gathered memory. "This . . . this is just
uncalled for." Lying on one shoulder, McNihil fumbled his
hand across the buttons of his shirt, trying to get his stiffened
fingers onto the weapon, not caring whether they were
watching him. "Not . . . friendly at all . . ."

He was starting to wonder if he'd misjudged the situation
into which he'd wandered. *Maybe they don't want me to find
out,* thought McNihil. Prowlers obviously had more secrets
than he'd known of . . . and maybe the prowlers wanted
them to stay secrets. If there'd been time, and some way of
clearing his head of the stuff the barfly's kiss had put in
there—the memory download went on unfolding like a
toxic flower, each petal made of human skin—he might have
tried figuring out what it meant. Something was going on,
that was way outside the original prowler design parameters.
Even the barfly—*She shouldn't have been able to pass for human,*
he decided. *At least not so easily.* The transference effect that
Harrisch had told him about—maybe that hadn't been just
an isolated occurrence between the late Travelt and his
prowler. Maybe it had been going on all along, with all the
prowlers and their users. *And maybe,* the thought struck him,
maybe Harrisch knew about it. Perhaps from the beginning; and

not because something was going wrong, at least from the viewpoint of that DZ executive bunch.

Another flower threaded its black stem through McNihil's skull. One that he was going to let remain un-opened, rather than forcing the hothouse blossom of revealed conspiracies. That was a particular garden path he didn't want to go down, at least not at the moment: the possibility that whatever was going on with the prowlers wasn't some-thing outside the original design parameters . . . but in-side. If they were becoming human, in whole or part, soaking up their owners' thoughts, minds, maybe even souls—maybe that was just what they were designed to do.

Those considerations tumbled through the murk inside McNihil's head, as though his fingertips were reading tactile Morse code on the tannhäuser's checked grip. *I'll think about 'em later*—he seized the weapon and dragged it out of his jacket.

"Oh, great," said the male prowler standing nearby. "Now look—he's packing." An anxious hubbub rose from the others at the little tables scattered through the bar. "Somebody should've taken that thing away from him."

"But you didn't," said McNihil. His legs still didn't seem to be functioning, as though some link down his spine had been snapped by the barfly's kiss. He managed to push him-self up on one elbow, raising the tannhäuser in the other hand. "Lucky for me." The gun wobbled as he swung its pendulumlike weight toward each of the hovering onlookers in turn. "Sorry . . . it's not in *your* plans . . ."

"It's your own that you're connecting up." The barfly looked down at him with mingled contempt and pity. "You came here to do a job—to get that job *done* and over with—and we're just trying to help you out, pal." The tough-girl persona from the old movies firmed up around her like a suit of armor, one made of cheap silky stuff molded to her ribs and hinged down the seams of her smoky-dark stockings. "Come on—that's why you came here in the first place. Because you knew that we could do that for you." Her smile held legions of superior wisdom. "Because you know that this is the door in."

"I changed my mind." McNihil flopped back against the bar's padded flank. He held the tannhäuser in both hands, trying to steady it. The implications about the prowlers—what they were, what they'd become—had gone spiraling out, despite his intent not to think about that. "I gotta fall back . . . and punt. I thought . . . I knew what was going on. Or at least part of it." The weapon had started sweating in his tight grip. "Plus what . . . I was going to do about it." The conceptual territory had shifted beneath his feet, as though the edges of one of the tectonic plates underlying the Gloss had broken through the asphalt and concrete, totally rearranging the map he'd stood on. "So it's been nice, but . . ." A little tingling sensation had returned to McNihil's legs; he made a tentative effort at getting them beneath himself. "I think I better be running along. . . ."

"I don't think so," announced the barfly. Contempt outweighed pity in her gaze. "You shouldn't make appointments you don't plan on keeping. There's somebody waiting for you."

"Somebody important." The male prowler loomed ominously above McNihil. Behind the prowler, the others had left their places at the bar's small tables and had assembled in rough, anonymous formation; the crowd of extras had morphed into an ugly mob scene, their muttering anger directed at the figure sprawled between the stools. "Somebody . . ."—the prowler's flat voice ratchetted down into a growl—"somebody you've needed to meet for a long time."

The words inside McNihil's head, the few that had been left after the power surge of the barfly's kiss, were replaced by quick, overriding panic. In instinctive self-defense, he raised his clasped hands up in front of his chest, the tannhäuser cranking into position as though on an invisible hoist line.

"Don't be stupid." The barfly shook her head in disgust. "That's not going to help."

McNihil let the tannhäuser take the initiative, whatever small mind it had inside its works substituting for his own exhausted one. The weapon spoke in true operatic fashion, a Wagnerian basso roar hitting the bar's walls as an orange gout of flame spat out of the muzzle.

"You dumb shit." In the fuzzy mists beyond him, the voice that spoke sounded like the male prowler who'd been getting so ugly with him. *He's still standing?* wondered McNihil. "There's a time," said the voice, "and a place for everything. This ain't it."

With the back of his head against the padding, McNihil opened his eyes as wide as possible, the furrows of his brow enough to bring the bar's contents into a discernible order. Only roughly so: between the aftereffects of the barfly's kiss, the engorged memories popping out from each other like an infinite series of Chinese boxes, and the still-echoing wallop of the tannhäuser, the things inside his head felt marginally connected, if at all, the synapses as ragged and wet as used tissue paper. The world of ancient movies encoded inside McNihil's eyes went soft and transparent, like a molecule-thick permeable membrane letting in the other behind it, the more-or-less real one. The gearing of his brain revved into a bone-held fever, trying to sort out the overlapping data and reassemble them into a coherent whole.

McNihil pressed his clenched hands, weighted with the tannhäuser, against his eyes, trying to shield himself from the chaotic stimulus rush. Even through his eyelids he could see what had been the bar, the dark hole both comfortable and threatening, with its diamond-padded door and leatherette-topped seats, the neon cocktail sign sizzling in the night air beyond, the rain slowly leaking down the stairs from the wet

streets and sidewalks jeweled with the moon's shattering reflection . . . and over and mingled with that a bleak metal
warehouse, industrial end-of-millennium chic, all exposed
bolts and scrubbed-bare sheet steel, black anaconda cables
looped over the girders and crawling around the space's lit-
ter-thick perimeter. Seeing even that much put a miasma of
chemical sweat and twitching O.D. vomitus into McNihil's
nostrils, the smell of grim fun aftermath. Places like this were
why he'd left one world for another, the annihilating real for
the endurable gone.

Wake up, he told himself, *and smell the burning corpses of
your dreams.* McNihil lowered the weapon in his hands and
looked up at the prowler standing before him.

The barfly had draped herself around the humanlike figure's shoulders, clinging like erotic seaweed to a jagged
shoreline rock. As though a wave had broken over the
prowler and drawn away only a few seconds ago; the front of
the figure's dark jacket was shining wet, blood seeping from
the hole torn through the upper chest.

As McNihil watched, and as the barfly smiled and
watched him in turn, the male prowler reached up and
hooked a forefinger in the bullet hole. The jacket's fabric
ripped away as easily as damp paper, exposing the pallid flesh
beneath. *No wonder,* thought McNihil, *it didn't fall down . . .*

Like a rock dropped into a gelatinous sea, the bullet
hadn't created a wound, but rather a rippling distortion, a
faint bull's-eye pattern that had spread over the prowler's
torso and faded. The bullet's entry point had been transformed by the black-ink tattoos that had swarmed and
inched their way from the prowler's abdomen and back, like
blind fish and bottom-feeding ocean creatures, attracted by a
sudden food source. The hole itself, edged with a small
wreath of pinkish erectile tissue, exuded a fluid clearer than
blood, but just as viscid and blood-warm, glistening like silvery snail tracks in a moonlit garden. When the prowler's

fingertips stroked the soft rim of the swollen non-wound, a tiny brass sun rose in its depths, just south of the ridge of collarbone. Shining wet, the flat end of the tannhäuser's bullet slid with minor grace from the hole, the surrounding pink-to-red tissue enfolding its steel-jacketed shaft. The prowler's thumb and fingertip grasped the exposed end of the cylinder; the humanlike figure's flat gaze shifted from where it had examined, chin tucked against throat, its adaptive flesh, up to McNihil's eyes.

"You see?" The male prowler spoke, its voice unaltered by pain or shock. "It's no big deal." The gathering tattoos, black hearts and black flowers, the names of martyred saints, nibbled at his fingertips. "As long as you're . . . *ready* for it." Slowly, the prowler slid the wet bullet back and forth in its receptacle of softly lubricated flesh. The black holes of his eyes, apertures in the mask that concealed no other face, narrowed as though savoring the slight penetration, the caress of the nerve endings just beneath the surface of the skin. "Just like you're ready." The prowler withdrew the bullet, slick with transparent mucus, and held it up before himself. "Whether you like it or not."

"You don't," murmured the smiling barfly, "have much of a choice." Her bruised-looking eyelids had drawn down to an expression of postcoital satiety. "Do you?" The barfly peeled her languorous form away from the male prowler; she stepped forward and knelt down directly in front of McNihil. "Because . . . it's all memory now. That's what we deal in here. We don't have any other merchandise . . . and we don't need any." She reached forward, past the tannhäuser in McNihil's doubled grip, and placed her fingertips on his brow, as though in blessing. "It's what you gave us. All of you; it's what we were created for. You wanted memories, memories other than your own, memories of things that hadn't happened to you, but that you wanted to have happen to you. All the pleasures of remembering and none of the risks." The barfly stroked his sweat-damp hair back from his forehead. "Maybe that wasn't such a good deal, though. Maybe you gave us more than you got back in turn. Maybe you really didn't get anything at all . . . and we got part of you." She wasn't smiling now; her voice had turned harsh and grating. "The ability to feel, and suffer . . . and re-member. Everything that made you human, that made you different from the things you created . . . that's what you gave us." The barfly's hand pressed harder against McNihil's brow, as though her lacquered nails could pierce the wall of bone. "It wasn't," she whispered, "a good deal for us, ei-ther."

He tried to push himself away from her, his spine in-denting the padded surface behind him. "I'm sorry . . ." McNihil raised the tannhäuser between himself and the woman. "But I wasn't the one . . . who did it . . ."

"No . . . you're not." The barfly gave a slow nod. "But you're the one who's here. So you'll do."

The bullet had dropped from the male prowler's finger-tips and rolled against the toe of McNihil's boot. In the bullet's wetly polished metal, he could see himself—his real face, the one without the mask that had been stitched on at the clinic; his face in that other world he'd left behind. That was what small, shining things had always done for him: mirror reflections that didn't synch up with all the rest that his eyes saw. Just as though the bullet had left another hole, which let the other world leak through.

There's more where that came from, thought McNihil. He placed the tannhäuser's muzzle against the kneeling barfly's forehead, the blond curve of her hair trailing across the bar-rel's black metal. "You know . . . I'd do this . . ." He folded one finger across the weapon's trigger. "If I weren't such a nice guy . . ."

"But you are." The barfly didn't draw away from the

cold circle resting just above her half-lidded eyes. "You're too nice. That's your problem."

"Maybe." McNihil lifted the tannhäuser from the woman's head, angling the muzzle toward the bar's low ceiling. "But I'm working on it."

Her gaze followed the weapon's new trajectory. "That's not a good idea," she warned.

"They're my memories," said McNihil. "At least they are now. So I can do what I want with them."

"We can't let you do that." The male prowler, nonwound still exposed on his upper chest, stepped forward, reaching for the tannhäuser. "It's not allowed—"

"But you must have." McNihil squeezed the weapon tight in his fists. "Otherwise, it wouldn't be happening. Or have happened—doesn't matter which. I wouldn't remember it happening." He managed a smile of his own. "But I can see it plain as day."

The tannhäuser roared again, as though it had suddenly recalled the second verse of its low-pitched aria. McNihil's spine jolted as the recoil knocked him back; a blinding spark, the same color as the flash from the tannhäuser's muzzle, jumped across the contacts inside his head.

"Watch out—"

He couldn't tell which of them shouted that. The barfly had scrambled away from him as soon as he'd pulled the trigger, as though she was desperate for shelter. Any kind of shelter; McNihil's eyes focused well enough that he could see where the bullet had struck the bar's ceiling. Fierce light poured through the hole, the radiance filling his vision and piercing all the way to the back of his skull. The doors of the small dark rooms inside his head shattered and tore from their iron hinges.

Above him, the ceiling grew more luminous, heat pressing against his face like a new kiss. The annihilating light flooded in as the bullet hole ripped open wider, the ceiling

giving way like the cheap fabric of the male prowler's jacket.
McNihil could no longer see that figure, or the barfly or any
of the others. The tannhäuser grew too hot for him to keep
in his hands; it fell and clattered away on the floor, pitching
and tilting now with the sudden upheaval of the earth. His
empty hands shielded his eyes, but with no effect; the light
passed through red flesh and shadow bones, relentless.

He could just make out the bar's ceiling falling away in
tatters, as a sky of flames broke over him.

"Now we're making progress."

She heard the medical technician speak, somewhere over
by the vital-signs monitor. November opened her eyes; she
had already propped herself up against the hospital-bed pillows, so she could watch whatever the techs and doctors and
nurses were doing, if she'd wanted to.

The tech glanced over at her. "Dreaming again?"

She nodded yes. The lights from the corridor outside the
room seemed unusually bright to her. *Because it was night,*
thought November. *In the dream.* She'd been someplace
where it was always night. Both inside and out . . .

There was only one of the med technicians in the room
this time; each visit the burn-ward crew had made, there had
been fewer of them. She supposed that was a good sign. This
one didn't ask about whatever dream she'd been having, but
just went about his work, reading off numbers from the various gauges and indices on the equipment screens, then
punching them into the little handheld data transmitter he
carried. He even hummed a little tune, barely distinguishable
from the sighing of one of the machines.

November laid her head back against the pillow. The
dream was still somewhat intact inside her head, the images
and general sense not as fractured as when she'd been
pumped full of the major anesthetics. Woozy drug sleep had
given way to fifteen-minute catnaps, which ended abruptly

when she felt her newly grafted skin tightening over her flesh. She missed being hammered underneath the big drugs; those pharmaceuticals had seemed to cancel gravity, sequentiality, guilt . . . everything unpleasant turned to sweet, filtered air. Getting detoxed from them, her bloodstream flushed out, the red contents scrubbed clean in something that looked like a miniature clothes washer and then I.V.'d back into her—that had been like returning to the orbit of some planet she wouldn't have minded seeing the last of.

The dream . . . With her eyes closed, November could view its basic setup. She carefully held her breath, fearing that any exhalation would shimmer and dissolve the image.

Not an ocean this time, or anything to do with falling: she'd dreamed of a building, a big one, an old one with rows of windows from top to bottom. It took a little while for her to recognize it, as she let her vision zoom in, movielike. *The hotel,* thought November. What was it called? Something terminal . . . the End Zone Hotel; that was it. Her spine contracted in a full-body flinch reaction, as the dream hooked up with her own memories. She remembered just enough—it was encoded in the deep layers of her nervous system—to sense again the heat of the flames, scorching down into her lungs. Even before the hotel's roof had given way beneath her, and sent her falling down inside, the place had been an exact hell. *Even before the fire,* she thought; just a different, bleaker kind.

Strangely, in the dream—she could see it now, in retrospect—the End Zone Hotel burned but was not consumed, as though some Old Testament deity had checked in. From her floating point of view, November could see the flames rising behind the grime-thickened windows, the glass either intact or shattered by the heat into shards diving like transparent knives to the street below. The tattered curtains went up in lacework of smoke and sparks; she could look past them just a little bit, enough to see a few of the sagging beds combusting, the smoldering mattresses coughing up the heavier, darker clouds of hourly rate passion. She couldn't see anyone there, though, whether sleeping in flames or beating a wiser retreat from the ongoing, apparently endless inferno. That made her wonder where they had all gone. The dark ocean she had seen before, maybe, with its gelled waves slowly lapping against the hotel's lobby doors . . .

"Won't be long now."

November's eyes snapped open. "What?"

"For you getting out of here." The med tech held up the black rectangle of the data unit. "See?" Green numbers tagged with a little happy-face symbol marched across the one-line screen. "You're rated in the top ten percent of all serious burn recoveries in the Gloss, or at least at the hospitals linked on this system."

"How nice. Does that mean you guys get a bonus or something?"

"Maybe." The med tech gave a noncommittal shrug. "Depends upon the year-end review for the whole division, and if the performance ratio comes in under the insurance companies' cost-efficiency targets. We're not doing too bad so far." He regarded the data unit with obvious satisfaction. "They're crunching your numbers down in Accounting right now; that'll probably perk up the averages quite a bit."

"So soon?"

"So soon what, sweetheart?"

She nodded toward the device in the tech's hand, as though the numbers had already spelled out good-bye. "I'm leaving here?"

"Of course. Did you think you were going to be here forever?" The med tech shook his head. "You're all put back together, believe it or not—"

"I don't." November instinctively wrapped her arms around herself, as though there were pieces that might fall off otherwise. "I feel like I've got needles all over my skin, the kind that aren't any fun—"

"That's a good sign. Means all the neuro work went off okay. It'll settle down after a while."

"And I'm still on that thing." She pointed to the I.V. drip; a clear tube ran from it to the bandaged patch on her arm. "How would I feel if that wasn't pumping away?"

"Honey, aspirin's stronger than what you're getting off on right now." The tech glanced at the label dangling from the dispenser's hook. "Baby stuff. You know the drill: you're at the point where if you want anything good, you're going to have to get it on the street."

The thought of it made her hands sweat, with both fear and anticipation. As good as the stuff in the hospital was, there was better walking around beneath the metal-raining skies. "I'm still not sure . . . that I'm ready . . ."

"Ready or not, you gotta trot." The med tech started punching off the displays on the gauges and monitors. "Your boyfriend, or whoever it was, didn't pay for you to become a permanent resident here. Even if he'd wanted to—" The latex-gloved hands tossed the data unit into the air spinning, and caught it again. "That's just not available. This is a hospital, not a hotel."

Hotel. She kept thinking about the one in the dream, her own internalized End Zone, after the med tech had left. Every time she closed her eyes, she could see it burning; the real one, she supposed, would've been ashes by now.

She heard someone's footsteps come into the room—probably another tech or the same one as before—and didn't bother to look. Maybe it was someone from the accounting department; she'd sensed the machines around her switching off one by one, the clicking and sighing noises falling silent, the electrical presence diminishing as the final data was processed down in the hospital's insurance computers.

The footsteps stopped by the side of the bed. "They told me—" The man's voice startled her when it spoke aloud. "That you're just about to roll. Right on out of here."

"Christ . . . it's you." She found herself staring up into the encompassing gaze and unpleasant smile of Harrisch. The burning hotel's afterimage evaporated like steam; November hadn't even been aware of the transition from closed eyes to open. For a confused half-second, she had wondered how the DynaZauber exec had come to be looking out from one of the End Zone Hotel's flame-shrouded windows, before she'd realized he was there with her, outside any dreaming. "What the . . ." November reacted by reaching up for the call buzzer that the nurses had pinned to the side of her pillows.

"Looking for this?" Harrisch held up the little box with the big red button, the wire dangling down to the floor. "There's really no need for it." He laid the buzzer down on top of one of the machines, well beyond November's reach. "I'm just here for a bit of conversation. I imagine you're feeling well enough for that. Aren't you?"

November pushed herself up higher on the pillows, drawing as far back from the exec as possible. "What do you want?"

"Why so nervous?" Spreading his empty hands apart, Harrisch let his smile fade. "Is there something I'm doing that's making you afraid? What is it?"

"You gotta be kidding—" November looked around herself for something she could throw at the exec, something hard rather than soft, that would do real damage. Musing about dreams and their meanings was over for the time being. "Get the connect out of here." She wondered if she could scream or shout loud enough to get the attention of anybody passing by in the corridor beyond. *That's the problem with hospitals,* November thought grimly. They were so damn loud, nobody ever knew what was going on. *No won-*

der people die here. "Just get out," she said again. "I don't want to talk to you."

"That's a rotten attitude to take." Harrisch appeared genuinely wounded. "What did I do to deserve that from you? Employed you, paid you . . . made your whole life possible, the way you wanted to live it. If it weren't for people like me, farming out the work outside the corporation, freelancers like you wouldn't exist. You oughta thank me."

"Your ass, connect-head." November's initial panic had been replaced with a simmering anger, the way it always was, given enough time. "I wasn't even working for you this time—you were just stringing me on with the *possibility* of a job—and you nearly got me killed." She reconsidered the words. " 'Nearly' . . . shit. You *did* get me killed. Cooked up like a connecting flounder."

"Seems rather a harsh way to put it . . ."

"Deal with it, pal." November felt the back of the hospital gown pull open against the pillow as she folded her arms across her breast. "You left me hanging out there, looking like yesterday's burnt toast. The only reason I'm alive—the only reason I've been brought back from the dead at all—is because somebody else popped for the bill here. Somebody who had a lot less reason to do it than you should have."

"Please." Harrisch sighed elaborately. "You might like to try to see these issues from my perspective. DynaZauber corporate practice is a strict implementation of Denkmann's Pimp-Style Management™ philosophy—or to put it another way, PSM is the codification of what we just do as a matter of course. We really wrote the book on a lot of those things, almost more than Denkmann did. The ego annihilation, the perpetual screw; all that stuff." A note of pride sounded in Harrisch's voice. "So you can just dispense with any notions about loyalty being anything other than a one-way street when you deal with DZ. We take, we don't give—even when you're on the payroll, that's how it works out. Anything else would violate the essential sadomasochistic underpinnings of our management style, and then the whole system falls apart. And we've got too much invested in it to let that happen."

"Aw, man. Spare me." *I'm lying here with a new skin stitched on because of these jerks*—she didn't need a lecture on why getting connected by them was supposed to be such a wonderful thing. "If getting connected by you people comes without lubricant . . . I'm a big girl now. I'll deal with it. Easier than listening to you sonsabitches."

"You know—" Harrisch sat down on a corner of the bed; November had to draw her feet up beneath the blanket to avoid him. "Some people come through experiences such as you've been through . . . and they're *better* people for it."

"Oh, I *am;* believe me." November glared at him. "I'm just not going to waste it on you."

"I see." The expression on the exec's face was one of sly assessment. "And who does get the benefit of your transformed nature? Or let's put it another way: who are you hoping will get it?" Harrisch leaned closer to her; he smelled of expensive cologne and adding-machine printouts. "Maybe it's that poor bastard McNihil. Because you're so grateful to him."

"Hardly." November wished she had found something to throw at this smiling apparition. "He's taken—remember? Even if I was interested in him, which I'm not. He's got that major bent for his dead wife. Not exactly the kind of thing it's possible to walk in on."

"True." Harrisch gave a shrug. "Unless . . . he wanted you to."

"Give it up." Her short laugh held contempt. "This

shows why you were having such a hard time recruiting him. You don't know how his mind works."

"And I suppose you do? Tell me then: why'd McNihil pay your bill, for the skin grafts and all the rest of it? He must've had a reason."

She regarded the DZ exec warily, then shook her head. "I don't know why."

Harrisch slowly nodded, deep in his own thoughts. "I don't, either," he said after a moment. "Kind of a mystery. I was really hoping that you might be able to clue me in on it. Because there's always a reason."

Like there is for your coming around here. The act wasn't fooling November. She could see inside Harrisch's skull with the same abstract X rays she used to turn on the men in the trains, the ones who'd wanted to press themselves on and into her previous skin. *They always want something,* she thought. Harrisch was no different in his wanting, his lust for connection, even if his eventual orgasm was wired into something other than his fleshy genitals, some part whose up-and-down movements were more accurately charted on a stockbroker's report.

"Like I said." November wasn't scared of the exec any longer; the twinge of fear had been rooted in some vestigial organ of her own body, childish and irrational; it would probably be a long time before a lit match wouldn't make her bladder tremble. "I don't know why he did it. Maybe McNihil thought he was responsible for what happened to me—"

"I doubt it," said Harrisch. "Asp-heads don't feel guilt. Everything's justified to them."

"Then he really should've gone to work for you. Without being pushed." She regarded the exec without flinching. "But I don't know the why of that, either. If the guy's got his reasons, he keeps them to himself. After all—" She tilted her head and looked at Harrisch from the corner of her eye.

"He didn't tell you why he was picking up my tab, did he? He just did it, that's all."

"True." Harrisch watched his own hand smoothing out a section of the bedsheet, then glanced back up at her. "But you'd like to know, wouldn't you?"

She felt as though she were looking down at the exec from some lofty mountaintop. "And somehow you're going to make that possible, I take it."

"Perhaps." Harrisch shrugged. "I just came to offer you a little . . . travel assistance. To go somewhere . . . interesting."

"With you?"

"Not necessarily."

Her eyes narrowed, as though sharpening her gaze enough to see into the DZ exec. "Is this a job offer? Because if it is, you're wasting your time." November had already made her decision, before this clown had shown up. "I'm not doing any kind of work you might be looking for. Not anymore."

"No—this is a freebie. Both ways." Harrisch stood up from the bed. "Let's just say that I'm the kind of person who likes to have things witnessed. Sometimes important things. Sometimes just . . ." He let his unpleasant smile show again. "Sometimes just personal things."

November's skin had stopped prickling; the sharp-pointed needles had gathered into a ball near her heart. "Which is it this time?"

The smile didn't fade. "It's both." Harrisch stepped around to the side of the bed, closer to her than when he'd been sitting down. "Of course," he said, "we can make it as personal as you want." He leaned down toward her, before she could react. One arm encircled November's shoulders, pulling her up from the stacked pillows; Harrisch brought his face right up against her, tight enough that she could feel his teeth through the thin lips pressing against hers. Harrisch drew back just a fraction of an inch. "Or it can be a job. You pick."

Her movement was one of instinct. She seized Harrisch's skull, hands on either side above his ears. November pressed as hard as she could, her eyes squeezing tight with effort, but nothing happened. Except Harrisch's laughter.

"Come on." He pushed himself away; standing beside the bed, brushing off his jacket lapels, he regarded her with amusement. "As long as that much work was being done on you, I didn't mind paying for a little extra. A little something to be removed. A pretty girl like you shouldn't have those kinds of nasty toys wired into her." Harrisch nodded slowly and judiciously. "Gives people the wrong impression about you."

Shit, thought November as she looked at her hands, with their now-ineffectual fingertips. "I spent a lot of money for those TMS implants—"

"Well, then." Harrisch shrugged. "Maybe you will be interested in a job. Or . . . some other arrangement." His ugly smile was like a bad kiss, overly familiar and nauseating. He stepped toward the room's door, pulled it open, then glanced back at her. "Soon as you're out, give me a call. Even if you just want to do a little traveling. You know where to find me."

Not where you should be, jerk. She went on glaring at the closed door long after the man was gone.

When November finally closed her eyes—it made more sense to get as much rest as she could, before they booted her out of the hospital—she saw again, without dreaming, the burning End Zone Hotel. This time, she realized something about it that she'd missed before.

That's where he is, thought November. One way or another—the burning hotel was where McNihil was at. Whether the hotel even existed or not; it didn't matter. That was why she'd dreamed about the hotel, seen it burning as it had been long ago, caught in that fiery moment. *Maybe,* she thought, *when he paid my bill, he bought my dreams as well.* . . .

Not dreams, but visions. She knew that now. With her eyes closed, she could feel the distant heat on her face. And was afraid . . .

But not for herself.

EIGHTEEN

TERRITORY THAT MOST PEOPLE ARE ABANDONING INSIDE THEIR HEADS OR THE GIRL ON THE BED OF FLAMES

You pretty much expected I'd be here, didn't you?"

McNihil looked at the Adder clome. Then nodded. "Yeah," admitted McNihil. "I pretty much did." To himself he thought, *There's no getting rid of some things*.

The two of them stood in the shabby corridor of the End Zone Hotel lined with numbered doors. For a few moments, when he'd first found himself here, McNihil had thought he might've been back at the cubapt building where he'd gone to see a corpse, a long time ago, in another world. That world, that building, had been transformed by the black-and-white vision in his eyes into something more or less like this one: a place of numbered doors and deep shadows, the cob-webbed lights overhead barely able to cut through the optical

gloom. Which was made even worse in this case by the black
smoke leaking out from beneath the doors and rolling across
the threadbare carpeting, then spilling down the stairs at the
end of the hallway. Traces of the smoke rose into the dense
air, stinging McNihil's eyes and gathering at the back of his
throat, thick enough to choke him. He could barely discern
the image of the other man, the clome from the Snake
Medicine™ clinic, standing in front of him; the clome's
voice, soft and insinuating, had identified him more than
anything else.

"But then . . ." The Adder clome spread his hands and
looked about the smoke-filled corridor—"this is the kind of
place that I'm always at. In some deep, fundamental sense."

"Big words." The air in the building had been baked dry
by the mounting flames; McNihil could feel his lungs shriv-
eling as the heat seeped inside him.

"They're true, though." The Adder clome tilted his
head, studying McNihil's reactions. "Do you remember the
name of this place? From when you were here before—out
in the other world, the world that isn't just memories that've
been kissed into your head."

"Sure." That much was a real memory for him; it had
actually happened. "The End Zone Hotel has always been a
real charming place." McNihil coughed and wiped his stinging eyes. "I had a lot of fun there. Believe me. So how could
I forget?"

"You should've learned to," said the Adder clome. "It
would've made it easier for you all along. And easier for us as
well. Your head's so packed with things—real things, plus all
that stuff that those messed-up eyes of yours make you
see—that it was hard for us to find room in there, to put the
things that we wanted you to remember. That you need to
remember. Even if they didn't happen to you—" The Adder
clome stopped and scratched his chin, as though momentarily confused. "Wait a minute. I'm not sure I'm getting that

across right. Well, I suppose it doesn't really matter." He brightened. "If you remember it happening—if you remember all this—" Both his hands gestured toward the narrowly spaced walls, barely visible behind the smoke. "Then it's just the same as if it happened. Or is happening. Or will happen. You see, that's one of the big breakthroughs we've made on this side. We've eliminated the notion of sequence as it applies to experience. No past, no present, just the eternal now. As in the sexual act itself." He sounded pleased with himself, as though personally responsible. "It's like doing away with gravity. All kinds of things are possible here."

"That's exactly what I'd be worried about." McNihil's throat felt raw from the smoke. "Maybe it's not a good idea to let some people's imaginations run free."

"Don't worry about it." The Adder clome acknowledged the personal remark with a shrug. "There's less to be concerned about than you might think. Even over on this side, there's limits. Anarchy—even the anarchy of the senses—runs eventually into a certain wall."

"Which is?"

"You'd know, if you were in the same business I am." With a tilt of his head, the Adder clome regarded his visitor with amusement. "Come on." One hand reached out and took McNihil's arm. "I'll show you around, and you'll see what I mean."

McNihil shook his head. "I don't have time for that. I came here to do a job."

"*Au contraire*. You have plenty of time. Or enough, at least. Since we don't deal in real time here—memory never does—nobody has any more time than you do." One of the Adder clome's eyebrows raised. "So it really doesn't matter, does it?"

McNihil let himself be tugged toward one of the hallway's numbered doors. The brass digits couldn't be read through the curtain of gray smoke that rose up from the doorsill, though the heat blistering the paint had turned the metal into dully glowing insignia. The Adder clome pushed the door open and stepped back, giving a partial, inviting bow. McNihil hesitated a moment—*Relax,* he told himself, *it's only memories,* not even real ones (*You're sure?* asked another part inside his head)—then stepped through the narrow doorway.

"You see?" The Adder clome's voice came from behind him. "Nothing to worry about. This could be anyplace. It doesn't have to be the End Zone Hotel—that's just a convenient metaphor we've decided to adopt. Just for you; a personal touch."

The ragged carpet was in flames beneath McNihil's feet. Smoke billowed up along his legs, swathing his abdomen and chest, its subtle rising force collecting under his chin. The hotel room was small enough that he could have spread his arms and put his hands flat against wallpaper writhing as though with fiery salamanders. An old-fashioned wooden bureau sagged and buckled as the flames leapt from drawer to drawer; the mirror hinged at the top looked like a bevel-edged slice of the sun's heart, but only for a moment. The glass's silver backing darkened and cracked, then shattered bomblike, mixing brighter slivers with the bits of broken window already scattered across the floor.

McNihil had raised one arm, the back of his hand shielding his eyes. Just as before, his flesh might as well have been altered to some redly translucent substance; he could see the room and its fire-lit, smoke-clotted contents as well or even better than if his eyes had been wide open. As an experiment, he took his forearm away from his face and reached out to the nearest wall, closing his fist upon the lapping flames. Rivulets of fire squeezed between his knuckles; McNihil felt the heat at the center of his palm, etching the lines written in the skin as though with a honed needle. The bloodless pain ran up his arm and burst inside his skull, the glare rendering him without sight for a moment. When he could see again, his hand was still clenched, undamaged and trembling, in the flames.

"Burns," said the Adder clome, "but is not consumed." He nodded toward McNihil's fist against the wall. "That's the territory you're in. That's the territory you're part of—or at least your memories, the ones we gave you. And besides . . ." His smile showed, Cheshire-cat-like, through the smoke and quick tongues of flame that moved between him and McNihil. "It's such a good metaphor, isn't it? All dreams and memories are metaphors at last, mere functions of language. Even without words—they still just exist in your head, in one of those little silent rooms you keep the key to."

"Metaphor . . ." McNihil drew his hand back from the burning wall and looked at it. The pain slowly ebbed from the soot-blackened flesh as he let the intact fingers uncurl of their accord. "For what?" He pressed his hand flat against his shirt, leaving its dark imprint above his heart. He glanced over at the Adder clome. "What's it supposed to stand for?"

"Come on. You know." This time, the Adder clome spread his arms out in cruciform posture. The flames and smoke billowed across him, like the tide of a red ocean turned vertical. "This world, the one that you always called the Wedge—but it's so much bigger than that. Bigger and older. Older than anything. What you thought was just the Wedge—some crummy bars and the places behind them, the rooms and streets where the prowlers hang out—you couldn't see those places for what they really are." The Adder clome's voice tightened fervently. "Temples and doorways. Doorways into another world, *this* world. But you couldn't see that. Because of the dark that you saw instead." Slowly lowering his arms, the Adder clome shook his head, as though struck with futile regret. "It wasn't just the darkness in your eyes, McNihil. It's in everyone's eyes. Everyone human, that is."

"Yeah, whatever." Unimpressed by the other's language, McNihil rubbed the rest of the fire's soot off against his trousers. "If we keep it dark, it's because we like it that way. We don't need to see some of this shit. That's what we have prowlers for." He realized where his own words were putting him: *I'm defending them,* thought McNihil. *All of them, Harrisch and Travelt and all the rest.* He didn't care. Some part of him supposed that he had more in common—still—with the humans than with the others, the ones whose masks just looked that way. "Let the prowlers walk around here," said McNihil with sudden vehemence. "It's their place, not mine."

"Not anymore." A certain triumph sounded in the Adder clome's voice. "You belong here now as much as they do. You've earned the right, pal. Enjoy it."

"I'm just visiting. And even that's under false pretenses." McNihil had managed to rub enough of the black from his hand, that he could see again the lined flesh of his palm. "Right now, I'm really just looking for the exit door."

"You don't have that option," the Adder clome sneered. "You came here to do a job—that's what you said, remember?—and you can't leave until it's finished." He reached out and gathered the lapel of McNihil's jacket into his own tightly clenched fist. "There's things you want to find out, aren't there? Connect Harrisch and his connecting job. Let's satisfy your curiosity, pal." The Adder clome bent his arm, nearly pulling McNihil from his feet. "You might as well have the whole tour. Or at least as much of it as you can stand."

The other's sudden force took McNihil by surprise; dizzied, he felt the Adder clome swing him about in the hotel room's close space, away from the smoke-outlined door and farther inside. *This is his turf,* McNihil realized, as the Adder clome knocked him back against the doorway leading to a minuscule bathroom. And payback time as well; this was

what came from his own violence back at the clinic, when
he'd been pressuring answers out of the other man.

"Take a look," said the Adder clome, "and get an education." He grasped both of McNihil's lapels and yanked him
away from the wall. The little dance inside the hotel room
had brought the two of them up to the bed shoved into the
corner by the broken window. "Tell me what you see, connector."

McNihil caught his balance as the Adder clome let go of
him. On a little bedside table, an antique-looking plastic
radio melted and sagged in the fierce heat. The room's flames
had engulfed the bed itself, the sagging mattress transformed
into a rectangular inferno, as though a trapdoor had been
opened down into the earth's molten core. Smoke, black and
viscous, rolled a choking thundercloud past McNihil's face,
obliterating the ceiling above him. The heat scalded his eyes
as he tried to discern the figure silhouetted in fire on the bed.

Something human, or close enough. And alive; the naked limbs slowly moved, writhing not in agony but in
dreaming bliss. McNihil could just make out the profile of a
woman's face, masked unrecognizable as his own. Her eyes
were closed, the eyelids trembling with the sight of whatever
moved inside her private dreams; her mouth parted as
though to draw deep inside her throat the flames' kiss from
the burning pillow. Almost a child, the fire sculpting her,
luminous and fragile; the fingertips of one hand rested between her negligible breasts, as if she had gathered the bed's
ashy smoke to herself like black-petaled flowers.

Another piece of memory, a real one, linked up with the
world in the hotel. He recognized the sleeping, dreaming
figure on the bed. *It's her,* thought McNihil. *The cube bunny.*
She looked the way he'd seen in the wet reflection on the
coffee percolator, back in the kitchen of his crummy apartment. That saddened him; for her to be here, something bad
would've had to have happened to her in the world outside.

"Dreams within dreams," said the Adder clome. He reached past McNihil and stroked the sleeping girl's hair, brushing what might have been softer flames away from her ear. "And metaphors that don't end." The Adder clome turned his head, looking up to see what effect the show was having on McNihil. "How do you like this one?"

"Not really my style." McNihil shook his head. "You should know that I'm a little more retro in my tastes."

"Really? She seemed to suit you well enough, at one time. Plus, there's always certain . . . novelties, shall we say . . . that could be of interest." The Adder clome ran his hand over the cube bunny's bare shoulder, then lightly drifted across her slow-motion ribs. "Take a closer look."

"I'd rather not," said McNihil. But did anyway. This time, he saw that what he'd assumed were shadows evoked by the flames and deposits of smoke carbon on the girl's skin were more of the drifting black-ink tattoos, the kind that moved. He watched as the Adder clome left one fingertip on the soft area above the cube bunny's evident hipbone, pressing just enough to indent the flesh. The images of lightly animated Asian tigers and weeping Latino prison madonnas clustered at that point, as though to suckle from his fingernail.

A moan escaped from the sleeping girl's lips. McNihil recognized the sound as coming from that place where wordless dreams shed their residual images, stripped down to endorphin flow and the involuntary contraction-and-release of muscle tissue. A shudder ran across the girl's body, her knees drawing up in fetal position as though the burning mattress's heat had sizzled some core tendon. Another heat pulsed from the terminus of the cube bunny's spine; McNihil could smell its radiation in the thick air, the coppery taste lodging at the back of his tongue like a mucus-wet battery.

"You know," mused the Adder clome, "for all the bitching I do about it, there's some real advantages to the corporate relationship with DynaZauber. It's a two-way street. Harrisch and his bunch connect you up the ass financially, but there's something to be gotten out of it. Those people have got bio-resources up the kazoo. You get access to materials and techniques that are utmost state-of-the-art."

"I can imagine." More than the smoke was making McNihil feel woozy.

"No, you can't. At least you couldn't until you arrived here this time." The Adder clome took a step back from the bed, spreading his hands with upturned palms, a parody of blessing. "Take this puppy, for instance. *Look upon my works, ye horny, and despair.* The latest thing—"

"Traveling tattoos? I've seen 'em."

"Don't be stupid." The Adder clome looked down with evident admiration at the sleeping girl's form. "Rev up to the present. Tattoos that move around, that even pass from one body to another—that's strictly old technology. Been there, done that, had the rusty nails driven through my hands and feet. This is something new. What we've got here—" A clinical finger pointed to the markings on the girl; they could be seen more clearly now that the muscle spasms had started to subside. "It's essentially a network of implanted receptor sites. In one grand conceptual stroke, we solve the age-old Theodora's-lament problem. Not enough altars at which to receive libations to the gods, as she put it? What nature didn't provide, science—or at least industry—can. There's a lot of unused territory in the human brain, just waiting to be hooked up to something fun. There's territory that most people are *abandoning* inside their heads—linguistic skills, higher-cognition faculties, emotional levels. Why leave all that just to become cerebral ghost towns, empty buildings, dust inside old closets? If you don't use 'em, somebody else will. Nothing remains uncolonized for long, not when there's corporations like DynaZauber around. They'll be happy to move their furniture inside your head. That's their business; that's how they make their money."

"You don't have to tell me about DZ business," said McNihil. "What I don't know about it, I'm not interested in."

"You should be." The Adder clome spoke with sudden vehemence, eyes bright through the smoke. "You're looking at the future here, pal; the future and the present and the past, all rolled up into one. The goal of commerce is to destroy history, to put its customers into the eternal Now, the big happy theme park of desires that are always at the brink of satisfaction but somehow never get there. Because if they did, the game would be over and everybody would go home. They might even move back inside their own heads and boot the happy corporations out."

"That's not going to happen."

"Yeah, well, I don't think so, either." Self-loathing seeped through the Adder clome's words. "That's why I sold out to DZ, joined up with them so hard it'd take a titanium crowbar to pry me loose." He passed his hands, fingers spread wide, a few inches above the sleeping girl, like a magician beginning a levitation act. "Me and the rest of the ones like me, plus everybody at the Snake Medicine™ franchise headquarters—we could see the handwriting on the wall. *Mene mene tekel up-your-ass.* Which is corporate-speak for *You've been weighed in the balance and we've found you worthwhile enough to buy, so you can either sell out now or go back to selling rubber vibrators at strip-mall discount outlets.* Not much of a choice."

McNihil had been there as well. "If Harrisch wanted you to have a choice, he'd have given it to you."

"Exactly." The Adder clome looked down at the sleeping girl, examining the naked form more critically now. "So that's why there's Snake Medicine™ fingerprints all over this concept; we were *happy* to get the consulting gig with DynaZauber.''

"Let me guess." Smoke had made McNihil's voice even raspier, painfully so. He nodded toward the cube bunny and her markings. "This is TIAC?"

"TIAC Mark Two; Two Point Five, actually. The DZ labs took the initial design revisions and did a little fine-tuning on them. Before they pulled the plug on the whole project."

"Why didn't they go to Three? Or even beyond that. It was my understanding that Harrisch and his crowd are always looking for new products to push." McNihil glanced down at the sleeping girl, then back up to the Adder clome. "Didn't this one work out?"

"Worked out like a champ." The Adder clome's own gaze was filled with longing, the girl's image that of unful-filled possibilities. "In some ways, better than they wanted it to. Maybe that was the problem; DynaZauber wound up with a kind of refutation of their whole turd-in-a-can mar-keting concept. Because this baby really delivered. Look here." The moving tattoos followed the point of the Adder clome's finger, like tropical fish in a skin aquarium, waiting to be fed. "It's not just the images, that's just what you *see*. You do see them, don't you?"

McNihil nodded. "Go on."

"There's a whole system here of transmission and recep-tion, sites and stimuli. The tattoos are triggers for previously implanted neural feed-through points. There's enough re-dundant, unused processor space in the human brain's occip-ital lobes, the vision centers, that a DZ surgeon—or a Snake Medicine™ clinic technician, for that matter, once the pro-cedure's been sufficiently dumbed down—can route a sub-cutaneous perception matrix to the deep limbic sexual areas." The Adder clome sounded enthusiastic now. "It's like having eyes all over your body—but a specialized organ; you couldn't read a book with your big toe or something. More like a frog's eye, adapted to perceive only a limited range of stimulus. In this case, the patterns of the traveling tattoos. A predetermined library of tattoo designs—some historicals, Rock of Ages–type stuff, some Iban primitivos, a lot of originals and public-domain stuff—is loaded into unconscious memory, using the basic prowler download technology. It's pretty versatile that way."

"So I've noticed."

The Adder clome rolled on, words coming faster. "Then you just have to load in the connections, the link between each tattoo and the subarea of the cortex that it should stimulate. All sorts of variations are possible: a basic Arrow-Pierced Heart with Banner Doves image is hooked up to a generalized, low-level stroke of the major pleasure centers, while an early-sixties Hot-Rod Demon, some classic Big Daddy Roth design, has a much higher-voltage, short-duration groin-chakra zap linked to it. The first gets you that warm-and-fuzzy bliss glow that lasts for hours, the other is your classic short-fast-and-hard number, twenty seconds or less standing up, from erection, insertion, and climax like a bullet to the center of the skull. Just like old-fashioned sexual encounters in that way: you don't necessarily know just what you're going to get until skin contact's been made."

"Sounds," said McNihil drily, "more like sexual disease than sexual encounters."

"Yeah, but this is the disease you *want*. Well, maybe not you—but somebody always does. They wouldn't put their tongues inside prowlers' mouths if they didn't want it. But with skin as the active, receptive element . . ." The Adder clome nodded slowly. "You add the public factor. People know what you've got, what you've done, what other skin you've rubbed up against . . . and what's rubbed off on you. Like trading cards, some of the tattoos are rarer than others; some are so rare as to be legendary, things to be whispered and conjectured about. Mysterious, sharp-edged emblems, pseudo-Arabic calligraphy, bleeding hearts-of-Jesus that can trigger cortical pleasure centers that nothing else can, soft gray padlocks that only one key can fit. If somebody's going to collect the set, they'll have to put some work in, chase down the missing pieces. There's a whole collector economy that develops off this system: people become major players by what they've got, what they can give you."

"Just like the regular world." A lot of this was stuff that McNihil hadn't heard of before, but it depressed more than surprised him. "It's all economics. Congratulations— between you and DZ, you've managed to complete the process of turning sex into a pure capitalist endeavor."

"You think so?" The Adder clome's sweating brow creased. "I see it going the other way. If Harrisch and his bunch hadn't shut down this project—if they'd gone ahead and put the ultimate TIAC on the market—it would've put the free juice back into sex. Taken it out of the cash registers and sent it on some deep wacko plane, straight out of D.H. Lawrence and Charles Bukowski, you know, those ancient erotic visionaries. Reading people like that was why I got into this business in the first place. I thought you could *do* something with this stuff, something *meaningful*."

"More fool you, then." McNihil wasn't interested in the other man's aspirations; he'd already lost most of his own. "Wake up and smell the—"

"Yeah, right," interrupted the Adder clome. "I've heard that line already. 'Burning,' we've got here; 'corpses' . . . maybe not. Prowlers are alive as you are; they just have different agendas. But what I said before is still true. There were possibilities here once."

"Harrisch hath murdered possibilities. But that's his job—to reduce possibilities to certainties. Late-generation capitalism isn't about speculation; it's all about making *sure* you get the money."

"Don't tell me about what I already know." One of the Adder clome's ash-smeared hands gestured at the surrounding flames and smoke. "This really doesn't seem like the place for an economics lecture. You're more connected-up in the head with Harrisch and his bunch of sub-execs than I am, and I've been on his payroll a lot longer. You're missing the sheer *wonder* of this system, the way all the pieces come together." He laid the flat of his hand against the sleeping girl's shoulder blade. The touch didn't evoke a low moan from her as much as did the Don't Tread on Me snake image slithering up under the Adder clome's palm. He glanced over at McNihil. "See that? Now that's a beautiful thing." The Adder clome pulled his hand away before the tattoo could migrate onto his skin. "A lot of value there. Maybe more than the DynaZauber corporation wants to deliver for the purchase price; that's probably why Harrisch and the others nixed it. Because of the repeatability factor: the effect produced by any one pattern diminishes over time, but for quite a while, as long as the subcutaneous optic receptors perceive it moving over the skin from spot to spot, there's still a measurable thrill derived from it. So memory is taken out of the head and moved onto the body, where it can really be appreciated." He gestured again toward the girl. "You can't say she's not getting something out of all this."

McNihil made no reply. His own body felt dehydrated from the heat of the burning hotel, his lungs and heart laden with smoke. The relief of ashes hadn't come, would never come in this place. The girl on the bed of flames could not even die as much as his dead wife had; she breathed in fire and breathed it out, her breasts like soft glass lit from within; her silken hair twined in the mattress's flames, like the mating of serpents, two close species coiling around each other. But was not consumed. *No death here,* thought McNihil. *Not*

even the littlest one. So the Adder clome was wrong. It didn't
have anything to do with sex at all.

"So this was the end of it?" McNihil pointed to the girl,
lost in the heat of her own dreaming, wordless and without
image, wired to pure coded sensation. "The end of the
TIAC project?"

The Adder clome nodded, mired in his own wistful
brooding, the contemplation of what might have been.

"But it wasn't the end," said McNihil, "of what Harrisch wants to do. Of everything that DynaZauber wants to
use the Wedge for. He may have cut *you* out of the loop—he
fires people as well as hires them, or just puts them on eternal
hold—but that doesn't mean he wrapped things up and left.
You know how they work. Once DZ has taken over a territory, they don't just hand it back."

"True." Another slow nod from the Adder clome. "The
End Zone Hotel—at least this one, in this world—it's pretty
much a DynaZauber property anymore. Owned and operated by, as it were."

"Harrisch and his bunch didn't leave; they just switched
operations. Didn't they?" McNihil watched for the other
man's reaction. "From TIAC . . . to TOAW."

A look of fright appeared in the Adder clome's eyes,
discernible even through the smoke filling the hotel room.
"Maybe you should drop it right there." The Adder clome's
voice had been scraped down to a whisper. "You don't want
to poke into TOAW. Not if you know what's good for
you."

McNihil's laugh felt like a lit match dropped inside his
throat. "Even if I ever did know that . . . I'm past caring.
Why would I be here otherwise?"

"It's your job." The Adder clome made a simple state-
ment. "Maybe Harrisch forced you to take it, but it's still
your job."

"I could've gotten out of it. There's ways; there's always

an exit door. You just have to decide which is worse. Besides . . ." McNihil held his palm just above the sleeping
girl's hip and watched the smaller tattoos begin drifting
toward it. "Maybe I've gotten to the point where I'm the
one who wants to know."

"About that poor bastard Travelt? And the prowler that's
got him inside?" The Adder clome shook his head. "Give it
up. It's gone someplace where, even if you do locate it,
you're not going to be able to communicate with whatever's
left of the human part. You're never going to find out what
you want." A sour, gloating tinge entered the Adder clome's
voice. "You might as well go back to Harrisch and tell him
that it's a wild-goose chase. It doesn't matter whether there's
anything of Travelt that's not dead yet. There are some places
that are even farther away than that."

"Like where?"

"Don't bother. Don't even *try* threatening me." Another
shake of the head, the Adder clome obviously savoring the
moment. "You can do whatever you want, wipe up the floor
with me—in a place like this, that might actually be
fun—and it's not going to help you now. Because there isn't
any *now*. This is something you're remembering. Remember?" That made the Adder clome smile evilly. "It's out of
your control—just like everything else."

"Maybe so." Unperturbed, McNihil let one fingertip
touch the sleeping girl's skin. The tattooed image of a single
tear collected under his finger, like a black raindrop that all
the fires couldn't evaporate. "But that doesn't mean it's under *your* control."

The Adder clome stiffened, drawing away from him.
"What do you mean?"

"Just what I said. Somebody else is running this show."
McNihil took away his hand from the cube bunny. "You
know it. And I know it."

A moan sounded, less of pleasure and more of pain. The

flames rose higher from the bed, catching McNihil's hand, sending a hot, quick stab through his arm. On the engulfed mattress, the sleeping girl writhed, barely visible through the fire that had finally penetrated her dreams. Inside her open mouth, the kiss-notched tongue drew back from the scalding teeth. Thicker black smoke billowed up into McNihil's face, the sudden pressure enough to push him into the center of the hotel room.

"You think you're so smart." The figure of the Adder clome and his glaring eyes could be seen past the flames that had suddenly vaulted from the floor to the charred ceiling. "I tried to help you—to warn you—but you wouldn't listen to me." A storm of ashes, black and etched with hot sparks, swirled through the hotel room; the last fragments of glass in the broken windows spat through the stifling air as oxygen rushed from the night outside. McNihil guarded the mask of his face with his hands as the sharp flecks stung his shoulders and upraised arm. "So have it the way you want," came the Adder clome's voice. "You want to talk to whoever's in charge? Fine. Just don't blame me if you don't like what you hear."

The firestorm knocked McNihil from his feet. He felt the heat of the burning carpet through his arched back, spearing his heart on the point of its white-hot tongue and straining it against the melting plastic of his shirt buttons. The flames rolled over him like a red tide, obliterating his sight of the hotel room. For a moment, his vision doubled; he could see, superimposed upon the wavering afterimage of the room's walls and ceiling, another space, darker and torn open to a night sky without churning columns of smoke. The glimpse of the bar where some other, more physical, part of him lay, evaporated into steam off his eyes.

In this room, at the End Zone Hotel, charred bones toppled to the floor beside McNihil, as the bed collapsed into itself. The moans of the sleeping girl had ended seconds

before, as though she had passed into deeper, dreamless sleep.
McNihil turned his face away, squeezing his eyelids shut as
the tattoos, freed of any skin, rose like heavy ash, edges curling in the heat.

"Say hello to her for me." The Adder clome's sneering
voice came from somewhere beyond the flames. "It's been a
while—but that's the way I want to keep it." The voice
faded under the roar of the firestorm. "Better you than me,
pal . . ."

PART FOUR

No soy yo quien veis vivir
sombra soy de quien murio.

Senora, ya no soy ya
quien gozaba nuestra gloria;
ya es perdido mi memoria,
que en el otro mundo esta.

El que fue veustro y sera,
sombra soy de quien murio.

I am not the one whom you see living;
The shadow am I of one who died.

Mistress, I am not he
Who enjoyed our glories;
The memory of me is lost
And dwells in another world.

I am not the one who was and will
be yours;
The shadow am I of one who died.

—ANONYMOUS RENAISSANCE LYRIC

NINETEEN

TO KEEP PEOPLE WITHOUT SKINS ALIVE

areful. You don't want to step in that."

November heard the cameraman's warning. She looked down at the catwalk below her feet, a narrow path without handrails or any other protective barrier. The interlocking planks were made of nubbly-surfaced recycled plastic, suspended a couple of meters above the street. At first, when the DZ limo had dropped her off as close as it could get to this zone, she'd thought that the city blocks had been flooded for some obscure purpose, an urban ocean bound in by a ring of prefab emergency dikework. Now she saw the slow, gelatinous nature of the substance filling all the spaces between the gutted buildings; the sight of it brought back recent memories of dreaming. The blackened nose of a

burnt-out 747 carcass poked through the transparent membrane covering the gel.

"What the hell is this shit?" A wave with no crest, rolling
heavily under the lake's surface, had splattered through a
break near the edge of the catwalk, enough to leave a few
rounded, snotlike drops on the toe of November's boot before subsiding. "It's disgusting . . ."

"Sterile nutrient medium." The cameraman rode with
his equipment on a small boom platform, angled out from a
cross-girdered pier planted in the middle of the street, the gel
substance rising and falling in slow motion around the base.
"Like they use in hospitals. To keep people without skins
alive."

That's where I saw it before. Not just in dreams, but in the
hospital reality, in the burn ward. And from the inside out;
she'd been floating in the stuff, her own charred body slowly
dissolving toward death. Whatever consciousness occasion-
ally sparked under the weight of the anesthetics, it had
looked out at the world through a vertical stratum of this
stuff.

"What's it doing here?" November had no option but to
wrap her arms around herself, trying to hold in her own
body heat against the chill wind sliding past the buildings.
The unseen Pacific was somewhere to the west side of the
city; she'd caught a glimpse of it as the DZ limo had driven
her out from the rail station. "So much of it . . ."

"It's only got one use, lady." The cameraman looked
even younger than she did, as though his cocky network
attitude postdated her own baby-new skin. "Just like I said:
keeping people alive." The wet expanse glittered in the dark
lenses over his eyes; the enduring clouds had parted for a
moment, bringing up enough light to trigger the glasses'
photochrome. He leaned forward in his perch, one elbow
against his knee, his earphones' coiled wire trailing behind

him. "Maybe I was wrong; maybe you should go ahead and step in it. Dive right in and join the party."

She looked down and saw what the cameraman meant. The thick liquid wasn't empty; there was more floating in it than just the ashes and dirt that'd been lifted from the streets' surface and out of the ground-level stories of the fire-blackened buildings. The shapes drifting in the gel were vaguely human in form, but with outlines blurred. *People without skins*—those words moved inside her head with the same wavering grace. *Poor bastards,* thought November, with no trace of irony. That was what happened when people got careless; she should know.

It took only a few seconds for the visions to hook up, overlap, and synch together; the one she saw below the narrow planks of the catwalk and the one she carried inside her head. The figures in the gelatinous liquid were the same that she had dreamed of back in the hospital's burn-ward chamber. She'd been too connected-up then, with the pharmaceuticals dripping into her own veins, to have reacted with anything more than mild, hammered, apathetic curiosity. Now, though, the sight drew her gut into a queasy knot and ran an ice probe up the links of her spine. Past her own reflection on the gel surface, she could discern white bones, whole skeletons turned as rubbery as life-sized novelty items, rib cages wavering like sea-anemone fingers, femurs and ulnas bending into shallow *U* shapes, as though boiled limp. Tied to the bones by loosened sinews and integuments were the glistening doubled fists and ovoids of the lungs and kidneys, spleen and gall; pericardial tissue shimmered and dulled with each heart's exposed pulse.

Just the same, thought November. She'd seen exactly the same in her dreaming, the softly eviscerated but still-living human clusters under the slow waves. But not a dream; she realized that now. The cameraman was the tip-off, along with all the other networks' news-crew gear that she'd seen at the gel's bounded perimeter. *I saw it on TV*—that made it even more dreamlike, in a way. There'd been a set in the hospital room, she remembered now, even in the chamber where she'd been floating on the other side of the infection-proof barrier, in the same nutrient-enhanced syrup as this. The video monitor had been up on a white-enameled bracket in the corner of the room, way beyond all the other equipment with its much more urgent and interesting displays of her various vital signs, the blipping tickers and green traces that'd gone up and down with her pulse and breath. Plus, McNihil's advance payment to the hospital apparently hadn't stretched as far as dialing in the video set to any of the premium sat-a-wire channels, so there had been nothing on it but the usual hammering dinfomercials and the FCC-mandated news-minutes. That was probably when she'd seen the coverage of this thickening human stew, the dissolving bodies wavering in their sustenant medium like spore colonies in watery agar, the streets of this city zone turned into one gigantic petri dish. The images transmitted by this camera-jockey and the others stationed here by the networks had infiltrated November's brain while she'd been out of it, her lidless eyes focused on the TV up in the burn-ward chamber's corner; when that nonsubstantial part of her had finally crept back inside her head, she'd assumed she'd dreamed all those liquid pictures.

"How long is this setup going to last?" Curious, she knelt on the catwalk and reached down to poke the gel with one careful fingertip. The semi-liquid rippled at her touch, the circles widening at a ponderous rate, but her finger didn't get wet. Just the same as in the hospital's burn-ward chambers, the transparent membrane encased the fluid, sealing it from both evaporation and infection. "This one's been here for a while." She figured that the layout must date from the blaze at the End Zone Hotel and the contagious rutting that had followed; some of the surrounding buildings were still marked with the residue of the fire-dousing foam that'd been used then. "When are you going to shut down and move on?"

"Are you kidding? This is the poly-orgynism of the century." The cameraman took a hand from the boom's controls and gestured across the small urban ocean. The far reaches, several blocks away, looked completely placid on the surface, the slowly writhing depths hidden beneath. "The ultimate connection, maybe. It doesn't get any better than this, at least for people in my business."

November knew what the cameraman was talking about. She'd never watched any of these real-time pornumentaries, not because she found them boring—just like everything else on the tube—but because she'd been able to calculate the sickly fascination of them. The sheer commercial appeal of this kind of coverage irritated her. Easy to see why the networks—and at least a couple of them were in whole or part owned and operated by DynaZauber—invested the setup expenses and devoted the on-wire time to these things, when and if they occurred. For the DZ subsidiaries, they probably got their share of the materials—the sterile nutrient medium, the barrier membrane—at cost from the mother corporation. The only real outlay was for a stake in the scouting pool with the rest of the networks, the constant search for and immediate response to the sex-fueled events.

If she'd been able to hang around awhile longer at the End Zone Hotel fire, instead of falling through the roof and several stories of burning building, November would've been able to watch the setup taking place, the godlike genesis of the poly-orgynism. She'd seen the prebirth, the first coition, the massing and interconnecting of the bodies still with their skins on, the human figures filling the streets around the trashed buildings and the open center area's downed airliner. The conflagration that the foam put out had started thousands of others, metaphorically speaking; November had

seen them from the burning hotel's roof, looking over the
edge while either waiting for McNihil or getting stiff-armed
by him. All that straight-on physical connecting, sweating
body on body, overlapping each other into all possible variations, daisy chains of filled, swollen and exuding orifices,
semen and blood striping flesh like knotted barber poles, the
massed radiation from the streets rising up into November's
face as hot as any flames coming up the End Zone Hotel's
stairwells. She remembered the building shivering before a
section of its roof had collapsed beneath her, as though the
thrashing limbs had triggered some deep seismic fracture.
The extinguishing foam sprayed by the low-flying helicop-
ters, nozzles stiff beneath the numbered fuselages, had been
all the extra ingredient needed, the only substance not produced by human flesh or imagination, making the connection between connections complete, the many organisms
into one compound animal, a colony of undifferentiated sen-
sual function. *E pluribus unum* was the creature's motto,
translated as "Let's connect ourselves to oblivion"; its flag
was the shredding tatters of skin, blood-edged, that chafed
and peeled away from the flesh of its once-separate components. That much heat was produced by friction as well as
lust; more skin-on-skin scouring, teeth-bared biting, and engorged piercing than human tissue could endure. *Maybe they
don't need scouts,* thought November, *on the prowl looking for
this kind of thing.* Maybe all that were needed were some
upper-atmosphere satellites, way beyond the reach of the
Noh-files, with thermal-imaging receptors trained on the
earth's surface. Any eruption specifically in the Gloss—if it
wasn't a volcano, then it was worth sending a hit-crew with
cameras and broadcast equipment.

Of course, there was more required than just the cameras
and the transmission antennae. November saw more of them
now, the strategic placement of their derricks and elevated
stations becoming apparent as she glanced up from the gel's

surface. The corporate medical teams had been here at the
start and were now long gone, maybe coming back every
couple of weeks to peel back a section of the barrier membrane and top up the sterile nutrient medium. Plus fish out
whatever parts of the poly-orgynism that had finally dissolved their personal gestalt to the point of no longer being
capable of maintaining even externally supported life functions.

"Hey, it's not like I'm not *ready* to leave." The network
cameraman's voice broke into November's thoughts. "I've
been out here on this particular tour of duty long enough to
develop calluses on my ass; I'd love to *rotate* home for a little
R and R. A decent meal and a hot shower would be heaven
right about now."

"A cold shower," said November, "would probably be
more like it." She could feel the frequency coming off the
slow ocean. The Sea of Sex; standing on the catwalk was like
being on the shore of some desolate terra incognita, gazing
out past where the continental shelf fell off into sunless
depths. The Pacific, wherever it was out to the west of this
Gloss section, was nothing by comparison. The wind sliding
over the gel's surface membrane cut past the nausea in her
gut, softly fingering hormone outlets lower in her groin.
This ocean had its trenches in the back reaches of the human
mind, which meant infinite. The poor bastards who had
dived into this harbor may or may not have known that, but
they likely wouldn't have cared, anyway. "That's what you
get," murmured November, "when you finally get what you
want."

"What'd you say?"

She ignored the cameraman. The sonuvabitch was just
passing the time, she knew, idling like the rest of the crews
here until the poly-orgynism worked itself up into another
thrash of broadcastable action. Just like the earth's oceans,
ones like this alternated between storm and doldrums; the

DynaZauber limo, the transport arranged by Harrisch, had let her off here at a relatively quiet moment. The skinless, partially dissolved once-were-humans under the membrane drifted on slow currents through the gel, mingling their soft bones and loose organs with each other in lazy pre- and postcoital suspension. What in other waters might have been tangles of seaweed, November discerned as the branching nets of nerve endings, hooked up and knitted together from one dike wall to the farthest. Some of the neural systems still retained a rough human outline, like a scrawled ink sketch surrounding the appropriate bones and organs; others, propelled by an innate longing, had disengaged from their origins and entangled themselves with others, threading throughout in an endless chain. That was what made the streets' contents a single entity: the boundaries between one body and the next had been erased, with no ability to tell where one left off and another began in the resulting soup.

They must put something in there, figured November. *The corporations' so-called medical teams.* Something to speed up the dissolution process, to hasten the shedding of the pink and yellow and brown rags, no longer necessary and impediments to requited desire. Or perhaps they didn't have to add anything at all; that was a scary thought. That given half a chance, people would slough off the soft, thin barriers between themselves and achieve a nakedness of the exposed flesh, perfect for nonstop connecting. What was that old song? *'Tain't no sin/To take off your skin/And dance around in your bones, your bones/And dance around in your bones* . . . Might as well forget the bones, too; they weren't needed for this horizontal tango.

She stood up on the catwalk and wiped her fingertip against her trousers, though nothing wet and sticky had gotten on it. Just the nearness of the thing in the thick liquid—she'd already dropped the plural in her own mind—the spark coming through the membrane, half warning *(As we are, so could you be)* and half invitation *(So why not join us today?),* evoked an uneasy response in her gut and spine. The sun had lifted a little higher, pooling her shadow around her boots; now she saw thin black shapes, like clots of ashes, sliding between the top membrane and the poly-orgynism a few centimeters farther down. An arrow-pierced heart with a Mom banner beneath, a cartoon devil riding a pair of dice—*The tattoos,* realized November. The permanent ones and those that traveled from body to body; the skins might've dissolved, but not the images that had been inked upon them. A side effect of the poly-orgynism's creation: the tattoos had been set free, achieving a new life in the habitat of the sterile nutrient medium. They swam about now like pilot fish, cutting knifelike through the gel, darting among the blind kidneys and lungs, past the loose ropes of nerve tissue. Another realization, a little glimpse of the future: *Someday they'll breed.* She could see it now, the intermingling of design and motivating codes. Another generation, and the laughing devil with rolling-dice eyes would climb up on the Rock of Ages, the neoprimitivist tribal tiger stripes would tie themselves into Celtic knots, the banner toted by mourning doves would read out the name of a yet-unnamed god . . .

"Stick around," said the cameraman. "If you can." He'd gotten a cigarette going, dangling from the corner of his mouth, and was amusing himself by flicking lit matches onto the surface of the sex ocean. The little flames, before they died, left puckered scars on the barrier membrane; a visible shiver ran through the interlinked components of the poly-orgynism beneath. "Me and some of the other guys—" The cameraman gestured toward the other boom-platforms' derricks, with their almost-identical network crew members watching from behind their dark lenses. "We've got a break coming up in a few hours; union regulations. We could skip the catering wagons and go straight to dessert, if you know what I mean."

"I was born knowing," said November. She couldn't even be bothered to make a display of weariness, recognizing the variations on the same old lines. The stuff she'd gotten from the businessmen on the trains, back when she'd been into all that, back in her previous life. "Maybe you and your pals should go for seconds this time." Sad to think that nothing ever really changed, for most people, anyway. These network guys were probably getting all sweaty from watching the poly-orgynism's action for so long. "Because," said November, "there isn't going to be anything else happening. Not with me, at least."

"Why not, sweetheart?" The cameraman leaned his elbow on the controls of his equipment. He knew he'd been blown off, but didn't mind making light conversation to pass the time. "Could be fun."

"Could be." November copped a line from McNihil. "But I've got a job to do." She started down the catwalk to the burnt-out shell of the End Zone Hotel. Harrisch and the exec crew at DynaZauber had some reason for ferrying her up here in a private car; she might as well find out what it was. "Catch you later."

"If you're lucky."

She didn't look back. As she walked, the surface of the gelatinous liquid rippled, as though the spread-out multi-creature below were scratching at the underside of the membrane, trying to tell her something.

TWENTY

THE DEATH SCENE IN LA TRAVIATA

Wake up and—"

McNihil opened his eyes and gazed up at the charred ceiling. "I don't need to hear the rest of it." He rolled onto one arm, then managed to sit up, pulling himself together piece by piece. He'd heard the woman's voice, but couldn't tell where she was just yet. "Besides . . . all my dreams were incinerated a long time ago."

"That's what you think," said the ultimate barfly. "Seems like there was enough to get this place going again."

He turned his head and found her sitting on the edge of a sagging mattress, blackened but no longer burning. She sat with her legs elegantly crossed, regarding him with cold and

casual amusement. A thread of smoke drifted from the cigarette held aloft in one hand.

"I thought you didn't smoke." McNihil pulled his legs
up and slapped dust and ashes from his trousers. "That's what
you told me in the bar."

"That's right, I don't." The barfly made no move to take
a draw from the cigarette. "I'm just doing it for your sake. To
set the scene. Complete the picture."

"Don't bother." The floor was covered thick in ash, the
hotel room's walls broken open by the long-ago fire, shattered plaster revealing the burnt beams and studs of the fram-
ing inside. The door stood open, showing its brass number in
the center and an expanse of similarly damaged hallway.
"I've got these." With a smudged fingertip, McNihil tapped
the corner of his eye. "They already show me things pretty
much the way I want them."

"Thank God." The barfly stubbed the cigarette out
against the narrow bed-frame. "It's a filthy habit." She
flicked the dead cigarette out into the rubble in the middle of
the floor, then tossed her golden hair back behind her shoulder. "I wouldn't have made it back then, in those old movies. All that smoking all the time—looks great, a real air of
mystery, but I would've started coughing and wouldn't have
been able to stop." The barfly smiled at him, eyes half-lidded. "Not very glamorous, huh?"

"Depends." He wasn't making much progress in clean-
ing himself up. His clothes looked as if he'd been rolling in
the ashes and charred bits of wood for hours, like some
rummy undergoing the DT's in an abandoned building.
"There might be a few lung specialists in the audience. They
always get a thrill out of the death scene in *La Traviata*."

"Yeah, I love that part where she says she feels so much
better, and then she croaks."

McNihil looked around the ruins of the End Zone Hotel. "This is stuff I'm remembering—right? From when I

kissed you." He figured this room must be on one of the upper floors; the brass number on the door started with a five. "I like it better this way. That fire shit was making me nervous."

The barfly shook her head in mock exasperation. "We work so hard on your behalf, and what do we get? Complaints. You should hear yourself sometimes. Bitch, bitch, bitch."

He ignored that comment. "What happened to the other one? The Adder clome?" McNihil stood up; he leaned over in a futile attempt to brush more gray ash from the knees of his trousers, then straightened. "He still around here?"

"That guy? The connector's a stone nuisance." On the barfly's face, the exasperation was genuine this time. "Always hanging around here—"

"What? In my memories?"

"No, you idiot." The barfly shook her head. "In the place where your memories came from—these memories, at least."

"Where's that?" McNihil tried to wipe the black traces of ash from his hands. "The Wedge?"

"Bigger than that," replied the woman. "Bigger and older. Come on—you know all about it. You must, or you wouldn't be here. You wouldn't have come around looking for me." She smiled, as if enjoying her own reminiscence. "You wouldn't have found me. And we wouldn't have had that kiss." A tilt of the head, the golden hair falling past one flirty eye. "*I* enjoyed it."

"I bet you did. Leaving men on the floor must be a kick."

Her smile broadened. "Maybe you should try it sometime."

"Yeah, in my next life." McNihil straightened out his jacket. He could feel the weight of the coiled cable dragging it to one side; he rummaged with one hand in the pocket, to

check if everything he'd been carrying with him was still
there. With all the banging around and getting decked sense-
less he'd gone through recently, there was a chance it might
have fallen out along the way. "If I get one."

"Shouldn't be that hard." The barfly shrugged. "All you
gotta do is finish up the job you came here for . . . and
then you can go wherever you want. And do whatever you
want to do."

"Where's 'here'? The Wedge? The ur-Wedge? Wedge
Beyond Wedge?" He couldn't think of anything else to call
it. "Or just the End Zone Hotel?"

"Like I've been trying to tell you." She leaned back,
balancing herself against the charred mattress with one hand;
her gaze radiated sultry languor. "We're very accommodat-
ing here. You can have it however you want."

"That sounds like the pitch the Adder clome was making
to me."

The barfly's gaze hardened. "I told you: that guy's a
nuisance. At least he is around here. We only tolerate him
because we have to."

"Why's that?"

"He's got the right." The barfly gave a shrug. "Somebody like that . . . he stands outside the gates of the palace.
Typical male mentality; half worshiper, half guardian. So he
serves a function, in his own way. Both here and on the
outside, out in that other world. He's the first circle you have
to pass through to get to where you want to go. If you can't
get past him—if you find the things you see at a Snake
Medicine™ clinic too scary or too disgusting to deal with, or
maybe you find them too fascinating to get past—then
you're not ready for the real thing. It takes a little courage.
Even a little wisdom." Her free hand gestured lazily toward
McNihil. "That's why you're here. You must have what it
takes. Even if you don't know it."

"I'll take it on faith," said McNihil.

"You pretty much have to. There aren't any other options. Not around here." The barfly pointed to the room's
single window. "Take a look outside. Tell me what you see."

McNihil picked his way across the rubble-strewn floor,
over water-soaked scraps of wall plaster, timbers that had
fallen from the ceiling, carpeting that had once been industrial gray and threadbare and was now crisped black, an
empty bureau that had toppled over in the fire, spilling its
drawers like a stack of lidless boxes lined with yellowing
newspaper. The glass had shattered out of the window frame,
leaving jagged splinters that crunched beneath McNihil's
steps. He brushed any sharp bits from the blackened sill and
leaned his hands on it.

Outside was the urban zone, a slice of remote-north
Gloss, that he remembered from before—from the world
outside, his real memories—when he'd come up here to take
care of another job, icing the would-be pirate kid. Like coming home: the remains of the kid, a living length of neural
and cortical tissue, were now the fat coiled loop in McNihil's
jacket pocket. The buildings looked the same, at least;
McNihil could see the one a couple of blocks down that had
the shabby movie theater on the ground floor, where he'd
done the hit on the kid, and from where he'd dragged the
face-muffled and squirming body back here to the End Zone
Hotel. And farther away, past the corner of the tallest building McNihil could see, was the open space where he'd
gotten panhandled via remote control from the burnt-out
'net-twit headcases in the downed jetliner. . . .

"Pretty good view from up here, huh?" The barfly's
voice was soft and patient. "You can see all sorts of things
. . . if you try."

The woman was right about that. McNihil's eyes felt
tense in their sockets, as though the pupils were somehow
being overwhelmed with the rush of optical information
from outside. A fierce clarity seemed to fill the air, as though

the smoke from the hotel fire had managed to scrub the
constant, obscuring impurities that had hung between each
atom of oxygen and the next. *I can see for miles and miles,*
thought McNihil. It had been a long time since that had
been the case. If the End Zone Hotel had been tall enough,
or if the *Noh*-flies would've let him ascend into the sky, he
could have seen all the way across the Pacific, to the far
shores of the Gloss, Kamchatka and Xinjiang. The godlike
headiness of the sensation rushed through McNihil's body
like pharmaceutical-grade amphetamine, sparking every cell
and setting his heart stumbling until it hit the right up-tempo
beat. *This is what Harrisch wanted,* he realized. *When he climbed
up on that cross.* To see everything at once, all the universal
data flowing into the receptors in your palms, like reverse
stigmata. Jesus bled for the world; Harrisch and the rest of
the execs at DynaZauber would improve on that, and let the
world bleed for them.

"Yes . . ." McNihil's voice was a murmur, words
tinged with awe. "I can see . . . everything . . ."

"Except for what's different. About how you see." From
behind him, the barfly pushed another hint in McNihil's
direction. "It's not just *what* you see. Come on. You gotta
think about it, pal."

Then he did see it. McNihil looked up to the sky, just as
the heavy, dark-gray-bellied clouds parted, as if on cue to
help him along, a hand parting the curtain. His gaze dropped
back to the zone's surrounding buildings; their shadows
etched sharp and knifelike across the streets and against each
other in a way that he hadn't seen for a long time. Long
enough to have forgotten.

"It's daylight," said McNihil. The realization struck him
with wonder. Ash slid under his palms as he gripped the
windowsill tighter, as though the view beyond it might slip
away if not held to him. "That's what it is. The sun's out."
He turned his head, glancing back over his shoulder toward

the woman sitting on the bed. "I haven't seen that . . . in years." How long had it been? That was lost as well, along with so many other things. "Because of . . ."

"I know, sweetheart." The barfly regarded him with outright sympathy. "Because of the eye thing. What you had them do to you. And the way you see. All that eternal-night business. But that was what you wanted, wasn't it?"

"Back then." McNihil slowly nodded, looking out at the bright window's view again. The direction of the building's shadows indicated early morning. *That makes sense,* he thought. Just as if a real night had ended. Hours or centuries could've passed while he'd been wandering around in this version of the End Zone Hotel; millennia—or sec-onds—since he'd met up with the barfly in that dive at the Wedge's neon-lit perimeter. For all he knew, he was still lying on the floor of the bar, hammered beneath the mem-ory load her scarred tongue had given him. His lips could be just parting from hers, the blue spark of contact fading into the taste of battery metal in his own mouth. He didn't know. *Just like a lot of things,* he mused. "You think you know," he said aloud. "What you want. And then you change your mind." He turned back toward the woman behind him. "Or you have it changed for you."

"You should be grateful." She gave a small shrug. "Most people aren't so lucky. They don't get the opportunity. They have to live with what they decide on. Usually, there's no going back."

The hotel room's window faced east; McNihil could see his own shadow now, black cast across the ashes and rubble. The top of his shadow, his head, just barely reached the tip of one of the barfly's spike-heeled shoes, as though genuflecting there. Not in worship of her, the vessel, the instrument of transmission. But what was behind her. The other one, that he'd had that momentary glimpse of, back in the bar. *Ver-*

rity—he'd never thought he'd actually see her. And for good reason.

"There shouldn't have been for me, either." The implications of what had happened, what he was able to see now, had started to work themselves out inside McNihil's head. With one fingertip, he touched the corner of his eye. "There's no way you should've been able to get inside here. It's private. It's locked in. What's in here—" He tapped the curve of bone at the side of his face. "It's not in this world . . . or the other. It's all my own, the way I see things."

"You should've known better than that." The barfly looked unimpressed. "You underestimate what—and who—you're dealing with. At least the other guy, the Adder clome, is up to speed on the situation."

"Really? So who am I dealing with?" McNihil knew he'd have to ask just this question, eventually. "If it's Verrity, then I've been here before."

"That's one name she goes by." The unsmiling gaze of the barfly annihilated the space between herself and McNihil. "There's hundreds of others. She's been around for a long time."

"But not going by the name of Verrity." It was McNihil's turn to smile, both grim and rueful. "That's something I know for sure."

"Why's that?"

"Because I made Verrity up," said McNihil. "She never existed. She was a lie. A fiction. The excuse I gave to the Collection Agency, about why my team of asp-heads and our investigation of the Wedge went wrong. Why we wound up getting our asses handed back to us." The words rasped in McNihil's throat. "And some of us worse than others. Some of the asp-heads—a lot of them—they died out here."

"And after all that happened . . . that many of your friends getting killed . . . and you thought that Verrity

didn't exist?" The barfly shook her head in amazement.
"What would it take to convince you?"

"It's kind of hard to believe in something when you
know you thought it up yourself." Telling his secret history
was oddly painless for McNihil; the story had lain next to his
heart for so long that it had developed its own calluses and
system of anesthesia. "And that's what I had done—way
before the Wedge investigation went wrong." The words
came easily, as though well rehearsed; he'd told them to
himself often enough, lying awake in the dark of his crummy
apartment, in a room not much bigger than this one, all
through those hours of the endless night. "I knew it was
going to go wrong, that there was no way we were going to
pull it off—"

"Because you knew it was bogus," said the barfly. "From
the beginning. It was a fraud, a number you were running on
the agency."

McNihil gave a quick, humorless laugh. "You must've
heard this story already."

"It's not much of a secret. Not from the side I come
from, that is." The barfly made a gesture with one hand that
took in all of the End Zone Hotel beyond the little room,
and beyond. "You may have fooled everyone you worked
for, everyone at the Collection Agency . . . but over here
in the Wedge, we knew what the score was. You were in
over your head, weren't you?"

He nodded slowly, keeping his silence.

"How far in debt?" The barfly peered closer at him.
"How much did you owe?"

McNihil shrugged. "Plenty. It doesn't matter." He
didn't want to talk about that part of the story, the bit about
his dead wife and how he'd connected her over. Leaving her
not quite dead enough. He hoped that the barfly, and the
others on this side, didn't know about that part. Not because
he cared what they thought about him. *I just don't want to*

hear it, thought McNihil. Not in their mouths. "There's always some way to owe money, and not be able to pay it."

"So you found a way," said the barfly, coolly and evenly. "To make the money. All you had to do was lie and hand a wad of bullshit off to the Collection Agency. You were smart enough to do that, at least. Fabricate the evidence that something was going on in the Wedge, that down among the perverts and prowlers, there was major copyright infringement going on, that the agency's clients were getting ripped off in a big way. Big enough to be worth doing something about."

"It was easy." Talking about this part wasn't so bad; he could still manage a certain feeling of self-congratulation, even though he knew how it'd all turned out, eventually. "Fooling the Collection Agency doesn't take much work at all. Or much brains. Because the agency *wants* to be fooled. That's its fatal flaw. The agency exists for the sole purpose of looking for copyright infringement, for theft of intellectual property; if it doesn't find that, it ceases to exist. So I wasn't the only one in trouble, if there wasn't enough work for us asp-heads. As a matter of fact, you could say I was doing the agency a favor by lying to it. In my own way—*I was keeping the Collection Agency alive.*"

"You . . . and how many others like you?" The barfly looked both amused and disgusted. "How many other asp-heads were doing the same thing, all through the agency? Going out and finding evidence of copyrights being messed with, agency clients not getting paid for use of their property, all of that, from little punks with a modem and a hokey encryption program to some bootleg polycarbonate being cranked out in the basement of the Gtsug-lag-khang in Lhasa. Once the bullshit starts, it's hard to say where it ends, isn't it?"

McNihil nodded. That had been one of his meager comforts, in those endless nights back in his apartment, with the water stains on the ceiling etching themselves into his sleep-less eyes. The comfort of knowing that he wasn't the only one, that there were others caught up in lies as deeply as he'd buried himself. Lies going both ways: the asp-heads lied to the Collection Agency, which in turn smiled its collective smile, and lied and said that it believed them. For all either side of the equation knew, the game would be over if it weren't for the mutual quasi-deceptions, the lies that the liars and the lied-to tacitly agreed not to expose. At this point, there might not be enough copyright infringement going on anywhere in the Gloss to justify the agency's continued exis-tence and the asp-heads' continued employment. Maybe the Collection Agency and its asp-heads had done their job too well; now, to find anybody stupid enough to violate intellec-tual-property rights, given the lethal consequences, they were reduced to scraping up idiot punk kids like the one whose strung-out brains McNihil was carrying in his pocket.

The big copyright-protection battles—the shutting-down of the Chinese bootleg factories, the absorption of the Vladivostok bourse and their *teneviki* holding corporations into the millennial Geneva agreements—had been fought and won; the wars were over. Or at least for the time being. Which was, McNihil knew, the age-old problem of the gar-rison state, applied to matters of intellectual property and its protection. Just because the war was over, that didn't mean you could disband the military; if that happened, there wouldn't be a convenient army of asp-heads to call on when the pirates, the big ones, saw a whole new world of opportu-nity lying before them, property rights that couldn't be de-fended against depredation. At the same time, if a standing army was going to be maintained, something had to be found for it to do; an unused gun turns to rust. So if the asp-heads, on their own initiative, concocted their own assign-ments out of thin air, all the better as far as the Collection Agency was concerned. Anything went wrong, the agency could deny responsibility, and the individual asp-head, the lying prime motivator of the fraud, was left hanging out to dry. *Just like I was,* thought McNihil. There might not have been anyone fooled at all, by what he'd told them.

"Except in your case, things went way bad." The barfly had read his thoughts as though they had gone scrolling down the blank mask of his face. "People—or at least other asp-heads—they died. Right here in the Wedge. And not very prettily, either." She casually examined the deep scarlet nails of her hand. "They were the ones who paid the price. Not you."

"I didn't know," said McNihil. "That there was going to be one."

"Then you're even stupider than you look. Even with your original face." The barfly's voice hardened, contemptuous. "You should've known, but you were too much of a smart-ass for that. What did you think you were connecting around with down here? A bunch of losers and perverts, all just banging away at each other all night long? Just so we could provide lots of sensory raw material for the prowlers to come down and pick up, so they could take it home to their owners? Real nice for *them,* I suppose, if that'd been the way it was; all the fun and none of the risks. But then, that's how the guy you're working for, that's how he pitches the arrangement, isn't it?"

"Pretty much." A slow nod. "That's how somebody else got roped in. Name of Travelt."

"You don't have to tell me about him," said the barfly. "I know all about that story. More than *you* do."

"That's why I came here. To find out what I don't know."

"How flattering." With a wry grimace, the barfly shook her head. "Really, pal—you don't have to come right out and *tell* a girl that you've got some other reason for putting the moves on her. Like I didn't know, or something. Like

I'm as dumb as you are. You couldn't let me keep a few illusions?"

"Why should I?" McNihil let the mask of his face show a thin smile. "Why should you get to keep them, when nobody else does?"

"You seem to still have a few of yours. That's either a tribute to your stubbornness . . . or your stupidity. Even that Travelt guy learned his lesson after a while."

"And what was that? What did he learn?"

"He learned," said the barfly, "that there wasn't anything he could *do* here. Not in this world. His bosses over on the other side—the same ones you're working for—they may have let him think he was a big deal, a take-charge kind of guy, somebody who got things done. But he was way out of his league here. Out of his league, and off his turf. The Wedge, and what's beyond it—that doesn't belong to the DynaZauber corporation, or to the Collection Agency, or anything from that other world you came from." The scorn in the woman's voice became more withering with each syllable she spoke, like acid going through a reverse titration process. "You're in *our* territory now, pal. The Wedge—everything over here—it belongs to itself."

"What about the other one I saw? What about . . . Verrity?"

"Who?" A wicked malice showed in the barfly's smile. "I thought she didn't exist. I thought you made her up."

"That's what I thought, too." McNihil spread his hands apart, a small gesture of surrender. "But I've changed my mind."

"Good. That shows you're learning. There's hope for you yet. Maybe that's why the Wedge is being so nice to you, letting you off the hook. Maybe . . ." With a tilt of her head to one side, the barfly gave him a newly appraising look. "Maybe you'll be as lucky as the other one. Maybe she'll do something . . . *nice* . . . for you. Like she did for that Travelt guy."

"What'd she do for him?" McNihil asked, though he already knew what the answer was going to be.

"Come on," chided the barfly. "I *know* you know. Your head's not too hard to get into . . . at least, not for somebody like me. I can walk around inside your skull like it's the hotel lobby. Easier, in fact, considering the present state of things around here. All this stage-setting, the heavy symbolism and shit—it really gets in the way, sometimes."

"How was it when Travelt came here?"

A dismissive shake of the head. "I don't even remember. It's hard to keep track of these things, when everybody's walking around with the same face, that prowler mask." She gestured with one hand toward McNihil. "Except it wasn't mask for that Travelt guy, the way it is for you; the Adder clome told me about the services he did for you."

"That's true." McNihil had expected that the barfly would be up-to-speed on that matter. "Travelt was actually inside his prowler. The transference had taken place. Enough of him had passed from one to the other. That corpse I was shown—there really wasn't anything left of him in there."

"Lucky for him. In a lot of ways." The barfly gave a slow nod. "He got a second chance. *To become real.* How many people even get one chance at something like that?" Her gaze weighed and judged McNihil. "That must be why you came here. Because you knew it was your big opportunity."

"You might be surprised," said McNihil. "I already had my chance." *And I took it,* he said to himself. There were some things that the barfly didn't know, despite this being her turf. Even when she'd kissed him, she hadn't been able to tell. The spark had passed from her mouth to his, this memory into his head; that was all that mattered. *They think there's only one mask possible*—they didn't know what he'd done to prepare himself for this journey. The ultimate mask, which concealed a difference greater than that between the human and the fake; no one had found him out so far. He might pull it off yet.

"Maybe you did . . . and maybe you didn't." The barfly drew her head back, studying McNihil as if seeing him for the first time. "I don't know; I'm not the one to decide. But if you're hiding something—if there's something you think you can keep from being found out—then you're playing a dangerous game, pal."

"Who am I playing against?"

"What?" The barfly raised an eyebrow. "Verrity isn't enough of a name for you?"

"No . . ." McNihil shook his head. "Not if it isn't the real one."

"Real, schmeal—that sort of thing just doesn't apply here. Not as far as names go, at least. There's a thousand different names for her, just like there are for the Wedge. It just depends on where you're coming from." The barfly's gesture pointed beyond McNihil. "Take another look out the window. A good look, this time."

The light had shifted outside; looking up as he stood at the window, McNihil saw the dark streaks of clouds cutting beneath the sun. Around the buildings, the shadows had diminished and grown less distinct, a slow fade into the graying daylight.

"Tell me what you see."

He didn't answer the barfly. McNihil leaned his hands against the charred windowsill, bringing his face past the shards of glass still embedded in the frame. The remains of the buildings' shadows had drawn his gaze downward. Now he saw what lay in the streets.

"I told you." The barfly's voice was a soft whisper from behind him. "I warned you. This isn't anywhere you want to be playing games. She plays for keeps."

When he'd been at the End Zone Hotel before, in that

other world he'd left behind, he'd looked down from the
rooftop. The building had been in flames then, real ones that
consumed both architecture and flesh. But past the fire and
billowing smoke, McNihil had been able to see the mass
overlapping and interconnecting copulation that had been
taking place down at ground level, the bodies writhing and
seeking each other's heat in the wet, sticky bounds of the
fire-dousing foam. All that motion had ceased, along with
any warmth, either fiery or body temperature.

The foam had been sluiced away, down the street's gutters and out to this world's hidden sea, by endless centuries
of storms. Leaving behind the remains, in this world, of what
had been alive in that other one. Whitening bones were
knitted together, a stiff tapestry of static coitus. The human
skeletons reached as far as McNihil could see, as though a
tide had receded from among the buildings, revealing coral
reefs at their base. Empty eye sockets gazed back at him,
darkness and silence inside the bone, hollow grins fixed in
transports of idiot delight. *We came here,* said the skeletons to
McNihil, *in more ways than one.* He could hear them inside
his head. *And it was worth it.*

"Sometimes she dances," the barfly said softly, "arrayed
in skulls. Those ornaments have to come from somewhere,
don't they?"

"I suppose so." This was part of the memory, he knew.
That they had given him in the barfly's kiss—*This is what they
want me to see,* thought McNihil. "I guess it's all part of the
gig."

"She has one name when she's like that. And one dread-
ful visage. Probably better—for you, that is—if you don't see
her in that form."

McNihil glanced back over his shoulder. "Do I have a
choice?"

"No . . ." The barfly shook her head. "Not really. Not
here. But you have luck; at least for a little while. You're

lucky you're from the Gloss, the real one outside. That's where her worshipers know her as Tlazoltéotl. Also Ixcuina, or Tlaelquani, depending upon whether you want the Nahuatl, the pure Aztec, or the original Huaxtec."

He'd seen that name, the first one, before. On the sandwich-board advertisements of the homeless marching single-file in nocturnal alleys, on a bishop's monitor and a dead man's stomach, revealed and hidden. McNihil supposed it'd been inevitable that he'd meet up with her someday. But not just yet.

"It doesn't feel like luck," said McNihil.

"You don't even know." The ultimate barfly slowly shook her head. "To have any encounter with Tlazoltéotl at all, to have seen her in my face the way you did, and still be walking . . . you're a totally lucky bastard."

"Why? Who is she?"

"Like I said." The barfly gave a shrug. "Different names, different forms. But always the Filth Deity—that's what the name means—the goddess of sexual impurity and deep, bad, annihilating sin. First a seductress, with no thought in her immaculate head other than connecting. Then comes her first destructive form, the one dedicated to gambling, risking and daring everything, including your own life. Then the redemptress, the form that can absorb and absolve human sin. That form can forgive sinners and remove all the world's corruption. But it's not her last form. The last form is the hag with teeth of iron, the destroyer of pretty youths and all innocence. Like, I said—everybody meets up with her eventually. But not many walk away."

"She's the one with the wild black hair? The crazy eyes?"

"Very good," said the barfly. "You'll know her when you see her again. The wild hair, the crazy eyes—and wearing the flayed skin of one of her victims." The barfly smiled.

"Rather appropriate for around here, I think you'd have to say."

"And this is her world," said McNihil. "Isn't it?"

"Of course it is." The barfly regarded him with amusement. "What else could it be? This business with the prowlers, people trying to protect themselves from the dark and scary stuff . . . what good does it do? Nothing at all. The prowlers can't help you. Nothing can. Just because you created a world without Tlazoltéotl in it doesn't mean it was ever going to remain that way. The doors will be broken down and the dark, scary stuff will come flooding in." One of her hands flicked a tiny gesture toward him. "Same way with your own little world. Yeah, you made up Verrity . . . but it didn't end there. You made her up—*and then you made her real.* You made the place for her, out of your own lusts and fears. And Verrity came to fill it. You should've known that was going to happen."

He knew she was right. But he still had a job to do.

"What about Travelt?" McNihil turned away from the window. "That's who I came here to find. That's my job. You said she did something nice for him. So I take it he's still alive?"

"Sure," said the barfly. "But that's not going to help you."

"You mean because of him being inside his prowler? I can deal with that."

The barfly shook her head and laughed. "He's gone way beyond that. He was looking for a place to hide. From everything. Just walking around inside a prowler wasn't going to do it for him. He knew they could still find him. Somebody like *you* could find him." She leaned back, smiling. "So he's gone where you won't be able to reach him. He had a Full Prince Charles done on himself. That's what she did for Travelt: he got it for free. On the house, as it were."

That was just what McNihil had expected. If somebody was going to run, they might as well run all the way.

"All right," said McNihil. He'd come prepared; that was what the stuff in his jacket pocket was for. "Take me to him. To where he is."

The barfly stopped smiling, and regarded him for a few moments in silence. "You're the boss," she said with a shrug, and stood up from the bed.

TWENTY-ONE

NECK OF SOME MECHANICAL BRACHIOSAUR

Nothing going on in there."

November turned and looked behind her. "What did you say?"

"You heard me." Another cameraman, different from the one she'd talked to at this slow ocean's perimeter, but with the same lazy-and-hip attitude—he watched her from behind an identical pair of dark-lensed glasses. November wondered if they were part of some network-issued uniform. "That wreck's all burnt out." He was perched in the molded plastic seat of a camera boom, extending across the expanse of gelatinous liquid and the catwalks below like the neck of some mechanical brachiosaur; the visual echo of a small microphone arced from his headphones. The cameraman pointed to the End Zone Hotel, or what had been the hotel before the fire. "Nothing's going on, because there's nobody inside. Gone, gone, gone—a long time ago."

"Yeah, I know." November had walked all the way across this contained sea, like Christ keeping his feet dry at Galilee. Around the catwalks' and derricks' pilings, little ripples and gurgles sounded, the sighs of bubbles that flowered, broke open, and disappeared with the heavy glacial quality of magma as she'd made her progress along the planks. "I was here when it happened."

"So was I." The cameraman tilted his head to listen to something in his 'phones, made a sotto voce reply into the mike, then redirected his attention to the woman standing in front of him. He'd angled the camera boom to impede, if not totally block, her way. "I was one of the first on the scene when the word went out. The combine had me up here so fast, I still had my toothbrush in my mouth and I was rolling tape. Been a while since the last big poly-org outbreak—that was the Goose-Pimpler up by the Bering Strait. I was on that one, too. We had to wire the whole place up with space heaters to keep the thing from freezing over and turning any exposed flesh blue. Got so hot up above that me and the rest of the crew were riding our gear in shorts and T-shirts. Like a summer day with melting glaciers all around."

"How nice for you." She hadn't come all this way—not just across the catwalks, but the hitch up from the hospital down south—to wind up listening to this idiot brag. At the same time, she didn't want to blow him off too fast, maybe arouse his suspicions about what she was doing here. There was probably some kind of security detail around here, sleeping on the job at the moment, but capable of being roused. "You don't seem to have that kind of a problem."

"Nah—this is the perfect setup." The cameraman turned a small chromed wheel, and the boom edged a few inches closer to November, as though the brachiosaur head had

come awake to sniff her human scent. "Nice, big one; getting some good shots off it." He patted the complicated flank
of his videocamera equipment. "I've seen some of the ratings. Worldwide, this is beating the pack. Those enhanced
Lucy reruns, with the Tarantino dialogue filters and the Peck-
inpah slo-mo death scenes—those were a good idea, but they
just really can't compete. People are just too hip to those
reconstruct jobs; you can't just add four minutes of ceegee'd
special effects and have people plotz like in the old days." He
gave an appreciative nod. "You want the numbers, you gotta
have something happening in real time. You get that event
factor, people think they're watching the news." The cameraman shrugged. "Plus sex, of course. That always helps."

"I'm sure it does." November put her hands on the forward edge of the boom, balancing herself as she tried to slide
around it on the catwalk. If she looked down, she could see
the soft bones, loose collections of vital organs, and skeins of
nervous tissue floating in the gel. "Give the people what they
want."

"Yeah, right." The cameraman angled his head so he
could look at November over the top of his glasses. His eyes
had the red corners and pinpoint pupils of someone who had
no way of remembering what sleep felt like. "Couldn't have
come at a better time, either. Sweeps week, you know." He
radiated a sweating intensity, excitement translating into a
vein ticking at the corner of his forehead, as though November had laid her hands on a portion of his carnal anatomy,
instead of just the machinery he controlled. "Sometimes it
makes you wonder . . . like whether they *plan* it that
way . . ."

She didn't make a reply. She'd gotten to the point where
she was half off the catwalk, holding on to the camera boom
rather than just using it for balance.

"So like I said. No point in going in *there*." The cameraman smiled and made another, tinier adjustment to the little chrome wheel. "All the action's out here."

The camera boom nudged her in the chest, pushing her all the way off the catwalk. November held on to the device's platform, both hands digging into the various bolts and flanges. Her boots dangled a few inches above the gel's surface membrane. Underneath, the outlines of the perpetually copulating forms grew more tangled and numerous, as though her shadow on the slow waves were a newly tattooed image, one that they hadn't seen before.

"Cute—" November looked up into the face of the cameraman above her. "But not very." It was made even more clear to her that she hadn't fully recovered from her hospital stay. The delicate new skin of her fingertips and palms felt as if it were about to shred apart from her desperate clutching of the boom platform. Plus, she was too weak to climb up and kick this smirking sonuvabitch's ass. "I'd appreciate it . . . if you'd put me down. . . ."

"What's your rush?" The cameraman leaned his elbow on the chrome wheel, as though it were the dial to a bank-vault safe. "There's more than one party possible at a time. Why should we let these folks—or whatever they are—have all the fun?" He nodded to indicate the gel and its interspersed contents. "World enough and time, sweetheart. Why miss the opportunity?"

"Thanks for the offer." November could feel her hands beginning to either sweat or bleed. "But I've got business to take care of."

"Bullshit." The cameraman's expression darkened, as though he were coming down from some minor chemical rush. Scowling, he picked up a handheld videocam from the platform by his feet; he held it to his eye, pointing the glassy lens toward November. The image of her face, in real time, showed up on the monitor mounted on top of the boom's bigger camera. "You see?" He lowered the camera from his face, still keeping her in focus with it. He pointed his thumb toward the monitor screen. "You look like somebody who could use a little relaxation. You're all tense."

"That's how I like it." November had managed to grab hold of some kind of cable socket on the side of the boom platform, giving one hand, at least, a secure purchase. "Now stop connecting around and put me down."

"All right, bitch." With one hand, he spun the chrome wheel hard, jerking the boom into a quick horizontal arc. "Your loss."

November clung to the edge of the boom until it slammed to a stop, harder than necessary. For a dizzying fraction of a second, she had an unnerving perception of the slow ocean below, blurred in her gaze, but with the things—or thing—inside it undoubtedly gazing up at her with inarticulate lust. The boom deposited her on the other end of the catwalk, closer to the ruins of the End Zone Hotel; the narrow pathway bowed toward the gel when she let go of the platform and dropped the few inches down. "Thanks."

"Whatever." The cameraman appeared seriously disgruntled; pushing a small black-knobbed lever in front of himself, he angled the boom away, without looking back at her. As though picking up on his disappointment, or expressing its own, the slow ocean roiled beneath the catwalk, its internal temperature taken up a notch from its previous simmer.

The lobby of the burnt hotel was flooded now, the gel extending past the former check-in counter with its steel grille—the open register book floated under the surface membrane like a preserved butterfly—and all the way to the wet stairs at the back. Standing on tiptoe on the swaying catwalk, November managed to reach the sill of one of the second story's windows. She jumped and scrambled her way

in, the front of her jacket scraping across the cindery wood,
and landed sprawling in ashes.

"Here you go, pal. You asked for it; you got it."

The ultimate barfly stepped back, pushing the hotel
room door farther open behind herself. She smiled and made
a sweeping gesture, half inviting bow and half magician's
display, toward the room's contents.

McNihil stepped in from the corridor, from the ashes
and rubble that filled the core of the End Zone Hotel. He'd
followed the barfly here from the other room, the metallic
fabric of her dress glittering across the sway of her hips like
the sparks of luminous insects, leading him on. *Die ewige
Weibliche,* he'd thought, amused by the literary allusion that
had popped inside his head. He doubted if Goethe could
have meant anything else but that familiar movement, the
kinder incarnation of Tlazoltéotl.

"Thanks," said McNihil as he walked in front of the
barfly. He could feel her behind him, standing in the doorway, watching him with that look of amusement, both
tender and contemptuous, in her golden-veiled gaze.

This room had the same dimensions as the other one,
with the single small window in the exact same position in
the wall near the bed. The essential room, McNihil knew,
was replicated throughout the hotel, space after space, distinctions annihilated in this world and the other one. He
could have been walking on a treadmill out in the hallway,
with the numbered doors going by him on some sort of
assembly line, a factory where bad dreams were bolted together.

Same furnishings as well: the narrow bed with its sagging
mattress, with the little table and the plastic Philco radio
beside it, the chest of drawers with the clouded mirror on
top. The fire that had consumed the other rooms seemed to
have only penetrated partway into this one; the wallpaper's

scowling cabbage roses, faded to the pink of consumptive lung tissue, could still be deciphered beneath the tapering wipes of smoke damage. The chest of drawers was still standing; McNihil saw the mask of his own face in the angled glass, the peeling silver behind making his image look like some ancient daguerreotype from the first American Civil War. The ashes on the floor were the ones that his own feet had brought in and trampled into the threadbare carpet.

He stopped in the middle of the room and turned to look back at the barfly. "This is the one?"

The ultimate barfly stood leaning against the side of the doorway, in a classic pose, a still from the old black-and-white movies that leaked out of McNihil's eyes. She had another lit cigarette, for his benefit, held down in one hand, her other arm crossing beneath her low cleavage and holding her elbow. "Of course." Her mocking smile made the image perfect. A wisp of smoke threaded past her breast. "Why would I lie to you?"

"No reason," admitted McNihil. "Nobody has to around here, to connect me up." He turned away from her, looking back toward the bed at the far side of the hotel room.

Lying on the bed was the same sleeping, dreaming girl as before. The cube bunny's eyelashes dark against her skin, her parted mouth almost a kiss against the thin pillow. The same girl, but different; it didn't take McNihil long to see that, even in the cloud-obscured light that seeped into the room. Her skin, from the bare curve of her shoulder to the sharper edge of her ankle, was unmarked. No tattoos, permanent or mobile, showed on her body. Her nakedness glowed, softly radiant, like a candle curtained behind transparencies of pink silk.

"She's lovely, isn't she?"

McNihil nodded slowly. He reached down and let his fingertips touch the girl, a soft, minimal caress of her shoul-

der. *Don't wake up,* he told her in silence. *Keep on dreaming.* It
would be better that way, if the cube bunny stayed in whatever world she'd found behind her eyelashes. The one outside probably hadn't been too kind to her.

He glanced over his shoulder at the woman standing in
the hotel room's doorway. The barfly looked older now, not
just in comparison to the sleeping girl on the bed, but in
some deeper, absolute sense. As though some part of her,
which turned the expression on her face weary with understanding, had connected to a carnal wisdom as old as this
world, as old as men's desires.

She's got it all wrong, thought McNihil. There were limits
even to that ancient wisdom. A current like electricity, a pale
fraction of the spark that had leapt in the barfly's kiss, passed
from the sleeping girl's skin and into his fingertips. But that
was all; the current didn't move down his spine, didn't connect with anything below the base of his stomach. He'd
come here—to this room, this bed, this girl, this dreaming—to do a job. And that was all.

"Why this one?"

The barfly shrugged. "Why not?" She gazed past
McNihil to the sleeping figure on the bed. "It had to be
someone. It could've been anyone. Any of them." McNihil
knew what she meant: *Any woman here in the Wedge.* "When
somebody—some man—comes looking for an FPC job, a
Full Prince Charles, the total and terminal—it's not necessarily with some specific woman that he wants it. It's with
women in general, *Woman* with a capital *W.*" Her look of
wry amusement showed again, as though she were aware of
what'd been in McNihil's head as she'd led him down the
hotel corridor to this room. "The eternal feminine—right?"

McNihil nodded again. "I guess so."

"No guessing about it, pal. You got some major psychological imperatives going on here. Exclusively a male thing;
women don't have to go looking for this, 'cause they're al-

ready carrying it around with them. A guy like this Travelt you're trying to find, even when his thoughts and needs and everything else—his soul, if you want to call it that—even when he's inside the head of a prowler body, he's still look- ing for what every member of the male species is always looking for. Way deep down inside. He's just brave enough to come out and say it, to ask for what he really wants. What all of you want, eventually. The complete and total reunion of the male and female principles."

He wasn't so sure about that. McNihil had heard the mystical, quasi-Jungian spiel about Full Prince Charles num- bers before, all that weird alchemical, revised neo-Platonic line; he'd never been overly impressed by it. *Nice place to visit,* he'd always thought, *but that doesn't mean I'd want to live there.*

Maybe Travelt hadn't, either. The fact that the former DZ junior exec, who'd left his real and original body lying dead on the floor of his cubapt, had come all this way into the Wedge riding inside a prowler, had made the right con- nections and had gotten an FPC done on himself—that didn't mean the guy had been operating out of some deep primal need. *Maybe,* thought McNihil, *he just didn't have any alternative.* He hadn't been running so much as he'd been chased here. To the best hiding place Travelt could find; the ultimate, really.

McNihil stroked the sleeping girl's bare shoulder; he'd sat down on the edge of the bed, his feet in the ashes smeared across the hotel room's carpet. The cube bunny's face was angled into the pillow, her profile hidden by shadows and the dark hair that fell loosened past the pink shell of her ear. This was what he'd come so far to find.

"You know just how it works, don't you?" The barfly's voice came from the doorway. "You're up-to-speed on what's involved with one of these?"

He nodded. Even if he'd never seen a Full Prince Charles before, in reality or dreaming or memory, McNihil knew all

about them. When he'd headed the Collection Agency's
abortive investigation into the Wedge, there'd been file cabi-
nets and databases full of reports on what the asp-heads
might run into there. The report on FPC's had even had
pictures, color photographs that had managed to filter
through McNihil's black-and-white vision.

Even the etymology, where the term *Full Prince Charles*
came from—he was hip to that as well. From that poor
bastard, the guy who may or may not have become the king
of the land he'd inherited from bloodlines and heraldry
charts full of other poor bastards, his predecessors, who'd also
never quite figured out the world they lived in—McNihil
wasn't sure of the exact history.

But there had been some details, that he'd read in the
Collection Agency's report on FPC jobs. That some poor
bastard other than McNihil, a long time ago and in a king-
dom by some other sea, had told his mistress, the royal girlfriend and other woman in the royal marriage, what he'd
really wanted. One of the lessons being, Never put it in
writing, especially if you were planning on being king someday. Particularly the embarrassing parts. Which was what had
been in the prince's love letters, one of them, at least: his
fervently expressed desire to be transformed magically into
his girlfriend's tampon, so that he could be with her forever,
constantly in place where he most loved to be. It'd been a
joke, McNihil had figured when he read the account in the
agency's report. Ancient history, and maybe an even older
joke. The stuff that Wedge lore was made out of, even before
there was a Wedge. *They probably told this one back in the caves,*
thought McNihil. The things that the Neanderthals had
wanted weren't any different, though maybe senses of humor
had changed over the millennia. Because even if it'd been a
joke, the joke of the poor princely bastard who'd gotten
tagged with it and a lot of other guys' joke as well, it was one
with a ring of truth to it. What men wanted; palaces and

cathedrals were all very well, but the goddess they worshiped was absent from those places, and they knew it. How much better to live inside the goddess herself, absorbed and yet still separate. Or just separate enough to be conscious, to know where you were . . .

That was the problem, though. Something else that McNihil was all too aware of. One man's joke was another man's wish. Joke, metaphor, or vision; it didn't matter. That was how McNihil had wound up, he knew, with that particular monochrome glamor inside his own eyes. *You take things too seriously,* he'd told himself before, *and it changes the way you see things. And it changes you.* Which was what had happened to that poor bastard Travelt: joke to wish to reality. McNihil doubted—and the Collection Agency report hadn't told him—whether the other one, for whom the FPC was named, had wound up like that; the surgical and neurological technology hadn't existed back then, for one thing. But now that it did exist, a lot of things were possible. Or enough.

McNihil laid his hand full upon the sleeping girl's shoulder. He could feel through his palm the motion of her pulse and breath, slow and steady, untroubled. And beyond that, another pulse and breath, a separate creature inside her, cradled and rocked in a different sleep, a different blurry wakening. When McNihil had been outside this world, when he'd gone to meet with Harrisch in the hospital burn ward—with another sleeping girl, or what was left of her, charred pieces drifting in the slow gel behind a transparent barrier—he'd passed by the obstetrics ward on another floor, and had glimpsed through a partially open door as a medical technician had moved the device in his hand over a pregnancy-distended abdomen, bringing up a ghostly living image on the ultrasound screen. That was what it felt like to touch this sleeping girl, and sense the form that lived, undeliverable and content, in her soft womb.

That was what the photographs in the agency report had

shown. Somebody must've put them in there, just to weird out anyone who read those pages. *Like a skinned rabbit,* thought McNihil, remembering the flat images. Skin taken off with a butcher's most delicate knife, instead of by fire. Skinned and reduced, taken down to essentials, the other parts thrown away, trimmed into the scrap bin under the sink. What wasn't needed could be eliminated; someone having a Full Prince Charles number done wouldn't need his (or even possibly her) arms and legs, and a good bit of the torso and the rest as well, not where he (or she) was going.

A lot of the same techniques were used in the Collection Agency's back rooms, when the techs were slicing down some would-be intellectual-property thief to appropriate trophy size. There wasn't much of that punk pirate kid in the cable looped into a coil in McNihil's jacket pocket. Same way with an FPC, though more than straight neural and cortical tissue could be retained; there was usually enough reduced bone and organ mass, according to the agency report he'd read, to make up a fetuslike entity, tucked and folded into a sleek, defenseless shape, tapered for easy insertion and capable of deriving sustenance not through an umbilicus but through its permeable skin casing. Even a little face, wizened as an old man's or an infant's, blind sight hidden behind fragile eyelids laced with red veins.

"He's in there." McNihil spoke aloud; he could see now what had been hidden from him before, by the room's shadows and his own focusing upon the sleeping girl's face. "I can feel him." He'd laid his palm gently upon the girl's rounded abdomen; nothing trembled there but the girl's own respiration, but he still was sure what he'd said was true. A long time ago, in that other world, he'd looked into Travelt's dead eyes, the black holes in the human body left behind. A little connection had been made; McNihil had seen something down there, in those empty eyes gazing up at the cubapt ceiling, and he'd taken it with him, along with the data-coded crucifax he'd pocketed. Just enough to make a positive ID, as though he'd known from the beginning that he was going to wind up taking on this job. He'd been this close to the corpse, and now he was just as close to the living man. "Or what," he murmured, "is left of him . . ."

"What was that?" The untouched cigarette was half burnt away in the barfly's hand. From the doorway, she gazed at McNihil and the sleeping girl. "I didn't catch what you said."

"Nothing important." He lifted his hand from the girl's abdomen. Without waking her, though he doubted if anything could have. Dreaming was that strong in this world. McNihil held his hand less than an inch away from the girl's body, as though its warmth were something he could draw into his own. "I was just thinking . . ."

"About what?"

"The job." He inhaled deeply, smelling the ashy confines of the room, the burnt reaches in the hallway beyond the woman watching him. "That I came here to do." Bit by bit, he assembled inside himself the remnants of his strength. There wasn't much left; he felt as though he'd walked all the way here, across the empty and the bone-filled streets. Fortunately, he was almost there, to the finish line. There was light at the end of the tunnel, even for somebody with eyes like his.

McNihil turned away from the sleeping girl. He reached over to the little bedside table and switched on the ancient radio. It didn't surprise him when the round dial lit up, despite the hotel's wiring having been stripped out and consumed in the fire; the radio was obviously connected to some other, deeper power source. The speaker behind the dial emitted the coruscating atonal scythes of the long-dead Stan Kenton band working through the charts of Graettinger's *City of Glass*. McNihil wouldn't have minded listening to that for a while, but he had work to do. He swiveled the radio around on the bedside table, reached into the open back, and pulled free a couple of wires. The tubes inside the radio stayed lit, but the music died. That was all right; he really just needed a hookup to the speaker.

The barfly watched his preparations with curiosity. "What're you doing?"

"Just getting things ready." McNihil dug his hand into his jacket pocket. "To do my job. I came here to find out what happened to Travelt. I need to know what he was running away from. So I'm going to have to talk to him."

"You're kidding." The cigarette dropped from the barfly's fingers as she tilted her head back to laugh. "That's great. I can't believe that." With the back of her manicured hand, she wiped a tear from one eye. On the floor, the cigarette stub continued to burn, a bright orange spark among the cinders. "You idiot. You can't talk to him—he's gone FPC. He's inside, where you can't reach him." The cigarette died, emitting a last thread of silvery gray smoke, rising slowly in the hotel room's enclosed air. "What're you going to do?" She pointed to the sleeping girl. "Induce delivery? Have her give birth to him? Take out your jackknife and perform a cesarean?" She shook her head. "The principle of What goes in must come out—it doesn't apply here. *Travelt is no longer a separate organism.* That's a given of a Full Prince Charles number. His physiology is totally dependent upon the host . . . that's her, you know. Like a mother and an unborn infant, maybe about the end of the second trimester in size, but a *lot* more delicate in terms of survival."

With the thumbnail of his other hand, McNihil scraped the decayed insulation from the tips of the radio's wires. "I've figured out what I'm going to do. You don't have to worry about it."

"You've figured it out, huh? I don't think you got what I'm talking about. Even if you've got some great idea, God knows what, of yanking what's left of Travelt and his prowler out of her, it's not going to help you any. It'll kill him. Her too, probably." The barfly's voice became tighter and more severe; she had pushed herself away from the side of the doorway. "Do you understand that? If you want to add murder to your job résumé, that's the way to do it. You'll wind up with a nice bloody mess and two dead bodies, a little one and a big one."

"What are you so worked up about?" McNihil glanced over at the barfly. "I thought that whatever's going to happen, has already happened. This is all memory, right? From your kiss into my head. That's what you told me. So it's all foreordained. Right?" He watched for any reaction from her. "Whether I wind up killing her and Travelt and the prowler or I don't; it doesn't matter. Because it'll be just the way I'm supposed to remember it. Won't it?"

A sullen expression clouded the barfly's face. "It doesn't work that way. There's some . . . allowance made. For variables. It's like a free-will thing."

"Yeah, right." *Figured as much,* McNihil told himself. There was undoubtedly some truth to what she'd told him; just not the whole story. Why should the ultimate barfly be any different from the others? "So let's just see how it goes, then."

"What . . ." Her voice twisted with concern. "What're you going to do?"

"I don't need," said McNihil patiently, "to take this FPC version of the prowler out of her. I don't have to do that just to talk to what's left of Travelt."

"You're not going to be able to do it with that . . . that piece of junk." The barfly pointed to the old radio. "Travelt and the prowler—it doesn't have any means of communicating with you. There's no vocal apparatus anymore; nothing that it can signal to you with. It can't even hear you; that stuff got all taken off in the Full Prince Charles conversion pro-

cess. You can insert a microphone, a little loudspeaker, anything you want, and it's not going to work." She regarded
him from the corner of one eye. "So that was your big
plan?"

"Not really." McNihil looked at the sleeping girl, then
back to the woman in the doorway. "I knew that if I found
what was left of Travelt, I wouldn't be able to communicate
with him in any . . . *ordinary* way. I knew I was going to
need some kind of interface; something that could hook up
with what was inside of the prowler, no matter what kind of
condition it was in. A translator; something to go between
me and Travelt, with its own intelligence built in. Something
that was a cross between a wire and a human nervous system."

"Wait a minute . . ." The barfly looked as if she was
just about to understand.

"It's all part of the job." McNihil pulled his hand out of
his jacket pocket. Looped around his fist was the cable he'd
ripped out of Turbiner's stereo system. The trophy that had
once been a would-be intellectual-property thief, skinned
down and reduced further than any Full Prince Charles
number. "And I got just the thing for it."

TWENTY-TWO

ALL SMOKE AND ICE AND
FATAL PERCEPTION

Y ou look like death warmed-over."

But also heavier than he looked. November slung the asp-head's arm around her shoulders and managed to get him to his feet. McNihil's head lolled back, a trickle of blood leaking from the corner of his mouth.

"That's . . . funny . . ." McNihil managed to open his eyes, the lids cranking back partway and then stalling, like defective machinery. "You look . . . great . . ."

"Yeah, like you'd know." No telling what McNihil was actually seeing. *Especially now,* thought November. His vision had been all connected-up before, and now he looked like somebody had been working him over with a crowbar. "Just shut up and try to walk, okay?"

She'd found him on one of the upper floors of the End Zone Hotel. Just getting up there had been a hazardous enough process. The building was little more than a burnt-out shell at this point, damaged as much by the dousing of the fire as the fire itself, most of the lower floors, above the lobby level filled with the sex-ocean gel, were tangled mazes of collapsed, charred timber and heat-twisted structural girders, their broken ends rooting snout-deep through strata of water-soaked carpeting and acoustic ceiling tiles mounded like crumbling dominoes. A lavalike flow of sodden ash, solidified into black glue, hid the steps of the hotel's central stairway; November had to clutch the swaying handrail, her careful weight producing groans of nails and bolts pulling free from the walls, and drag herself upward, boots miring and slipping beneath her.

What had kept her heading upstairs, after climbing into the End Zone Hotel from the catwalk outside, was first the impression, then the certainty, that there was someone else in the building. Despite what the cameraman on the boom platform had told her, she could hear voices coming from the dark reaches overhead, faintly at first and then with increasing clarity. She recognized one of the voices. *That's him,* November had thought. *That's McNihil.* A perfect memory of the asp-head's voice remained in her head, from when she'd been in the hospital burn ward; somehow it had managed to leak in through the transparent barrier while she'd been floating in the sterile nutrient medium. She'd stood somewhere around the End Zone Hotel's second or third floor, gripping the stairway's wobbly handrail while the wet ash had crept across the steel toes of her boots, and had listened. She couldn't make out what he'd been saying; the words were muffled by distance and the intervening layers of wreckage.

There had been other voices she'd been able to hear as well, faint and fragmentary. A woman's voice, husky and

almost as low-pitched as McNihil's. For a few seconds, November had wondered if he was watching one of those old
movies up above, the kind that had been inserted into his
eyes and optic nerves, that made everything look dark and
moodily dramatic to him; maybe on a portable monitor and
videoplayer, though she couldn't imagine what the reason
would be for that. Her imagination had provided another
scenario, as she had worked her way up the tottering stairs.
Maybe the old movies had finally leaked out from McNihil's
private universe to the world at large, so that everyone could
see them at last the way he did. And hear them—that was
what the woman's voice had sounded like, even from the
distance November had caught it. Like one of those killer
broads from the old thrillers—November had watched a few
of them, part of her own research on McNihil and how his
mind worked. Possessed of a murderous glamor, all smoke
and ice and fatal perception. If that was what had happened,
if those cinematic archetypes had gotten loose—*Then we're
all in trouble,* November had thought as she'd climbed the
stairs. *Even more than we already are.*

A third voice, high-pitched and whiny, like a teenage
boy's, had sounded as if it'd been coming over a wire, crackly
with static and sunspot interference. That one had been even
less intelligible to November, though she'd been able to pick
up on the rapid, stammering urgency in its words.

She'd been relieved to find McNihil all by himself. Unconscious, passed out on the shabby bed in one of the rooms
nearly to the top of the hotel. A dead radio sat on a little
table beside the bed, a thick, metallic-sheathed cable dangling out of its back like a baby boa constrictor with bare,
unattached wire for a head. The room itself and the rest of its
furnishings were scorched by the long-ago fire, but not completely destroyed; enough of the original carpet showed that
November's ash-muddy boots could leave prints on it. No
video equipment, but no mystery woman, either, though a

trace of scent, tobacco mixed with a cheaply heady perfume, filtered through the airborne cinders. As November stepped forward from the doorway, the toe of her boot dislodged a cigarette butt from the rubble on the floor. Fresh gray ash fell from the tip. Either somebody had been here with him, or McNihil had taken up smoking since she'd investigated his personal habits. She doubted the latter.

"Let's go," said November. "One foot in front of the other." She pressed a hand against McNihil's chest, trying to keep him from toppling over on her. "You can do it."

"Where we going?" The trickle of blood from McNihil's mouth had gone all the way down his throat and under his shirt collar. "Maybe . . . I don't want to go . . ."

"Sure you do, McNihil." She pulled him toward the hotel room's doorway. "This place sucks. Not first-class accommodation at all."

"Wait a minute." He halted, planting himself unmovable in the middle of the room. His heavy-lidded eyes gazed at November with half-conscious obstinacy. "How do you know?"

November sighed, feeling his weight growing more oppressive against her. "Know what?"

He touched the side of his mouth, took his hand away, and stared uncomprehending at the blood on his fingertips. His gaze refocused on her. "How do you know . . . it's me?"

"What're you talking about? I'm looking right at you. Of course it's you."

"But . . . I've got a mask on . . ."

"Connect you do." November swung him around toward the room's chest of drawers; he swayed unsteadily against her as she halted. "Take a look for yourself."

The mirror mounted on the chest was just clear enough to reflect McNihil's image back at him. The asp-heads on either side of the glass peered at each other, bending slightly forward, eyes narrowing to slits. Suddenly, McNihil tilted his head back and laughed, hard enough to make the mirror shiver.

"Those sonsabitches . . ." He wiped his mouth, smearing the blood across his chin and fingers. "That's really good. They really had me going there . . ."

November braced herself, keeping McNihil upright. "Who? I don't know what you're—"

"It's what you get for going to a Snake Medicine℠ clinic. You wind up getting connected, one way or another." McNihil pulled himself up straight, maintaining his own balance for a moment. "That sneaky little Adder clome—he was in on it, along with everybody else on that side."

"That side of what?"

"Never mind." McNihil shook his head. "It's a Wedge thing. You don't need to understand."

November figured she understood already. *I was born knowing.* If not the specific details, then the general picture.

"The anesthesia's worn off," said McNihil. With one hand, he poked himself in the side of his face, fingernail digging in to leave a little bloodless crescent-moon mark. He winced—unnecessarily—at the self-inflicted pain. "That I got shot up with at the clinic."

"I don't see any marks." November still had his arm slung around her shoulders. "Except what you're doing to yourself."

"That's the way it always is." The eyes in McNihil's face had cranked open another couple of increments, though the gaze inside them didn't look much less muddled. "You *remember* stuff happening—they make you remember—and that's supposed to be enough." He looked over at November close to him, bringing her into focus. His expression turned puzzled, as though he were trying to remember who she was. "Why'd you come here?"

"I'm beginning to wonder," said November sourly. The guy was getting on her nerves again, the way he had before, when she'd had any contact with him at all. Her skin might've been replaced at the hospital burn ward, but nothing had been done to her own memories, the ones that were coming back to her, like the furnishings of the ruined hotel. It didn't make any difference that the skin she wore was McNihil's money transubstantiated—it was still too thin to keep her from feeling annoyed. "Why I bothered. I was told there was some bad shit that was about to happen to you. That you didn't even know what kind of trouble you were in—"

"Maybe." McNihil rubbed his thumb across his bloodied fingertips. "But I found out soon enough."

"I must've thought I owed you one." She watched him smear the blood off onto the front of his shirt. "You bought this much help from me."

"Who told you I was in trouble? Was it Harrisch?"

She nodded. "At the hospital—he came by to brag, among other things."

"Yeah, well, he'd know, all right." McNihil gave his head a shake, as though trying to dislodge the last remnants of sleep. "Since most of this particular bad shit comes from him." He almost had to admire how thoroughly the DZ exec had made himself the latest incarnation of a long line of corporate evil-mongers. *There'll be others after him,* thought McNihil. "Though *this* much bad shit—Harrisch must have problems keeping track of it sometimes."

"Not when I talked to him." November slid out from beneath McNihil's arm. The guy still looked wobbly, but at least he didn't appear to need help standing up anymore. "Harrisch seemed pretty on top of his affairs. At least to hear him tell it."

"How long ago was that?"

November shrugged. "Maybe . . . about twelve hours

or so ago." She'd lost track; the only way she could calculate it was by figuring how long the journey up to this section of the Gloss might've taken. "Something like that."

"Then he should be showing up pretty soon." Using the sleeve of his jacket, McNihil wiped the rest of the blood from his chin and the side of his mouth. He turned away and spat a red wad out into the rubble on the floor. "Count on it."

She believed it as well, but wanted to hear how McNihil could be so sure. "How do you know?"

"Because," said McNihil simply, "the job's done. That I came here to take care of for Harrisch. It's all nailed down for him, but he'll still want to hear all about it. That's how his mind works. He wants to look straight into my eyes and have me tell him. That's his kind of trophy. Bragging rights. He can't just have what he wants; everybody's gotta know about it, too."

That was also true, November figured; it was probably part of the reason that Harrisch had come by the hospital and bent her ears about what he was planning on doing. Something wasn't quite right about the explanation, though.

"Wait a minute." November set her hands on her hips. "How would Harrisch know that you succeeded? The job he wanted you to do was to find out what happened to that Travelt person—the whole business with his prowler and where it disappeared to." She studied the figure in front of her more closely. "Even if you did find Travelt's prowler—how would Harrisch know that?" November's gaze swept around the hotel room. "Is this place wired or something? Hidden watchcams?" She didn't see any signs of it, any telltale lenses glinting among the cinders. "Or did Harrisch put some kind of tracking device on you, a bug so he'd know what you were doing?"

"No bug." McNihil smiled and shook his head. "Harrisch would know better than to try and hook me up with something like that. Asp-heads don't like being followed

when they're going about their work; cramps our style.
We've got ways of finding those little devices and getting rid
of them. All you gotta do is flush 'em down the toilet and
then all the people on the other end are listening to is the gas
bubbles popping down in the sewer."

"Then what?"

"You're underestimating our mutual friend Harrisch."
McNihil still looked weary and beat-up, but he managed to
keep the smile from completely fading away, as though it
were some ragged medal he'd won on the battlefield.
"There's things you don't know about this little job of his. If
you had known, you wouldn't have wanted it so badly, no
matter what it payed. If Harrisch had told you, he wouldn't
have had his backup system ready, in case he wasn't able to
push me into taking it on."

"So?" November was unimpressed. "They *never* tell you
everything about the job. Nobody does. They always want to
connect more out of you than what they pay you for."

"This one," said McNihil, "would've connected you
right into the ground."

"Really?" That pissed her off. Even with this delicate
new skin of hers—*I could kick your ass,* she thought. "And
you pulled it off, I suppose, because you're so much connecting tougher than I am."

"No . . ." The last of the smile faded as McNihil shook
his head. "It nailed me into the ground, too. Even before I
started the job."

She wondered what the hell that was supposed to mean.
But she didn't get a chance to ask him. A shudder ran
through the End Zone Hotel, as though the remnants of its
structure were giving way at last. Ash and ancient dust sifted
down from the ceiling; November could hear, out in the
hallway beyond the room, a few of the beams pulling free
and crashing in the darkness.

"What's going on?" November pushed past the asp-head

and looked out the single window. "Shit—" Past the jagged fragments of glass in the frame, she could see what was going on down below at street level. The gelatinous sea, which had appeared so relatively peaceful when she had traversed the catwalks over it, had changed since she had climbed up into the building's ruins and found McNihil.

Now the slow ocean looked storm-tossed, with swells rising beneath the transparent surface membrane, high enough to rip the catwalk sections loose from each other; the sections of broken pathway tumbled down the gel's nearly vertical flanks like the timbers of a capsized ship. Around the sea's perimeter, just visible beyond the farthest buildings, the booms of the networks' video equipment tilted upward, the cameramen on the platforms furiously working the position controls to stay out of the swells' mounting reach. Scattered throughout the gel, the derricks between the buildings swayed with each ponderous roll of the surrounding element, the camera operators riding out the dizzying, nausea-producing motions at their perches; they desperately clutched their vid equipment, both for safety and to swing the lenses down toward the furious action below.

"Check it out." Standing behind her, McNihil pointed toward the scene surrounding the hotel. "That's what's causing it all."

It took a moment for November to see what he was talking about. A wave larger than all the others had slammed in slow motion against the building; a section of the hotel's brick facing, charred and weakened by the long-ago fire, sheared away from the structure and crashed across the sea's membrane. The impact vibrating through the hotel's fragile structure threw November against the wall beside the window; her knuckles snapped out a splinter of smoke-darkened glass as she grabbed the frame for balance.

She held on and saw what McNihil had meant. The surface of the gel was being peppered with fiery bits of metal, white-hot shrapnel raining down from the skies above. The pieces hit the gel's surface like incendiary bullets, sending sharper ripples across the membrane from the partially melted impact scars. Underneath, the exposed, interwined nervous systems of the poly-orgynism visibly responded, overloaded synapses sparking and neurons writhing in excitement both painful and pleasurable. The swarms of free-swimming tattoos darted about, as though the shadows of the heated metal bits had struck and passed through the membrane, taking on a new life of their own.

November leaned out the window, turning her head to see where the shrapnel was coming from. A jagged bit, trailing fire, tumbled within inches, its momentary heat perceptible against her face. Up above the urban zone's buildings, and beneath the churning, dark-bellied clouds mirroring the sea below, the air was filled with the darting forms of Noh-flies. November heard now their keening, nasally whining shrieks; their demon faces, like a European's nightmare remembrance of a bad night at the Peking Opera, flashed across her vision. "Jeez . . ." The sight appalled her. "I've never seen so many of them at once . . ."

"That's because you've never seen them down this low before." Standing behind her, McNihil sounded calm enough. "Usually, they make their attacks higher up in the atmosphere. They must've been tracking a low-flying jet, something with a state-of-the-art margin control system, so it can zip among the buildings and do all the necessary evasive maneuvers."

"Plus—it's got drones." November spotted the other shapes, bigger and slower than the Noh-flies. "Decoys." Most of the hot metal fragments were coming from those, as the little terrors screamed and swarmed over them. As she watched, a couple of the drones came apart under the aerial siege, engines and ragged wing sections arcing toward the ground. "Those must cost."

"Yeah, they don't come cheap. So you know it's a high-level exec appearance. Just the kind that Harrisch likes to make. He should be showing up any second, now that his flying defense systems have cleared a path for him."

There wasn't time to watch for the approach of any DynaZauber corporate jet. The rain of hot metal had whipped the gelatinous sea around the bases of the buildings to a greater frenzy. November was thrown backward from the window, toppling against McNihil, as another swell hit the End Zone Hotel, the wave's bone- and nerve-filled mass coming several stories up the side of the charred structure. The exterior wall collapsed completely, taking the window frame and a good portion of the hotel room with it. McNihil pulled her back from the tilting precipice that had suddenly appeared beneath her feet, as the dresser toppled over onto the buckling floor with a crash of glass and splintering wood. The bed slammed against November's legs as it came sliding away from the farther wall, winding up dangling halfway out the opened face of the building.

"Come on—" McNihil shoved past her and grabbed the thick cable dangling from the back of the silent radio. With his thumbnail, he split the metallic sheath near the exposed brass tip, then ripped the cable further open. With his crooked forefinger, McNihil dug out what looked like a set of miniature batteries and other small electronic components. A set of LED's on the cable's surface blinked and died as McNihil snapped the hard, metallic bits away from something wetter and softer inside. "The guy earned a reprieve," said McNihil in response to November's puzzled glance. He gave no further explanation, but threw the dead cable across the bed's upturned edge, just before it toppled and fell out the window. The dingy mattress was pelted with the hot shrapnel rain as it turned end over end, sheets fluttering and catching fire. McNihil pushed November toward the door. "Time to move."

Outside the hotel room, the corridor whiplashed around them, the floor rolling in exact echo of the next wave that hit the building; the numbered doors swung open or ripped free of their hinges as the blackened walls came apart like a cheap film set being struck, shooting over. McNihil's shoulder broke through water-soaked plaster as he was thrown against the baseboards; a distorting web of burnt timbers and beams opened around him. November grabbed his forearm and yanked him to his feet. Keeping her head down against the clouds of dust and ash, she shoved him toward the unseen stairway.

TWENTY-THREE

FURTHER, TO THE NUCLEUS ACCUMBENS

Τhere they are."

The pilot, one of the best in the DynaZauber transport pool, nodded toward the cockpit's windshield. He took one hand from the controls and pointed.

Harrisch followed the direction of the gesture, leaning forward from the seat behind the pilot's. The interior of the jet was a cylindrical coffin, cramped and unluxurious; the craft was built for speed and low detectability, not comfort. "I don't see anybody . . ."

"Right there." The pilot pointed again, indicating, the roof of the burnt-out End Zone Hotel. "By the stairwell exit." Large sections of the roof were gone, caved downward into the building's ruined floors below; the remaining areas

were being pelted with new fire, debris from the jet's accom-
panying drones as they were shredded by the *Noh*-flies.
"They just came up."

Coming out of a banking turn, the jet avoided an ugly-
faced contingent of the antiaircraft devices. Harrisch looked
through the side of the cockpit at the tilting urban scene, this
time spotting the two human figures on the hotel's roof.
They hung back in the small sloping structure with the
sprung door, peering out at the bits of fiery metal coming
from the sky, as though waiting for the storm to pass.

That's a relief, thought Harrisch. He would've hated to
have come all this way, and under such hazardous conditions,
for nothing. To get here and find that McNihil hadn't made
it all the way through, finished his job and survived,
would've been somewhat depressing. Not that it would've
changed anything; McNihil had been connected as soon as
he'd taken the job, and if he'd died in the performance of it,
the results would have been the same for DynaZauber. *Because that's the way we like it*—Harrisch didn't have to remind
himself of that. He'd constructed the operation, the whole
TOAW project, that way. Other people had to deal with
win-or-lose situations; he'd made sure that his own contained no possibilities other than winning.

"So you can put me down there?" Harrisch nodded to
indicate the rooftop, now swung back toward the front of the
jet. "There's enough room?"

"Not a problem." The pilot pushed the jet's rudder forward. "I can do a vertical drop, and then hover long enough
for you to get out. As long as I don't actually touch down, it
should be okay." The ruins of the End Zone Hotel were fast
approaching. "But I won't be able to hang around. These
little connectors—" He meant the *Noh*-flies swarming in the
air around them. "They've already latched on to me. I'll have
to swing out and pick up another fleet of drones. Just hit my
pager number when you're ready, and I'll be back for you."

The wash from the jet's flow-directed nozzles was enough to bend the roof of the hotel ruins; Harrisch felt the structure flexing upward again as the jet ascended from where it'd deposited him. Beneath his feet, the burnt-out building continued to shift even after the corporate jet moved off horizontally, dragging the remaining drones and the shrieking *Noh*-flies along with it. The hotel trembled as though from a giant hammer, the impact stretching through a few seconds. *It's the sea,* realized Harrisch. For a disoriented moment, he'd thought he'd missed something when he'd been up in the jet, that the actual Pacific had somehow gone tsunami, a tidal wave thundering this far inland and inundating the streets. Then he'd remembered the poly-orgynism that had been established in the zone; he'd seen the network ratings on the DynaZauber morning balance sheet, the viewer figures and advertising revenues. That was as much of the creation as he was interested in.

Another wave hit, almost knocking Harrisch from his feet on the hotel roof, smelling of tar heated up by the bits of molten metal strewn around. If the mess of gel and interconnected human tissue down below was getting agitated—and the last wave had been bigger than the first one he'd felt—he supposed that would be good for the corporation's numbers. Just what the Gloss-wide audience liked. *Maybe not so good for me,* thought Harrisch. *Not at the moment.* He was starting to entertain some misgivings about having gotten out of the jet.

"Come on—ride it out!" A voice called to him from across the rooftop. "Don't be such a pussy."

He looked over and saw McNihil. The asp-head had stepped out from the small stairwell enclosure; the former burn victim and fast-forward November stood behind him. She had to keep one hand on the open doorway to keep from being knocked over by the increasingly violent shock waves running through the structure. McNihil, on the other hand, stood with his arms folded across his chest, legs slightly spread as though bracing himself like a sailor on a storm-tossed ship.

"Well . . . good to see you." Through sheer force of will, Harrisch swallowed down his own nausea and apprehension. "Glad you made it."

"You didn't have to worry about me." The dark clouds overhead let through just enough light to reveal the angles of McNihil's face. His real one—if there had been a mask at one time, it was gone now. "You should spend your time worrying about your own ass."

The self-assured tone in McNihil's voice had the opposite effect on Harrisch. *Something's up,* he thought. What could've gone wrong? By now, the asp-head should've known just how badly he'd been connected over—in degree, if not in detail. But McNihil was acting like he was completely in charge of the situation; he even *looked* bigger, as though the skies' dramatic backdrop were some special-effects number out of the movies magnifying McNihil's shadowed outline.

"Big talk." Harrisch felt his own pulse revving up, pushed by fear and adrenaline. "You don't—" A section of the rooftop, inches from his feet, split open, the ancient tar paper ripping apart to show the blackened planks and beams underneath. Harrisch managed to keep back from the gaping hole, holding his arms out for balance. "You don't even know what you're talking about."

"The job," said McNihil flatly. "The job's done." He didn't even sway as another deep tremor ran across the rooftop. "Now it's payday."

Harrisch heard other voices, shouting in the distance. He realized that it was the cameramen and all the other network technicians, down on the equipment platforms at street level. They were shouting to each other over the basso groans of the gel and its thunderous impacts against the mired buildings. Harrisch couldn't make out their words, but he knew

what was happening: they were abandoning their posts, leaving the toppling camera derricks and booms, scrambling
across the buckling catwalks to safety at the sea's bounded
perimeter.

From the corner of his eye, he saw a section of the roof's
raised edge crumble away, the bricks and mortar sliding guil-
lotinelike down the hotel's shattered front. He looked back
toward McNihil, who'd taken a few steps away from the
stairwell enclosure, out into the center of the rooftop.

"We pay off on performance," said Harrisch, converting
some of the adrenaline inside himself to courage. "Did you
find Travelt?"

"Oh, I found him, all right." McNihil's voice turned
harder. "Whether you wanted me to or not."

"What . . . what're you talking about?" Another wave
hit the building, sending Harrisch sprawling onto his hands
and knees. He looked up to see McNihil walking forward,
stepping across the open patches of roof, until the asp-head
loomed right in front of him.

"It didn't matter," said McNihil, voice grating like stone
on stone. "Whether I found the prowler that still had Travelt
inside it. Because either way . . . you got what you
wanted."

"You're crazy." But he knew the asp-head was fear-
somely sane. Inside himself, Harrisch felt the molecules of
adrenaline breaking into some other, frightened chemical,
oozing out of his pores and draining into his bladder. *Time to
go,* the still-thinking portion of his brain announced to the
rest. "Maybe we should talk about this later." *Much later.* "I'll
make an appointment for you." Harrisch let his words go
rattling on, unhooked from any thought processes, hoping
that McNihil would be sufficiently distracted. He reached
inside his coat and started punching a familiar number into
his tight-cell phone. "You can tell me all about it—"

"Not a good idea." McNihil leaned down, his hand

striking and grabbing Harrisch's wrist. "You're pissing me off." Without straining, McNihil pulled the captured hand toward himself, the phone loosening in Harrisch's grasp. McNihil took the phone, letting Harrisch fall back onto the rooftop's rolling surface. "Looks like something on the DZ switchboard." McNihil looked at the digits on the device's LCD readout, then back down at Harrisch. "Calling for a ride home?"

Something in the look in the other's eyes terrified Harrisch; his spinal column contracted like a spring-driven mechanical device. It was only a momentary relief when McNihil turned and slung the phone in an underhand pitch, back to November. She caught it in both hands.

"Hang on to that," instructed McNihil. "Don't hit the *connect* button just yet."

November had followed McNihil's example, managing to let go of the stairwell enclosure's support. Standing near the center of the rooftop, surrounded by the gaping holes that had already been torn in the structure, she rode out the building's shuddering motions, knees slightly bent for shock absorbers. "All right—" She'd glanced at the phone before tucking it inside her jacket. "You need help with him?"

This has all gone wrong, thought Harrisch, somewhat dazed. Control of the situation had slipped out of his grasp, or had been snatched away as easily as the tight-cell phone. *I wasn't expecting this.* The notion of having a final confrontation, all by himself here with McNihil, was seeming less of a good idea by the second. Obvious now, but he still wasn't sure how it'd come apart like this. There had only been, at best, a fifty-fifty chance that McNihil would still be alive now, let alone in any kind of functioning condition; Harrisch had actually entertained the notion that he might have to bring along some kind of medical crew, a first-aid team to scrape up whatever might've been left of the asp-head, inject him with whatever cardiac and cerebral stimulators were necessary to bring him to even partial consciousness. But that would've brought on the scene more potential witnesses than Harrisch would've been prepared to deal with; he'd been glad that it'd worked out that the DZ corporate pilot had had to split for the time being, leaving him here on his own. It was one thing to have somebody like that November person around as a witness; she could be eliminated if she somehow became trouble afterward. But if he'd had to take out people on the DynaZauber payroll, like pilots and med techs, the corporation's human-resources department would've given him more grief than it would've been worth.

"Naw—" McNihil shook his head as he called over his shoulder to November. "But thanks for asking." He turned back to Harrisch at his feet, reached down, and pulled the DZ exec upright. "Me and this guy go back a ways. We know how much—how far—we can trust each other."

"You're not scaring me—"

November watched as Harrisch snarled at the asp-head. McNihil's fist at his collar choked some fragment of determination through the exec's throat. She didn't figure that what he'd said was true, but it looked as if Harrisch was at least determined not to let McNihil walk over him without a show of struggle.

"You don't—" Harrisch gasped for breath. "You don't even know—"

"Know what?" McNihil lifted the exec up onto tiptoe, then back down a couple of inches, relaxing the pressure against Harrisch's windpipe. "What is it you think I don't know? Because by now, believe me, I know a lot of things."

"You idiot." Chin thrust back by the asp-head's knuckles, Harrisch still managed to get a sneer up and running on his own face. "You don't know just how badly you've been connected over. By me. You were connected even before you took the job."

"What's he talking about?" November came up beside McNihil, maneuvering her way across the bucking rooftop. The moans and shuddering low-octave noises from the street level grew in volume and intensity, like a real ocean scudding into white-topped waves, as she peered at Harrisch. "He told me the same stuff, about you and this job, back at the hospital."

"It's TOAW." McNihil didn't look over at her as he spelled out the acronym. "That's what it's been all along. That's what the job was about all along." He let go of Harrisch, shoving him a step backward. "His big secret, that he didn't think I'd be able to figure out."

"What if you did?" Rubbing his bruised throat, Harrisch glared venomously at McNihil. "Even if you did find out, *there's nothing you can do about it*. Not now." A wild sense of triumph seemed to surge up inside Harrisch's chest. "It's too late. And you made it happen that way, just the way I wanted it to. Just by your being here—that was all you had to do."

" 'TOAW'?" That puzzled November. "What's that supposed to be?"

"His big secret," said McNihil disgustedly. "And his little joke. It's the kind of thing that these high-level corporate minds think is funny. It's connecting hilarious, all right." He nodded toward Harrisch. "You want to tell her what it stands for? Or should I?"

"Be my guest." Harrisch left his own hand at his throat. "Why should I care?"

"It's what came after DynaZauber's TIAC project," said McNihil. "You know that one?"

November nodded. "Heard something about it."

"They got this fixation at DZ. Schoolyard humor." McNihil shook his head. "TIAC stood for 'turd in a can.' It was DZ's notion—at least back then—of their ultimate consumer strategy. A general principle, to just make sure that the customers get the least amount of goods or services for their money. Max out the packaging and you can forget about the actual contents. But it wasn't enough." He'd glanced over at November beside him, then turned his gaze back to Harrisch, "Was it? There's always room for improvement; their kind of 'improvement,' at any rate. Thus, we go from TIAC to TOAW. The *T* stands for the same thing—you guys down at DZ must've thought all that was hilarious, huh?"

Harrisch shrugged. "Anything that gets the point across is good communication. Short and sweet."

"Short, maybe; sweet, I'm not so sure about. Since the whole thing stands for 'turd on a wire.' " McNihil gave a tilt of the head toward November. "Maybe a little poetic reference there as well; these aren't totally uncultured people, you know—"

Suddenly, the whole building seemed to turn onto a pitched angle. Catching herself against the asp-head's shoulder, November saw Harrisch being thrown onto one side, sliding across the roof's crumbling sheets of tar paper; the exec managed to dig his fingers in, stopping himself just short of one of the broken gaps, as the echoes of the wave that had slapped the building rumbled away.

"Maybe," said November, "we should talk about all this at some other time. And place."

"Call the jet—" Harrisch pushed himself into a sitting position at the gap's edge. "You've got the phone. The number's already punched in, just do it—" He sounded as though he was verging on hysteria. "This thing's going to go any minute—"

"Oh, I think we've got time." McNihil pushed November away from himself. "There's always time for the important things. And this won't take long, anyway. It's really pretty simple."

"We'll all be dead before you finish talking."

"Maybe." McNihil reached inside his jacket and pulled out a fistful of weighty black metal. "But let's see if I can hold your attention, anyway." He aimed the tannhäuser at Harrisch's forehead.

"You *are* nuts." Harrisch gaped at the weapon extended toward him. "You really are."

"No . . ." McNihil shook his head. "Maybe just overly given to classicism. This is the way my old friend Turbiner would've done it in one of his books. Having long conversations at gunpoint is such a perfect *noir* thing."

"You connecting idiot—"

McNihil ignored his last comment. "The good folks at DynaZauber had a great idea, you see." The asp-head spoke calmly, despite the sounds coming up from the street level and the ongoing collapse of the End Zone Hotel. "It's not enough—it doesn't achieve *ultimate profits*—to sell people shit in a shiny can. Metaphorically speaking; shit being all those products that get sold in the cheap-'n'-nastiverse. Because even shit costs something to produce, and the can—the advertising and all the rest of the pretty package—that doesn't come free. If DynaZauber's going to achieve the perfect ratio between price and product—which, of course, is one hundred percent to nothing—they needed to come up with something even more of a scam-job than their previous TIAC program."

"Hey." That seemed to piss Harrisch off, enough to cut through the panic enveloping him. *Smart-ass sonuvabitch,* he thought. "It's a competitive business environment we live in, pal. You can't stay still and just hope to survive."

"Survival's another issue," said McNihil sourly. "We'll get to that." McNihil glanced over at November. "So when our friend here, and the others like him at DynaZauber, put together the next level, when they created TOAW, they went to the best business model they could think of. Which, of course, was pushing addictive drugs, licit and illicit."

"How's that an improvement?" November frowned. "For them, I mean. Drugs cost, just like any other consumer

product. Believe me, I'd know." For the moment, she let her
earlier concern, about the building collapsing underneath
them, fade to the background. "And not just for the end
user," she said. "The manufacturer and the distributor have
to shell out *something*. You never get down to absolute zero."

"You do, if you're DynaZauber. And you've got smart
people like this one running the show." McNihil gestured
toward the exec still sitting on the rooftop. "Or at least that's
what you can shoot for. A lot of the research that went into
the TOAW project goes back to before the turn of the century. DynaZauber bought it out and has been working on it
for years."

"If we hadn't," said Harrisch stiffly, "one of our competitors would've."

"What research?" November's impatience manifested itself. "What're you talking about?"

"I can just about cite you chapter and verse." Legs
braced against the hotel's motion, McNihil looked down at
Harrisch. "The mesolimbic dopamine system, right? That's
where the action is. That's where TOAW gets rolling, isn't
it?"

Harrisch stared in amazement at McNihil. "Where did
you . . ."

"It's all connected," continued McNihil. "From the specialized structures in the human orbital frontal cortex, up
near the top, to the amygdala, that little almond-shaped bit in
the center. And further, to the nucleus accumbens—that's
one so small, it doesn't even show up in positron-emission
tomography scans, does it?"

"No . . ." The words produced a deep fascination in
Harrisch. "That's what the old researchers used a long time
ago. But we've got better methods now . . ."

"I bet you do." McNihil gave a disgusted shake of the
head. "Who says mankind doesn't progress? Every day brings
us whole new methods of connecting people over."

"Wait a minute," said November. "What's all this brain stuff got to do with anything?"

"And the ventral tegmental area . . ." Harrisch spoke with a woozy dreaminess. "Don't forget that. That's the most important part . . ."

"He's right about that," McNihil said to her. "This is all deep-level addiction research. Like I said, it goes back a long way before DZ ever got hold of it. But those silly-ass scientists back then, they didn't know what they had. They thought they might find some deep biochemical *cure* for addiction. And where's the money in that? You want to go for the long-term profits, the ultimate merchandise—the turd on the wire—you want to see about *enhancing* addiction. Making it perfect, a thing in itself, completely separate from any substance, any production or distribution cost."

Just from hearing the asp-head talk about it, a radiant joy seemed to burst inside Harrisch's heart; his face suffused with sudden rapture. "And that's what we did. We found it. The final product." The waves of the gelatinous sex-ocean below sang along, a heavenly chorus fallen out of the skies. "All profit and no cost, not to us, at any rate. It doesn't get any better than that."

"They found the neural engine," said McNihil. His voice sounded flat and emotionless. "That drives addiction. That chemicals—pharmaceuticals, white powders, whatever—are just crude hammers to evoke. Like banging on the rear bumper of a car with a fifty-pound sledge, to get it to move. How much more efficient, when you think about it, to find the key to the car's ignition—the key to the brain—and get in and switch it on, and just drive it down the highway until the wheels fall off. Or until the money's all gone."

"The wire." Harrisch appeared to be musing from blissful memory. "That's the axon from the ventral tegmental area neuron to the nucleus accumbens neuron. A wire or a highway—it's all the same. A little passage for information, billions of little passageways. Stuffed with neurofilaments like pavement, the dopamine path. Which can be made wider or narrower—if you know how. That's really where the action is; that's the ultimate valve of commerce. You get inside people's heads, squeeze those axons down or shut them off completely, a state of absolute dopamine deprivation . . ." A shudder ran through Harrisch's frame, the effects of his rhapsody as strong as the forces battering the End Zone Hotel. "Then you've got 'em. That's when you've got your customers right where you want them. And no production or distribution costs at all. You're right—it's perfect."

"That's what the DZ labs found. What they'd been looking for." McNihil turned his face toward November. "The way to separate the dopamine flow down the axons from any physical source. A technology of regulation; the hand on the valve, the key in the ignition. So that all DynaZauber would have to do would be send out the right signals, on whatever wavelength they chose, and the customers would respond. Turn the valve one way—send the shutoff signal—and the axons between the ventral tegmental area and the nucleus accumbens start to narrow, constrict the dopamine flow from one neuron to the next, even close down completely. The result being the classic symptoms of drug-addicted systemic collapse, the crash of the individual neurosystem below normal operating levels. And the resultant urge, the overwhelming drive to reestablish homeostasis, to pay any price just to feel back to normal again."

November gave a slow nod; enlightenment was beginning to come. "Been there," she said. "Done that." *Threw up on my shoes*—

"Everybody has. It's the basic algebra of need." With his thumb, McNihil pointed to Harrisch. "But what he and his bunch found was a way of reducing their side of the equation—what they'd have to supply—down to zero, and still having their customers' numbers crunch out the same. They tried it before, with the whole push to get people on the telecommunications wire, have them value bits of information as much or more than the atoms of the real world, have them pay to be mesmerized by the pretty colored lights on their computer screens. That would've taken the suppliers' costs down to zero as well. Only that equation didn't work out; eventually, the boredom factor sets in with the customers, and their interest in the colored lights drifts down to zero as well. What DynaZauber finally put together was TOAW, the perfect equation."

"You have to admit—it's a cool thing." Harrisch drew his legs up, resting his folded arms on his knees. Watching him, November figured that back at the boardroom, and in the DZ executive lunchroom, he and the rest of his bunch must've been fascinated by discussing the philosophical fine points of this TOAW project. "It's really the refutation through economics of established physics principles. The laws of thermodynamics, all that stuff, they no longer apply. We've transcended reality—*we've found a way of generating something from nothing*. TOAW is not just a new stage in human evolution, it's a transformation of the universe itself. It's what the wired-up telecommunication theorists were trying to achieve, but could never pull off. Well, we did it." Harrisch raised his chin defiantly. "And proud of it."

"I don't get it," said November. "How's it supposed to work?"

"It's a replicating system." McNihil continued his flat recitation of the facts. "Operates on basic viral-contagion lines. Plus some more brain-research material that DynaZauber bought up. More stuff before the turn of the century: the way people think can produce actual physiological changes in the structures of the brain. In this case, one of them is the orbital frontal cortex." McNihil tapped the side of his head with a finger. "It's right over the rear of the eye

socket; it basically functions as the error-detection circuit for
the rest of the brain. I already knew about it, because it's part
of what was changed inside my own head, so the way I
wanted to see the world wouldn't get automatically rejected
by the rest of my mental processes. But what TOAW does is
hook that up to things way inside the human brain, the
caudate nucleus and the cingulate gyrus structures. Those are
a couple of your basic fear and anxiety circuits. TOAW sets
up a feedback loop among those brain structures, which gets
stronger every time the brain takes in and processes information."

"Until it's unbreakable." Listening to the asp-head, Harrisch couldn't refrain from boasting. "That's the beauty of it.
Or part of the beauty, at least."

"Yeah, it's connecting lovely, all right. Especially when
it's hooked up to the other loop, the one running through
the axons from the ventral tegmental area to the nucleus
accumbens. Because then you don't just have a *valve*, you've
got a *stranglehold* on the human brain and how it works—and
what it wants. The classic junkie neural engine, driving all
behavior, minus the necessity of actually having to shovel the
drugs into the system. Because with TOAW, all that's
needed is a signal, a pretty colored light, a bit—and you get a
response in the infected human neural system that's stronger
than what anything in physical reality could have produced.
The axons narrow or shut off, the caudate nucleus and the
cingulate gyrus structures fire up and go into a feedback
spiral, and you just have to have a slot in the corporation's
front door for the customers to shove their money
into—they'll do anything to get the countersignal, the
counterbit sent out, to get those axons loosened up again, to
get the fear dogs inside their heads to let go for even just a
little while. Until the signal is sent out once more, setting off
the process all over again."

"Oh, it's better than that," said Harrisch smugly; the

discussion also appeared to have drained his fear away, for the time being. *This place could fall out from beneath him,* thought November, *like some massive practical joke, and he wouldn't care. Not now.* "TOAW's got it all," continued Harrisch. "The feedback loop it sets up inside the head contains its own signal-generating ability, which doesn't require any further input from us. The infected brain produces its own signals and countersignals; it's the translation into reality of all those Foucauldian theories of self-surveillance. The brain watches itself and administers its own stimuli and rewards, with DynaZauber as the beneficiary. And really—let's face it—money is just a crude bookkeeping device in a system like this. Money is for people who have options, and the whole point of TOAW is to eliminate options. It's the height of mercantile capitalism: you chain your customers to their lathes and running-shoe assembly lines, and you throw the key to the padlock down the black hole you've put inside their heads. So who needs even the *concept* of money? All you really need is enough of an uninfected elite at the executive level to rake off the profits, and the whole thing runs itself." Harrisch unfolded his arms, spreading his hands apart. "What could be more beautiful than that?"

Another wave hit the building at street level; a far corner of the rooftop disappeared with a rumbling crash, bricks and structural beams tearing loose to fall down the hotel's flank. "Maybe I better make that call," said November, looking nervously over her shoulder at the increasing damage. "This isn't looking so good—"

"Never looked better," said McNihil. "To me, that is. This is one of those classic situations, right out of the old movies inside my eyes. It's what you're always supposed to get at the end: a nice long explanation of everybody's crimes."

"I'm sure that'd be fine, but I don't think we have *time*

for that." November glanced around the rooftop, or what was left of it. "You know?"

"There's always time." The asp-head's voice sounded eerily confident. "Plenty of it. Once you get to a certain state. Nothing but time, you might say."

"Excuse me, but . . . I'm beginning to agree with her." Harrisch pointed to November. His face appeared gray and anxious, as though the pleasant high that came with recounting TOAW's details had started to fade. "This is an untenable situation, in my opinion."

"Really?" The look in McNihil's eyes was further evidence that whatever had happened to him out here had been enough to take him over the edge. "I'm enjoying it."

"You shouldn't be," said Harrisch. "Since you lost. It's all over; you might as well admit that. We've got a vision, and it's not just limited to DynaZauber; it's all of us." The exec's voice heightened to a fervent pitch. "What was it Orwell said would be the future? A vision of a human face, and a boot stamping on it forever. He was wrong, of course. The future is a bloodied human mouth, with a cock shoved down its throat, the perfect connection forever and ever, world without end. Amen, asshole. And you helped make it all come true. Like I said before, you were connected over before you began." Harrisch's thin smile looked even uglier and more woundlike. "You realize that, don't you? So it shouldn't surprise you too much, if I've decided that your usefulness to us is at an end." Harrisch suddenly reached inside his jacket, to the other side from where he'd kept the cell phone. His hand came out with a darker and heavier device. He aimed the weapon, a snub-nosed parsifal, straight at McNihil. "Consider yourself unemployed."

The shots leapt out of the gun, one after another, a tight pattern in the center of McNihil's chest. The first knocked McNihil off his feet; he landed hard on one shoulder, the hole the bullet had torn in his shirt and chest exposed. A few yards away, the tannhäuser skidded to a stop, knocked from McNihil's outflung hand. Harrisch continued to fire until his own gun was empty. The repeated impact of the bullets, in a tight pattern around the first one, shoved McNihil back against an aluminum ventilation duct.

When there was silence again, the noise of the weapon fading into the smoke-heavy air, Harrisch lowered the empty weapon in his grasp; he stared, aghast and amazed, at the figure across from him—who was still alive. Slowly, McNihil stood up.

November had already turned, following the bright tracery of the parsifal's bullets. Now she gazed at the torn front of McNihil's shirt and jacket, the fabric ripped by the bullets, a few shreds dangling like frayed ribbons. There wasn't even any blood, though enough of McNihil's flesh was exposed to show that he hadn't been wearing any body armor, Kevlar mesh, or anything capable of stopping the hot, fast metal.

Her gaze moved up to McNihil's face. A simmering anger showed there.

"That really pisses me off," grated McNihil's voice. "When you do something stupid like that. I'm *trying* to keep it together. For a little while longer, at least."

TWENTY-FOUR

CORPSES KICK ASS

You shouldn't be standing . . ." Harrisch gazed up in fear at the figure looming in front of him. "Not anymore . . ."

Standing, hell. November had watched in amazement as the asp-head had strode across the hotel's buckling, crumbling rooftop. *He shouldn't even be moving,* she thought. McNihil looked in even worse shape now, with the front of his shirt all torn up from the bullets out of Harrisch's weapon, than when she had found him downstairs in the hotel.

McNihil reached down and plucked the emptied weapon out of the exec's trembling hands. "You don't need this," said McNihil. He flung it away, over the side of the collapsing hotel, past where his own tannhäuser had skittered across the roof. "You should've asked, before you started going off like that. I could've saved you the trouble."

"Wait a minute." November's gaze moved between the two men. Or man and whatever McNihil had become. *A corpse?* she wondered. *Corpses kick ass like this?* "What's going on?"

"It's simple." McNihil glanced over at her. "All this stuff about the job—that was all crap. It was never the important thing." He gave Harrisch a sharp nudge in the shoulder, jabbing a fingertip at the other man. "Was it?"

Harrisch shrank back into himself. He nodded, as though trying to mollify the specter standing before him. "That's true," he said in a quavering voice. "What we wanted out of you wasn't the job—we didn't care whether you completed it or not. Just your taking it on was enough for us to win. All you ever amounted to was a delivery system."

"I know all about that." McNihil showed his version, even uglier, of the other's smile. "I know that I wasn't the first, either. The first one was Travelt, wasn't it? Only he found out what you were doing with him; he figured out that you'd made him into the vector, the infectious agent for the TOAW project. That was the only reason you gave him the prowler he used. The transference of his personality, his core essence, into the prowler wasn't an accident, something that wasn't supposed to happen; it was planned that way from the beginning. His prowler was specifically designed that way, to receive Travelt's essence and carry it into the Wedge. Because he'd already been infected with TOAW. With Travelt aboard, the prowler could sneak TOAW in past whatever defenses the Wedge might've had, infect and spread TOAW throughout the whole Wedge until it was one big vector pool. Like a venereal disease, only a custom-built one. Anybody going in or out of the Wedge, whether they were using a prowler to have their fun or doing it in their own skin, would be infected. Pretty neat."

"True . . ." Harrisch gave a weak shrug. "The Wedge and its . . . *inhabitants,* let's say . . . they were our pilot project. The idea was to see how it worked out with that subject population, assess the results, and refine the technology, see how we wanted to go on from there."

"But it didn't work out that way." A measure of satisfaction sounded in McNihil's voice. "Travelt's prowler, with Travelt's contaminated essence, went into the Wedge—*but nothing came back out.* It didn't matter whether Travelt or the prowler ever showed up again, and it was just as well if they didn't. As a matter of fact, you made sure it was a one-way trip for him; once the transference between Travelt and the prowler had been made, you had his original body killed, right there in his cubapt. Or did you do it yourself?"

"That's not important." Harrisch's expression turned to a scowl. "But you know there are some things better left . . . undelegated."

"Doesn't matter to me," said McNihil. "And the result was the same for Travelt. But what you weren't expecting was that there was no indication of TOAW having been delivered into the Wedge by Travelt's prowler. Within days, there should've been some signs of infection spreading. The first victims should've been turning up, both inside the Wedge and outside, all through the Gloss. But nothing happened. That's when you knew something had gone wrong. That's when you figured you'd need another delivery system." McNihil's voice tightened, harder than it ever had before. "And that's when you came to me."

"We wouldn't have had to," muttered Harrisch, "if that little connector Travelt had done things right."

"What you mean is, if he'd done what you'd wanted him to. But somehow he figured out what was going on, that he'd been infected with TOAW, that he'd been turned into a vector for spreading the contagion. *And he found a way of containing it.* Of *not* spreading it. So you *had* to come to me.

Not because you wanted me to locate Travelt's prowler, or
find out what'd happened to him, or any of that line you
handed to me. Like you said, all I had to do was take the job,
just go into the Wedge and try to find out what happened to
Travelt, and that'd be enough. Because you'd made sure I
was infected as well, that I'd become a TOAW vector the
same as Travelt and his prowler had been. You figured that
somebody—or some *thing*—in the Wedge had caught
Travelt's prowler on the way in and eliminated it, so it
wouldn't spread its contagion. But you knew I'd be smarter
and tougher than Travelt and his prowler, and I'd get past
whatever barrier had been put up for the Wedge to defend
itself. That would've been a real good plan," said McNihil
with grim vehemence. "If it'd worked."

"What do you mean?" A new apprehension appeared to
rise inside Harrisch. "Of course it worked. It had to. You
went into the Wedge—you were carrying the TOAW infection—"

"You dumb connector." McNihil's voice tinged darker
with contempt. "You screwed up with Travelt because you
didn't realize that the prowler you laid on him would also
give the game away. There was something in the Wedge, all
right; something that could figure out what you were trying
to do. Something a lot older and smarter than all of your
corporation put together. It read out Travelt's prowler and
what it was carrying like a neon sign on a dark night; you
could've put it on a billboard and it wouldn't have been any
plainer. So even before the transference took place between
him and the prowler, he knew something was up. He knew
you'd connected him. And he found someplace to go."
McNihil's voice softened, as though still impressed. "Someplace where the contagion would be locked up, where
TOAW wouldn't spread from him to the Wedge. Someplace
where you wouldn't be able to find him, where he'd be . . .
safe. And even happy. Someplace where you'd never be able

to find him. But I found him, all right. And he told me all about it. Everything. Some of it I knew before. And the rest? It just confirmed all my suspicions, about you and DynaZauber and TOAW, about all of it. Believe me; there weren't many secrets left when Travelt and I got done talking."

"Then you should've realized," said Harrisch, "that *you're* the one who's connected. Just by being here, you've spread TOAW into the Wedge. And from here, it'll go everywhere. The Wedge is now the perfect vector pool for us—"

"That'd be true . . . if I hadn't taken a few little precautions. To keep the contagion from spreading. To eliminate my vector potential."

"How could you do that?" The asp-head's words seemed to baffle Harrisch. "If you didn't find out about it until you went into the Wedge and found Travelt, and talked to him—it'd be too late by then!"

McNihil slowly shook his head. "You're assuming too much. I knew enough about it—about the contagion—*before* I got to the Wedge. When I came and met up with you at the hospital, I had already taken care of it. It was too late for you then. I had already done what I needed to do."

"But . . . that's impossible. You wouldn't even have known you were infected with TOAW. How could you do anything if—"

"Because I did know," said McNihil simply. "I knew I'd been infected, and I knew how it'd been done. What the vector agent was, that I got TOAW from. The same one you used to give it to Travelt. The comparison of TOAW to a venereal disease, something that's sexually transmitted from one individual to another, isn't just a metaphor. Travelt and I caught it from the person that we'd both had intercourse with—that little cube bunny, the one that hung around his cubapt; and then, when you had me come over to look at

Travelt's corpse, she followed me back to my place and put the moves on me. You must've had her down at the DZ labs, getting her ready to be a contagion vector, long before you hooked her up with Travelt." The shake of McNihil's head was slower and sadder. "Poor little thing. I didn't even find out her name. She did her job, and she was gone. I suppose you took care of her, too."

"Like you said. She'd done her job."

Nice, thought November. She didn't even know who they were talking about, but she could figure out that whatever had happened was entirely typical of the way Harrisch operated. *Somebody—some poor little thing—always gets it.*

"But still—" The look of confusion didn't disappear from Harrisch's face. "How could you tell you were infected? It doesn't show; TOAW doesn't work on a visible basis."

"Not for you," said McNihil. "But you forgot. *I don't see things the way you do.* Some things that are real and visible for you, I don't see—and vice versa. TOAW as a contagious disease is a metaphor—and I can see some of those." McNihil tapped the side of his face. "My eyes are different. You knew that, but you forgot, or you didn't think it was important. But it is. Because the way I see things, that kind of vision . . . it translated your TOAW-as-disease metaphor into something visible for me, something I could see. An actual disease, a physical contagion, with symptoms I could see and feel right on my own body."

"Yeah?" November was both repelled and fascinated. She couldn't see anything wrong with him. *But then,* she realized, *I wouldn't be able to. I don't have his eyes.* "What kind of disease?"

"Come on. What do you expect?" McNihil displayed no embarrassment. "The designers at the DynaZauber labs put together TOAW using a venereal-disease model—so naturally I'm going to see it that way. One of the classic varieties;

the symptoms are pretty hard to mistake. But just to be sure, I had to get checked out—or tried to." He glanced over at Harrisch. "That was another reason I wanted to meet with you at the hospital. Killing two birds with one stone. Before I came up to the burn ward for our little conversation, I had time to swing by the communicable-disease clinic on the ground floor; it's their job to find out who's come down with what. And they couldn't find anything. They couldn't even *see* it—not the way I could. That just confirmed what I'd already pretty much figured out. That something else was going on. Something that had DZ written all over it."

"You knew," marveled Harrisch. "You knew that much—and you still took the job."

"Why not?" McNihil shrugged. "It was the only way to get you off my ass. That's what you wanted, isn't it? The cube bunny had done her job, and now I was supposed to do mine. And then everything would've been just the way you wanted it, with TOAW successfully inserted into the Wedge. With everybody lining up, to come in and get contaminated. That's a fine old tradition with these sex-based industries, isn't it? Historically, you're going with the flow on that one; even making a profit from disease isn't that much of an inno-vation." The contempt in McNihil's eyes turned to pure loathing, something that appeared to November as deep and instinctual, the gaze of a human creature toward a particu-larly noxious arachnid. "It would've all worked out so well for you and everybody else at DynaZauber, except for one thing. *I found a way to keep the contagion from spreading.* There may be diseases in the Wedge, but none of them are TOAW."

"That's impossible." Harrisch stared wonderingly at the asp-head. "If you went into the Wedge at all, if you had any contact with anyone there—you would've spread it. Sex isn't necessary for the transmission."

"Why not before?" The unquieting thought had just

occurred to November. She instinctively drew a little farther
away from McNihil. "If you were already infected—why
wouldn't you have been passing it on before you went into
the Wedge?"

"Because TOAW's got a lock on it." McNihil glanced
over at her. "You don't have to worry. The DynaZauber labs
wired a bonding inhibitor into TOAW, so they could mess
around with it all they wanted back at DZ headquarters and
not worry—or at least not much—about anybody catching it
there." He pointed with his thumb toward Harrisch. "That's
why this connector's not worried about catching it. He's got
the bonding inhibitor as an adjunct to his immune system,
like a vaccine. Just another way that TOAW is such an improvement over all those old-fashioned type diseases; with
this one, only the right people come down with it."

"Yeah, well, that's great for him." A surge of anger
welled up inside November. "But I don't have any kind of
inhibitor." *If I'd have known*, she thought viciously, *maybe I
wouldn't have come to this little party*. "I'm running around here
without protection."

"Simmer down," McNihil told her. "You don't have
anything to worry about, either. It's not a problem for anyone. Not now. Like I said, I took care of it."

"You're lying." Trembling, Harrisch rose up on his
knees. "There's no way. At the clinic—the Adder clome
showed me the proof that he'd disabled the bonding inhibitor on you. As soon as you walked out his door, you were an
active infectious agent. A TOAW vector—"

"He may have taken out the inhibitor—but just doing
that wouldn't make me a vector carrying a transmittable disease. I'm way ahead of that one." McNihil gave the exec a
grim fraction of a smile. "You and the TOAW designers
back at DZ headquarters overlooked something. You made
TOAW communicable between humans and humans, between prowlers and humans, between prowlers and prowl-

ers—you thought you'd covered all the bases. But it's still essentially a *biological* disease. A disease for the living."

"Wait . . ." November reached her hand toward his arm, as though there were some way that she might intervene in what had already happened. "Don't . . ."

The identical surmise flashed behind Harrisch's startled gaze. "You're crazy—"

"Probably. But that doesn't change things." With both hands, McNihil pulled open the front of his shirt. "The dead can't infect the living. Not that way."

November could see the wound, the bullet hole above and through his heart. He would've had to have used his own weapon, that monstrous tannhäuser he was always carrying around, to have done that kind of perfect damage. It looked like it'd stopped bleeding a long time ago, an old wound, something that would've decorated the inhabitant of a stainless-steel morgue drawer.

"Of course," she murmured. "Now it really does make sense . . ." The pieces had already started to fall together; now they flew toward one another even faster. "That was why you went into hock, to pay for the skin grafts and everything else I got at the hospital. It wasn't just to keep me alive, to put me back together and out on the street. It was the debt; it wasn't a drawback to the arrangement. It was what you wanted." She had talked to the dead before, in another place far from this one; she'd gotten used to it. And to what they said. *They always tell the truth,* thought November. Maybe because they no longer had anything to lose by it. "To be in debt," she mused, thinking about McNihil's words. "To be so far into the hole, owing so much money, that your own death wouldn't get you off the hook. You'd be one of the indeadted, a walking corpse—like those ones down in the south of the Gloss."

"Exactly." McNihil gave a quick nod. "And when you're reanimated because of outstanding debts, you're automatically assigned to whatever ongoing job you might have that has the highest possibility of making enough money to pay off what you owe. I already had this gig with DynaZauber, so I was allowed to go ahead with it. Only the job I had been given was to find out what happened to Travelt and his prowler—and I did that. It's not my problem if what these people really wanted was for me to infect the Wedge with their TOAW project. Because that didn't happen; the vector modeling after a venereal disease was too close; it can only be transmitted from one *living* thing, a human or a prowler, to another. They forgot about the dead. But that's all right." This nod was slower, with obvious satisfaction. "I didn't forget about them."

"You didn't do it for me at all." November was amazed at how much clearer that made things. "You just needed to rack up the debt—and doing it at a hospital is the fastest way. Everybody knows that."

"It's nothing personal," said McNihil. "And you got something out of it."

"No, no—it's okay. I don't mind." The thought struck her, that he'd already been dead, entering into the land of the dead and making it his own, when she'd been coming back from it. *He must've done it,* she thought, *right after he finished talking with Harrisch at the hospital.* When he'd been by himself again, up in that shabby little apartment of his. *Just took out his gun and—did it.* When they'd been putting her back together, fitting a new skin to her, he'd already had a hole drilled through his heart. A real one at last, to match the metaphorical one. "As long as . . . it's what you wanted."

"Connect this." Harrisch's snarling voice broke in. "I don't care if you think you did the job we hired you for or not—you're not getting paid. You're not getting a penny from us. That debt you're carrying around? It's yours for good. If you think you're headed for a quiet grave, that you're not going to be indeadted forever—you're really con-

nected. Anybody connects around with us, gets a long time
to regret it."

"Maybe so." McNihil's voice softened. "I'll have a long
time, all right. All that skin didn't come cheap; what I owe
now, I can't even generate the interest payments on. But I
don't know about regrets—"

His voice was drowned out. For a few moments, November had forgotten about the slow sea, the gel filled with
soft bones and human neural tissue, surrounding the building, extending out farther than she could see. The rooftop of
the End Zone Hotel had become a little world in itself, the
place where the last words were being spoken, the final ex-
planations given. As if they—or it—were listening, the poly-
orgynism had quieted itself, the waves subsiding for a time.
In that quiet, the clouds overhead had grown darker and
heavier, another ceiling rolling nearly within reach. The next
rain wouldn't be fire, but ice and steam mingled together.
The sound that swallowed up McNihil's voice was like thunder and earthquake, the coming together of earth and sky.

The flat world tilted, the rooftop with its gaping holes
and solid sections swiveling into a forty-five-degree angle as
one entire side of the building collapsed. Falling, November
heard the rumble of bricks and girders sliding in chaos onto
the gel below. Her spine hit tar paper that flexed like a
drumhead with her impact, the edges tearing loose from the
surrounding material. She rolled onto her side, head downward, scrabbling desperately for anything to hold on to.
Grabbing on to the broken end of a structural beam, jutting
out from the collapsing depths of the hotel like the bowsprit
of a foundering ship, November found herself shoulder-to-
shoulder with McNihil. The dead asp-head's fingers had
clawed a purchase onto the sharp knife's-edge of a ripped-
open ventilation duct; with a kick of his legs, he got his chest
up onto the corner of the thin metal.

"I think . . . she got tired of waiting . . ." There was

no need anymore, for McNihil to gasp for breath. "She can get . . . impatient . . ."

"What?" November stared at him. "Who are you talking—"

She didn't get to finish the question. She'd braced herself for the slam of another wave building up in the slow ocean beneath him, but was unprepared for the butt of a human hand striking her between the eyes. Her head rocked back, as her fingers gripped tighter on their own accord. Through a net of her own blood, November saw Harrisch above her, one of his hands grasping an insulated electrical cable like a mountain climber's belaying rope. His thin, ugly smile showed as his other hand reached and fumbled inside November's jacket.

"It's been great talking to you." Harrisch's voice spat out the words, as his hand came up with the tight-cell phone. "But I've got another agenda to take care of."

November heard the tiny beep of the phone's send button being hit, as Harrisch clambered up the cable with furious agility. The far edge of the rooftop had reared up, a straight-line peak against the darkening clouds. Storm winds hit the DZ exec full-force, but he managed to let go of the cable and jump, clinging to the highest point; the phone, no longer needed, tumbled like a smooth stone down the roof's skewed surface.

Beside her, McNihil tried to clamber farther onto the ventilation duct, but the flat aluminum was too slick for him to work his fingertips into. "Relax," said November. She'd managed to get one bootsole onto the edge of the gap behind and below her; with that and the beam, she got herself back on the slanting roof. What was left of it shook beneath her hands and knees, as more of the shattered building fell away. "I'll settle his account."

Harrisch was too busy watching the skies, looking for the corporate jet that had brought him to the End Zone Hotel.

He didn't hear November's clawing approach, masked by the gel's rumbling impact, until it was too late. Using one of the smaller gaps as a handhold, she reached up and grabbed his ankle, jerking him back down from the rooftop's edge.

Startled, he managed to hang on, sliding only a couple of feet down toward her. His kick caught her on the chin, loosening her grasp for a few seconds, letting him scramble back up, farther than he'd been before. Enough to push himself upright into the open air. Beyond him, November saw fiery sparks falling in the distance. The DynaZauber jet, surrounded by drones and swarming *Noh*-files, banked into its approach run.

November made another grab for the exec's ankle, but missed. Her handhold gave way, letting her slide painfully across the rooftop's jagged surface before she could dig in and stop herself.

She looked up and saw Harrisch, out of her reach, climbing up onto the exposed crest of the roof's highest angle. He took one hand away from the ridge, signaling frantically to the still-distant jet. That was enough; that, and the next wave that rose up and hit the building. Hot scraps of metal swept across the rooftop as it rolled with the impact. November flinched, shielding her face against one shoulder; she saw only a glimpse of Harrisch's face as he lost balance and fell over the building's side.

When she reached the edge, fingertips digging into the crumbling tar paper, November looked down and saw where the exec had hit. The gel of the soft, slow ocean had cushioned Harrisch's impact; he was still alive and moving, legs and arms splayed out, dazed face looking up unfocused at the dark sky. Across the surface membrane were the scattered pieces of the network crews' catwalks and equipment booms; none of the cameramen were in sight. *You're missing it,* November told them inside her head.

The bits of half-molten shrapnel had weakened the slow

ocean's surface, the membrane studded with scars and hissing, cooling bits of metal. She could see that Harrisch had hit
with enough force to split the transparent layer underneath
him; the gel oozed up through the narrow opening. Below,
the gel swarmed thicker with the tangled, interconnected
form of the poly-orgynism; the new sensation, like a whiplash sharp enough to draw blood, had drawn the strands and
knots of the excited neural tissue, the thin black tattoos darting among the nerves and cortical material like quick shadows.

Silently, the tear in the surface membrane lengthened,
like Harrisch's own thin, ugly smile. The exec had recovered
enough consciousness to roll onto his side and try to grab the
retreating edge of the opening, as the gelatinous liquid
welled up around his legs and torso. His fingertips missed;
the shallow wave that rolled through the slow ocean was
enough to slide him under the other side of the membrane.

Clinging to the rooftop's edge, November watched,
wondering how long it would take for the exec's skin to start
dissolving. *Maybe it already is.* She couldn't tell; she'd only
been able to see Harrisch struggling for a couple of minutes,
before the stranded net of the poly-orgynism, shivering with
the advent of an addition to its substance, had pulled Harrisch deeper and out of view.

"Here. Take this."

November turned her head and saw McNihil beside her.
He held on with one arm over the rooftop's crest; with his
other hand, he extended the black shape of his tannhäuser
toward her. The asp-head's face was wet; she realized that
real rain had begun, the storm clouds' contents hissing
downward with the hot metal bits.

"Take it," repeated McNihil. "When the jet gets here,
put it up against the pilot's head, and have him take you
wherever you want to go. I don't think he'll give you any
argument."

Obediently, she took the weapon. "But what about you?" November watched as the asp-head began working his way back down the angled rooftop. The heaving motions of the slow ocean below had subsided; the building still trembled and shook, but held its remnants together. "Where are you going?"

McNihil had reached a gap large enough to lower himself down into the unlit reaches of the hotel. He stopped and looked back up at her. "Don't worry about me," he said. "I've got someplace else to go to." He smiled. "I've always had it."

He dropped down inside the building, where she could no longer see him. November could hear him for a few moments, then those faint sounds were gone as well. She turned away and looked up, watching the jet as it approached, surrounded with fire.

AFTER

The fundamental element of the fox-trot derives from mechanisation, suppressed eroticism and a desire to deaden feelings through drugs.

—ANATOLY LUNACHARSKY
(1875-1933)
Peoples' Commissar for Education,
USSR

TWENTY-FIVE

THE KIND OF THING THAT HARDLY
EVER HAPPENS ANYMORE

Tell me a story," said the professional child.

"All right." November laid her hands on top of the briefcase in her lap. The Asian shores of the Gloss rolled by outside the train. She took a deep breath before starting. "Once . . . there was a man and his wife. And they died."

"That's sad." The professional child's lower lip trembled. "Did they die together? At the same time?"

"No, they didn't." November gave a slow shake of her head. "She died quite a while before he did." Her hands smoothed across the expensive leather surface of the briefcase. "But it's not really so sad. Because they didn't die the way people are supposed to. In some ways . . . they're not really dead at all."

"I know what you mean."

A nod. "And because he died for her—kind of—now they *are* together. Forever and ever." November managed a smile. "So he got what he wanted. That's the kind of thing that hardly ever happens anymore."

"No, it doesn't," agreed the professional child.

"So you see—" November wiped the corner of one eye. "It's not really a sad story at all."

"Then why are you crying?" The professional child sounded genuinely concerned for her.

"Just for myself." She let the smile turn embarrassed. "Because I'm not as lucky as those people are."

"Nobody is." The professional child regarded her with a wise, ancient gaze. "Nobody ever is."

She gave the professional child the standard fee, and let her skip down the passenger car's aisle to the next customer. November closed her eyes, leaning her head back against the padded seat. At the edge of sleep, or something like it, she felt the motion of the train's iron wheels, the ocean's stately tide, the meshing of all the earth's gears.

ABOUT THE AUTHOR

K. W. JETER is one of the most respected SF writers working today. He is the author of over twenty novels, including *Dr. Adder, The Glass Hammer, Wolf Flow,* and *Farewell Horizontal*. His previous novels, *Blade Runner 2: The Edge of Human* and *Blade Runner: Replicant Night,* achieved international bestseller status.

After residences in England and Spain, he and his wife Geri, currently make their home in Portland, Oregon. He owns two pairs of Dahlquist DQ-10's, but none of them are wired with human neural tissue—yet.

An essay on the copyright issues raised in his novel NOIR can be located at http://www.europa.com/~jeter/copyrights.html